WITHDRAWN

A FRIEND IN POWER

A
FRIEND
IN
POWER

BY CARLOS BAKER

CHARLES SCRIBNER'S SONS

NEW YORK

TO

DIANE, BETSY, AND *BRIAN*

IN LOVE AND LOYALTY

"I had been looking forward," said Pangloss, "to a little discussion with you on cause and effect, the best of all possible worlds, the origin of evil, the nature of the soul, and pre-established harmony."

At these words the dervish leaped up and slammed the door in their faces. —VOLTAIRE, *Candide*

A FRIEND IN POWER

ONE *OCTOBER*

I

THE brazen-tongued bell in the chapel's Georgian tower was
already striking five as he walked, not hurrying, down the
campus path in the failing October light. Even with the sun
nearly gone, the day stayed warm. His tweed jacket, which
had seemed necessary in the cool fog of the morning, now
felt like a blanket. Searching the inside breast-pocket for his
tobacco-pouch, his left hand ran into a temperature of ninety-
odd degrees and—finding the pouch where it belonged
—quickly withdrew. The outside air, playing over the withdrawn hand, was maybe just beginning to take on the first
hint of evening freshness.

And of fall. All the freshnesses, he thought, lifting his head
to sniff the air in which the smell of burning leaves faintly
hung. Freshness of the fall-time, not yet crackling with frost
but mild, not yet sere in the icy nostrils but rich and warm,
like the odor of fresh apples under the orchard trees. Freshness now of the evening, descending in long shadows among
the buildings. Freshness of the college year, unjaded still, full

3

of ambition, eager with talk—not as it would be in the early darkness of winter-time, when you walked home under the bare boughs, stripped of morning energy, tired bone-deep, hunching up your coat-collar against the seeping cold.

Freshness, yes, of the woods in the spring, the smell of wet pine-needles, the suck and gurgle of water receding underground, spring pools reflecting the young blue of the sky. Freshness of the summer sea, those days the wind blew stormless from the northeast or the southwest, and the tide high and the water cold, and the sweet, sweet, ineffably sweet smell of the salt ocean, borne in to where you stood on shore, flowing all round you like a gulfstream in the atmosphere.

But this, now, was also good: this far fresh perfume of an aging year. Somewhere in town a man was standing in his backyard, rake in hand, contemplation in his eyes, bending over the year's first crop of brown windfalls, regulating the blaze, his clothes redolent even now with the acrid sweet smoke which rose and spread, was borne in time all over town, to be sniffed appreciatively by scores, probably hundreds, of the homeward-bound.

Off with the old, on with the new. Off with the old, anyway. The new would have to wait while seven moons waxed and waned. Then the green haze like a mist around the tops of trees, then the mouse's ear, and finally the full, veined, velvety, still undusty expanse of the maturing leaf. Off with the old while we wait for the new. Meanwhile we can enjoy the distant perfume of the old leaves' decease. "The only dead thing that smells good," he had said to Cos Cobb, biologist and woodsman, when they paused for a breather—the sawn log-chunks around their feet—in the September woods beside Moose Lake.

"Only dead thing that smells good?" Cos said. "Oh, I don't know. How about a good steak?"

Hunger stirred in him like a small animal. He stood for a moment at the top of the broad granite steps to Enfield Hall, turning for another backward look. Across the green, five hundred yards away, Trask bulked sturdily, catching in its highest windows the red of the sunken sun. Turner and Bishop Halls, flanking Trask on either side, showed a few luminescent oblongs here and there: a philosopher or two still laboring, no doubt, in Bishop; some of the social scientists winding up the day's bout with statistics inside the bowels of Turner. Not ten minutes ago, in his own office on the second floor of Trask, he himself had pumped the hand of the last student, turned out the desk lamp, shrugged into the too-heavy tweed jacket, slapped his breast pocket to see if a pipe was there, locked the door, and headed for the October faculty meeting.

That student, now. The black-haired soccer-playing Fenelosa. He chuckled, thinking of the conversation in the quiet office. For some reason Fenelosa had come in with the idea that he could prove in his senior thesis that Voltaire was really a Christian.

"I'm sorry to keep you, sir," said Fenelosa. "We had an early practice today and I ran up here, hoping to find you in."

"Here I am," he had answered. "And it's October, and it's high time you got going on the thesis."

"I think it's a pretty hot idea," said Fenelosa. "I fooled around with some other topics this summer, but this one is really exciting. Do you think the department will approve?"

"Why not?" he had answered. Fenelosa would find out soon enough how crazy the notion was. But in the process he would find out more about Voltaire than—obviously—he knew now. "Why not?" And he had given Fenelosa a list of definitions to look up in the *Philosophical Dictionary*. A list, he hoped, that being read would cause Mr. Fenelosa's ears to burn with shame at his present ignorance.

Ignorance, he thought. The great foe of us all—and the collaborating friend. All year long we will fight it, in all the forms it takes. This is what we are about: this is our job, our private war, our engagement once again renewed, as it is every fall, year in and year out and down the centuries. This year will hurry past like all its predecessors, and outwardly there will be no great excitement, no cataclysmic events. We will win some football games, the prophets say. There may be a riot in the spring. Someone will fall asleep on a couch and his cigarette will start a small fire. There will be some verbal quarrels in the public prints. A group of sophomores will agitate against compulsory chapel, protesting, though their peers may feel otherwise, that they are mature enough to judge their spiritual needs. But the real events would happen inside: the bombshells, the hoisting petards, the hidden mines you didn't know were there and which, exploding in your consciousness, left you different from the man or boy you had been. Nothing exciting. Nothing special. Just a perpetual war perpetually renewed in all the classrooms and offices and laboratories, with time your ally and time your adversary, too.

Time, the adversary, he thought with a sigh. His eye swept from south to north across the green, past the Phoenix sundial which now, lapped to the top in October shadow, indicated no hour, and up to the lighted clock in the chapel tower, which did. Five-eight post meridian. Come on, professor, if we're ever going to get to the faculty meeting, now is the time.

Turning, he stepped through the Enfield doorway and tiptoed across the marble hall. The high double-doors to the faculty room were already closed, but outside them, looking in his direction, already bending towards the huge brass door-handle, his clean white shirt resplendent in the gloom, his purple sleeve-holders regally contrasting, was Joe Grandi the Enfield Hall janitor.

"Giovanni," he said, keeping his voice low. "How are you?"

"Just fine, Puffess Tyler. Just fine."

"They've already begun inside, have they?"

"Just begun," Joe said. "You going in? Is plenty seats, don't worry."

"Yes, Joe. I hate to be late. I'll see how little noise I can make. How's your wife, Joe?"

"Just fine, Puffess Tyler. And yours?"

"She was in good shape when I left home this morning, thanks. I hope she has supper ready when I get out of here. I'm hungry, Joe."

"Me, too, Puffess Tyler," said Joe, grinning. "We hope they keep this short."

"The shorter the better, Joe," said Tyler. He moved past Joe Grandi and went in.

II

Ionian white and gold, dignified but not gaudy, rich with polished furniture, the maroon plush on the seats worn as

7

threadbare as the faculty's pants, the faculty room was only, Tyler saw, about half filled. In the attitudes of some old painting—"The Anatomy Lesson," say, or "The Signing of the Declaration of Independence,"—the faculty sat, white-haired, gray-haired, brown or black or blond or bald, in the mahogany seats which ranged like elongated pews down either side to the room's focal point.

There, on his throne, its high back ornately carved, flanked by the American flag and the official banner of Enfield University, the president was presiding, looking, as he always did, somewhere between owlish and eagle-ish, and gazing out at his faculty over the great silver sword of his office, never to be wielded except metaphorically. Through the hush of the room came the voice of Milton Fletcher, Clerk of the Faculty, reading the minutes of the September meeting. All the heads were half-turned in Milton's direction except those few who heard Tyler coming and glanced in his direction, scowling, smiling, or simply looking over curiously to see who the latecomer might be.

"Boom," thought Tyler. "Bah! Suppose I let out a yell— a war-whoop, a high Indian hoot, a gorilla-scream, or the old Enfield locomotive. What would these dignified characters do?" But he slipped as silently as possible into a seat on the left-hand side, settling gratefully onto the maroon plush while Milton Fletcher droned through the minutes like a bumblebee. Old Bill Waggoner of the Art Department shifted slightly to give Tyler room, raised a hand in wordless greeting, smiled briefly, and shifted his gaze back towards the platform where Milton was standing, tall as a church-warden.

8

OCTOBER

Crossing his legs and mopping his brow once with his handkerchief, Tyler settled down to listen to the minutes. "There being no nominations from the floor," Milton was saying, "The Chair declared the nominations closed and, upon motion, the Clerk was instructed to cast one ballot. . ."

While the voice droned on, Tyler let his eye roam over the faces in Enfield University's House of Lords, if lords they were, and you sometimes wondered. The Founding Fathers, eternized in dark oils, looked benignly down from the white and gold walls. Under the combined light from the west windows and the four glass chandeliers, the faces glowed handsomely, the living and the dead, the young and the old. Across the room sat the usual battery of social scientists, natural scientists, and engineers. Many of the faces looked grim in repose. Jim Sloane's jipper-jaw stuck out like a bird-perch. Paul Eaton's firm mouth clamped vise-like, gathering to a point all the vertical lines in his face. Even Cos Cobb, biologist and woodsman, still tanned from his last week-end at Moose Lake, had his brows contracted as if listening closely to what Milton Fletcher was saying. Some of the bodies slumped with evident fatigue, others slouched easily. A few sat straight, alert and attentive, as if this were not the end of a long day. In general, though, thought Tyler, they looked damned distinguished under the benison of that westering light.

On his own side—such was the unwritten custom—sat the literary people, the historians and philosophers, the art-historians and musicologists. They faced the scientific brethren on the opposing side as by symbolic intent. Here and there, of course, you could spot the individualist who scorned or

9

feigned not to recognize the unwritten law. Like Lindsay
Howard, Dean of the Chapel, a tall brown quiet man who
sat among the engineers far up near the president's throne.
Lindsay, no doubt, had opened the meeting with prayer, as
was the annual habit. Now he sat like the others, long fingers
laced together, meditatively listening to Milton Fletcher.

Milton ended his reading of the minutes. There was no
Clerk's business, and the president began to call for the reports of the deans.

"The Dean of the Faculty." Bob Schaeffer's handsome
white head rose into view from his seat on the Dean's Bench
near the platform. His tall figure bowed briefly to the president and his harsh mid-western voice echoed in the room.
"Nothing to report, Mr. President." He sat down.

"The Dean of the Graduate College." Phil McClure's
craggy head appeared, his thick mustaches discolored with
the coffee he drank from morning to night, the pale-gray eyes
snapping behind the rimless glasses. He had the usual list
of "Visiting-Fellows-by-Courtesy-of-Enfield-University" which
required faculty action. The list, he said, was long, some
twelve or thirteen names, and he would read them if called
for. The president harrumphed, cocking his old eagle's head.
"The Chair hears no call," he said, and rapidly got the list
approved by voice vote.

"The Dean of Students." George Woodruff lurched to his
feet, papers in hand. Tyler thought he looked exhausted already. His thin, seamed face was the color of old parchment;
the wispy hair shone like a coronal under the light; the
scholar's hump stuck out between his shoulder-blades like a
compensation for the concave chest. But all that was de-

ceptive, Tyler knew. George was as tough as nails or shoe-leather. He had to deal with the succession of young men who waited each afternoon on the worn bench outside his office, coming in one by one to sit on the judgment seat, contrite or defiant or just plain scared, to be questioned, harangued, warned, or punished. It was too early in the fall term for any cases of intoxication, destruction of university property, rape, bad-check-passing, failure to give correct name to the proctor, stealing, or simple assault, to be reported to the faculty. All George had were some changes of grade to report, accumulated over the summer from the June examinations.

The faculty perked up to listen. This would be mildly funny. The humorous evidence of human fallibility, the brilliant professor who can't add or multiply, the justice done at last after the now antiquated mistake.

"In the Department of Astronomy," George Woodruff said "Astronomy 204. Mr. Zoltan Moorian. Change of grade from C plus to A minus. Reason: error in computation."

The faculty chuckled. Bill Waggoner leaned to Ed Tyler's ear, the smell of his pipe heavy on his breath. "The astronomers were star-gazing," he said with a grin.

"Department of English. English 306. Mr. Harold Pingry. From a C minus to a C plus. Reason: term paper finally submitted after grades had been reported to the Registrar. Department of History. . . ."

The dean worked down his list. Tyler glanced at the president, who seemed to be paying close attention, laughing with the faculty. They were all waiting for the Math Department to come up, but there was only one case this time. A

Mr. Theodore Jones (Tyler knew him slightly) whose grade was to be changed from an E to a D. "Reason: error in computation."

The faculty laughed loudly, expectation fulfilled. Here was your academic humor, cropping up among the official dullnesses, lighting the grave faces. Some little freshman like Teddy Jones borne upwards on the wings of justice from the limbo of E to the passing status of D. "Department of Mathematics. Error in computation." Ha ha ha!

George Woodruff sat down, grimly smiling, conscious of having provided momentary amusement. There were no reports of standing committees. There was neither old nor new business. Tyler glanced at his wrist-watch. Five-twenty-five. They'd be out by five-thirty, into the October evening and its business or its pleasure. Home to their wives and families, if any; back to the kids struggling with their homework or raptly watching television cowboys; washing their hands for what was called dinner or supper according to the decision of the wives; home for an evening of talk or work in living-rooms, bedrooms, paper-strewn studies. Cos Cobb pushing back his chair, brushing his strong white teeth, smacking his wife on the rump, swinging out of the door for a few more hours in the laboratory among his fruit-flies and guinea-pigs. Bill Waggoner stumping home to a glass of sherry, a light repast of scrambled eggs, an evening poring over his modern French prints. Distantly, the chapel bell struck five-thirty.

"If there is no further business to come before the faculty," the president was saying, "I should like to ask you to bear with me for a few minutes while I make an announcement of some importance."

12

The faculty had stirred at first, expecting adjournment. Now they glanced at watches, recrossed legs, and settled back again in the mahogany pews. What was it? Tyler wondered. Somebody give us a million dollars? Some new study of the curriculum coming up? The president was getting to his feet, going to the lectern, shuffling two narrow sheets of paper in his plump old hands.

"I shall not detain you long," he said, "but I have felt that the first faculty meeting of the new academic year would be as good an occasion as any to remind you that time, as it eventually must with all of us, has now caught up with me. According to the faculty rules and regulations, a man must retire at seventy. By the next Ides of March, I am planning to attain the age of sixty-nine."

All eyes were on the Old Roman, rolling out his phrases: Homer Virgil Vaughn, erstwhile archaeologist, longtime president, widower of ten years' standing, his muscular paunch in its well-draped vest just visible behind the low lectern, his Phi Beta Kappa key glinting as he mildly gestured, his powerful voice rumbling in the room like peals of distant thunder.

More than ever tonight, thought Tyler, Uncle Homer resembled Grover Cleveland, if you shaved off Grover's handlebar mustaches. Like Cleveland he had grown a public face, marked with the marks of power, dignified as something carved on the sides of Mount Rushmore. Indeed "Old Rocky Puss" was one of his nicknames, a mark of the esteem in which he was generally held, a tribute to his years of public service. But the name that had held for years was simply "Uncle Homer", the Enfield Jupiter with the mildly fierce countenance of an aging eagle. How long had he been in office, any-how? Tyler did a rough computation. It would certainly exceed twenty-five years.

"For a classical archaeologist," rumbled the president, "you will agree that sixty-nine is no great age. For example, the Roman Forum is by all accounts a good deal older than I." (Jovial academic laughter). "Still, next June's commencement will round out for me a full thirty years in office. That may well be enough. The laws of symmetry, to say nothing of a mild indisposition that sooner or later may require surgical attention, suggest to me that thirty years from the beginning is a good time to stop."

Tyler heard the slight stir and rustle which was rising, like a tide on a quiet beach, among the men in the pews. The deans, advised no doubt ahead of time about the president's intentions, did not join in. But among the rank and file of the faculty, the low-pitched gabble had commenced. From this date onwards, you could expect the whispered speculations, the wise observations over the lunch-tables, the gossip at cocktail parties, the half-founded or unfounded rumors that would continue like the hiss of geese all through the fall and winter—and for as long after that as it took the trustees to locate their man.

Cherchez l'homme, thought Tyler. *Cherchez le président.* From now to June is eight months' time. Roughly nine months to the close of the fiscal year. Even nine months seemed too short a gestation period for the birth of a new president. Unless, of course, as the man said, nothing succeeds like duress. Unless the trustees discovered some selective magic that would cause the new Enfield Jupiter to spring full-

armed from the broad forehead of this old one. It was even
conceivable that Uncle Homer had his successor in mind.
That would—might—become clear as time passed. Off with
the old, like the leaves of autumn, and we'll wait for the new
one, whoever he may be, in the time of the leaves in the
spring.

"Naturally," Uncle Homer was saying, "I have discussed
this matter at length with our Board of Trustees. I have
warned them that at my age senility may overwhelm me at
any time, possibly next week. They have read me the law
about that matter. I am instructed to stave it off by an act of
will—and of course I shall strive to follow orders." (Laughter). "The trustees are not greatly impressed by the argument about symmetry. One of them pointed out that to retire at 70 after 31 years in office would be just as symmetrical
as to retire at 69 after 30 years in office, an argument which
caused me to draw back momentarily and lick my wounds."
(Laughter). "For the time being, however, I prefer to think
that they will find a new president by June without great
hardship. And yet, gentlemen, such are the contradictions of
the human spirit, I know that when June comes, I shall be
no more anxious than any of you would be to be turned out
to pasture. Though I have eaten little of it since my early
days as an instructor, my appetite for meadow grass is strictly
limited." (Enthusiastic laughter, a scattering of applause).
"Still, I hasten to assure you that I do not intend to stand in
the way of my successor. In the conduct of the exciting process
of finding a new president, my one operating rule will be to
keep clear. From this day forth, *Hands Off* is my motto. This
is strictly a problem for the Board of Trustees."

"Attaboy," Tyler murmured, overheard only by Bill Waggoner, who looked up seriously and nodded. That was how it should be. No president, even the nation's, should pick his successor. You wanted a clean sweep, a new deal, a change of venue. Good, on the whole, as Uncle Homer's administration had been, one was foolish to imagine that the same conditions could or should be perpetuated under the new man. Let them scour the country, find a new Rocky Puss— though his puss wouldn't at first (Tyler supposed) be quite so rocky as the Old Roman's. Then support him while he learned to run the whole damned complicated show.

"The Board of Trustees," the president was saying, "has authorized me to approach you with a very important request. Like the members of the Board, you will have to live with the new president, whoever he may be, for a number of years. Further, since this is a democratic institution, it is only right that you should have a voice in the selection process. I do not wish to be misunderstood. The final choice, by University Charter, must and will be made by the Board. But they wish me to say to you that they both want and need your help. Therefore, assuming the faculty's concurrence and (I hope) their interest, I have asked Professor Fletcher, as Clerk, to draw up the necessary plan. Mr. Clerk, will you be good enough to explain the procedure you have worked out?"

Professor Fletcher would. While the clock outside bonged six in measured strokes, Milton Fletcher, equally deliberate, explained his plan. Ballots would be sent out on Wednesday next. Faculty to enter two nominees in each division: Humanities, Social Sciences, Natural Sciences (including engineers). Deadline: next Monday at five. Milton would then prepare a second ballot containing twelve names, the four men in each division who had been nominated most often. You'd be asked to vote for two in each division, and in a couple of weeks, before the end of October, you'd have a six-man committee. The name of it, Milton said, would be the Faculty Committee Advisory to the Board of Trustees on the Selection of a New President. He doubted, he said, if anyone could alphabetize that committee the way they'd done with NATO and ASCAP. But Milton, with a faint gleam of humor, said he guessed it would probably get to be known as the Committee of Six.

III

"Committee of Six, is it?" As they passed the sun-dial on the green, now obscure in the gathering darkness, Paul Eaton hopped and skipped once to fall into stride with Tyler. "It didn't take old Milton long to put a title to it. But why six? Don't they know the magical powers of seven and nine?"

"I was thinking in faculty meeting," Tyler said, "that nine months is a pretty short gestation period for a new president. How can they find themselves a man between now and June?"

"Oh, they can find a man all right," Paul said, in his tough, clipped voice. "They can find any number of men. In nine months they can whelp a whole litter of men. What they want, though, is not *a* man but *the* man. The one man in the whole country who can fill Uncle Homer's well-polished and capacious shoes."

"Whoever they find will have to grow into them. It'll be

17

like my son Toby walking around in mine. He takes two
steps before the shoes catch up with him. Uncle Homer's
feet have been expanding for thirty years. The old boy covers
a lot of ground with them now. He's got a toe in every campus
pie."

"What an unlovely figure of speech," said Paul, grimacing.
"He can keep his toes out of my pie, thank you. In fact he
has. With great and continuing skill. For an archaeologist he
certainly shows damn little interest in sociology. Unless it's
the sociology of the Greek city-state and the Roman Empire."

"Sociology wasn't invented then," Tyler said. "It's one of
those things we have dreamed up in modern times."

"The hell it wasn't," said Paul. "They just didn't call it
sociology. Roman rule in Asia Minor was one of the greatest
sociological experiments ever undertaken up to that time.
Ever read the great Princeton professor's treatise on the
subject?"

"Who would want the job?" Tyler exclaimed. "There's a
sociological problem for you."

"There'll be plenty," said Paul. "Don't kid yourself. At
nine o'clock tomorrow morning, the Old Roman's mail is
going to be full of courtly missives from all corners of the
campus. Men telling him how they regret to see him going
into retirement. Men gently hinting that since there will be
a vacancy in the White House, they ought to be considered.
They are experienced money-raisers, good personnel men,
able administrators, first-class hotel-keepers——"

"Hotel-keepers?"

"Sure," Paul said. "The dorms and the dining halls are
hotel business, and the Dean of Students is the head bell-hop.

And then they'll point out how good they are as budget-manipulators. Wizards of finance will suddenly grow up like weeds. Not to mention that they are good at holding hands, patting backs, and offering sturdy shoulders for the weak to weep on. Human nature abhors a vacuum. Long before Uncle Homer has vacated his spot, there'll be dozens ready to rush in."

"To rush in?" said Tyler. "Where angels fear to tiptoe? Who would be fool enough? What a job. What a life."

As they passed under one of the Enfield Avenue street lamps, he could see Eaton's lined face turned intently towards him, the firm mouth closed like a trap between sentences. "Maybe not fools," Paul said. "Certainly not angels. But plenty of men. It's not only a vacuum. It's a power-vacuum. I'll lay you a bet right now. That faculty meeting hasn't been adjourned ten minutes yet. Already a dozen men are walking home right now. Entertaining dreams of glory. *Ecce homo.* Behold the man. And that man's face, the new president's puss, looks very surprisingly like the face they see every morning in the shaving mirror. They're already imagining themselves up there in the Parthenon, ordering the butler around, entertaining the president of Harvard or the president of Princeton the Saturday of the big football game. But mainly wielding power, slashing off the heads of nitwits with the old presidential sword, dealing out largesse with a beneficent hand."

"You really think so?" Tyler said.

"Sure I think so. As a sociologist I ought to spend the evening getting up a questionnaire—one that I wouldn't ask them to sign—to circulate among the faculty tomorrow while the dreams of glory are still red, white, and blue. Can you imagine yourself as President of Enfield University? Do you think you would be good at the job? What are the special qualifications which, in your candid opinion, would fit you for the post? When I got around to tabulating the answers, you'd be surprised how many of them would offer a list of qualifications as long as your arm. Hope springs eternal. As long as you didn't ask them to sign their names to the questionnaire, they'd come clean."

"What makes you think the trustees will pick a faculty man? Wouldn't they be more likely to scour the country for an outsider?"

"Oh, sure," Paul said. "That's what will probably happen. They'll get themselves an unemployed general, or a former director of the New York Stock Exchange, or steal a young president from some other college. But that won't affect the local dreamers. Each man will be thinking of himself. Remember when Stassen was here in the last campaign?"

"I guess I was out of town," Tyler said. "What happened?"

"Well, they had this big political rally for him. Over in the North Quad. You know the place is sort of like an arena. It was packed with people. The Students-for-Stassen had been working it up for a couple of weeks. The University Band played 'The Stars and Stripes Forever.' Eight o'clock in the evening. Big floodlights hanging on the buildings. A public address system rigged by the student electricians. You know, all the usual build-up. So Stassen arrived with a motor-cycle escort. Only thirty-five minutes late. He made his pitch, not very inspired. A claque raised big cheers. Then there was a forum on the issues of the campaign."

"So there were issues in that campaign?"

"You can always dream up an issue," Paul said. "Someone asked Stassen where he stood on colored margarine versus dairy butter. I forgot his answer, but it was to the general effect that he put colored margarine on one side of his bread and butter on the other. From where I was, up in one of the dormitory windows, you couldn't hear the questions from the audience. So Stassen would listen intently, and then repeat the questions through the P.A. system. There was this woman down in the front row under the platform—"

"A margarine girl or a butter girl?" Tyler asked, grinning.

"Neither," Paul said. "Or maybe both. You could see her way down front there in the glare of the floodlights. She was wearing a tight white sweater, well sculptured for the part. What do you Frenchmen call it?"

"*Embonpoint?*"

"Yes, *embonpoint*. She also had a point. It took her quite a while to say it. From where I sat, you could see her mouth flapping away for a full minute. Stassen listened politely, and then you could hear him chuckle. 'The lady down here,' he said, 'has just asked a rather complicated question. Perhaps she will allow me to attempt to repeat it in a somewhat shorter form. She points out that according to the latest census there are about a hundred and sixty million people in the United States. She then goes on to say, Mr. Stassen, out of a hundred and sixty million people, only one of whom can be president, how did you happen to choose yourself?' "

Tyler laughed. They had reached the front walk of his small house now, and the light from the street-lamp fell slantingly across Paul Eaton's lined sardonic face. "How did Stassen get out of that one?"

"That was easy," Paul said. "He answered, as I recall, that

21

he hadn't really picked himself. Some experienced party leaders had asked him to run for president. After long deliberation, he had finally agreed. Not without real reluctance, of course. It represented a considerable sacrifice. But the thing that had finally decided him was the opportunity to serve the good people of the United States. The highest service a man could render. You gathered that, though he was very humble and self-effacing as a regular thing, he had felt morally obligated to rise to this notion of service. It was a smooth answer from an experienced politician. A nice mixture of margarine and butter. And that's where my questionnaire comes in."

"How does it come in?" Tyler asked.

"I mean that these men walking home tonight are saying to themselves that of course they don't covet power. Far from it. What would make them answer in the affirmative, if they were offered the job, would be that ideal of service. A golden opportunity—why is opportunity always golden?—to serve their fellow faculty-men, to advance the cause of liberal education in America. And so forth."

"Maybe. Maybe," Tyler said. "I know what I'd write on your questionnaire. In big letters. PLEASE LEAVE ME ALONE."

"Oh, don't worry," said Paul. "Or rather, start worrying. You're a proven administrator, sitting on top of that barrel of monkeys or prima donnas they call the Modern Language Department. You're well liked on the faculty. You may not be too good with figures, but you can always get advice from some financial wizards on the Board of Trustees. You'll be a candidate. Never fear."

22

"I don't fear at all," Tyler said, laughing. "You're just gabbling through your hat, like all sociologists. An obscure Voltaire specialist in the Parthenon? That's just one of your sardonic jokes."

"I'm not so sure. Didn't your man Voltaire have quite a reputation as a reformer? After a thirty-year regime, there are bound to be changes that ought to be made."

"That ought to give the sociologists a golden opportunity," Tyler said. "How about yourself? Think of the wonderful chance to run studies of the faculty from the front office. By the end of the first year, you'd have so much sociological dope on the departments that the trustees could hardly keep up with the proposed reforms. Bigger salaries for all, two motor cycles in every garage, a roast of prime beef in every faculty oven at least once a week——"

"Not me," Paul said, moving off into the shadows, his briefcase dangling at the end of one long arm. "You know me. The fifty-two-year-old sociological bad boy. The goader of the administration. The Guy Fawkes of Enfield, setting off his firecrackers on the Parthenon porch. Strictly the outsider, sociology and all. Give my distant regards to the Committee of Six. So long, Ed."

With a wave of his unencumbered arm, he hurried off down the sidewalk. Tyler stood for a moment looking after him. "Good night, Paul," he said.

But you'd better be wrong, he thought. No more committees, please. I'm on enough committees, as it is. Everything from the Committee on Discipline to the Committee on Honorary Degrees. They say it's the price you pay for democratic government in a university. And the places that don't

23

have committee-government are always trying to get it. But who pays the price of scholarship? Who writes the books on Shakespeare, Sophocles, Voltaire? No books were ever written while a man sat at a committee table. Correction: no good books. The writing of good books is an individual matter. Like choosing a wife. Name me a wife that was ever selected by a committee. A good wife. You can't. At least not recently, unless you count the Queen of England. To hell, he thought, with the Committee of Six. I've got enough to do. I've got what my grandfather used to call a great plenty.

He sighed briefly and took a deep breath of the evening air, which was growing sharper now, and was still, he noticed, faintly scented with the smell of burning leaves. Two blocks away, in one of the yards, a small fire burned redly in the dark of descended evening. Henry Armstrong, probably, who prided himself on the neatness of his tiny estate, and was always policing, raking, clipping. Smoke rose in a slow column, fanned outwards, and diffused. He could smell it strongly now, and his quiescent hunger stirred again within him. He turned towards his own house, where a light burned over the door. Home, he thought. To hell with all committees. The tweed jacket felt none too heavy now. There was a suggestion of a chill in the autumnal air.

IV

A lamp burned in the living-room. The books looked silently down from the walls. Alice's best silver tray glinted from a side-table, and the pair of wine-glasses on it winked in the light. After Eaton's machine-gun monologue, the quiet

24

of the house descended like the wings of a dove. Some pleasant pigeon of Languedoc, dipping down to the evening tree.

The day's mail, so much sparser than the mail at the office, was stacked neatly on the polished surface of the antique table which served as a desk. Tyler glanced it through, dropped the advertisements into the waste-basket, saw that one of the envelopes contained a bill from the garage, and slid it unopened into the pocket of his jacket. Tonight we will not think of money. He read the badly mimeographed post-card which gave notice that the next meeting of the *Cercle Français* would be honored with a paper by Professor Harry Porter on the journals of André Gide. He put that into his pocket beside the bill from the garage. Tonight, he thought, we will not think about André Gide, either. He shucked off the jacket and hung it, with his tie, over the back of the desk-chair. No, he thought. Let us take shelter under the wings of that dove of Languedoc in the evening tree. The wine-glasses winked at him in the light. On the mantel above the fireplace, the Dutch clock busily ticked. Its bland face showed six-thirty-five.

From somewhere upstairs Tyler heard a muffled shout and the sound of splashing. He went to the foot of the stairs.

"Anybody home?"

He heard the bathroom door open. Alice's heels clicked along the hall. "Hello, Ed," she called. "How's my boy? Your other boys are having a bath." Her voice strengthened as the bath-tub splashing recommenced. "Tommy. Tom-mee! No more splashing, Tommy. You're getting the floor all wet."

Looking up the dark stair-well, he watched with satisfaction as her trim figure came into sight and the heels clicked rapidly down. In that perspective she looked taller than she was. Her face and arms were still brown from the summer in Massachusetts. She was wearing a light green dress, and her hair was brushed back from her ears. It was brown, with flecks of gold in the light. She stopped on the last step but one, her face flushed prettily, and leaned forward to kiss him.

"How was your day?" she said rapidly. "You ought to see the boys. They stayed out in that pine tree until after dark. They're both covered with pitch. I've had to scrub them almost skinless to get it off. They say they're building a tree house. Some kind of fort up in the pine. They say they're going to sleep out there next spring."

He saw that her dress showed splotches of water. "So they got you all wet," he said.

"They certainly did," said Alice. "My dress is a mess."

"Not so," said Tyler. "You look like a naiad."

"I'm a little better dressed than a naiad," said Alice. "Or a dryad. I wonder if dryads get themselves covered with pitch."

Tyler took her hand. "Dryads stay out of pine trees," he said.

She linked an arm through his and led him into the living-room.

"It's a good thing you were late tonight, Ed. What kept you?"

"We had the October faculty meeting this afternoon. It ran on for some time. Big doings."

Alice pushed her brown hair back from her forehead, back from her ears, stuck out her lower lip and blew a small blast of

26

air up over her face. "I'm hot," she said. She picked up one of the letters from the desk and fanned her neck with it. "That bathroom is like a Danish steam bath. And Tommy is developing into a splasher. You'll have to speak to him or one of these days the dining-room ceiling is going to fall into our laps. What a day this has been! Mrs. Lawrence came in about four-thirty to talk about my joining the Garden Club."

"I see you ladies lapped up some sherry," Tyler said. He took her left hand and pulled her down on the couch beside him.

"Oh, no," said Alice. "Not Mrs. Lawrence. You know she never touches anything alcoholic. Though I think she must drink in secret. Her nose. You know that ball on the end of it. Today it was red as a cherry. Really like a sunset. I couldn't keep my eyes off it. Anyway, I told her I thought I would like to join. And all I could think of, watching her nose, was cherries." Alice laughed merrily, in the husky contralto he loved. O dove of Languedoc. "Cherries. So I asked her about planting cherry-trees. You know, for the spring blossoms. That was good for at least an hour's lecture, with a lot of talk about how you have to dig the hole, and the humus, that's manure, and then——"

"With a couple of George Washingtons like Toby and Tommy, no cherry tree would ever reach maturity around here," Tyler said. "We'd better stick to pine-trees."

"Stick is right," Alice said. "All that pine-tree pitch. I scrubbed Toby's arm so hard he says he's got to have a band-aid on it. And then I was just going to call the boys in when the doorbell rang again and it was Giorgio—Don't, Ed, you're squeezing my rings." She reached over with her right hand and gently pulled her left from his grasp. "You don't know your own strength, Professor Tyler. Here, wait a minute and I'll get you some sherry. Poor Giorgio!"

She put a hand on his shoulder and got up, and Tyler saw the patch of wetness on the hip of her skirt as she went into the hall. "Toby. Tommy. Time to get out now. And please rinse out the tub." Her rapid heel-clicks receded towards the kitchen. A pan rattled on the stove, a cupboard door slammed.

"Giorgio looked like a lean and hungry wolf," she said, coming back with the wine-bottle and a glass. "Well, no, not a wolf. A fox. Or any half-starved small animal. He seemed quite distressed that you weren't here. I told him you worked all the time, and he said he knew it. But then he seemed to take it as some kind of slur on his own working. Does he work hard?"

"Moderately," Tyler said. "Moderately. When his wife will let him alone. Naturally he had forgotten all about the faculty meeting."

"Well, so had I," Alice said. "We sat around waiting for you to appear. And when you didn't come, he seemed so restive and nervous, I asked him to have some sherry. One glass made him so loquacious, I'm sure he hadn't had anything to eat since breakfast."

"Maybe not," Tyler said. "He sometimes eats at the Faculty Club, but I didn't see him there today. Doesn't she even feed him?"

"Giulietta? Not Giulietta. You know her. The Italian intellectual who doesn't shave under her arms. One day I was over there paying a departmental call, being a good chairman's wife, and we were in the kitchen for some reason. She opened the refrigerator door to see if there was anything to offer me for refreshment. And do you know what was in it? Manuscripts. Piles of typewriter paper in the refrigerator."

Alice laughed her low, throaty chuckle. She filled Tyler's glass and her own. "By the way, we're having pressure-cooker beef stew tonight. With all my late afternoon callers, there wasn't time for anything more elaborate."

"It sounds good," said Tyler.

"It's almost done," said Alice. "Don't say I don't feed *you.*"

"I won't, as long as you keep on doing it. What was eating Giorgio?"

"Oh, he wouldn't say what was eating him. Though something obviously was. Probably Giulietta. He looked moony. You know that Italian mooniness. We just talked about his Dante book. After his first burst of talking, though, he kept sighing. His eyes would go dead and sometimes he'd forget to answer."

"It all sounds pretty inspiring," Tyler said.

"Really, it was sort of pitiful," said Alice gravely. "But it didn't look to me like anything a square meal wouldn't take care of."

"Or a little attention from Giulietta," Tyler said. "Maybe she sleeps in the refrigerator, too. Along with the manuscripts."

"More likely she makes him sleep there," Alice said. "Without any blankets. I wish she'd wash her neck. Well, anyway, he gave up waiting for you about six o'clock. He said he'd see you in your office tomorrow. By the way, did you get your Guggenheim application sent off?"

29

"At last," said Tyler. "Though I had so many interruptions all morning, I couldn't get it off until around noon. I went over to see the Dean—"

"Which one?"

"Oh, Bob Schaeffer. He was very nice about it. He said he would see the president tomorrow and put through a year's leave of absence for me next year. At half salary."

"He'd better," said Alice belligerently. "The way you work around here. Is the application actually in the mail?"

"In the mail, yes," said Tyler. "At last it's on the way. Bob Schaeffer said it wasn't too late. They just announce the early deadline because they know how professors and artists and composers and novelists and poets are. Procrastinators. Procrastinators all. It's an occupational disease. I have another occupational disease right now. A bad case of it. I'm hungry. Alice, as Cal Coolidge used to say, where's muh suppuh?"

Alice drank off her wine and stood up. "At your service, bossy," she said. She leaned over and kissed the part of his forehead where the hair was beginning to recede. "Would you do me a favor and see that the boys wear their bathrobes and slippers? They'll be coming out of a very steamy bathroom, and we don't want head-colds yet." She took the damp part of her skirt in thumb and forefinger, pulling it away from her body, shaking it slightly. "Those monkeys got me all wet," she said in her husky voice. "Would you get them now because we're almost ready?" She carried the wineglasses into the kitchen.

"You bet," said Tyler. He rose and moved towards the stairs. Beside the open window at the top landing he paused

30

to sniff the evening air. It still smelled pleasantly of burning leaves. From far up the street he heard the bell in the chapel tower striking seven deliberately. He was halfway down the hall before he suddenly remembered that he hadn't told Alice the news about the Old Roman and the search for a new president.

I

SHINING blobs of what looked like grease floated on the surface of the two kettles sunk in the steam-table. One was pale yellow, the other tomato-colored. A matching tomato-colored splotch adorned the apron of the Negro girl behind the lunch-counter.

"What's the red one?" Tyler asked.

The girl gazed past his right shoulder, rolling her eyes. Funny, they wouldn't look right at you. Trained not to look at the enemy from childhood? Maybe a conditioned reflex? "That's the vegetable-beef," the girl said.

"I'll have a cup of the vegetable-beef," said Tyler. She filled the cup too full, the soup-ladle too large for the cup, and some of the liquid slopped into the saucer. Tyler slid his tray along the steel slideway to the cashier's desk.

"Forty cents," said the student cashier. His white coat was daubed, too. Old coffee-stains. Tyler paid and moved off down the room towards an empty maroon-and-white table. Its top was crumby and the ashtray overflowed with cigarette-butts and gray ash. He swept the maroon top clear with a paper napkin and sat down, his tray before him, looking with distaste at the lunch he was about to eat. Out of the loud-speaker high in the basement wall the beautiful blue Danube was flowing. Thank God they had turned the spigot low. In the gaps between notes Tyler could hear erratic coughing all down the long cafeteria. Outside the Student Union, across the dank brown grass of the campus, over the town, over the whole state, heavy clouds rolled eastward, laden with rain. Huffle, Snuffle, and Wheeze, the demons of November. Snow White and the Seven Coughs. Tyler burned his tongue on the first spoonful of soup and sat back to let it cool.

Fenelosa went by, balancing a tray containing three sand-wiches, a cup of coffee, a carton of milk, and two scoops of ice cream in a large waxed-paper bowl. Over its side marsh-mallow dripped. The boy's cheeks and chin were covered with a two-day bristle. Voltaire should see him now. Voltaire the Christian. Fenelosa hadn't been back for a couple of weeks. Not since the afternoon of the faculty meeting. Now he did not look in Tyler's direction. Still balancing his laden tray he moved to the far end of the room. He sat down at a table under the too-bright mural, where impossibly husky Enfield crewmen in their gleaming shell feathered their ma-roon-and-white oars over an impossibly blue lake under a sky in which impossible marshmallow clouds somnolently drifted.

"Mind if I sit down, Ed?" said the voice at his elbow. Tyler half turned to see Milton Fletcher standing beside him, peering down from his seven-foot height, his neat, small-featured rubicund face politely bent forward above the

polka-dotted bow tie and expanse of spotless shirt-front. "May
I join you?"

"Hello, Milton, yes. I've just begun. If you can stand this
slop-joint and the beautiful blue Danube. And that mural."
Tyler nodded his head towards the stalwart crewmen feather-
ing away under their marshmallow sky.

"I'll sit facing away from the mural," Milton said. He
examined his chair-seat for crumbs and, finding none, sat
down. "How do you like this weather. November chose to
enter like a lion."

"Or a dripping dragon," Tyler said. "To hear the coughing
in here, you'd think he had his fangs sunk in everybody's
throat."

"There do seem to be a lot of colds around," said Milton,
seriously. He neatly unwrapped his sandwich—egg salad,
Tyler saw—and opened the flap on his carton of milk. "I told
Mary this morning I thought I'd come home for lunch. Not to
eat in public places where germs congregate. But then I
looked out at the rain and thought how wet I'd get going
home. I concluded it was six of one and half a dozen of the
other. Is you family well?"

"Tommy is in bed today with a slight fever," Tyler said.
"How about yours?"

"Mary is fine. At Hill School—you know Larry is at Hill
School—they have what they call a hat-coat-and-rubbers rule.
For the boys *and* the faculty. You can't go out in late fall or
winter without all three. They enforce it, I believe, by
demerits for the boys and fines for the faculty. It has cut
down seventy-five percent on days missed from classes."

Milton sounded, Tyler thought, exactly as if he were read-

34

ing the minutes of the last meeting in the faculty room. From
where he sat, back away from his cooling soup, he could see
Milton's enormous feet under the table. They were carefully
shod in rubbers.

"It's a good idea," he said. "We ought to try it here. Two
of my graduate students were out with colds this morning.
But in a university you can't enforce that sort of thing. Or
anything else, even a clean cafeteria." He tried the soup
again. It was now, he found, too cold.

"It wasn't exactly enforcement," Milton said, "but I was
surprised at the way the faculty followed our plan for the
election of the advisory committee on the new president.
What I call the Committee of Six." He smiled gently, proud
of having named it.

"I followed like a faithful sheep," Tyler said. "What surprised me was the absence of talk about it. How is it coming?
I thought the election results were supposed to be in before
the end of October."

"They were supposed to be. Unfortunately there was a
delay in printing up the second ballot. I couldn't keep precisely to my timetable. Now, I am glad to say, the results are
tabulated, the committee is elected, and the announcement
went out yesterday. November the first."

"Announcement?" said Tyler. "I didn't see it. When was
it announced?" He gulped down his lukewarm coffee, set
down the mug, and lighted a cigarette.

"The general announcement," Milton said, "will be in the
Eagle tomorrow morning. But there is also a special letter to
the men elected to the Committee of Six, and a circular
printed letter to all senior members of the faculty. They

35

went out yesterday afternoon at four o'clock by campus mail. You should have gotten yours this morning."

"I had a graduate seminar all morning," said Tyler. "So I haven't seen the mail. It's probably in my office now. What happened? Did you scare up a good committee?"

Milton Fletcher's face took on its serious look. He inserted a straw carefully into the square gap in his milk-carton, drank, glanced around to see who was at the nearby tables, cleared his throat, and leaned forward confidentially.

"Why, yes," he said. "It appears to be good. Now I can't say that it is exactly the one I would have chosen if the choice had been up to me. There are one or two names that—well—" His serious face warmed momentarily into a grin. "The choice, however, was not up to me. The results we have represent, I think I am safe in assuming, the will of the faculty. *Vox populi, vox dei.*" His lips wore the Latin tag like the polka-dotted bow tie.

The close-mouthed Milton was not, Tyler saw, going to reveal the names of the new Committee of Six unless he was asked point-blank. And Tyler, examining his own state of mind, found there no inclination to ask. He would find out soon enough from the envelope in his office. His eyes fell to his tray where the unopened package of saltines lay beside his saucer. He put it into his pocket to take home for Tommy and stood up.

"Did the voting show any evidence of electioneering?"

Milton's brow contracted seriously again. "No. Not that I could see. That would not always be true, of course. But this time it was. The interesting thing was the size of the vote. A very good percentage of the ballots was returned in each of the mailings. Something like sixty-eight percent on the

36

first mailing, and close to that same figure on the second mailing."

"Is that good?" said Tyler. He could not repress a yawn. "I'd have called it rather low." He mashed out his cigarette in the crowded ashtray.

"Anything that exceeds a fifty percent return I would call good," Milton said. "You know how the faculty is. They will fight to the death for a principle—for the right to vote, say, on a particular issue—and then they get so wrapped up in what they're doing professionally that they forget to mail in their ballots on an important issue like this. Or sometimes mail them in unmarked. Or wrongly marked."

"Or too late for your deadline, Milton. I'm afraid I'll have to go. My deadline for office hours is coming up."

"Yes, Ed. Go right ahead." He sipped his milk through the straw, tipping the carton to get the last drops. "And wear your hat, coat, and rubbers."

Tyler carried his tray to the wheeled cart and lowered it in among the noisome debris of other men's lunches: the soiled paper plates, the half-eaten hot-dog rolls splashed with mustard, the aluminum box of dirty silver. "Where the hell are my rubbers anyway?" he thought fiercely. "They ought to provide them for all the people who wade through this slop-joint." As he went through the coatroom to find his hat and his trench-coat, he noticed that the song on the loudspeaker was the Merry Widow Waltz.

II

He should have worn his rubbers, wherever they were. The rain had stopped. For the moment. On the esplanade

before the Student Union, uneven flagstones held puddles
the color of lead under that scudding sky. At the draughty
corner of the library, grabbing for his hat as a gust wrenched
at it, he nearly ran down Giorgio Renzulli, walking just
ahead of a cluster of colleagues, gesticulating over his shoulder
about something or other, not paying any attention to where
he was going. Why, Tyler suddenly wondered, had the Dean
not done anything about that raise for Giorgio? Probably not
enough time had gone by. The mills ground slowly. Giorgio
and the others saluted him, but the wind tore their greetings
out of earshot as soon as they were uttered. Holding their
hats and belted caps, coat-tails flying, the little group moved
off like crows across the wet flagstones.

To talk, no doubt, like the young intellectuals they were,
about last night's paper on Gide's journals. As if that matter
hadn't been gone into with scalpels at Simeon Strong's apartment after the formal meeting of the *Cercle*. Porter's essay
had been no more than fair. Wit, as usual, masqueraded as
substance. Long quotations from the master, some wonderfully perceptive, some merely uninformed, some woefully
prejudiced. Then Strong's polite invitation: "Could you
join a few of us afterwards at my house for a drink?" Men
standing in groups in the crowded living-room of the apartment. Others sitting on the rug arguing with someone on the
corner of the divan among the turkey-red cushions. The
usual Van Gogh reproduction on the wall. Highballs clinking, one glass overturned, Strong mopping up with a kitchen
towel. Smoke in the air like fog on the New Jersey flats. All
the foreign accents. Sliced salami and salty rye-bread. Cheese
hastily daubed on crackers. Academic Bohemia.

38

Climbing the stairs to his office on the second floor of Trask, Tyler felt the familiar sagging in the muscles of his calves and thighs that meant he had stayed up too late the night before. Signs of the times that meant you were past forty. No head-ache, no malaise, just that dull ache in the leg-muscles which followed too much smoking and too little sleep. And the one concentrated ache, halfway up the back of the right thigh, where the ligaments had been ripped and the muscle torn when the mine-fragments caught up with him twelve years back. Tyler reached the second-floor landing and unlocked the door with his name and title on it. The cafeteria coffee lay like a lead ball in the pit of his stomach.

He peered through the gloom at the familiar furnishings: desk, desk-chair, visitors' chairs, the faded draperies at the windows which Mrs. Rhodes had been trying to persuade him to replace. And of course the books, all the books, yes the books, lining the walls, piled four deep on the old table, ranged in rows on top of the filing cabinet, gathering dust on the floor in one corner, shoulder to shoulder between bookends against the cracked plaster behind his desk. The bust of Arouet, called Voltaire, peered back at him with blind eyes from the top of the bookcase. Tyler dropped his eyes before that pale stare.

The air, it occurred to him, smelled like the interior of the Bastille in 1760, and he went to the window to lift it an inch or two. Dissuaded by the blast of wind and a spatter of damp, he lowered it again and stood looking sourly out towards College Street. The wind and the rain. *Entendez-vous le vent qui jase, et qui s'arrête à chaque phrase.* . . . The old rhyme went through his head and out again as he watched a black car like a hearse moving north on College Street, its tires throwing up a visible spray. The leaves, he saw, were going fast now under the joint attack of the horizontal wind and the vertical rain. Already the tall columns across the front of the Parthenon could be seen among the bare branches of the maples on the slope of College Hill. Wonder how Uncle Homer likes this weather. One lonely old widower, one butler, one cook, to fill that huge Greek Revival mansion. "What a life!" said Tyler audibly. Under the cheerless November sky, the residence of Enfield's presidents looked more like a mausoleum than ever.

The story sprang into his head of the old housekeeper Uncle Homer had had before the war, how she loved to answer the telephone, how she put on her most haughty voice to say the magic words: "President's residence." Accenting the final syllable of each word with a nasal twang. Tyler chuckled. Where was the old girl now? Gone with the snows and the crows of yesteryear. Like Uncle Homer after next June thirtieth.

He turned from the window and switched on the overhead light. His desk was neater than usual. Mrs. Rhodes, he saw, had arranged the morning mail in a pile on his blotter, and he began to sort it through. Three publishers' advertisements. The big manila envelope from the Modern Language Association: another essay on Diderot from some young scholar, probably. There had been a run on Diderot lately. Contents to be judiciously appraised and returned to the editorial office. The small one was a colored picture postcard so nearly illegible that he flipped it over to see if the picture offered a clue. Ah, Don Drake at that little Campbellite college in Wisconsin. Tyler snapped on his desk lamp and bent over the card to decipher it. "Having ugly time," Don had written. "Glad you're not here." The next words were heavily under-scored. "*I do not like it. Quel dommage!* Students are nincom-poops. No liquor allowed!" And the sprawling signature, like a French admiral's.

Near the bottom of the pile was one buff-colored envelope, distinguishable from the others by the narrow band of maroon ink which meant inter-office mail. This would be Milton Fletcher's official notice to senior faculty members about the Committee of Six. He ran his index finger under the flap and opened the envelope.

III

"Dear Professor Tyler," he read. "As Clerk of the Faculty, I have the honor to inform you that the recent balloting to determine membership on the Faculty Committee Advisory to the Board of Trustees on the Selection of a New Presi-dent has now been completed, and to declare elected the following six men. It is expected that at their first meeting they will elect a chairman and a secretary. Their names are here set down in alphabetical order:

Cos Cobb, Jr.	Biology
Paul Eaton	Sociology
James B. Sloane	Chemistry
Edward B. Tyler	Modern Languages
Abel Vincent	Economics
W. W. Waggoner	Art

I have notified the Chairman of the Executive Committee of the Board of Trustees, Mr. John A. Martin, of the election of those named above, and he will shortly get in touch with committee members to arrange a first meeting. I have also notified President Vaughn of the constitution of the committee, and he sends his best wishes for their success in the fulfillment of this heavy responsibility."

At the bottom of the letter was Fletcher's signature in fresh blue ink, as neat as his polka-dotted bow-tie. Tyler dropped the letter to the blotter where the other postal débris lay helter-skelter, spoiling the neatness of Mrs. Rhodes's arrangement of the desk-top. He stared at it moodily. So that was it. There it was. Of course, Milton Fletcher, wearing his clerkship like an academic gown, would never have tipped a man off in advance. His motto was like the old housekeeper's: a place for everything and everything in its place. Everything according to form. Everything official as hell. Everything symmetrical. He picked up the letter and looked at the names. Two scientists, Cobb and Sloane. Two social scientists, Vincent and Paul Eaton. And the two humanists: Waggoner and Tyler.

At least he knew most of the committee. Cos Cobb, old fishing companion. Paul Eaton, who called himself the Guy Fawkes of Enfield. The man with the barrel of verbal gunpowder under the House of Lords, itching to blow up the joint. Leader of his Homeric Majesty's Disloyal Opposition. Well, not disloyal exactly. Just watchful. A viewer with alarm. A writer of letters to the *Times*. Then old Bill Waggoner, mild as May, art historian and collector. Now he could start collecting names of candidates. Tyler knew the organic chemist, Jim Sloane, but only slightly. And Abel Vincent he knew scarcely at all. An able economist, no pun intended. Tall, cadaverous, with a large mouth full of crooked yellow teeth; sleepy eyes; a perpetual pipe, and fingers always slightly soiled from the pipe-ash he kept ramming down into the bowl, while the thin smoke issued from deep in his throat after its journey through the slender lungs.

So here were the king-makers. The philosopher-king-makers, if one could be found in this day and age. The pickers and choosers. The screeners and gleaners. Tyler's courage, as he stared at the cold rain trickling down the window-panes, quailed before the task.

It was going to be, as Milton had indicated, a hell of an obligation. How did you go about it? Would the trustees themselves have ideas? Had they, in fact, already found their man, with this new faculty committee only a polite bow in the direction of democratic procedures? You could only wait and see. Perhaps the committee would turn out to be a rub-ber-stamp outfit. Not, though, certainly, with Paul Eaton aboard. He delighted to stamp on rubber stamps, or blow them sky-high with his verbal squibs. Never a dull moment with Eaton. Like the Old Howard Theatre in Boston in its burlesque days: "Something Doing from One to Eleven." And all the Harvard undergraduates down near the stage, cheering on the strip-tease artistes.

The real trouble was, when you looked at this thing ob-jectively and from the point of view of the faculty man, that this was just one more committee surmounting an already topheavy schedule of ad hoc committees, standing committees, departmental committees, and outside committees. And the scientists, of course, with their consultant jobs in industry. And the economists hopping the train to Washington every

week. If this new committee met often—and they would have
to in order to find a new president in eight or nine months—it
would become the extra bale that cracked the camel's already
overloaded vertebrae. The afternoons and evenings in the
smoke-filled rooms. The trips to New York for conferences
with trustees like John Martin, who was a busy man himself.
And then the getting behind in your other work—teaching,
writing, running the department, writing reports, editing for
the learned journals—just to stay on top of the new job.

Like old John Henry Norton's squall. Tyler remembered
the wizened figure of John Henry astride the lobster-trap
amidst the various ripe smells on the wharf. Fish-scales on his
shoes. Gnarled and scarred hands whittling a stick. Looking
out across the glittering coastal waters towards the Gay Head
end of the Vineyard, while his aged eyes squinched up against
the glare, and the jaws worked between words and the quid.
"I member one time we was out in the dory," John Henry
said. "We was trying to get in our traps, some of them, for
the winter. The boy was along. 'Twas rough. Dory all
aslosh. The wind was blowing hard's it could blow. Couldn't
blow no harder. Nen, all of a sudden, up come a squall. We
was damn near tipped over. But you know these dories."

Yes, the dories, like the faculty, were hard to tip over. But
it could be done. Tyler remembered the sudden storm half
a mile off the Hen and Chickens lightship. Wind like iron,
waves like green dragons. He broke an oar trying to head
into it and in a minute, in a second, there was the shock of
cold water, bitter in the throat where you had gasped it in,
heavy as lead in your stomach until you had vomited it up,
lying across the coast-guardsman's knees in the surf-boat
twenty minutes later. The water turned from green to gray.

NOVEMBER

It was hard to keep your head above the surface. His old black lunchbox bobbed for a moment before it sank. And the odd, enormous look of the dory-bottom rising and falling beside him, covered with the black stuff John Henry called monkeyturd, half awash in the viscous gray swell. But not sinking. The Hen and Chickens crew had a pair of binoculars on him. Sixteen-year-old Tyler had hung on until they came. How, he wondered, would the forty-four-year-old Tyler hang onto the pitching dory through the rough months ahead?

"Don't dramatize it," he told himself. You can dramatize the dory-story for Toby and Tommy, watch their eyes pop as they picture their father valiantly striving with the wind and waves. But don't dramatize this committee. "Many brave hearts lie asleep in the deep, so beware, so beware." Beware of what? Well, beware of unemployed generals and ex-presidents of the Stock Exchange. Otherwise, let the wind blow where it listeth.

Tyler lighted his pipe and picked up one of the freshman themes. They had been reading La Fontaine's Fables this week and the assignment had been to write four hundred words on the master's model, using a beast to point a moral or sharpen an irony. The title of this one, neatly printed with a stub pen, was *Antaeus in Parvo*. Tyler remembered the boy's face, long as an El Greco, brown eyes, glasses, thin light hair: Jimmy Lawlor, a true introvert. "I shall not follow," Jimmy had written, "the model of La Fontaine. Instead I will tell a true anecdote about an ant I saw last summer. He was so strong for his size that he reminded me of the giant Antaeus in classical mythology. But he was just an ordinary black ant, neither very large nor very small.

"When I first saw him I was sitting on the lowest of a

45

flight of nine stone steps in a neighbor's garden. Over the top of the book I was reading I saw the movement of something white. It was an ugly, ghostly thing; it seemed to be the front part of a bleeched-out grasshopper's body. The feelers were missing and both the eye-sockets were empty. Of course the only reason it was moving at all was that my friend the ant, who was about one eighth its size, had clamped his jaws firmly on one of those pale legs and was dragging his prize back home, walking backwards all the way. While I watched, he backed his way up the first riser. The grasshopper-body must have been much heavier on the vertical than it had been on the horizontal because now the whole dead weight hung free from the ant's jaws. But the ant backed right up the riser of the second step as if nothing could ever stop him.

"The ant had real trouble getting the body over the square edge of the second step. He had to yank and yank, then move sidewise, retreat a half-inch down the vertical plane to get another start, and then yank some more before he found a place where he could get real traction. He must have worked for three or four minutes right on that edge alone. At last he heaved the body onto the horizontal plane of the second step, and you expected him to stop, get out his handkerchief, mop his brow, maybe look back over the great distance he had covered. But he didn't. He never even stopped. He never relaxed his hold and he just kept on pulling.

"I must have watched him work for five minutes. Then I forgot about him and read my book for ten minutes. At first, when I looked again, I couldn't see the ant at all. Then halfway up the sixth stone riser I saw the moving fleck of white, and I knew the ant was still pulling away, heading up the nine steps. Each of them was as big for him as a mountain would be to a cliffdweller lugging home the front half of a cow. I saw him once more just starting up the seventh riser, then I didn't see him any more. But I have not forgotten him.

"He did not speak, like the animals of La Fontaine. His mouth was too full of grasshopper-leg, and if ants breathe he must have been puffing hard. But he is an insect who could represent something to mankind. Go to Antaeus, thou sluggard. He is a fable in himself." The theme was signed neatly at the bottom: *James Whitcomb Lawlor.*

Tyler corrected the spelling of "bleached" with a red pencil. "A," he wrote at the top. "This rates a top grade because you have both observed and written a genuine fable on the theme of indefatigability. It could apply very well to a variety of situations."

It could, too, thought Tyler as he wrote the words. Add one more step and it could represent the scholar lugging the corpse of the past through a decade of laborious scholarship. Or keep the nine steps, and it could be a professor moving through the school year, October to June. He put the essay into the manila folder and reached for the telephone. Better call Alice, see how Tommy's temperature was doing.

IV

Tyler filled and lighted his pipe and reached for his telephone to call Alice. Just as he lifted the receiver from its cradle, the buzzer sounded from its black box.

"Yes?"

47

From her office down the hall, Mrs. Rhodes's voice came, crisp, polite, secretarial. "Professor Tyler. Dean Schaeffer is calling." Then the Dean's harsh voice, which contrasted so oddly with his smooth tanned face, his clean white hair.

"Oh, Ed. Do you have a minute? Is anyone with you?"

"Yes. No, Bob. All clear."

"Two matters," the Dean said. He was systematic always. Had to be in that job, or your dory would turn over in a trice. "Two matters," he'd say, and tick them off, interrupting you patiently if you got longwinded. "Three matters." Then he would lay it on the line. You knew where you stood with the Dean, which was a comfort.

"First," the harsh voice said, "as to your own leave for next year. Did I tell you about that?"

"Yes, sir, you did," Tyler said. "Sometime early last week. You said that the president had approved the leave, conditional of course on my getting the Guggenheim. Which of course is not at all certain. This was outside our regular schedule of leaves for next year. Our other departmental leaves were taken care of last June, you recall. I—"

"That's right," Schaeffer said. "Now the second matter. Ed, just how much of an emergency, in your judgment, is that Renzulli case?"

"No more than usual, I guess," Tyler said. "You remember I told you that Giorgio came into the office a week or two ago. He seemed very nervous and depressed. He said he was thinking of leaving the profession because he couldn't get along on his present salary. You know Giorgio is quite a linguist. Not only Italian, his native tongue, but three or four others, including Russian. He had had some kind of a nibble from—as I recall—Radio Free Europe. A friend of his, I believe—"

"Does that work pay well?" asked the Dean.

"I have no idea what it pays," Tyler said. "And I'm not sure Giorgio knows, either. But he's an idealist, and I suppose he thought—"

"You can't eat idealism," the Dean said. His harsh laugh crackled in the receiver. "Ever try it fried? Or soft-boiled?"

Tyler laughed back. "They say hard-boiled idealism is very nourishing. But no, sir, I think Giorgio is probably discontented for a number of reasons, and I guess it occurred to him that a little more money might help to take off the rough edges of his discontent."

"Spoken like a poet," the Dean said. "Maybe he could buy a few more bottles of *grappa*. Isn't that what they call it?"

"Giulio drinks more coffee than wine," Tyler said. He thought of Alice, feeding Giulio the glass of sherry, making him talk in the living-room at home. "He says wine sours his stomach."

"Maybe he's got a case of spiritual sour stomach," said Schaeffer. "You know him far better than I do, Ed. Would you call him a malcontent?"

"No, sir. Not a malcontent. Maybe a discontent. Or a noncontent. I don't know what the proper phrase is." Tyler did not enjoy the analysis of a departmental character in the presence of the dean. At least not today. He felt his own stomach souring. "Giorgio, you see—"

"How are things at home?" asked the Dean, as if to short-circuit a lecture on Giorgio. Perhaps, Tyler reflected, the Dean was not enjoying this either.

"You mean at Giorgio's home. All right, I guess. Though my wife says she thinks Giorgio looks like a famished wolf. She—"

"Doesn't he get fed?" Schaeffer asked quickly.

"In a manner of speaking." Tyler was becoming a little tired of the fast interruptions. Busy as he was, Schaeffer ought to let a man finish a sentence. Tyler rapped out that one phrase, "In a manner of speaking," and let it lie.

The Dean's voice took on its generalizing tone, a few notes up the scale from his usual speaking-range. "Would we have here, do you think, Ed, a case of wife-trouble? Of course in this job I see a certain amount of it. I call it wife-trouble just as a generic term; it's shorthand for a multitude of problems. All kinds. Financial worry or debt. Death in the family, or illness of some sort. Nervous breakdowns. Accidents in the house or in the car that lay the wife up in some way. Social ambition. Plain shrewishness. Husband drinking, worrying the wife who clamps down on him. Husband playing around —of course not on *this* faculty—" The Dean interrupted himself, this time, and the harsh laugh came again.

"Nope, not here," Tyler said, and clamped his mouth shut again.

"What I was leading up to," Schaeffer said, "was to ask you what about Mrs. Renzulli. Do you know her? What is her name?"

"Giulietta."

"Oh, Julietta, is it? Like Shakespeare's heroine." The Dean, an American historian by profession, was proud of his literary attainments. "Well, Ed,"—the crackling laugh came again—"how does she treat her Romeo?"

"No better than she should, I believe," Tyler said. "You may have put your finger on the real cause of his discontent. Except that he's one of those brilliant personalities, a very good Dante scholar"—never lose a chance to plug the men in your department—"who is all wrapped up in what he's doing. And he's not making as much progress as he feels he should be. You know the frustrations."

"Yes, yes," the Dean said kindly. References to the difficulties of *la vie intellectuelle* often touched him.

"And then," Tyler went on, "Giulietta is something of a scholar herself. A translator. She's working on some Tasso translations, and she probably forgets to put the pasta on the table precisely at seven o'clock every evening. They eat out of cans, I have heard, at least part of the time."

"Well, now, Ed," the Dean began. Here, Tyler thought, comes the decision. Schaeffer was a good administrator, humane and kindly. He investigated his cases, talked them over frankly with his subordinate administrators, satisfied himself that he had his finger on the situation's pulse, made up his mind, then moved in fast with his decision. "Ed, you tell Giorgio—I mean, the next time you have a chance you might want to say to him that our teaching budget is pretty well frozen for the current year. Except, of course, for emergency cases, outside offers, and the like. You can tell him, if you want to, that the chances for a raise in salary are good next year. If you like, and if your department wants to recommend it later on this fall or winter, you can tell him that you will put through a recommendation for a raise for him, effective next year. Do you think that will hold him? You see, Ed, Renzulli has been pretty well treated. I have my book here on the desk. Let's see. One, two, three raises in the last five years."

"It may hold him and it may not," Tyler said. "I don't know how serious the competition is from Radio Free Europe. But I'll talk with him and see. Thanks very much for all your trouble."

"No trouble, no trouble," the Dean said quickly. "How are *you*? I see you were elected to the Committee of Six. That's quite an assignment."

"I guess it will be," said Tyler. "I see my Voltaire book receding into the distance."

"Don't worry, Ed," said the Dean. "You'll have the Guggenheim next year. You can rest up and write about Voltaire."

Tyler laughed. "You call it restful. Voltaire isn't restful, Bob. He's whirling in his grave, waiting for me to whirl back. And anyhow, the Guggenheim is by no means a sure thing."

"Don't worry," said the Dean again. "Voltaire's in his grave and the Guggenheim's in the bag."

"The first is right," said Tyler. "I wish I were that sure about the second."

When the dean rang off, Tyler put down the phone and lighted the dead ashes in his pipe. "Rest up, indeed," he muttered, half aloud. Schaeffer could be slightly obtuse on matters of scholarship. Still, he was a fine dean. If we do as well with the new president, thought Tyler, we will be lucky.

He picked up the phone again and dialed his home number. Alice's low voice vibrated along the wire.

"You sound sleepy," Tyler said.

"I *was* asleep," said Alice. "Fast asleep on the living-room couch. Mrs. DeNew was here all morning, cleaning the house.

And talking. You know how she talks. Full of stories that go on and on. What time is it, anyway?"

"Ten after three."

"I'm supposed to call the doctor a little after five and report in."

"How is Tommy?"

"He ate his lunch well," said Alice. "At two o'clock, his temperature was down to a hundred and one. He was lying in bed drawing pictures of airplanes and listening to a soap opera on the radio. I think he's coming all right. Goodbye, Ed. I'll go and check his temperature."

"Goodbye, Alice. See you later."

Alice's voice stopped with a click just as the first student of the afternoon knocked on Tyler's door. "Come in," said Tyler, swivelling in his chair to face the door. If it hadn't been for the student, Tyler would have telephoned Alice again to tell her about the Committee of Six assignment. But she would be upstairs now, one hand on Tommy's brown head, the other placing the thermometer under his tongue. The news could wait for the evening glass of sherry.

v

By the morning of Guy Fawkes Day, the three-day blow had done its best—or its worst—and had departed. All along Enfield Avenue East, Tyler noticed, the maples stood bare, well-washed blue sky showing through their black branches. Underfoot lay the leaves, mashed and crushed by passing feet, drying out now on the brown lawns of the fraternity houses, still heaped damply in the gutters. The grizzle-headed old yardman at the Alpha Delt house plied a wooden rake. Already two piles, neatly coned, were waiting to be gathered up in the square of burlap, braced with sticks on two sides, which leaned against one of the maple-boles near the sidewalk.

"Good morning," Tyler said. "Getting set for a little burning?"

"Too wet to burn yet," the yardman said. "But if I don't get them up now, they going to spoil the grass."

"The storm really took them," Tyler said.

"Not that oak." The old man gestured with his rake-handle to a young tree which stood by itself, branches still covered with fawn-colored leaves. "They tough. Those leaves going to stay on all winter."

We're all tough, Tyler thought, walking on. We're all going to stay on all winter. After the wet dark days the morning seemed populous. The morning colloquy, Tyler thought. The bright energy of the new day. Feet dry for a change. Pants pressed. "Wear your best suit," Alice had said as he came out of the morning shower. "It's just been dry-cleaned. You want to look nice for the trustees." She had even straightened the knot in his tie as he kissed her good-bye. Now he glanced down at the well-creased trousers, the fairly well polished shoes. Left, right. Left, right. Moving briskly up the sidewalk.

The meeting was set for four in the conference room of Bishop. Martin's letter had been polite, almost deferential. "Time," he had written, "is of the essence if we are to work out a solution to our problem." He had named the other members of the Board of Trustees who would participate in the search: Dr. Norman Macy of Presbyterian Hospital;

54

Robert F. Sibley, a banker or investment man from Philadelphia; Jarvis Eames, who was something in Standard Oil of New Jersey; the Reverend Harrison Caldwell of the Massachusetts Theological Seminary. Five in all. Farther on in the letter, Martin used the word "task-force." Military terminology, Tyler reflected, had now invaded the business world up and down the country. And from there it was trickling into education. Task-forces, strikes, concentrations, dispersions, operations. This was Operation Parthenon. Post-Homeric Task Force. That was better than the language of Madison Avenue, anyway. There, evidently, you were always wrapping things up, giving someone a rundown on something, or promoting package-deals. Or finalizing. There was a word for you. Let us finalize the new president. Or the old one.

He took the Trask stairs two at a time and opened the door with *Department of Modern Languages and Literatures* painted on the glass panel. Mrs. Rhodes's typewriter was already clacking. A single rose stood on her desk in a small green vase.

"Good morning," Tyler said. "Where'd you get the rose? I thought they were all gone long ago."

"Good morning, Mr. Tyler. Isn't it nice? Just a little overblown. Mr. Strong brought it in a few minutes ago. From his garden. The last rose of summer," said Mrs. Rhodes. In the streaming light from the east windows her white hair made a nimbus.

"More like the last rose of autumn," Tyler said. He leaned over to sniff it and noticed that it had almost no odor. "Has the mail come yet?"

"Not yet," Mrs. Rhodes said. "Ernie should be here any

55

minute. Mr. Tyler, a student was asking for you. I told him you would be in pretty soon. Fenelosa. He went over to the Student Union to get some breakfast. About ten minutes ago. He should be back shortly. Can you see him?"

"Yes, I'll see him. Would you send him in when he comes. Any messages?"

"No messages," said Mrs. Rhodes, turning back to her typewriter. Clack. Clack. As he went down the hall to his office, he heard her shift into high gear. Like a distant machine gun. A good woman. If she weren't too old, we ought to consider electing her president. Never had a woman at the helm. Petticoat government. Shake the old place up like Guy Fawkes's gunpowder. Tyler was whistling as he unlocked his door and opened the windows to the bright air. "You may not feel so gay after the trustees' meeting," he thought. "Better enjoy it while you can."

Fenelosa, when he sidled in a few minutes later, was apologetic. "I won't take much of your time, sir." He had shaved, Tyler noticed, and his black hair was freshly combed. "It's about that Voltaire subject. I've been looking into it and I'd like to change the approach."

"Good," Tyler said. "I was hoping you would come around to that. How did you happen to get the idea in the first place? I mean the idea that Voltaire was a Christian."

Fenelosa's cheeks flushed slightly. "I have a confession to make, sir," he said. "When I saw you before, I was just casting around for an idea. My room-mate—well, I hadn't really read much Voltaire. My room-mate had some lecture-notes from last year. A history course on France."

"Eighteenth-century France?"

"It covered the whole history of France," said Fenelosa. "Anyway, he showed me some notes about Voltaire taking communion. I forget the date."

"The late 1760's," Tyler said. "Did your room-mate say Voltaire was a Christian?"

"Not exactly, no. But he thought Voltaire was maybe, you know, getting converted in his old age. So I began to read around some, and I found out why he did it. Took the communion, I mean."

"Why did he do it, do you think?"

"Well, he said it was to be an example to the poor people. The peasants. But I think he really did it because he was afraid of being burned at the stake."

"The scholars argue about that," Tyler said. "Some say it was fear. The old guy loved life, and there really was some danger. Others say he was just thumbing his nose at that bishop. His enemy. The Bishop of Annecy. I don't want to rub it in, Fenelosa, but to call Voltaire a Christian, you'd have to ignore most of the years of his maturity, and you would have to ignore the *Philosophical Dictionary*, and you would have to ignore—"

"Don't go on, sir," the boy said, laughing and blushing again. "I get it. In fact that's why I'm here. I already got it. But I'd like to know a good modern life of Voltaire. One that says a lot about his ideas on religion."

"There aren't too many good ones," said Tyler. He took down a red volume from the shelf beside his desk, blew the dust off the top, and handed it to Fenelosa. "Here's one you can borrow. By John Morley. A little old now, but still good. The prose is—well—noble."

57

Fenelosa riffled through the pages. "Thank you, sir," he said, getting up. "I won't take any more of your time." He departed happily, the book under his arm, his conscience clean and bright as the morning. Probably a lot cleaner, Tyler thought, than Voltaire's conscience when he took that bread and wine. Fenelosa was a good kid, a high C or a very low B student. Not as naive as he sounded. Just uninformed. The book would put him on the right track. Concentration of truth. Dispersion of error. Voltaire's watchword and the teacher's bright reward.

Outside in the hall, hasty steps sounded, paused at his door. Through the mail-slot three or four envelopes appeared, plopped to the floor. Ernie the campus mail-carrier. His steps receded down the hall, and Tyler scooped up the envelopes. Today the mail would be no problem. He dumped the insurance advertisement and the Buick Garage postcard into the waste-basket. The round file, Mrs. Rhodes called it. The card with the maroon band around it gave notice of a meeting of the Faculty Committee on Discipline. Four-thirty p.m. Monday. Tyler entered it on his desk calendar as a reminder, and got out his small green appointment book. Monday looked clear. He wrote it in with a pencil: "4:30. Discip. Com. 108 Enfield." And dropped the card into the waste-basket. The remaining envelope was heavy: obviously a wedding invitation. Former student, likely, taking himself a bride. Yes, from Florida. Mr. and Mrs. Arthur Parsons Wilder request the honor of your presence at the wedding of their daughter, Sally Anne, to Ensign Peter Alfred Adams, U.S.N.R. So Pete Adams and Sally Anne were tying the knot. You learned how to tie knots in the Navy. He was thinking of

Pete's breezy California manner, his impossible French accent, when the buzzer made him jump.

"Ed. Eaton. Paul Eaton. Ed, you'll be at the trustees' meeting today."

"Command performance, I thought," said Tyler.

"Commando performance," Eaton said. "Sneak ashore in the dark of the moon. Worm through the bushes. Kidnap the Harvard president. Tape his mouth, bring him out to the submarine on a rubber raft. Hold a Luger against his belly. Offer him the presidency of Enfield at a cool fifty thousand per annum. If he says no, shoot."

"Is that what the president makes?" Tyler said, laughing.

"Probably closer to twenty," Eaton said. "With the butler thrown in. But you have to pay income tax on the butler's salary. Say, Ed, you remember Milton Fletcher's letter to us? I have a copy here. First paragraph, quote: 'It is expected that at their first meeting they will elect a chairman and a secretary.' That's us. Now I ran into Abel Vincent at lunch yesterday, and we sort of reached the conclusion that Bill Waggoner ought to be chairman of our committee. He's the oldest of the bunch. Also level-headed."

"Sounds good to me," Tyler said. "I'd vote for that. Have you checked with the others?"

"You're the first one I called," said Paul. "I don't expect any argument from the others on this. With the possible exception of Jim Sloane. I seem to remember that he and Bill don't hit it off too well."

"They should," Tyler said. "My scientific friends tell me that art is a process of organic chemistry. I'm sure that Bill—"

"Oh, it isn't Bill Waggoner I'm worried about," Eaton

said. "It's our jipper-jawed friend. But I think he'll go along with our proposition. I'll call him next and find out. Now about the secretary. I suppose it ought to be someone with a literary flair."

Tyler saw it coming and side-stepped. "How about Cos Cobb?"

Eaton made a humming noise into the mouthpiece. "How about Ed Tyler? Frankly, Ed, Abel and I were thinking of you."

"I expect you made the suggestion and he agreed," said Tyler. "I hardly know Abel, and I don't think he knows much about me. Our paths haven't crossed often. But this secretaryship doesn't call for a literary flair, does it? Why not one of the secretaries—the office secretaries—to take down all the golden words in shorthand?"

A sound like a small whirlwind came out of Tyler's phone. It was Eaton's mock shushing. "Shhhh! Remember the commandos. This is all highly secret stuff. Top drawer. Under the rose. Hidden under a bushel, and all that."

"Cos is your man, then," Tyler said. "He's not only a good secret-keeper. He's also a good summarizer."

"All right, Ed. If you say so. I'll call the others and suggest those two names as our slate. Waggoner and Cobb. Unless I call you back, that will be settled. Then we can formalize it this afternoon."

"I still feel a little glum about the whole business, Paul. Not our officers, but the whole affair. It's going to take a terrible lot of time."

"Absolutely," said Paul. "You compute it in terms of our salaries, and it will amount to a pretty sum before we're done.

Picking a president takes time and money. So does serving as a president. Anyhow, I assume the present slate of officers is settled."

"I don't think you'll run into any trouble," Tyler said. "Except that the candidates themselves may want to argue. So now—the conspiracy begins. Officers lined up and agreed on before the meeting even starts. Paul, do you know what day this is?"

"Sure, November five."

"I mean what holiday? In England?"

"Bastille Day?" said Paul. "No, that's France. August Bank Holiday? No, that's in August. You've got me, Ed, what holiday is this in England?"

"I'll clue you, as Toby says. The year is 1605. The reigning king is James I. The place is—"

"Guy Fawkes Day," yelled Eaton into the phone. "How fitting! But I seem to remember they did something fairly rough to the conspirators when they caught them. Boiled them in oil, or something. Cut off their ears and gave them to Uncle Jacobus. Can you picture our gang spread-eagled out there on the Phoenix Sundial? Would you care for a slice of the rump? Those are pearls that were their eyes, or however it goes. But enough! I dodder in my morning dotage. See you this afternoon. Where is the meeting?"

"Conference Room, Bishop Hall. Nothing too good for our trustees. You know the room was just done over last summer."

"Nothing too good for us, you mean. We're the Committee of Six. We are the boys who say 'Nix!' " Eaton chuckled to signify irony. "I'm really hanging up now, Ed. A bientot."

"Thanks, Paul." Tyler put down the phone and swiveled his desk chair so that he faced away from it. Now, he thought, to hell with that committee. For the rest of the day, at least until four, he would put the trustees' meeting out of his mind. Let the idea of it, the advance imagination of it, stay in its corner. Let it mind its business, period. Because meantime there was plenty of other business to mind. The daily business by which you earned your daily bread. Business like the eleven o'clock lecture he must soon go to give to the fifty-odd undergraduates who were taking his course in the literature of France in the eighteenth century.

He glanced at his watch, which showed ten-thirty-five. Time now to look over his lecture notes. Today he would deal with satire and irony, try to demonstrate the multiple profundities of Montesquieu in the *Lettres Persanes*. Out of these notes—these pencil-scrawls, these patches of typing with their interlineations, these scribbled marginalia, these after-thoughts which had become forethoughts, these forethoughts that became afterthoughts—would have to come the urbane and finished product. The notes were the rough quarry from which he must extract the block of marble. And then this mass, to be worked over for fifty minutes, to be carved with words into the proportioned statue, the Galatea. And finally, hardest of all, this statue to be brought alive by any verbal magic he could muster. Not only brought alive but borne alive into the heads (and if possible the hearts) of those four dozen yawning, alert, scratching, attentive, surreptitiously-*Eagle*-reading, argumentative, girl-dreaming, out-of-window-gazing undergraduates who would straggle in to take their places when the chapel-bell struck eleven.

62

An impossible task, to awaken Galatea. Impossible but necessary. Necessary and therefore—somehow—possible. Sighing slightly, but also beginning to feel the first stirrings of the slow pulse of his enthusiasm for the subject of the lecture to come, he got out the notes (too dog-eared, he thought, he must take time to organize them better) and bent in the bright morning to his proper work.

VI

"Gentlemen," John Martin said. "It is now four-ten and I know that some of us must catch the five-thirty train back to New York. So with your permission, we had better get this show on the road." Under the close-cropped gray hair, the gray eyes looked genially round the table. That head, Tyler reflected, looked like Oliver Cromwell's life-mask—or was it death-mask—which stared down from the wall in one of the classrooms in Trask. Large, powerful, with that great beak of a nose; the big, full-matured head; the great ears; the clean-shaven cheeks and broad chin.

"I ought to say first what a privilege it is for us to be able to work with you gentlemen of the faculty on this important assignment. We are going to be leaning on you heavily for advice and counsel. We are all agreed that we want to find the best man in the country to succeed Homer Vaughn, President Vaughn. Speaking for the Trustees' group, and of course we are only the executive arm of the whole body of twelve trustees, it is fair to say that we have not yet thought through any special ways and means for the conduct of this search. After all, we aren't called on every day to select a new president of Enfield. I don't think any of us were on the Board at the time President Vaughn was chosen. Professor Waggoner, I believe you were the only faculty man, you *are* the only faculty man here this afternoon who has served under two presidents—Dr. Lawford and Dr. Vaughn."

Bill Waggoner nodded politely and fixed his eye again on the yellow pencil on the blotter before him. Jim Sloane raised his hairy hand.

"Correction," he rumbled. "I was here under Lawford. I had just come a year or two before his retirement."

"Yes, and Professor Sloane," Martin said. "So the point is that we have no special precedents to go on. I don't myself feel that we should be bound by any precedents. We can hammer out our rules and procedures as we go along. By the way, I forgot to say as we began that Bob Sibley had to send his regrets that he could not be with us today. He had a last-minute call to Washington. I think we all know each other, that we had a chance for a few moments of talk before the meeting started. But I will just go round the table once to make sure. Dr. Macy, just here to my right."

The great surgeon from Presbyterian, Tyler thought. Heavy-set, powerful, conservative horn-rimmed glasses, strong surgeon's hands, fingernails closely clipped.

"Next to him, Professor Sloane of Chemistry. Professor Eaton of Economics next to him."

"Sociology," Paul Eaton said.

Martin's big face flushed. "Of course, sociology. Excuse me." He glanced at the papers in front of him. "Professor Vincent of Economics. At the end of the table, Mr. Eames, of the trustees' group. Professor Tyler of the French Department.

Professor Cobb of Biology. Professor Waggoner of the Art Department. And finally, at my left here, Reverend, Doctor, Professor—what is your title, anyway, Harrison?—of the Massachusetts Theological Seminary."

"Mister will do," Caldwell said.

"Mr. Caldwell, then," said Martin. "And I'll call on Mr. Caldwell to speak to us on the matter of qualifications."

"Well, John," Caldwell said. "And gentlemen." His long clean fingers played with an ashtray on the table before him. "We thought it might be well to begin with a rough blueprint. It goes without saying that we cannot expect to find a replacement—a younger replica of President Vaughn. As we all know, he is unique. He has grown up with the university. Thirty years is a long time. He probably knows—certainly knows—more about the innermost workings, the side streets and alleys, than anyone else. We cannot, should not, expect to duplicate him: there is only one Homer Vaughn."

Eames, the plump, broadshouldered man from Standard Oil, looked at Tyler and smiled and nodded. Tyler smiled and nodded back. What Caldwell had said was perfectly true.

"Now," Caldwell went on, his almost hairless head bent forward, his fingers still pushing the ashtray a few inches to the right, then back again to the center, then an inch or two to the left, "now we come to the blueprint. It is quite simple. We would like to find a man of excellent character, with some experience as an executive, and with at least twelve to fifteen years to go before retirement."

"In other words," Jim Sloane said, "he should be somewhere between fifty-four and fifty-seven."

"That's right, but he need not be that old. Other things

65

being equal we would certainly consider a man in his middle fifties." As he spoke, Martin pointed his big nose directly at Jim, his big shoulders hunched forward aggressively. Does he know, Tyler wondered, that Jim is aggressive, too? Does he counter force with force?

Cos Cobb cleared his throat. "Excuse me, Mr. Martin. Do you have a floor on this: I mean a lower age-limit?"

Martin had continued for a moment with his eyes on Jim Sloane. Now he turned deferentially back to Harrison Caldwell. "Harrison, excuse my interruption. Professor—er—Cobb has asked—"

"Nothing absolute about it," Caldwell said, mildly. "The man is the thing that counts, and his age is secondary. We would be prepared to go as low as thirty-nine or forty. That was about Homer Vaughn's age when he took over. Our criteria would be maturity of outlook, administrative experience, and the like. Could a man of thirty or thirty-five do the job? Probably he could, in time. But he would have to learn an awful lot awfully fast."

"But you would not automatically exclude a comparative youngster?" Cos said.

"Certainly not," said Caldwell. "Now as to the other qualifications: we think that, ideally, the candidate should have some connection with Enfield. A graduate of the university, say."

"How wide do you swing on that, Harrison?" asked Paul Eaton. "For example, would a graduate school product count? An A.B. from some other place who got his doctorate here?"

"Oh, yes, Paul," Caldwell said.

Jim Sloane leaned forward, his jipper-jaw protruding.

66

Tyler recalled a remark by somebody that Jim used his lower lip like a boxing glove. "What about current or former faculty members?" Jim rumbled.

"Oh, yes," said Caldwell, again. "We thought they would loom up very prominently in the picture."

Sloane nodded, grunted, and settled back in his armchair.

Caldwell looked at Martin, who nodded for him to continue.

"Finally on this point," Caldwell said, "there are outside candidates. People who have no connection with Enfield. While our primary preference would be towards an Enfieldian, we wouldn't want to exclude qualified men who had made their marks in other places, other parts of the country."

Tyler said: "Would that mean retired generals? Business men? Presidents and deans in other institutions?"

Martin smiled. "Harrison, let me answer that one. Professor Tyler, it might, but it very probably would not. I'm not sure how happy some of our sister institutions have been with that kind of administrator. I won't name names—"he looked genially around the table—"but there have been a few bitter experiences in recent years. The Lorelei of Washington have been singing loud enough to be heard. No, we—"

"You may have heard the story about one of these administrators," Eaton said. "One of the men in our department is a refugee from one of those universities. He tells of a philosophy chairman who went to the president and said he would have to have a metaphysician. The president looked blank. 'Metaphysician?' he said. 'Metaphysician? Why, yes, if you need one, procure one!'"

In the middle of the laughter, Tyler saw Martin glance at his watch. "We are agreed, gentlemen, and this point is of the utmost importance, that we would prefer a man who is a proven scholar—"

From the faculty members there was a murmur of approbation. "Good," Tyler thought. "Good." He looked at Martin admiringly.

"One who has made his way in his profession by his own brainpower," Martin said. "One who has written books."

Jim Sloane leaned forward slightly again. "Or made scientific discoveries?" he asked. Still, Tyler noticed, with that air of implied aggressiveness.

"Scientific discoveries would qualify certainly as very important scholarship," Martin said, pleasantly. He watched Sloane settle back in his chair, and again turned his head towards Caldwell.

"Now, Harrison, can you give us a quick fill-in on those other points?"

"Well," Harrison Caldwell said, "let's see. We have covered age, administrative experience, the desirable but not mandatory Enfield connection, proved ability as a scholar. The other matters have to do with character, mainly."

"What about religious affiliation?" said Abel Vincent. He had not spoken before. His sleepy eyes, encircled by the dark discolorations of the heavy reader or the worrier or the insomniac, were like slits under the bony brows. In the brown light of the conference room, his skull-face looked, Tyler thought, Dantesque.

"I don't believe we had even thought of that question," Caldwell said. "In any case, it should not be primary. Probably he should be a Protestant. All previous presidents of Enfield have been Protestants. But we need not feel bound by this tradition. There are many able Catholics, many able men of the Jewish faith. For the right man, we would break the tradition."

Again, from around the table, the murmur of approval came.

"Finally," said Caldwell, gently smiling, "as to his personal character. We conceive of a broad-ranging mind, absolute integrity, nobility of motives. A deep concern, of course, for the welfare of liberal education. The kind of man the alumni would respect. A man without ambitions on the national scene. A man of settled religious convictions. He should be adaptable to a variety of situations, and should have a capacity for back-breaking work. This means a healthy and vigorous man. Someone, too, with a good personnel sense, because a strong faculty must be constantly rebuilt and infused with new blood. He must be absolutely devoted to the two great tasks of the university: the education of young men and the extension of the boundaries of knowledge. One who will fight for principles. A man of moral courage to do the right as he—"

Dr. Macy had been moving his powerful frame and making as if to speak. Now, when he opened his mouth, his voice came slow, and Tyler noticed that his big hands were trembling. Was the great surgeon shy?

"Harrison," the doctor said deliberately. "Your description reminds me of the time, I think it was in 1940, when I happened to be on the board of one of the medical foundations. We were looking for a new director." Dr. Macy's slow voice paused, the hands still trembling, for so long that Tyler wondered if the story was over. But he noticed that Martin still watched Macy with interest. "A new director," said Macy at last. "And the qualities wanted were a lot like those you mention. Finally one of the men said, 'We are licked before we start!' He said, 'The only man who could possibly qualify on all those counts died on the Cross nineteen hundred years ago.' "

Martin laughed loudly, hitting the table with his fist, and beamed round the company. Like a big searchlight, Tyler thought. Even Sloane looked pleasant. Dr. Macy was leaning towards him, repeating the punch-line in his deliberate voice: "Nineteen hundred years ago."

"We don't have to go quite that far," Martin said, jovially. "We will settle for something a little short of God."

"If we should want to get God," Paul Eaton said, "we wouldn't have to look far. I understand they've got Him giving a course in religion at Princeton."

Again the male laughter roared in the room. Tyler glanced at Harrison Caldwell, who was laughing with the rest. The whole company sat relaxed, companionable, the line between trustees and faculty suddenly erased. Martin wiped his eyes and glanced again at his watch.

"Now our time is growing short," he said. "Some of us have to hop that train. Perhaps you men have further questions. Professor Tyler?"

"How did you want us to proceed?" Tyler said. "Will you give us a list of possible names? Or do we prepare a list? We need some instructions as to how to begin."

Martin's face turned back to business. "We hadn't reached any firm outline on that. I can only offer a few suggestions.

First, we thought you might want to get organized. A chairman and perhaps a secretary. We could then communicate through your chairman and save time. Second, you might prepare a list of Enfield-connected people and boil that down. And the same with outside possibilities. We want to leave you a free hand. As I said, we are going to lean on you heavily. Though, of course, we'll be looking around, too."

"And what about the time-table?" Tyler said. "The time between now and June is short."

"We hope to keep the pressure on right through the winter," Martin said. "If we come into June with empty hands, we will not worry too much. We will just keep on after that for as long as it takes. Any other questions."

There were none. The trustees shouldered into their topcoats and shook hands. Through the hubbub of goodbyes, Paul Eaton's voice cut like a knife. "If the faculty committee can stay a few minutes more," he was saying, "we can settle the organization problem right now."

With the trustees gone and the door closed again, the conference room seemed larger. Eaton, a good no-nonsense operator, wasted no time. In five minutes the slate of Waggoner and Cobb had been elected. Waggoner, looking gloomy, took the seat at the head of the table.

"We have an uncomfortably free hand," he said. "Now, as we used to say in the first war, where do we go from here, boys?"

"We'd better set a time for a meeting while we're all together," Cos Cobb said. Out came the six appointment books. Monday the eighth was too soon; they rapidly settled on Monday the fifteenth.

"Where shall we six meet again?" Waggoner intoned. "If

I may, I'd suggest my own house, a quiet conspiratorial spot. We won't be interrupted in our dire prophecies. I even own a copy of *Who's Who in America*. Somewhere in those pages our candidate lurks, waiting for the weird sisters to point their skinny fingers. Are you willing to agree on my house at eight on the fifteenth?"

The five heads bent over the appointment books, pencils scribbling. Sloane got to his feet. "Are we all set?" he said, moving towards the coat-rack.

Outside the night had fallen and the wind was rising. The men dispersed rapidly, buttoning their coats.

"Going my way?" said Tyler, as Paul Eaton emerged from the doorway, struggling into his coat.

"Not tonight, Ed," said Paul, hurrying down the walk. "I'm meeting Marianne at the Student Union. We're going to eat and go to the first show."

"How can you stand the Student Union?" asked Tyler. But he saw that Paul was out of earshot, heading across the campus.

Walking down Enfield Avenue alone, facing the rising wind from the east, Tyler felt his gloom returning. The bright morning seemed far off. Looking up, he saw that the sky was overcast again. A few drops of rain fell on his upturned face. "Not more rain," he muttered, half aloud. "Not again." Passing the Alpha Delt House, he turned up the collar of his coat. The young oak-tree, he saw, still held its fawn-colored leaves. Under the light from the Gothic lamp-post beside the fraternity walk, they tossed in the east wind. But they did not fall.

THREE *DECEMBER*

I

As HE came down the stairway from the main reading room of the University Library, Tyler saw Cos Cobb's broad-shouldered figure sidling through the turnstile at the checker's desk, wearing a red-checked woodsman's shirt and carrying three or four books. His close-clipped brown hair—"lichen on a granite ledge," Polly called it—almost matched the color of his skin, and his long legs were encased in the khaki pants which had been for ten years the daily uniform of most Enfield undergraduates, as well as the engineering and science faculty.

"Cos," Tyler said, "I'm surprised to see one of you scientists in the library. I thought you never read books."

"Just returning these for Polly," Cos said, his brown face wrinkling in a grin. He did not state the fact, which was that he read very widely, often late at night, a habit he had formed in the Navy. "Polly's been catching up on last year's best-sellers. What are you doing here? I thought departmental chairmen just wrote reports and conferred with deans."

73

"That's roughly it," Tyler said. "Right now, though, I feel very virtuous, after a morning—a whole morning—on recent Voltaire scholarship. Two or three years of it, and most of it not worth a hoot. How's the keeper of the minutes?"

"Wait till I drop these books upstairs," Cos said, "and I'll tell you if you're interested." He took the broad marble stairs two at a time. Tyler leaned against the balustrade, idly watching old Gosse, leaning confidentially towards the blond girl at the checker's desk. The girl tossed her head and looked away. Probably, Tyler guessed, old Gosse was giving her details on his World War I experiences in France. It was good for an hour of your time whenever he got you cornered: how he had felt as he wrestled with the broken hose of his gasmask while that greenish cloud of mustard gas rushed nearer and nearer. Tyler had heard it several times in the ten years since Gosse's retirement. Now Gosse really had a captive audience; the girl checker couldn't leave her desk; the skinny old man bent forward again to give her some more details. Tyler glanced into the back of the green volume in his hand. Yes, he had remembered to get it stamped at the circulation desk; the red ink had smudged and dried but the date was still legible: "Dec 4."

"What time is it, anyway?" said Cos behind him. "My watch stopped."

"I left my watch at home this morning. The Saturday noon whistle just blew a few minutes back. The Keeper of the Minutes, are you?"

"I'd rather keep that kind of minutes than the kind I'm keeping," Cos said. "The Committee of Six minutes would already choke a horse."

74

They came out into the bright air and stood looking north across the campus. The white sun-dial, topped with the phoenix writhing in its cold marble flames, seemed to point like an index finger at the chapel clock beyond and above it. The black hands said twelve-ten.

"I'm groggy with minutes," said Cos. "Do you have time to listen to some complaints? Think it's warm enough to sit on the sun-dial bench?"

"Yes, and yes," Tyler said. "This is hardly Christmas weather."

"Give it time. Christmas is still three weeks away. That gives the elements time to aggregate, as we say in the Navy."

"What's the trouble with the minutes?" asked Tyler. "Are we all too long-winded?"

"Too many names, for one thing," Cos said. "We've got to start cutting down. That first night at Waggoner's we went through half the catalogue like a hurricane. Names flying left and right. I was using the catalogue itself, making checks in the margins, drawing lines through names, making notes on a clip-board. No chance to weigh the merits of our faculty brethren. In the end I had, by actual count, sixty-two names. And the second session was worse. Bill kept turning to me and telling me not to cross out a name that everybody had agreed ought to be axed, and I haven't even counted up the survivors in the second half of the catalogue. On top of that was your own rundown on the regular alumni and the graduate alumni."

"Keep your courage up," Tyler said. "My list was only the alumni in education and educational administration. We still have all the other alumni, and then all the outside people, to be screened. Console yourself with the thought that you are not only the keeper of the minutes, you are also your brothers' keeper."

"My complaint is that my brothers are too numerous," Cos said. "Bill Waggoner is such a kindly man that he's very reluctant to cut the list down. Sooner or later that will have to be done. The trustees clearly can't take time to investigate a couple of hundred possibilities." He sat down on the marble bench under the sun-dial.

"Maybe we ought to spend the next session just boiling down the lists we've got," Tyler said. "Like maple-sap in your native woods."

"Sap is right," Cos said. "We want the true maple sugar, the golden nuggets. We can let the saps go up in steam." He swiveled on the marble bench to face the Parthenon, partly visible between Trask and Turner, bulking hugely behind its woven screen of leafless maple-boughs. "All this palaver to fill that mausoleum with one new man," he said. "First the session with the trustees. Then two meetings at Waggoner's house. Another Waggoner session coming up next week. Doubtless another coming up after that. And then January, February, March, April, May—" He laughed ruefully. "My fruit-flies are complaining, too. I have to ignore them unto the third and fourth generations while we generate a new administration."

Cos straightened his backbone and stretched in the sun, grinning, his even teeth glinting white against his brown skin. "All right, Ed. End of belly-ache. I'll be my brother's keeper, whoever he is. We're just not making enough progress to suit me."

76

"It's slow work," Tyler said. "I think Bill is right in not eliminating too many people at the start. Jim Sloane goes too far the other way: he seems to want to veto every non-scientist whose name is raised."

"Hell," Cos said, "we don't want a scientist in the White House. Those names he's been suggesting between vetos— I know most of them, and they're a pack of nags."

"Part of it is Jim's feeling about Bill Waggoner," Tyler said. "Anything in the realm of art strikes him as decadent. And Bill, as a famous collector of French prints and painting, seems doubly decadent, as if he somehow was corrupted by the pictures he collects. It's a real feeling with Jim. One day he asked me very seriously if I didn't think the French were a nation who asked to be raped by the Germans, once every generation. Rape with tacit consent, and so forth. Others have had that theory, but Jim seemed to take it seriously."

"Speaking of rape," Cos said, "do you know that young couple who rent Bill Waggoner's back apartment? You remember there was a noise outside during the last meeting at Bill's, and Sloane was all for going out to investigate it. He thought it might be someone listening in on the Committee of Six."

"Bill said, as I recall, that it was just his tenants coming home," Tyler said, smiling. "Nary a spy."

"Well, I was sitting against the wall on that side of the house," Cos said. "Taking the minutes. They hadn't been home for half an hour before the damndest sounds began to come through the wall. One light voice, female; one dark voice, male. And bumpings and thumpings. And squeals. It was rough on the minutes."

77

Tyler laughed. "I don't know who they are. Some engineering instructor and his bride, I think. They have only been married a few months."

"How does Bill Waggoner stand it?" said Cos. "It could become embarrassing if he was giving tea to some polite old lady who was about to give the Art Department a picture."

"That's life," Tyler said. "The raw material of art."

"It was raw, all right," Cos said. "But if he can take it, I can. Maybe the engineer should be a presidential candidate; populate the White House with numerous progeny." He got up and stretched his arms. "I ought to move on home. Polly and I are going up to the lake this afternoon with Cornie. I have to cut some wood. How about going up for some fishing this spring?"

"I'd like to," Tyler said. "Maybe we can hook into a new president up there. If we don't find one sooner. So long, keeper."

"So long, brother," Cos said, moving off. "See you Thursday."

Tyler watched his receding figure until it disappeared around the corner of Enfield Hall. Cos ought to be a candidate. Were the members of the Committee of Six automatically excluded? If so, it was a foolish exclusion. Cos could easily develop into a forceful leader. Distinguished Navy record in the war, running that supersecret show. Underwater soundwaves. Sonar they called it. Submarine identification. A topflight biologist now. Started before the war out in the California Sierras. Widely known and respected. Always traveling off to learned colloquiums. Decorated two years ago with some kind of medal by the national organization of biologists, whatever they called it. A complicated character. But simple in the best sense. Liked the woods, liked working with his hands. Age around forty. That fitted the trustees' prescription. Wife, Polly, one small daughter, Cornie. Cos had been married before. Never mentioned his first wife. Some war-time *mesalliance*? Alive, now, or dead? There was a story, there, probably not a dramatic one, but Cos had closed the book. For the better part of ten years he and Tyler had served on committees together, played bridge with Alice and Polly every month or so, fished, cut wood, drunk whiskey together. Talked for a grand total of many hours in that ten years. But not a shred of information ever volunteered about that first wife, that disembodied wraith somewhere in the past. "Don't dramatize it," Tyler said to himself, half aloud.

It would be worth raising the question of Cobb for president. Quietly, with Bill Waggoner. The idea, which had crossed his mind once or twice before during the fall, now began to grow, to acquire depth and roundness, to knock with a kind of fresh insistence on the door of consciousness. Or was it the door of conscience? Your conscience came in for examination, too, on the Committee of Six. What, you asked it, is best for the university? What combination of powers does the job of president demand? Integrity, the trustees had said: the power of moral invulnerability. Courage. One of the three main requirements for leadership, they used to tell the boys in cadre school. Tyler remembered the handsome young West Point shavetail lecturing the privates and corporals on leadership, pointing to the words on the blackboard, each in a different color of chalk. Courage was red. Then Justice, in blue chalk. The young lieutenant had his spiel to go with each quality, each color. The deep seriousness of his analysis, exactly four minutes to each quality, three minutes at the end for questions. What was that third quality of the good leader? Red courage, blue justice, and—? Well, no matter. You had it or you didn't. Cos Cobb had it.

Tyler reached into his pocket for the tobacco pouch and his fingers met the envelope, the unanswered—the unanswerable —letter from yesterday morning's mail. Poor old Turcotte. Tyler put the envelope down beside him on the marble bench while he filled his pipe. The crabbed address: "M. Le Professeur Tyler, Université d'Enfield." That was all. The Post Office Department had done the rest. Apparently it had even come through without a stamp. The front bore the official purple legend: 3¢ postage due. Wouldn't they even give the old man postage stamps, so he could write his friends? Twenty, thirty years ago, Turcotte's correspondence must have been immense as his reputation. The great French biographer of the young Voltaire. *La Jeunesse de Voltaire.* Now, how long? At least since the war, the arteries in the old brain had gradually filled and tightened. The sedimentation of senility, someone had called it. The great Turcotte was now, in a short and vulgar American expression, nuts. Lived with his married sister somewhere on Manhattan Island. No visitors, please. Professor Turcotte is not himself these days. Exercise: a walk with his gaoler, some local New Yorker, a man hired for the purpose, once a day in good weather. No telephone, please. "My God," his sister said, "if we would let him, he would call California, even Paris. *Transcontinentale, transatlantique*: to him is all one. Poor man!" She wept, the goodhearted ugly widow in the black dress. "We must watch him all day, all night. That man has craft. He gets out, he may be killed. Who can say? Sometimes we think he is out, he is only hiding inside. Sometimes we think he is hiding: 'Alcide! Alcide!' we call. He is gone out. Later, *voici*. He has been riding two hours in a taxicab without *monnaie*. We pay the chauffeur."

Tyler opened the letter. The cheap paper like a child's tablet, blue lines across it, written in pencil and in French: "My dear Professor Tyler, Once more the time has come for my annual lecture to your students on our beloved Voltaire. I shall come at the usual time, and, never fear, this time I shall bring my own gown. In preparation for this visit, please assign them to read all the tragedies. Until then, my dear Tyler. Turcotte."

Poor man, poor old man. Nothing ahead of him but that final closure in the narrow arterial pipes, sedimentation completed. And probably, in between, a period of virtual imbecility. No more parades. Nothing like Voltaire's Parisian *triumphus,* which probably, by its excitement and fatigue, hastened his death, though there was that glass, smelling of laudanum, by the final bedside.

Tyler sighed and stood up. "My only complaint," Cos Cobb had said, "is that my brothers are too numerous." Yes, Tyler thought. Too numerous and too humorous, or not humorous enough. Too old or too young. Too rich, too poor. Too powerful, weak, hungry, ambitious, suspicious. Too senile. "All the tragedies." He went over and looked curiously at the Roman numerals on the sun-dial. The shadow fell at one o'clock.

II

"And that's the news," the announcer said, "from the WABC Newsroom. Seven-ten on your dial. We'll be with you again with late headlines at eight o'clock."

"All right, Tommy, you can turn it off now," Tyler said. "Thanks for letting me listen. As usual, it wasn't worth listening to. Toby, get under the covers. I'm going to open the window, and you don't want to catch cold. What do you guys want for Christmas? You heard what the announcer said: fifteen shopping days until St. Nicholas."

He watched their small clean faces, their gesturing small hands, as they told him what they thought they wanted— Toby insistently first, claiming his right as the elder. The red bicycle, the first baseman's mitt, another car for the train, a candy cane. Many balloons also wanted: "a big package," Toby said, spreading his hands. Except for the train, Tommy's list was an imitation of Toby's, but Tommy wanted automobiles—the tiny replicas, built to scale, that were always underfoot in the boys' bedroom. Week in and week out, untiringly, eyes intent, Tommy pushed them along the floor, simulating engine-noises with high internal humming, puffing his lips as the mimic engines raced or, if there seemed to be ignition trouble, duplicating with pleasure all the plosives of the cold engine. Their wide blue eyes (like Alice's) snapped and blinked as they spoke, sweeping round the room as they searched their minds for Christmas ideas: those gleaming images of what they hoped would appear under the tree, that splendor of enamelled metal, pristine horsehide, varicolored plastic, or inflatable rubber—the treasure-trove of the real and tangible after all the imaginations.

Alice, humming to herself, came in to lay out their school-clothes for the morning. She stood for a moment behind Tyler's chair, her warm right hand massaging the nape of his neck.

"How are you, boys?" Alice said. "All you boys."

"They're saying what they want for Christmas," said Tyler. "Do you want to know what I want?"

"Tommy, do you have gym tomorrow?" said Alice. "Tomorrow is Thursday."

"Nope," Tommy said. "Friday. Where is my gym suit?"

"It's in your bureau drawer," Alice said. Her hand left Tyler's neck and rested on the back of the chair.

"More," said Tyler. "More of the same, please."

"Who are you," Alice said, "Nicholas Nickleby or Oliver Twist? Don't be greedy." But she let her hand rest for a moment on his shoulder before she went to the bureau, swiftly selected the boys' clothes, and leaned to tuck the blankets around their shoulders. Tyler watched her admiringly as she bent over the beds, first Tommy, as the younger and obviously the sleepier; then Toby, who leaned bright-eyed, reluctant as always to close the day, supporting himself on one elbow. Gently, bending to brush his forehead with her lips, Alice forced him down, smoothed the blankets, and turned to the light-switch.

"There are two of the boys bedded down," she said. "Good night, fellows."

"Good night, old boys," Tyler said, getting up. "Sleep

well." As he reached the door he could smell Alice's perfume plainly, and he brushed close to her going past.

"I'm going to put the car away," he said. "Will you be here when I come back?"

"Very likely," Alice said. "In fact almost certainly."

The night air was sharp. The thermometer above the mail-box by the door registered thirty-four. The car stood silently where it had been left, shining under the streetlight. It responded quickly as he pressed the starter, roused to life by the leaping spark, warming to enthusiasm in a minute. He drove it into the garage and lowered the overhead door. Through the tall pine in the back yard, a single star winked. He came gratefully into the warm kitchen.

He snapped the lock on the back door, stripped off his necktie, hung it and his jacket over the back of a chair in the dining-room, and turned the catch on the front door. Alice, when he came into the living-room, was in the big chair, a magazine in her lap. He thought, but he could not be sure, that she had brushed her brown hair and put on fresh lipstick.

As he sat down on the edge of the couch, Alice said, "Who's the new president?"

"Eisenhower. And the Vice President is Nixon."

"No, silly, I mean of the University. How are you boys doing? Have you got one yet?"

"Man by the name of Loopenhicker," Tyler said. "Former director of the Asbury Park Beauty Contest Winner's Protective Association. Southern Branch."

"Those southerners need protection," Alice said. "No, seriously, haven't you found a man yet?"

"We decided on a woman," Tyler said. "Ida M. Tarbell. Clean up the place. Petticoat government."

"I thought you had decided on Giorgio. How is Giorgio, by the way?"

"We're nominating him. For a raise," Tyler said. "Next year."

"Poor Giorgio," said Alice. "How does he look these days?"

"Haven't seen him lately," said Tyler. "Not since I gave him Bob Schaeffer's message: no raise this year, Dr. Renzulli. He's keeping to himself. He minds his business and I mind mine."

"Poor Giorgio," Alice said.

"Do you know it's cold outside?" said Tyler. "I'm developing a crick in the back of my neck."

"That's from sleeping in the refrigerator," Alice said.

"No, seriously, Alice." He turned his head from left to right. "I'm afraid it's stiffening rapidly. It needs massaging."

"I already massaged your neck," said Alice. "Don't you remember? Up in the boys' room."

"But not enough," said Tyler. "That was just the beginning."

Alice laid the magazine on the rug beside her chair and stood up, smoothing down her dark green dress over her hips. "All right," she said, smiling. "You tell me who the new president is, and I'll massage your neck."

"We're thinking seriously," said Tyler, "of a double president. The Walrus and the Carpenter. Walrus in the front office, trying to look like Grover Cleveland. The Carpenter on Grounds and Buildings."

"That would never do," said Alice, her fingers firm and warm on the nape of his neck. "Remember what happened to the oysters."

"Eaten," said Tyler, grinning. "Swallowed up. A parable

of administration and faculty in the twentieth century. The way of all flesh."

"Now you're on another book," said Alice.

"Nope. Just another tack. It's got nothing to do with books or presidents. Do you think maybe we should get to bed? They tell me a crick in the neck is often the sign of a cold coming on."

"Are you being coy about a basic urge?" said Alice.

"Not coy. Never coy. Circumlocutory, perhaps, like Flaubert. Beating around the bush with words."

"Please stop," said Alice, laughing.

"Stop what?"

"Beating around the bush with words."

"Deeds she wants. Deeds it will be."

"When?" said Alice.

"At your immediate convenience, you bold young thing."

"Did you lock the back door?" said Alice.

"Yes, and the front. All safe."

"How is your neck now?"

"It's coming along, but it still needs treatment."

"Mine, too," Alice said happily.

III

"I was just about to wind the clocks," Bill Waggoner said. "Do you mind? I make a kind of nightly ceremony of it. Sit down, Ed. I think you'll find cigarettes in that box beside you."

"Sure, Bill, of course, go ahead. I'd like to watch." The old bachelor and his clocks, Tyler thought, his mechanical

Tobys and Tommys. "You've got quite a collection. Do they all strike together?"

"Some of them don't have chimes," Waggoner said, with affection. "Those that do strike show, I'm glad to say, a certain amount of originality. Like the Committee of Six." He laughed his old man's laugh—the single "huh," like a stag blowing through its nose. "They remind me of those clocks in Thomas Hardy's village. Dorchester. Casterbridge, he calls it in the novels. I was there once, thirty years ago. Charming little town. In one of the novels he has a wonderful sentence, maybe a paragraph, to describe the village clocks as they strike. I once had it memorized." He paused in the act of winding a small Dutch clock of blue-and-white china, tapping his forehead with the hand that held the key, knitting his brows in recollection. "I used to quote it, but it's gone from me now. The older I grow, Ed, the worse my memory is."

"Mine, too," said Tyler. "I even forgot to bring my lists along tonight."

"Candidates, you mean?" said Waggoner. "Never mind. I have all the lists we've made so far. And Cos will bring his."

"I ran into Cos last week," Tyler said. "He thinks it's about time for us to begin boiling the lists down to some feasible size. I came a little early tonight to find out how you felt about it."

"It is early, isn't it? I was wondering where the others were," Waggoner said. He picked up a small black clock, its case inlaid with gold, and wound it slowly. "They should be along in a few minutes. Probably Cos is right. Let's see, this is December—"

"Ninth," said Tyler.

"December ninth, yes. And we've been at it for about a month, now. A month and a few days. In the first month, Ed, I thought it was best to start big, and then cut. That way, I thought, we would stand a better chance of not missing the quiet but effective man who may turn out to be our dark-horse candidate." Waggoner finished his evening round and sat down, looking with evident satisfaction—even paternal pride, Tyler thought—around the comfortable and well-appointed room with the handsome prints on the walls and all the mingled clock-voices.

"Speaking of dark horse candidates," Tyler said, "there's another problem I wanted to talk over with you beforehand. I'm not a politician, and I don't mean to speak out of turn on this, but would you say that members of the Committee of Six are automatically out of the running?"

"Well, at my age, I certainly am," Bill Waggoner said, accenting the pronouns and laughing again. "And it had naturally occurred to me, though I haven't brought it up, that some of you young fellows, the pick of the campus so to speak, ought to be included in the overall consideration."

"Not me," Tyler said quickly. "I'm no college president. But just the other day I was thinking of Cos Cobb as a possibility. A strong possibility."

"I should think he might be," Waggoner said. "Cleancut young chap. You know him better than I do."

"Don't get the idea, please, that I'm pushing for him to the exclusion of others," Tyler said. "I don't think we should. But he has had real administrative experience in that underwater sound program, his age is about right, he has a nice little family, he's a first-rate scientist—"

"That ought to make him popular with Jim Sloane," Waggoner said. "Jim seems to be going on the notion that only a scientist could possibly run the ball for dear old Enfield, or however the song goes."

"Cos Cobb is an exceptional scientist," Tyler said. "His interests are much broader than most of them have. He's well read. He's something of a philosopher. Well, I've spoken my piece."

"I'm glad you did," said Waggoner. "I need to have that kind of information. I'll buttonhole some of the others on the Committee privately, and see how they feel. If they all agree, or if most of them agree, I'll pass the word on to Johnny Martin."

"You and he sound close, now," said Tyler, smiling. "Johnny."

"Bless you, young man," Waggoner said. "I taught the bloke when he was a sophomore. Jumping Jack Martin they used to call him. Damn good quarterback, I remember, but no ability in languages at all. I was teaching French, then."

"Yes, you were," Tyler said. "We claim you proudly as a departmental alumnus who went on to finer things than irregular verbs."

The doorbell rang and Bill rose to answer it. "I remember that Jumping Jack Martin had an awful time with the verb *craindre*. I finally had to tell him that he knew no fear. Which was true in both senses." He disappeared into the hall.

From the mingled voices outside Tyler distinguished the rumble of Sloane and the clearer New England intonations of Cobb. There was a scraping of coat-hangers along the rod in the hall closet, a bustle of coats and scarves being stored.

First two humanists, then a pair of scientists. Eaton the sociologist and Vincent the economist still to come. The old
historical sequence: humanists, scientists, then our redeemers,
the social scientists. The doorbell sounded again, soft chimes
that played (incongruously) the notes of "How dry I am."
The draft of cold air from the open door streamed round
Tyler's ankles, and he heard Eaton's staccato delivery, followed by the lower, slower voice of Vincent.

Two by two, Tyler thought, like the animals climbing the
ramp of the ark. Tonight we are traveling in pairs. Like
Sister Mary Madaleva and the other one. They were two nuns
who came to take his course in French literature at the summer language school that time in Vermont. Sister Mary was
young—at least younger; under those outfits it was hard to
tell. She was also the intelligent one—very quick on the intellectual draw, skilled in debate. She seemed to have read the
whole of Voltaire, and could discuss it with objective fervor.

The old one was like a delicate crow, her rimless glasses
shuddering on her nose, almost visibly shaken at every mention of the Encyclopaedists. But brave, too. Or persistent.
From time to time, whenever there was a gap in the discussion, she would ask in her dry light voice for the right to
speak, raising the wrinkled hand like a child in school. "Voltaire, we must conclude, did not know how to think correctly.
Now there are three ways in which we may come to know
God—" And she would count them off on her fingers, trotting
out the arguments as if by rote, glancing right and left at the
other students, fixing Tyler himself with her old converter's
eye.

Bill Waggoner was talking about one of his prints which
hung by the hall stairway. Tyler opened the box on the table

beside him and lit a cigarette. Who would convert who to-night? Correction: Who would convert whom? How do we come to know the new chief god in the Enfield pantheon—the new academic Prometheus bringing the torch of wisdom to Mankind, Enfield Division? Careful, Tyler, he thought, you're mixing images again.

"Evening, Ed," Cos Cobb said. His face was ruddy from the cold, and he was rubbing his palms together. "Sitting alone in lordly magnificence?"

"Just waiting for you men to finish your art discussion," Tyler said, "before we turn to more important—or is it less important—things."

"Sometimes I wonder," Cos said. "I'm in favor of tangibles, though: Bill's prints, trees, grass, guinea pigs."

"How did you make out with the trees last week-end?"

"What trees?" Cos said. "Oh, the wood at Moose Lake, you mean?" He held up his hands for Tyler to see, but the light in Bill's study was too dim.

"What you got?" asked Tyler. "Athlete's hands?"

"No, I've got blisters. Some very tangible blisters. I spent most of Sunday hacking around in our woodlot." He lowered himself into one of the deepest chairs. "I'm still stiff. But I have the satisfaction of having dealt with tangibles. Not all those intangibles we're about to spend the evening on."

"What is more tangible than a man?" said Tyler.

"What's less tangible than his qualities?" Cos said. "Who really knows? Who knows how he will turn out if he is given power? Who knows if his courage is really courage, or just temporary confidence induced by a good dinner? Did you speak to Bill about cutting down our lists?"

"Just briefly," Tyler said. "Will ten or a dozen names seem

more tangible to you than a hundred or a hundred and twenty?"

"Somewhat," Cos said, "but even then, how do you know what your man is really made of?"

"A man is made of potentials which get to be actuals under the stress of circumstance," Tyler said. "All we can do is take a bet on potentials."

"And what is less tangible than potentials?" asked Cos. "Can you weigh them, measure them, taste and feel them?"

"You just know what they probably are," Tyler said. "In a way you feel them, in a way you see them, in a way you can measure them. They're the intangible tangibles, the provisional judgments we make every day."

"I know, I know," Cos said. His face was serious. "But I get sick of them sometimes. When I get too sick of them, I go hack at some fallen trees, and carry my tangible woodchunks home in a wheelbarrow. I just feel sorry for the men who survive on our final list. Think what they're being condemned to: when they feel like chopping wood, they have to go make speeches to the alumni; when they feel like fishing, they have to go fish up some more money instead. That's what Henry Adams meant. Poor Henry."

"What Henry Adams? Oh, you mean *the* Henry Adams. What did he say about fishing?"

"Very little about fishing," Cos said. "No, I was thinking of what he said about friends. A friend in power is a friend lost."

"Lost to what?"

"Lost to his friends," Cos said. "Lost to his job. In this case, lost to the alumni, the campus building program, the million hours in committees. Lost to his laboratory if he's a scientist. Lost to his readers if he's a writer. Lost."

"Who's lost?" said Paul Eaton, coming in briskly. "We almost got lost in the realm of the fine arts. We country boys have just been getting an education. A trip through the Waggoner Art Museum with gun and camera. Downstairs, upstairs, through the dining-room. Bill even has a fine engraving in the lavatory."

"My little joke," Bill said, chuckling. "The Water Carrier by Velasquez."

Tyler watched them settle down, Vincent already fingering his deep-bowled pipe, Eaton and Sloane in voluble talk about something he couldn't hear, Waggoner gathering up the papers, lifting down the copy of *Who's Who* from the shelf, Cobb inspecting a blister on his right hand. Here were friends in power, power of a sort. Friends called to judge their friends, weigh their intangibles in intangible scales, find them wanting. Or find them—what was the word?—ready, ripe, the good risk. Was ripeness all? Could you take them up like canteloupes, press gently with the thumbs around the stem end, pick the ripe one that you wanted to carry home? Not likely. How many times had you been stung when you cut open the canteloupe you had carefully chosen? Cos Cobb, with his love of tangibles, ought to consider the analogy of the university president and the canteloupe.

Bill Waggoner cleared his throat. "Some of us have begun to feel that it's time now to cut down on these enormous lists of names we have assembled in previous meetings. I'm afraid the length of the lists is mainly my fault. I was anxious that we should not pass over any really likely candidate in our haste to get through the lists. And I didn't want to send anyone to the executioner's block without due process of discussion. If nobody objects, I think our job for the evening should be to try to arrive at a tentative list of a dozen or fifteen names—men who, in our judgment, fit the qualifications of the Board of Trustees."

"Get out your axe, Cos," Tyler said.

"Too many blisters already," said Cos, grinning. "Can't we use some more delicate instrument like tweezers?"

IV

For what seemed the nine hundredth time that week, the telephone rang at his elbow. Even on Saturdays, Tyler thought, they can't leave you alone. Even Alice, who seldom complained, had made a mock stab at the telephone wires only yesterday.

"Shall I snip?" she said. "Before we all go deaf?"

The tempo always accelerated around this time of year. Committee chairmen, anxious to get in one more meeting before the Christmas holidays; Dean Schaeffer's secretary, saying that the Dean was most anxious to assemble the departmental recommendations on promotions and salary increases so that he could study them over the Christmas recess. The man calling from the hardware store to say that the new skates for Toby had arrived. Invitations to cocktail parties, eggnog parties, the rare invitation to dinner with one of the young instructors or assistant professors. The people who called to ask if you were planning to attend the Modern Language Association meetings after Christmas. The graduate

94

students wondering politely if you had assigned a due-date for the term papers; the undergraduates who called at ten or eleven in the evening to say they were sorry they hadn't been in lately to talk about their senior theses but would appear right after vacation. The insurance salesman, the Railway Express office. Departmental wives wanting to speak to Alice; the quick small voices of Toby's friends; Tommy's younger friends who thought they had to yell to be heard: "Hello, hello. Is Tommy here? Is Tommy Tyler here?" The Library asking if you would bring that book back as it was wanted by another reader. Bill Waggoner calling to say that he had written to Jumping Jack Martin about Cos Cobb as a candidate. The long-distance calls from fledgling Ph.D.'s who wanted to arrange an interview with you at the M.L.A. meetings.

This was probably another of those. As the phone rang insistently, Tyler folded his newspaper, laid his pipe in the silver ashtray, and leaned over wearily to pick up the receiver. "Yes," he said.

"Professor Tyler? Inskip. Joe Inskip, you know, manager at the Inn?"

"Yes. Oh, yes, Joe. How are you?"

"Fine and dandy. Sorry to call you at this hour."

"It's all right. What's on your mind?"

"Not on my mind," Joe said, laughing. "Sort of in my hair. What there is of it. Mr. Tyler, we've got a man here who says he is going to give a lecture on the campus tomorrow night."

"He'll have a small audience," Tyler said. "The students' vacation started yesterday afternoon, and tomorrow is Sunday. Almost all the students have gone."

"What I thought," Inskip said. "He says it's under your auspices. The Modern Language Department, isn't that you? Have you authorized anyone to stay here tonight, with your department picking up the tab?"

"Not as far as I know," Tyler said. "And I suppose I would be the one to know. Who is he? What does he look like?"

"I haven't seen him," Inskip said. "He's down in the bar. Why I called was that the bartender just called me. The old man is getting slightly crocked, if you know what I mean. He's not known to the bartender. I phoned our front desk a minute ago and he checked in sometime late this afternoon. They didn't see any luggage. He gave Sue your name when he registered."

Tyler felt his stomach gather into a knot. "Do you know his name?" he said quietly.

"It's illegible. I'm looking at the bar-check. He was finally —he signed it a few minutes ago downstairs. The name looks like *Swater* or *Sweater*. I don't know. *Puckett? Lucette?* There's a first initial which is clearly an A."

Tyler pushed back at the sinking feeling in his midriff. "Would it be Turcotte? Alcide Turcotte?"

"As I say, the first initial is an A, all right," said Inskip. "How do you spell that last name?"

Tyler spelled it, already trying to work out what to do. How had the old man escaped? "My God," his sister said. "We have to watch him." This was one time they had gone to sleep on the sentry's post. Poor people.

"Look, Joe. Can you hold him there?"

"He doesn't show any signs of wanting to leave," Joe said. "The bartender just doesn't want to serve him any more liquor. That, and the report from the front desk, the fact

96

that he gave your name when he registered, is why I called you."

"Has he had any dinner?"

"Not that I know of. There's no dinner-check here."

"Joe, would you try, or get the bartender to try, to get the old man to order some dinner? Is your kitchen still open?"

Inskip said it was.

"Maybe the bartender can persuade him to eat," Tyler said. "How many has he had?"

"Four, it looks like. Type of drink not specified on the check."

"All right. It's all right. Thank you for letting me know. If there's no danger of his leaving right away, I want to call New York City. Then I'll come up."

"We'll hold him," Inskip said. "Vertical or horizontal. But no more booze, right?"

"Right," Tyler said. "And if you could try to get him to eat. I should be there in ten or fifteen minutes."

Driving up the cold street twenty minutes later, bumping over the ice-hummocks which were all that remained of Wednesday's snowfall, Tyler planned his next few moves. Poor old Alcide. In the old man's mind some foggy vision of a lecture-hall, crammed with students and faculty, great applause as he stood up, hushed attention as he spoke, laughter at the Gallic jokes, the finespun witticisms, the pince-nez glasses on the black cord, the hands grasping the lapels, moving out in quick gestures, the roar of clapping hands when he finished and sat down. The composite memory of a hundred such lectures swimming and merging now in the old brain. Tyler took a left on College Street, following the slight downward gradient towards Main. Madame Langelier, the sister, had been astonished and relieved. "Thang God," she had said several times. "Thang God. You have him there. In Enfield. Thang God. He has craft. He found my money. In my boudoir. It is hidden but he finds it. Our man, Alcide's guardian, was out for bread. We have no bread, he goes to the bakeree to get a loaf for the dinner. In that little time, Alcide is gone. Since three or three-thirty."

Tyler had reconstructed it now. Turcotte, searching the dresser in his sister's room, finding the bills, letting himself out the back door, hailing the cab two streets away, buying the train-ticket at Penn Station. Going down there to give his lecture, lave his ancient ears in that applause.

"Our man will come," Madame Langelier had said. "He will catch the next train. You tell me where he should go."

"I have a time-table here in my billfold," said Tyler. "There is a train out of Penn Station at nine-thirty-two. It is only a thirty-minute trip. I will meet the train down here. What is the guardian's name?"

"Longo," she said. "Larry Longo. He is short, strong. He wears a brown overcoat. Larree, what color is your hat? His hat is light brown. Nine-thirty-two. And you meet his train there, that's good."

Yes, on the cold platform where the dirty newspapers whirled and subsided in the night wind, Professor Tyler would meet Madame Langelier's emissary, the short man named Longo in the light brown hat. Her brother's keeper. "Thang God." Meantime, there was just meantime enough, he would park by the Inn curb, find the old man in the bar, eating alone at one of the tables, the colored waiter solicitous.

"Ah, Tyler, forgive my not rising to greet you. How are you, Tyler? As you see. I decided to come one day early, spend the night in the arms of your hospitality, to rest up before the lecture."

And how would you handle that one, Professor Tyler? Oh, just say the lecture had to be called off. Say that circumstances beyond the department's control had necessitated postponement. No, better not say that. The old boy would be hopping another train in the spring. The sister's brother's keeper would have to come down again, wearing the brown hat but not the overcoat, a fleur-de-lis in his lapel for identification.

The traffic light at the corner of College and Main turned from red to green. They would have to stay overnight now, the crocked old man and his keeper, and take the train back in the morning. Tyler swung the car into the parking-lot behind the Inn and got out, buttoning his overcoat across his chest. Check on the old man first, then meet the train from New York. His brother's keeper.

I

OPENING the window on the night air and leaning forward to take a final lungful, Tyler heard the chapel bell strike once. "Hear that?" he said. "One o'clock. Latest we've been up in a long time. Rough on the old folks."

Alice was already in bed, brown arms akimbo, hands behind her head, staring at the ceiling. "Don't count me among the old folks," Alice said. Usually she made such remarks with mock asperity, softening them with her wide-mouthed smile. This time Tyler thought her tone held—though he could not be sure—the merest hint of an edge. Tired, probably. He said nothing, but scuffed into his slippers and went softly down the hall to the boys' room.

In the light from the hall he could see them both, Toby flat on his back, mouth slightly open, breath coming soundlessly. Tommy had kicked off the covers and had his thumb in his mouth. Pulling gently, thumb and forefinger around Tommy's wrist, Tyler dislodged the thumb and straightened the blankets. "Start the New Year right and proper, Tommy,"

100

he said under his breath. "Give that old thumb a rest." Tommy sighed and turned onto his stomach. He did not awaken.

Outside the window moonlight lay thick as frosting on the frozen grass and the fronds of the tall hemlock. Standing there for a moment, looking out at the moon-paled streetlight, Tyler said the prayer he said at night whenever he remembered. "Sir, help us to raise them strong and well and whole and wise and true-hearted." Turning in his sleep, Toby murmured something unintelligible. Tyler went out and closed the door.

Alice was still as he had left her. "You know," she said, as he kicked off the slippers and swung his legs into bed, "I think that something is wrong with Polly. She didn't seem—not normal tonight."

"Probably simple nervousness," Tyler said.

"Nervousness?"

"I mean at the responsibility of having twelve ravenous people for a New Year's Eve dinner. No, eleven. Not counting herself. A New Year's Eve dinner is the roughest of all; the hostess knows she can't get her shoes off until after midnight. It's a long pull."

"That kind of thing doesn't usually bother Polly," said Alice. "I think it was something more important. When we got there tonight, you remember Cos met us at the door, and I was carrying the big plate of fried chicken. Cos held it while I took my coat off and then I took it out to the kitchen to arrange it on the platter . . ."

"The chicken I had must have been yours," Tyler said. "It was excellent."

101

"You were just hungry," Alice said. "How did you ever wait until nine-thirty? You're usually starved by six sharp."

"Surreptitious nibbling," Tyler said. "It's an art. You begin with dry cereal and milk before you leave home."

"And when I got out to the kitchen," said Alice, "her eyes were red. I'm sure she had been crying. She saw that I noticed it, so she laughed and said it was from the onion she had chopped up to make the French dressing. I told her to douse her eyes in cold water. I said it was the only way to get rid of the irritation from the onion-juice. She knew I knew she'd been crying, though. Later on in the evening, she took me aside and told me she was tired, and that sometimes when she is tired she cries. It rests her."

"I thought," Tyler said firmly, "that she seemed quite gay all evening."

Alice looked over at him sidelong, as from a distant mountain peak. "You weren't looking carefully enough. It was the kind of gaiety a woman can put on like a dress."

"Or lipstick," said Tyler. "Cos seemed gay enough, too."

"Cos wasn't really very gay," Alice said. "After I saw Polly's eyes in the kitchen, I watched Cos now and again. It might have been nothing more than a lover's quarrel. But they hadn't quarreled. I know. From the way Cos kept looking at Polly, as if he were trying to buck her up. No, Ed, it is something else."

"It isn't something we can probably lay our fingers on tonight," said Tyler, yawning hugely. "Tomorrow is Sunday. Let's give ourselves a break and sleep until eight o'clock."

"Or even eight-thirty," Alice said. "The boys don't have to be in Sunday School until twenty of ten." She leaned over, as she always did before she slept, to kiss him. "Happy New Year."

"Happy New Year, my dear." The light switch was on his side. He flicked it and settled down. He knew that it would be a good while before he got to sleep, but he lay quietly, courting it. The one time that he looked towards Alice, in the moonlight that came through the open window, she was lying quietly, her arms akimbo, her hands behind her head, staring at the patterns the reflected moonlight made on the ceiling.

II

A light rain, falling steadily from the clouds which hung almost as low as the chapel tower, was melting the inch or more of snow the night had brought. On the sidewalk between Trask and Bishop, already shoveled clean by the Grounds and Buildings crew, Tyler stamped his shoes, shaking off the small toe-caps of wet snow. Incredible slop, he thought with disgust. That was no doubt what the students were thinking, back now to the grind from wherever they had spent their Christmas holidays, streaming now across the campus towards the classrooms, cursing the Enfield custom which began the instructional day at eight, some breakfastless, some with the warm ball of Student Union coffee pleasantly central in their midriffs, hunched in the fur-collared olive drab jackets which (along with the khaki pants, high-laced brogans from the Army and Navy Store, and the imaginative variety of their hats) made up their usual workweek attire. A boy in a green mackinaw loped past, wolfing one of those chocolate-covered ice-cream bars they sold from the automatic machines in the Student Union, heading for a sociology class in Turner. "Ugh!" Tyler said, half aloud. One of the sociologists ought to do an investigation, with statistics, on the breakfast-eating habits of Enfield students.

The gray weather lowered. You could smell the imminent snow. The morning *Times* weather-column predicted more snow, possibly turning to sleet. Sitting over his second cup of coffee in the kitchen half an hour ago, Tyler had looked at the weather-map, not pausing to read the text: something about a stationary cold front, slanting from Boston southeastward out over the coastal Atlantic, and a warmer air-mass slogging in from the west. This was the kind of morning, with the gray clouds, the light rain, and the lowering sky, that they had had thirteen years ago off Casablanca, scrambling down the ladders into the slow-pitching LST's, roaring in through the lead-colored November swells, all of them scared as hell, all the white faces seen in profile, ducked low against the dark bulkheads. And the boy miserably vomiting into his helmet. Tyler shuddered as he climbed the stairs to his office.

From the humidor on his desk he filled his pipe and sat back to contemplate the week ahead. The calendar showed nothing today until 1:30. Beside that hour, in Mrs. Rhodes's neat handwriting, was the name of Fenelosa. She was good at keeping his appointments straight, logging them in on the master-calendar in her own office, entering quietly each week-day morning as soon as she had hung up her coat, making the duplicate entries on the hour-lines of his chairman's calendar, adding, in parentheses, some memory-stirring phrase. Fenelosa must have made the appointment before he went home for Christmas. All right, he thought, and what else are we doing this week?

From among the paper matches in his pocket he extracted his small green appointment book—as uniform among the faculty as O.D. jackets among the students. With one of the freshly sharpened pencils (Mrs. Rhodes again!) he entered Fenelosa's name under Monday the ninth. Tuesday the tenth: 4 p.m. Committee on Discipline. Wednesday the eleventh: departmental meeting at 3:30 to finish the cases of instructors who were up for reappointment next year.

The next entry meant nothing for a moment: Thursday the twelfth at eleven in the morning, and the words "Schuyler rep." Then he remembered the letter which had come during the holidays: two men from the small women's college in New York state who were revising their underclass curriculum. Wanted to talk about Enfield's methods in language instruction. Had read Tyler's text on language teaching in the Army of Occupation training programs. Would appreciate an hour of his time if possible. Then at 3:30 Thursday afternoon, a conference with Dean Schaeffer. Departmental matters. Who gets promotions, who gets raises? Friday was clear, both in his book and on his desk calendar. Not, he thought, a very exciting week. The usual round of classes, committees, student conferences, administrative bottle-necks, minor departmental head-aches. The every-other-day dictation to Mrs. Rhodes: "Dear Professor Soandso: I have your good letter of January soandso." And so forth, et cetera, *und so weiter*. And maybe, with luck, a couple of hours in the library, reading and making notes for another book on Voltaire. It was a good life, thought Tyler, returning his appointment book to his pocket. Nothing to squawk about except the way your scholarly enterprises kept getting the short end of the stick.

At the sound of the key in the lock, Tyler turned to see Mrs. Rhodes coming in, calendar and pencil in her hand, white hair neatly waved, her thin frame draped in the gray skirt, the fresh white blouse.

"Good morning, Mrs. Rhodes," he said jovially. "Only it isn't, is it?"

"Good morning, Mr. Tyler. No, it isn't. And the radio says more snow. I can remember, as a little girl, when I really prayed for snow. The older I get, the less I like it. It's such a gloomy morning for the boys, coming back to classes."

"Gloomy Monday," Tyler said. "I see Fenelosa has a date for a conference this afternoon."

"Yes," said Mrs. Rhodes. "He was in Friday. That boy's been working hard. He said he went home just for Christmas Day, and has spent all the rest of the vacation working on his thesis."

"That's good," Tyler said. "I was afraid he was getting behind the eight-ball on that thesis. He was late getting started."

"I wanted to check your calendar against mine," Mrs. Rhodes said, coming forward. "The Fenelosa is down already. Tomorrow you have Discipline Committee, Wednesday the departmental meeting, Thursday the conference with Dean Schaeffer——"

"And the visiting firemen from Schuyler College," said Tyler. "You must have that. Thursday morning."

"Yes, I have that." Mrs. Rhodes put down his desk-calendar and held out the newspaper. "Have you seen the *Eagle* this morning? They have something about the Committee of Six. On the front page."

"Thanks, no, I hadn't seen it," Tyler said. He watched

Mrs. Rhodes tiptoe out, gently closing the door behind her. The Enfield *Eagle,* the town's weekly newspaper, was probably the only one in the state which came out Monday morning. Coghall Edwards, the crusty old editor, was proud of the distinction. "It's the ideal time for a weekly," he had often argued. "You sweep up last week's news, and look forward to events coming up. And you have all day Sunday to put it to bed."

The small headline in the lower right-hand corner said: "FACULTY GROUP SCREENS MANY." Tyler's eye skimmed through the type underneath: "Enfield University's faculty committee has now settled on four local men as candidates for the position of twelfth president of the University," it said. "Continued on page 2." Tyler turned the page. "Informed sources told the *Eagle's* representative that the successor to President Homer Vaughn, who completes his term of office next June, may well be a member of the University faculty, although a persistent rumor has had it that the Board of Trustees might name an outsider. Prominently mentioned in the local sweepstakes were Professors Oliver Buell of the Department of Astronomy, now on leave in Europe; Cassius A. Daniels of the Department of Chemical Engineering; Geoffrey Balder, Chairman of the Department of Physics; and James E. Howarth of the Department of History."

Where did old Coghall run that down? Tyler wondered. Somebody was babbling. Edwards, an old-line Enfieldian born and raised in the town, had a lot of lines out. Tyler had seen him at one of the eggnog parties just before Christmas, wearing the bright tattersall vest he always affected, pretending to listen to the aged matron who held him possessively by one coatsleeve, but all the while sweeping the room with his ancient gray pouched eyes, maybe even looking for the man or the woman whose internal censor might have been relaxed by the eggnogs, and from whose idle babble Editor Edwards might extract the one grain of information he needed, the golden glister of truth in the sandy pile of verbiage.

The next paragraph said that Jeff Balder was "the popular Physics Chairman, and internationally known authority in the study of light"; that Jim Howarth was a specialist in the history of the American Revolution, official historian of the University who "is now well into the research for his book, which will be published in connection with the University's Bicentennial Celebration in 1961"; and that Cass Daniels was "a former business executive" who had joined the University faculty in the School of Engineering after distinguished service to the United States Army in the Pentagon. The term for Buell was "mathematical theoretician"—vague enough, Tyler guessed, so that no-one would be able to guess what Oliver was really doing, far out on the borders of the known universe.

The rest of the column was a rehash of last November's story about the election of the Committee of Six, naming the names, summarizing the committee assignment. A concluding one-sentence paragraph said that the *Eagle* had not been able to extract any comment from John Martin, Chairman of the Executive Committee of the Board of Trustees at Enfield University.

Somebody had talked. Old Coghall Edwards had called the shot in three out of four cases. Of course there were half a dozen other men whose names had been submitted to the trustees after the last meeting. And Jeff Balder was not in the running: he had been eliminated early on grounds of his age. Nor did the *Eagle* name any of the "outsiders" whom the trustees (according to *whose* persistent rumor?) were said to prefer. It looked like one of those verbal cocktails Edwards often ran in his weekly: two parts rumor, one part invention, dash of truth, shake well, and serve. Here, though, the usual proportions were different. Three of the men named were actual candidates, even though not (except Jim Howarth) the strongest.

You could not even tell whether it was a faculty member or a trustee who had let those three cats out of the bag. The tentative list of faculty nominees had been forwarded to Jumping Jack Martin almost a month ago. Maybe the trustees had been nosing around the campus, checking on this man or that man, and someone had put two and two together. Maybe a couple of the trustees were having a holiday highball together at the University Club while some jug-eared faculty member inadvertently listened in from the table in the next alcove. Maybe one of the Committee of Six had been unwise enough to tell his gossipy wife who the leading contenders were. Or had put leading but transparent questions to one of his colleagues. There were a dozen, maybe a score, of possibilities. Well, the best thing to do was ignore it. Let Coghall Edwards have fun with his rumors. No harm done, except embarrassment to the men whose names the morning *Eagle* carried. Candidates and Committee both. Embarrassing the candidates because they hadn't heard about it before, embarrassing the Committee members because they *had*!

Tyler went to the window, half expecting to see crowds

of students and faculty milling around the sidewalk, arguing and discussing the big *Eagle* newsbreak. The gray rain was still falling, the clouds still lowered over the Parthenon, a fuel oil truck sizzled through the slush heading south on College Street. But in all that dismal vista not one person was visible.

III

Filled to the edge of the page with Tyler's fine small scribble, each paragraph dominated by the printed date, the red limp-leather daybook lay open before him on the desktop. It was, he thought, his pen poised in his hand, something like a trail in the forest. When you looked back over them, some weeks and months did seem to show a rough kind of direction. Not that the shape of things ever became totally clear. The rambling curvature of daily events, meaningless in themselves, always helped to obscure the grand design, if there was one. Still, over a period of six months or a year, if you looked closely enough, you could sometimes discover the beginning of a sequence, watch it weave in and out among contributory or irrelevant events, disappear for a while, reappear, and at last reach some (seldom dramatic) conclusion.

Like the forest trails he used to follow those occasional summers in Vermont. The pine-needled track, climbing the low eminence, dropping away over granite outcrops to the logger's road in the next valley, would be easy to follow for a while. Then it would be obscured by the fallen trees, the dried brushpiles the loggers had left, the high grass that sprang up wherever sunlight penetrated the gloom under the tall evergreens, the mountain freshet, bringing its small avalanche of loose stones and gravel, cutting a channel for itself across the trail, misleading the searching eye. Looking for the trail again, you stumbled out in a semicircle around the great fallen tree-boles, wove back and forth in the brush like a hound off the scent, ducked under low branches, straddled over rotting moss-covered logs, ran your face itchingly into the invisible spider-web, wet your boots in the black muck of a bog, and then finally—just ahead and to the left—there would be the trail again, stretching out through the sun and the shadow, its direction plain for another two hundred yards.

This sequence on the search for the new president, now. It might show, over all, a few ironies, a comic touch here and there, a poetic or an actual justice, a certain ultimate logic. On top of the low pile in the filing-cabinet drawer, still dustless, last year's day-book had lain for a week or more. Filled with the fine script of a busy year. Or almost filled. There were always the blanks to mark the times when he had been pre-occupied or busy or lazy or (once or twice) sick. But there, in the main, lay last year's trail of ink, including the beginning of the—what would you call it?—the presidential sequence, and such development as it had had through November and December. The new volume, open here and waiting like a tabula rasa, was still young. Young as the new year, showing only a week of entries. Yet sometime, somewhere in the middle of the volume—in March or April, in May or June, possibly as late as July or August, he would be setting down the name of Homer Vaughn's successor.

Monday, January 9. The pen, moving slowly, left its thin

trail of ink across the page, drying quickly in the heat of this morning's sun. "Rain foll. by snow," he wrote. "Incredible slop. *Eagle* breaks presidential story. Who leaked it? Lunch Faculty Club. Old Mercer boresome on SAR. I hate genealogy. Fenelosa makes apptmt, fails keep it, leaves note. Now settled and rolling. Will do Voltaire & Jefferson, Ferney and Monticello. Good idea. Spent pm on Wed. lecture, revising Rousseau Savoyard Vicar material."

A boring day, except for the *Eagle* story. Maybe some old men were not bores: Picasso, Clemenceau, Thomas Aquinas. But old Dr. Mercer, pearl stickpin in tie, false teeth gleaming, had run on like an eight-day clock about his membership in the Sons of the American Revolution. Tyler, captive to etiquette, squirming in his chair, had finally interrupted the genealogical monologue. "You remember what Lincoln said. I say, you remember what Lincoln said," he shouted, startling the colored waitress in the corner. "He didn't care who his ancestors were, but he cared everything about who his descendants were." And old Mercer, chomping his teeth once or twice, opening and closing his watery eyes behind the dirty bifocals: "President Lincoln—had no cause—no cause 't all—to take pride in his ancestors. Sorry lot, by all accounts. A sorry lot." No use to argue with a deaf old man. Tyler had left after shaking the old man's hand, slender and dry as a bunch of twigs.

Outside the Faculty Club, the fine cold rain of the morning had turned to snow. As predicted. Large flakes fell lazily. Tyler had skidded on the slick granite steps, saved himself with a quick clutch at the iron rail. The old wound in the thigh muscles began to throb angrily. He had hurried, limping, across College Street and up to his office in Trask. In lieu of Fenelosa he found the note in the office door. Very sorry. Forgot dentist's appointment in Philadelphia. Could he make another conference date for later in week? Had stayed in Enfield all vacation, worked hard. Thesis now shaping up. Had decided to compare Voltaire at Ferney with Jefferson at Monticello. "*Amazing* parallels," thought Fenelosa. And did Tyler know the poem by Auden attached herewith, which Fenelosa had rather sloppily typed out for his professor's edification? "I'd like to know what you think of it, sir." End of note. End of Monday, January ninth.

Tuesday the tenth. Searching his memory, Tyler drew a complete blank. Had anything happened Tuesday? He flipped back the pages of his desk-calendar. Oh; yes. Yes, indeed. The Committee on Discipline had met that Tuesday afternoon. In what used to be called a solemn conclave, Dean Woodruff presiding. A very much shocked Milton Fletcher had kept the minutes, though the Lord knew what he put into them; Dr. Maynard represented the Department of Student Health, if that was the word for it; and Professors Webb, Sloane, and Tyler were the other representatives of the faculty.

"This," George Woodruff had remarked, "is a rough one." He squinted round the table at his five committee-men, rubbed his rough hair furiously, and gestured towards Maynard with his pipe-stem. "I'll leave it to the doctor to acquaint us with the facts. Reg, could we have them?"

Maynard cleared his throat. Lean and brown, his age betrayed only by his white hair, he shifted uncomfortably in his chair.

"I can summarize quickly. They were all infected by the same—er—woman—er—girl on the same day—er—night. The evidence became apparent to them all after the medically expectable interval. They came loping in to the infirmary. We tested them. The result was four positive Wassermans. The young men have begun the prescribed course of treatment."

"And I can add, gentlemen," said the dean gently, "that they are a fairly contrite lot. Contrite, surprised, chagrined, and damned uncomfortable. On the advice of Dr. Maynard they were all sent home."

"Wow," said Webb quietly. "How far?"

"Three of the four live in New York City," said the dean, "though I don't take that as a reflection on that fair city. The fourth is a very much astonished Philadelphia boy from the Main Line. So it was not hard to send them home, though hard on them. Nor was it hard to bring them back. They're waiting in the next room in case we have any questions."

Webb looked at Maynard. "Isn't four quite a crop?" he asked.

"Luckily we don't have much of this," Maynard said. "Why it doesn't happen oftener is anyone's guess. It lies, so to speak, in the lap of the gods."

"The goddess, Reg," said the dean. He chuckled and looked round the table again over the tops of his glasses. "The lap of Venus."

Everyone smiled except Fletcher. When he spoke, his voice was shocked. "I don't remember anything as bad as this in the two years I've been on the committee." He sat slumped in his chair.

"Last year," said Maynard, "we seem to have escaped entirely. One case the year before withdrew from the university voluntarily and immediately and has not attempted to come back. We listed him simply as withdrawal for medical reasons."

"What do we do with these kids, George?" said Tyler. "I assume they have been punished enough already."

"They've been punished, all right," the dean said. "If only by the shock, as you might say, of recognition. We have also notified the young lady's parents. Our boys were too angry to be chivalrous. They gave us her name, address, and telephone number. I think we may safely say that she is hors de combat. No pun intended."

The committee laughed, quietly, so as not to suggest to the boys next door anything like unseemly levity.

"What do you recommend as a penalty?" said Webb. "I mean other than what they've got."

"Obviously we can't have them around until they are untainted," the doctor said. "That, with modern medical treatment, needs roughly two weeks. What you add to that is the committee's affair."

"What classes do they belong to?" asked Tyler.

The dean grimaced and sighed audibly. "As you might expect, Ed, three are sophomores. The fourth, I'm sorry to say, is a formerly starry-eyed freshman on his first escapade."

"Wouldn't it fit the case," asked Tyler, "to send them away for the rest of this year and consider them for straight readmission, if healthy, to next year's freshman and sophomore classes? They'd lose a full year, and that's rough. But it might be the wisest plan."

"I'll buy that," said Webb.

"Do you want to talk with them before we act?" said Woodruff.

Milton Fletcher looked up from his minute book. "I don't see that that's called for," he said stiffly.

Jim Sloane's jaw thrust forward. "What was the point of getting them here if we aren't to see them?" he said aggressively. "I don't see it. They ought to have a short lecture."

"For what?" said Tyler. "For being foolish? They're boys. George has already lectured them. And they're getting other lectures through the business end of a hypodermic. There will be, I imagine, plenty more of the same."

"They ought to learn—" Sloane began.

"I say they've learned, Jim," said Tyler. "Let's send them along home. I move my motion."

"Second," said Milton Fletcher in a choked voice.

"I'll ask for a show of hands," said Woodruff.

So we prevailed on that one, thought Tyler. We sent them home to sweat it out. He picked up his pen. "Two inches of snow," he wrote in the daybook. "And still overcast all day. Meeting Discipl. Committee. Venus on the half-shell without benefit of Giorgione. The quality of mercy is not strained."

He held the pen poised over the page. Anything else for Tuesday the tenth? Any other great revelations? Ah, yes. Bill Waggoner had telephoned, summoning the Committee of Six for Friday afternoon. Jack Martin had been disturbed by the national publicity given to the presidential sweepstakes after the *Eagle* broke its story. Could the members meet to

116

discuss the problem? *"Times* reprints *Eagle* story," Tyler wrote. "Martin summons Committee of Six for Friday the 13th. Date ominous."

Anything else for Tuesday the tenth? All right, Wednesday the eleventh. Tyler's calendar showed only the departmental meeting in the afternoon, where they had quickly reappointed the whole slate of instructors for next year. Even Double-trouble Eliot, who always put his foot in his mouth, but might (his long-suffering but kindly peers suggested) make the grade with another year's experience. Was that all for Wednesday? Well, he had taught all morning, dictated to Mrs. Rhodes after lunch, run the departmental meeting, and walked home with Paul Eaton through the crisp and frosty evening. "Weather clearing during day," Tyler wrote. "Cool & crisp. Dept. meeting reappoints all instructors."

Thursday the twelfth. That's today. We are caught up now. Tyler blotted the last entry and put the daybook into the top drawer of his desk. "Weather clear and sunny," he would write in the book tomorrow." Conference on language teaching with Ronald and White of Schuyler College. Conference with Dean Schaeffer on dept. affairs."

A dull week, generally speaking. Well, what do you want, Tyler—a three-ring circus? Thanks, I have a three-ring circus. A dull three-part round, sung in a January monotone. A Gregorian chant, all on the same note. Or did they run up and down a note or two? He was speculating on the problem when his buzzer sounded and Mrs. Rhodes said, "Professor Tyler. Can you see Professor White and Professor Ronald of Schuyler College now?"

Professor Tyler could. He put on his jacket and went to

117

open the office door as the approaching heel-clicks sounded
in the hall corridor.

IV

As soon as the two men appeared in the doorway, Tyler
recognized White. That leonine head, with the finely carven
features, regular and symmetrical as an idealized statue's, and
with the clean lines of his closely shaven jaw, the small flat
ears, and the thick hair with every strand in place, gave White
the air of an actor—all ready with well-memorized lines,
anxious to begin the second act of some serious comedy—the
part of Caesar, say, in Shaw's play. The head and the face
were unmistakable, thought Tyler, though he had met him
only once before, at one of the M.L.A. meetings where White
had read, with great urbanity, a paper on La Rochefoucauld.

The other man, William Ronald, had the excessive shyness
Tyler had sometimes noticed in tall men. When White intro-
duced him to Tyler, Ronald's prominent Adam's apple
bobbed up and down and he mumbled (almost unhappily)
the shortest of replies before he sat down in one of the chairs
on the other side of Tyler's desk. During the first ten minutes,
as White swiftly described the way foreign languages were
now taught at Schuyler, Ronald sat perfectly still, uncomfortably large for the small chair, his sloping shoulders unmoving,
the big hands quietly folded in his lap. Whenever his companion looked towards him, pausing momentarily in the
fluent development of an idea, Ronald would nod his head
the fraction of an inch, the craggy face impassive, only the
veiled eyes alert.

When Tyler, urged on by White's questioning, launched

into an extended description of the Army Language School he had organized just at the end of the war, White's cameo-like face recorded every turn in the conversation—sympathetic, responsive, smiling or grimacing as the occasion seemed to require, shaking his head, moving his quick white hands, interjecting a word here, a phrase there, paying the closest attention, it seemed, not only to the individual words but also to the merest change of intonation in Tyler's voice. Ronald, on the other hand, seemed to be peering round the room, trying to read the titles in the farthest bookcase, looking away when Tyler looked at him, his veiled eyes pausing only momentarily on Tyler's face at times when he thought Tyler was not watching him.

At the end of twenty minutes, half from curiosity, half from pity, Tyler spoke directly to Ronald. "How do you like the Foulet discs for teaching conversation?"

Ronald flushed pink up to his eyes and glanced quickly at his companion. His Adam's apple jumped in agitation, as he half mumbled, half blurted, "Well, you see, I teach mathematics." Now he fixed his eyes unmovingly on White, like one demanding rescue. For the first time that morning, Tyler felt uncomfortable. What was up, anyway? His palms were sweating, and his face prickled with what he suspected was a blush of his own. He, too, looked directly at White.

White's fine-cut features opened into a quick smile. "I wonder, Mr. Tyler, if you know our college well."

"Not well," Tyler said. "I have seen it. My wife and I were up that way a few years back. We drove past it. A handsome set of red brick buildings off by itself on a plateau beside the river."

"That's right," said White. "Although they're not all as

handsome as those you see from the highway. Like every college, we have a few architectural errors. But we think we have one of the most beautiful small campuses in America. It's historic country, too, as I'm sure you know. The Battle of Saratoga, and so on."

"And the battles still go on, don't they, at the race-track?"

"Yes," said White, flashing his quick smile. "Mostly, I believe, in July and August. The school year is fairly quiet."

"My wife and I were there about the middle of July," Tyler said.

(Should he tell them about that evening at the races? Alice pregnant then, looking across the stretch of greensward to the lighted grandstand beyond. "O, Ed, I've always wanted to see a horse-race. Couldn't we stop?" Tyler, humoring her, swung the car into the parking-field and helped her bulkingly out. It was a long walk to the admission gate for one in her condition. Heavy with the child, Alice was puffing when they arrived, but her eyes were bright. They bought the programs and settled into a grandstand box, the finish line just below them. On the nut-brown track, under the floodlights, the horses who would run the first race were limbering up, the drivers hunched forward in the two-wheeled gigs, their silks varicolored.

"Aren't they wonderful?" said Alice. "They look so small and trim. Aren't you glad we came? I wish I were small and trim."

"It won't be long now until you are," Tyler said. "Not long till the first race, either. Are you going to bet?"

"Where do you bet?" said Alice. "Yes, we'd better bet. Isn't this exciting? Let me see what the horses' names are."

*"Down under the grandstand," said Tyler. "I believe you
go to one of the windows and get some kind of a ticket. What
do you say on this first race? Who's your little nag?"*

*Alice picked Number Four, a horse name Superb Wellesley,
and Tyler had just returned with the two-dollar ticket when
the announcer said, "Ladies and gentlemen, our national
anthem."*

"O," said Alice, "I can't get up. You be patriotic for me."

*But she did get up and held Tyler's hand while the pre-
liminary ceremonies went smoothly ahead. At last the horses
gathered on the far side of the track. "Here they come," said
the announcer in his hill-billy intonation. The gleaming
starter's car spread its bird-like wings, gradually increasing
its speed as the horses, trotting smartly, rounded the turn
into the straightaway, small hooves pounding, pace steadily
quickening. Then the starter's car shot suddenly away and
the horses bunched at the near turn. "They're off," said the
announcer, and Tyler looked at Alice.*

"O, Ed. I can't stand this. It's too exciting."

"Don't have the baby yet," Tyler said.

*"No, not here," Alice said. "Not yet. If our horse wins,
we'll call the baby Superb Wellesley."*

*When they flashed under the half-mile wire, Alice's horse
was neck and neck with a small black one called Little Joe
Clancy.*

*"Better look out," Tyler said, "or we'll have to call the
baby Little Joe."*

*"No," said Alice. "No, no." Her clenched fists pounded her
knees. "Come on, Superb Wellesley," she cried.*

"Take it easy," said Tyler. "It's only a horse-race."

But Alice was watching the clumped horses on the far straightaway, only their heads visible, too distant to identify, shooting like automatons towards the last quarter. Suddenly they exploded around the final curve and drove towards the finish line.

"Come on, come on," cried Alice, as the crowd roared. "Wellesley, come on, come on."

Superb Wellesley came on, her driver glancing back over his shoulder, the slender whip flicking her haunches, and won the race easily by a length and a half.

"We won. Wellesley won," Alice said happily and flung her arms around Tyler's neck. Later, of course, they had lost all but eighty cents of their winnings on a horse called "Dat Wumman." But Alice still spoke occasionally of Superb Wellesley).

"We have a faculty," White was saying, his leonine head back, "of about three hundred, and there are seven hundred girls. So we think the ratio of faculty to students is one of the best in the country."

"Known to be," Ronald said warmly, looking at Tyler directly. "Statistics show it."

"The endowment," White went on smoothly, "is large and steadily growing, the trustees are a very thoughtful group who have the welfare of the faculty very much at heart, and the physical plant is up to date, with no major building program required for the immediate future. To run all this, we have been fortunate in having had, since the war, an excellent president, a woman."

Tyler nodded. He knew Mrs. Gaskell, Mrs. Honora Gaskell, by reputation. Following a wartime command in the Women's

Army Corps, she had taken the presidency of Schuyler. What was White leading up to? Did they want to move in and take one of the Enfield nominees?

"Unhappily for us," White was saying, "her husband's professional obligations require that he move to the west coast. In fact he has already gone. Mrs. Gaskell naturally must be with her husband, and has given us notice that as soon as we can find a successor to her, she wishes to resign. So we are in the same position as you down here. We are in search of a new president."

Tyler saw that Ronald's veiled eyes were still watching him closely. "Yes," he said, "our Board of Trustees is at work now. We have a faculty committee. Six men. Elected by the faculty as a sort of advisory group. Did you want—"

"We are your equivalents at Schuyler, Dr. Ronald and I," said White quickly. "Except that we have only the two. Our Board of Trustees has been very active in combing the country, especially its chairman, Mrs. Eames. I believe you may know her husband. She is a Schuyler alumna who happens to be married to a member of Enfield's board. Mr. Jarvis Eames."

Tyler nodded again. "I know him only slightly." All right, Lion, he said to himself. All right, White Lion. You want one of our men. Just bring him up, and I'll give you the old fight-talk.

"In arranging this meeting today," White went on, "we really had a double purpose. First, we wanted your advice on the language program. But secondly, we have been authorized by Mrs. Eames to ask you—" White glanced momentarily at Ronald, the merest flick of an eye—"to ask you if you would be interested in being considered for the presidency of Schuyler."

The sentence exploded in Tyler's head the way those Saratoga ponies had exploded around the final curve of the racetrack. You couldn't see, on the backstretch, who was ahead. They were all bunched, unidentifiably, at the beginning of the turn. Then they burst into sudden view and you saw, five or six trotting strides later, that (astonishingly) the horse in the lead was your own. With this difference, though. You were not betting on this particular race. Your horse was not even competing.

Tyler absorbed the blow silently. With Ronald's eyes on him, he was determined not to move a muscle. Did they think you would leap at the chance? He looked over at White, the smooth interlocutor, the tactful diplomat. An hour at least, he thought, must have elapsed since White had spoken. "This doesn't—" he began. "I don't—"

"I know this has come to you as a surprise," said White quickly. "And of course, we cannot presume to ask for a split-second response. Still, Dr. Ronald and I ought to say to you that Mrs. Eames and the rest of the Board are most anxious that you will give our proposal your serious attention." He smiled and spread his white hands in a controlled gesture. "This day," he said, "this hour, comes as a kind of climax to many days and hours of work on our part. We have been on the job for more than a year, ever since we knew that Mrs. Gaskell—" He paused, with just that touch of dramatic poise that Tyler had noticed in him from the beginning. "I can assure you," he said, smiling kindly, "that your qualifications for the post have been very thoroughly investigated. We are unanimous in our belief that the chairman of Enfield's Department of Modern Languages, and the very able organizer of the Army's Language Program at the close of the war, could, if he would, do the kind of job we want done at Schuyler."

Tyler opened his mouth again, but was stopped by White's raised hand. "The form in which I have broached the invitation," said White, "is of course the usual form in such matters. We are not asking you to accept the position; we are asking whether you will consider—whether you are interested in being considered for the position." He dropped his hand and sat quietly.

Now it's my turn, Tyler thought. How many people has he said this to already? How many times has he been turned down?

"You're very kind," Tyler said. "It's a very great honor even to be asked. But I'm afraid—I mean I think your investigation—" He stopped to gather order. "Forgive my fumbling," he said, "but I'm afraid I'm not your man. By the time a man is past forty, he has a pretty clear idea of what he's good at and what he's not so good at. I'm a teacher, of sorts, in language and literature. And when I can get the time, I try to be a scholar. This is my life, this is what I think I'm best qualified to do. My administrative experience, even in the Army, is practically nil."

"Of course, you are chairman of your department," said Ronald, shifting his weight in the small chair, hardly moving his lips.

"Chairmanship is nothing," said Tyler, "but a glorified secretary's job. Not too glorified either. You just oil the wheels of the departmental machinery." He grinned tightly. He could feel the tightness in the muscles around his mouth. "And when parts wear out, you try to replace them. Also, it ought to be said that I never raised a nickel in my life. Except selling magazines for the Boy Scouts thirty years ago."

"The President of Schuyler," said White, smiling, "has almost no money-raising duties. It's a little different in a women's college than in a great university. Our Board of Trustees devotes more time to money-raising than to anything else. The president is left free for administrative and educational duties."

Tyler, filling his pipe and leaning forward to light it, found that his mouth was bone-dry. He had never, he thought, been more uncomfortable in his life. Spiritually, that is, he corrected himself. How did you tell them tactfully that you wouldn't touch a presidency anywhere with a ten-foot pole?

"We are not asking you for a decision now," said White. Again his voice was kind, his sympathy apparently sincere. "Certainly you would have to see the Schuyler campus, meet the trustees and the faculty, find out more about the current problems, though they are not many, before either Schuyler— or Tyler—came to any final terms. We have only come today to ask you to think about the proposal, and if possible to set a date on which it would be convenient for you and your wife to pay us a visit." He took a small notebook from his pocket. "Naturally we hope it would be soon. Even late this month or early in February. The procedure would be for you to drive up with Mrs. Tyler on, say, a Friday afternoon. The trip takes about five or six hours in good weather."

"I'd allow six," said Ronald.

"We would have cocktails and dinner on Friday with the

members of the Board," said White. "To give them an opportunity to meet and talk with you. On Saturday, you would
talk with Mrs. Gaskell and then have lunch with her and with
our departmental chairmen. And then in the afternoon there
would be a faculty reception." He glanced again at Ronald,
that mere flick of the quick eyes. "I am sure," he added,
"whatever the outcome, that we could guarantee you and
Mrs. Tyler a very pleasant week-end. You could return home
Sunday."

He opened the small notebook. "I wonder if you could
arrange it for as early as Friday the twentieth." He smiled at
Tyler. "Or, failing that, Friday the third of February."

Oh, God, Tyler thought, what do you do now? Do you say
you'll go, when you know damned well you would turn them
down if they ever offered you the job? Do you waste their
time and your own with a sleeveless errand? Or do you say,
flatly and now, that you cannot do it? Do you plead previous
engagements for both dates, only to have him propose a third
date which you cannot pretend is already filled. Sweating
there in his desk-chair, he hoped not visibly, he puffed furiously at his pipe and found that it was out. The worst of it
was, and he was much shaken to notice it, that along the outer
edges of his consciousness the faint glow of something like
ambition was beginning to be visible. "Why not?" said the
small voice from the midst of the glow. "Who says you can't
do the job? They have clearly checked you out and found a
man they think they want. The great Nielsen of Smith met
the same kind of proposition. He did a great job at a women's
college. He's a major figure in American education. Do you
really mean that about professoring all your life?"

For something to do, while his head began to throb and

the cold sweat-drops fell uncomfortably, irritatingly, inside his undershirt, Tyler got his appointment book out of his jacket pocket. Friday the thirteenth showed the meeting of the Committee of Six. But Friday the twentieth was clear and so —he was not surprised to see—so was the third of February.

"Both dates seem to be clear," he said. "Of course I would have to check with Mrs. Tyler—she may have something that would keep her from going."

"Yes, of course," White said. "We recognize that this is rather sudden, rather short notice."

Turn them down, said Tyler to himself. Don't fool around any longer. It's a dirty trick to pretend you're interested, even for the sake of politeness. Now is the time. Say the word. He opened his mouth and drew in a quick breath. Like a fish, he thought, like a damn trout flapping on the grass, gills working, body writhing, desperate to be back under the brown surface, under the tree-roots in the shelving bank, hidden again in the cool water.

"Would you agree—at least tentatively until you have had a chance to call Mrs. Tyler—to drive up on the twentieth? I am sorry to be so importunate," White said. "But this is a matter of some consequence."

The glow out on the edge of Tyler's mind brightened for a moment. "Yes, I can understand that," he said. "I think, yes, we could probably come." What the hell made you say that, now? Repeat the point about wanting to be a professor. You're wasting their time. You would never take the job even if you got the offer. Maybe Alice would like to go, though. She liked people. It would be fun for her. She would make a first-class president's wife. She could have a maid, not have to work so hard.

Stop it, he told himself. You're just hiding behind your wife, now. Your pride is touched and you know it. You're flattered. You want to go and be admired. You want them to offer you the job so you can have the pleasure of turning it down.

The hell I do, he thought. I just want to be left alone. I will do the best I can with the job I've got here. It's more than enough for a satisfactory life. Alice likes it. It's a nice town. We have good friends here. And what was it Cos said, the remark by Henry Adams: "A friend in power is a friend lost." You're lost. You're lost if you take that job. You're lost if you go up there.

"Forgive me," he said to White and Ronald. "I guess you realize that this is a hard decision."

White smiled his tactful smile. "Naturally. But I would point out that it is hardly final, hardly irrevocable. No offer has been made as yet. And I would be less than honest if I pretended that we are not also considering several other possibilities. We cannot," he said jocularly, "put all our eggs in one basket, or cross our bridges before we know which way the river flows."

"Of course," Tyler said. This would not be final. Probably they would make the offer to someone else in the end. He felt relief for the first time. It would not be so bad. A week-end in upstate New York. On the way there he and Alice could drive past the race-track where Superb Wellesley had trotted home without a break in her handsome little stride. Then they could trot home again, with pleasant memories of Schuyler College, and that would be it. All courtesies duly entered into and completed. Nobody's feelings hurt. Back to the professor's life with the professor's wife.

"Under those circumstances," he said, with only a touch of dry misery in his voice, "I think we could arrange to come on the twentieth."

White and Ronald both smiled together and stood up. "Thank you for all this time," White said. "I'm afraid we have demolished your morning. And we will look forward to seeing you and Mrs. Tyler on the afternoon of January twentieth."

Tyler helped them on with their overcoats. They shook hands warmly and went off down the corridor. Tyler closed the office door and opened the window as wide as he could, leaning out to breathe the fresh air. The sky, which had been clear blue when he walked up Enfield Avenue that morning, was beginning to cloud over. He sat down in the desk chair— still warm, he noticed. "The hot seat," he said half aloud. "Now what in the name of God made you say you would go up there?"

v

Crossing the campus towards Enfield Hall a little before three-thirty, the Schuyler business heavy in his pocket, he came near stopping to rest on the sun-dial bench. Where's your energy? he thought. Somewhere inside him lay the lunch he had eaten with Cos Cobb in the Faculty Club dining-room. What had he eaten, anyway? Poached egg on corned beef hash? No, that was sometime last week. Maybe even last year. Whatever the lunch was, it hung suspended somewhere within him, like cold pancakes in a haversack. His feet dragged on the pebbled path. Three-twenty, the clock said. No harm in sitting here for five minutes. The clouds had moved off to the east now; overhead and to the west the sky was blue. He slumped down on the marble bench under the phoenix.

"Sit down, Ed," Cos had said. "You look gray in the face. You work too hard. By Thursday you're licked and every Friday you die. Some day Saturday is not going to fix you up again. The layman doesn't know what professoring really is."

"Nothing but a rocky morning," Tyler had said. "I'll recover. There were a couple of visiting firemen from an upstate college in New York. They wanted to talk about language-teaching."

That was true, he thought. No need to lie. They had talked about language-teaching—for at least twenty minutes.

"Maybe you'd like a drink," Cos had said. "The bar's open. Dr. Mercer is having his noontime snifter."

"Not today. Have a conference about the department with Bob Schaeffer this afternoon. A drink would put me to sleep. I'll just stick with the coffee."

"What we need," Cos said, "is a little exercise. How about shooting up to the lake next week-end to cut some wood. Can't go tomorrow on account of Jumping Jack Martin and the Committee of Six. But Friday the twentieth is clear. We've got a lot of fall-downs in my woods. They should be sawed up and split before they start to rot. We can go up Friday, come back late Saturday."

"Not next week-end," Tyler said, hating himself. "Alice and I may have to be out of town next Friday and Saturday. Sorry, Cos. Maybe we could make it up there a little later."

"Oh, sure," Cos had said carelessly. "Lots of time. No rush. How's Alice?"

"Fine," said Tyler automatically. Would she be fine when she learned about the Schuyler business? For ten minutes before he met Cobb for lunch he had sat staring at his office telephone, wondering how to broach it to her. He knew, of course, that she would take it well. What really made him hesitate was the state of his own emotions. Then he had suddenly remembered that she wasn't home anyway: this was the day of the Thursday Club. She was there for lunch and wouldn't be home until she had picked up the boys after school.

"How is Polly? Alice thought she seemed nervous New Year's Eve."

"Tired," Cos said, with a touch of gloom. "All those parties to go to around Christmas, and one Polly thought she ought to give for Cornie and her small pals, and then our own New Year blast. Though the New Year one wasn't so rough, with everybody else contributing the food. Polly's a country cousin, like me. We can't take the heavy social whirl. Probably should have spent a quiet Christmas at the camp. But little old Cornie, naturally, wouldn't hear of it." He looked quickly at Tyler, then looked away. "Just social strain," he added. "Passing thing. Nothing we—nothing she won't recover from. What are you going to have for lunch?"

Tyler had eaten whatever it was he had eaten and walked back across the campus with Cos. Climbing the steps of Trask was a lift-and-drag operation. "Social strain," he had muttered to himself, "takes many forms, and one of them is what you do when they want to offer you a presidency. Correction: when they ask you to come up so they can see if they *want* to offer you a presidency."

There they had sat, he thought, coming into his empty, Bastille-dungeon-smelling office. White Lion White was there. William the Silent Ronald had sat there. And in the middle, like a trout on the hook, had sat Edward the Undecided, wrestling with his ambitions.

"The hell with it," he had suddenly said. "The very hell with it. Nothing doing. First impulse was the right impulse. You are not presidential material, and don't ever fool yourself by thinking that you are. You should have had the guts to turn them down then and there, flat and pronto." Nice guys, of course. They had been very decent about the whole thing. But that wasn't the point. The point was that Edward Bennett Tyler would not, under any circumstances, consider a presidency. He had thought several times, half jokingly, of submitting an article to the Bulletin of the American Association of University Professors. Title: *Why I Turned Down the Presidency*. First two sentences: "It goes without saying that I have never been offered the presidency of a college or a university. Should that very remote contingency ever arise, however, these are the reasons I would turn the offer down."

Now he could never write such an article, even in fun. But the reasons still held. Here was something that wasn't exactly an offer, but close enough. Too close. So what do you do, Dr. Tyler? You stop fooling, and you write them. You write them now, politely, firmly, and finally. You say no.

Tyler sighed with fatigue and glanced up at the phoenix, white as a gull against the blue sky. Well, the no was said. In his pocket was the letter, addressed to Professor Alfred White of Schuyler College, all stamped like a love-letter with an air-mail and a special delivery, ready to take flight. Beat the boys back to Schuyler, even, if they had some other candidates to see.

However they felt about it when they saw it, it was the best letter he could write. From one to three he had wrestled with it, scribbling, tearing up, typing, tearing up. His waste-basket in the office was half full of Schuyler College confetti. He had tried to say it rightly, tried to say it as impersonally as possible, tried to keep it (as far as you ever could with these things) on the philosophical plane. Now it was finished. Nothing to do but drop it into the red and blue mailbox in front of Enfield Hall, feeling only slightly like a heel, and let the man from the post office pick it up at four.

The clock on the chapel tower struck three-thirty. Tyler stood up and stretched. Time to see Bob Schaeffer about those raises for Simeon and Giorgio and the other men in the Modern Languages Department. He hurried over to the mailbox and dropped the letter into its dark mouth. As he mounted the steps to Enfield Hall, his legs felt lighter. Definitely lighter.

FIVE *FEBRUARY*

I

STANDING gratefully in the pool of warm sunlight by the back door, Tyler watched the neighbor's cat picking its way slowly across the wet snow. It had not yet seen, perhaps would not see, the squirrel. Every few steps it paused to lift its head, pointing its pink nose sunward like a flower, seeming to sniff the air. Busily, in staccato stops and starts, the squirrel searched along the bare ground under the shadow of the pine tree. Tyler leaned back, his shoulders against the wall of the house where leafless stems of climbing ivy clung tenaciously to the rough brick. A melting icicle, losing its hold on the eaves-trough, fell and smashed on the cement walk beside him. He jumped slightly, and the cat, startled, turned its green eyes swiftly in his direction, saw in a moment it had nothing to fear, and resumed its slow progress, paws lifted, shaken, and then delicately set down, across the stubbled snow. The squirrel, nosing among the pine-needles, found a buried acorn and sat up, holding the prize in its front paws, just inside the edge of the tree shadow.

The cat stopped still, one front paw lifted like a setter. Now
it saw the squirrel: its black tail began the slow switching;
its haunches contracted like springs. The squirrel was un-
husking the acorn, turning it in his paws, the jaws moving
hastily. Head low, eyes concentrate, the cat took one carefully controlled step. Tyler clumped a handful of wet snow
into a ball, aimed at the cat's broad back, tossed underhanded
—and missed. But the cat's concentration was broken, it had
become aware of the enemy, it looked back over its shoulder
with something like disgust. Then it loped across the yard
and disappeared through the privet hedge. When Tyler
looked again, the squirrel had finished its lunch and gone.
"And I've finished mine," he thought. "Time to get going."

"I saw it all," said Alice's husky voice from somewhere
above his head, and he jumped again. "Aren't you ashamed?"

Moving away from the warm brick wall, eyes squinting, he
looked up to see her head and shoulders framed in the window, sunlight gleaming on her smooth brown arms. "The
idea," she said, smiling her enigmatic smile. "Hitting poor
Penelope that way."

"I missed," said Tyler smiling back. "And besides, poor
Penelope is no friend of mine. I'm for the underdog—or the
under-squirrel. You saw what poor Penelope was aiming to
do."

Alice bobbed her head, still smiling the mysterious smile,
looking sleepy and luxurious in the sun. "I saw it all," she
repeated. "I know about you and Penelope. You're secretly
in love with her. That was nothing but a lover's quarrel. Did
you finish your lunch?"

Tyler nodded back. "Very good, too. Not even a crust

left, or I would have fed my friend the squirrel. My true friend, the squirrel. I was just getting up courage to return to the Trask squirrel-den, Room 208, when your lovely head appeared. Now I think I'll stay. It's very pleasant here."

"Isn't it?" said Alice. With her palms she pushed back her hair and exposed her small ears. "I'm kneeling on the bedroom floor. Like a sun-worshiper. If my knees were more comfortable, I'd stay right here and get a February sunburn. When are you going to take down that platfom in the pine tree? It's too dangerous. I don't want the boys up there."

"Soon," said Tyler. "After we get the new president picked and I have a spare Saturday. Have they been playing up there?"

"Not this winter," said Alice. "Pretty soon they'll discover it again."

"And get covered with pitch again, I suppose." He suddenly remembered the October evening. Long ago now.

"It's the height, not the pitch," said Alice. "That platform is forty feet up."

Tyler measured the height with his eye. Probably twenty feet. "I'll take it down," he said. "But first, I'll have to prepare the ground with Toby and Tommy. A little advance propaganda. They're proud of their work. It shouldn't disappear without warning." He made another snowball and threw it towards the platform.

A crow rose, complaining raucously, from the pine-top into the cerulean sky. They both looked up, blinking in the sun. Diagonally, high above the yard, cumulus clouds sailed eastward, slow and majestic as full-rigged schooners. Pearl-gray and pearl-white nearby, they deployed like a fleet as they receded towards the horizon. Cut flat by steady air-currents, their undersides might have been gray waterlines on the broad hulls of cruising ships. All their tops clumped high like billowing sails, pile on pile, moving out to sea, seen from a harbor shore.

Tyler stretched wiry arms in the sun. "Back to the squirrel-cage," he said. "Have a good sunburn."

"Not for long," said Alice. "The Garden Club meets at two. A man is coming to tell us how to prune roses. Don't work too hard, Edward."

"Not me," he said, moving off. "See you around six."

He had just emerged from the black cinder-mud of the back driveway and was scuffing his shoe-soles on the Enfield Avenue sidewalk when he heard brakes squeal and looked up to see Cos Cobb's face leaning from the car window. "Ride?" Cos said.

"This is no day to ride," said Tyler. "What's the old woodsman coming to? You ought to be walking all over the countryside, searching for spring." He went around the car and climbed in. "What are you doing down in this end of town?"

"Just dropping Cornie at the nursery school," Cos said. In the afternoon light his eye-sockets showed dark and his skin looked drawn and sallow. "I have to catch a plane out of Newark at four, and Polly's driving me to the station in half an hour."

"Where to?"

"We have a big symposium cooking on the west coast," said Cos. "I'm reading a paper in the genetics section. The conference will run all next week. That's one way to use up a leave of absence. My guinea-pigs wept when we said good-bye this morning."

"Cos, if you're flying west, why do you have to leave Thursday?"

Cos glanced out of the car window on his side and shifted his hands on the wheel. "Little business in Chicago this week-end," he said. "I'll fly out from the Midway Airport Sunday night."

"Some more genetics?"

Cos laughed oddly. "It might come under that head, yes. Some more genetics." He glanced out of his window again and cleared his throat. "I'll be back from the coast on the eleventh," he said. "How's the Committee of Six?"

"You know as much as I do," Tyler said. "All quiet, I guess. Nothing since that meeting with Jumping Jack Martin last month. The meeting of Friday the thirteenth, when he gave us the little lecture on keeping our mouths closed."

"Very politely," said Cos. "It was a fine little lecture. And the topic was embarrassing. How did he know one of the trustees hadn't leaked the story to the *Eagle*?"

"Even the *Eagle* has been quiet lately," said Tyler. "Maybe because everybody is now closed up like clams."

"It's a good idea," Cos said. "I'm in favor of the shut mouth. No sense in advertising your dirty linen. Where do you want to hop out?" He had slowed down for the College Street intersection.

"Right here is fine," Tyler said. "Have a good trip, Cos."

Cos smiled faintly. "You bet," he said. Under the brim of his gray hat his eyes looked sardonic. He waved his hand and drove off down the sun-dappled macadam.

139

Tyler stood for a moment looking after him; all the buildings shone clear in the strong February sunlight; the elms and maples cast angular shadows on the walls and the sidewalks, sharp edges fading when a cloud moved across the sun's face, then coming clear and stark again as the covering cloud moved on and the light once more intensified. He wondered if Alice still knelt at the upstairs window, drinking in the sun. Probably not. In the quiet bedroom she would now be laying out her dress and shoes for the Garden Club meeting. And in the quiet back yard, while the white cloud-galleons moved past, the cat Penelope might be stalking that squirrel again. But I hope not, Tyler thought. I hope not.

II

Paul Eaton spooned the powdered coffee into a thick green cup and filled it with boiling water from the tea-kettle on the hot-plate. "I thought you'd worked enough today, Ed," he said, the spoon clinking as he stirred. "Sugar? No? I hope you don't mind being pried loose from your office for an hour or two."

"Thanks," Tyler said, accepting the cup. "It's a good time. Nothing was happening. I went home for lunch today and since I got back I've just been going around in circles. If someone calls, Mrs. Rhodes has your number." He glanced at Eaton's neat book-cases, the single Gauguin reproduction on the green wall above the desk, the desk itself—perfectly empty except for a single sheet of paper. "This is a very shipshape office, Paul. After my unpoliced den, this looks positively austere."

"You're speaking about my desk," said Paul. "Everyone does. It shows what an able executive I am. At the end of the day, I just sweep stuff off the desk-top into this drawer. When the drawer's full, I empty it into the wastebasket. Good system, saves hours. Luckily I'm not one of you departmental chairmen. The need of answering letters would kill me inside of a month."

"It's really the white man's burden," said Tyler, sipping the coffee. "I may adopt your system any time."

"Don't," Paul cried, throwing up his hands in mock horror. "Tyler follows Eaton and the whole of Enfield will come apart at the seams. But just to show you I can be systematic, too, I've got me a little list here. At the top it says *Tyler Topics*. More coffee? No? Then prepare to talk." He leaned over the sheet of typewriter paper.

"Item one," he said crisply. "The strange case of our mutual friend, Mr. Ducky Drake. Sometimes known as Donald Duck."

"Don Drake?" said Tyler. "I heard from him this fall sometime. A postcard. He said he didn't like that little Campbellite college worth a damn."

"That little Campbellite college doesn't care for Donald Duck, either," Paul said. "He wrote me a letter a couple of days ago. He has been canned."

Tyler grimaced. "Poor Donald," he said. "He hasn't told me about this yet. If he ever does. What happened?"

"It appears," said Eaton, "that he made the mistake of asking a student around for a cocktail. The student, a farm-boy from the prairies, took one too many and went wavering off across the campus into the arms of the dean. A Dean Baer, I think his name is. One thing led to another and young Mr.

Drake was called onto the carpet. It was late the next afternoon and our hero had taken another slug, just to whet his
courage for the entrance into the Baer's den. Result: twenty-
four hours later, Donald must be out of town, bag and bag-
gage. Drinking, sir, we will tolerate in extreme moderation.
Drinking with a student is the most heinous of crimes."

"That's too bad," Tyler said. "I had hopes that Don would
be taken in at that place. He's a good teacher, but he's such
a perfectionist as a scholar that I doubt if he gets out a book
until he's eighty. If that. That's why we had to can him here
—I mean, that's why we were unable, as Bob Schaeffer prefers
to say, to renew his contract."

"I know," said Paul sympathetically. "Don't I know! Those
years when he was living in our third-floor apartment, he used
to drop into our living-room late in the evening. Often for
a beer. Then he'd talk and talk about what a wonderful place
Enfield University is. The very cream of all the Ivy League
colleges, he thought. Not big like Harvard, not wealthy like
Yale and Princeton, not roughneck like Dartmouth and
Brown and Columbia, not too small like Amherst and
Williams. But just right. Donald Drake had one of the worst
cases of Enfielditis I've seen in years. It's that, more than
anything else, that did him in when he got out to the little
freshwater college. Homesick for dear old Enfield, where
the roof doesn't fall in if you offer a student a drink. Or does
it?"

"It might," said Tyler. "But as long as Don was here, the
problem didn't come up. He was happy among his colleagues; they might have a beer or two in the evening—the
young bachelors, I mean. And because Don was a pretty good-

looking young man, with that wealth of taffy-colored hair and that habit of quoting the *Fleurs du Mal,* he was well-liked by the younger departmental wives, to say nothing of a couple of older ones with marriageable daughters. Jim Sloane's wife had an idea Donald might hit it off with her daughter Janet— you know the one that got out of Vassar a couple of years ago, the dark one with the handsome eyes. But Don's contract expired before the romance had burst into bloom. Maybe Janet is well out of it, after all."

"It was a topic in some of our late-evening confessionals," Paul said. "I'm afraid I wouldn't want Mr. Drake for a son-in-law. Well, that's item one. You may hear from him. He may want your help in getting another job. More coffee?"

"No, thanks. I'll look over our file in the office tomorrow and see if there's anything suitable," Tyler said. "Where is Don now? It's a bad time of year to get him a job. The second term has already begun."

"He's gone home to Omaha, evidently. There might be some opening in one of the places that runs on the quarter system. So he hopes."

"Maybe so," said Tyler, sighing. "He's probably a misfit, of sorts. Like old Gosse. Did you hear about Gosse's latest exploit? You may want to write another limerick about him. I heard about his latest adventure from Bob Schaeffer a couple of weeks ago, and I was trying to recall your limerick. I could get it started, but the end was all fogged in."

"Oh, that," said Paul. "It's not one of my better limericks. Do you really want to hear it? Let's see; it commemorates the time he decided to go in for riding as exercise.

Anthony Emerson Gosse
Bought himself an Iranian hosse,
But she threw him and ran
Back to where she began,
And the losse showed old Gosse who was bosse."

"The man must be accident-prone," Tyler said, chuckling. "You'd better try a limerick on this one, too. Schaeffer thinks it was intentional. He said the other day that he was walking along that sidewalk between the library and Wilson Hall. There's a manhole about halfway down, and it was open that day. Some men were down inside, repairing the steam lines or something, and they had put up one of those fences with a red flag on it, practically surrounding the manhole but leaving a little space for them to get in and out. Schaeffer said he was walking along just past Enfield Hall when he saw old Gosse strutting up the sidewalk fifty yards ahead of him, moving towards the fenced-in manhole. When he looked again a second later, Gosse had disappeared. So he checked a little more closely, and there was Gosse, head and shoulders sticking out, but legs and torso down in the manhole. Schaeffer rushed up and they yanked the old man out, yowling and moaning that this was a disgrace—they shouldn't have open manholes on the campus walks, and so on. The Dean thinks Gosse walked into it deliberately, edging through the fence and stumbling in. He's sure the old man is going to bring suit against the university."

"I wouldn't put it past him," Eaton said, laughing. "One of these winter evenings I'll have to immortalize that one in my matchless verse. Old Gosse is a misfit with a certain flair. Some style and imagination. Not like your man Renzulli."

"What's the matter with Giorgio?" asked Tyler. "I thought he had quieted down."

"I don't know what's eating him," said Eaton. "But I seem to be cut out for the confessor's role. Maybe I should have been a padre. Giorgio was around last week. Maybe two weeks ago. He'd been reading my book on the institution of marriage in America, and he seemed to want me to interpret some of the statistics. You know I have a whole bunch of tables in the back—divorce rate by decades since 1900, chief causes of marital disorders. That kind of thing. He hemmed and hawed. Said he was working on a similar problem for Italy, only from the literary point of view. Just what, I don't know. His questions were not what you would call strictly scientific."

"What's eating Giorgio, I'm afraid, is his wife Giulietta," said Tyler. "He's also troubled about an outside offer he's had from Radio Free Europe. He put in for a raise on the strength of that this fall. I had to tell him finally that the raise would have to wait until next year. Giorgio has always been something of a misfit. But a brilliant one. His book on Dante, what he's done of it, is wonderful. The trouble is it goes along so slowly."

"Down the manhole," Paul said. "Down the manhole with Donald Drake and his Campbellite cocktails. Down the manhole with Anthony Gosse and his Iranian horse. Down the manhole with Dante Renzulli and his marital statistics. What feuds we mortals see! Well, that's enough on misfits—" He leaned forward to look at the sheet of paper on his desk. "What frankly worries me, Ed, is the possibility of a misfit in the presidency of Enfield. That's mostly what I wanted to talk to you about. Have you heard from Bill Waggoner lately?"

"Not a peep," said Tyler.

"I have," said Paul. "We were speaking on the phone about something else a few days ago, and he dropped a hint about the trustees' current interest in outsiders."

"Outsiders, eh? Were any names named?"

"Yes, I've got them down here on this sheet. A Louisiana dean named Olin Ochs. Can you imagine an Enfield president named Olin Ochs? He is said to be a ball of fire in Louisiana educational circles. Very able money-raiser. I've never heard of him, but he's in *Who's Who*. I looked him up. Forty-three years old. A physics professor before he became a dean. In Washington during the war. Then there's Joe Naylor. Not strictly an outsider: he graduated from Enfield in 1927 and is president of Tecumseh College in North Carolina. Aged fifty. Waggoner remembers him slightly, and thinks he's a pretty good man. The third one the trustees are said to be hot on is a foundation man, one of those anonymous wielders of great financial power. Name of Henry Fuller. Yale man, about the Class of 1922. That's the lot. Waggoner thinks the trustees are moving in the direction of these men, rather than the men on our faculty list."

"Does that worry him?" asked Tyler.

"Not much," Paul said. "On the other hand, he thinks the faculty group we have named to the trustees is still too big. A whole bunch of names is bad policy. When the faculty committee refuses to differentiate, to individualize, the trustees can't do it, either. Result: they begin to turn towards the outsiders whom someone has taken the trouble to individualize

146

for them. It's Mr. Ochs, Mr. Naylor, and Mr. Fuller—all individuals—against a large group of faculty people who remain only names. Until we cut the list in half, maybe cut it by two-thirds, and then give the trustees very thorough biographies on each of the leading possibilities, the faculty candidates are likely to suffer by comparison. It's the great, empty, staring face of group-man. And group-man never got to be president of anything."

"Maybe Ochs and Naylor and—who is it?—Fuller are good men," said Tyler.

"But so is Cos Cobb," said Paul. "So are the others. At least two or three of the others. I told Waggoner I would talk to you, and if you agreed that we had better take action, start pushing the trustees a little to give the local boys some consideration, then we would take action. Very shortly."

"We can't get Cos Cobb for a meeting," said Tyler. "Not right away. I saw him this noon, and if he made it, he took off from Newark for Chicago about half an hour ago. He goes from there to California, and won't be back until the eleventh."

"All the better," Paul Eaton said. "It was my idea that we ought to meet without him anyway. We need a meeting where we can take a straw vote on Cos and the others, and then make a strong preferment of a few men—the few we want to push above all others—to the trustees. Then, if the trustees want to go ahead with an outsider, well and good. But we will have done our advisory duty."

"I can't see any objection to that," said Tyler. "First we weed out, then we fertilize. Is that it? Cos Cobb has been my leading candidate from the beginning. I haven't felt we ought to put his name in all by itself. But the name of Cos Cobb at the head of a small group of topflight candidates would suit me down to the ground. And I think it would suit the trustees, too. After all, they are looking to us—I hope—for sound advice."

"Good," Paul said. "I'll line up the others tonight. Bill Waggoner had to go to Washington yesterday for a museum directors' meeting. He's due back Monday. Have you got your little leather book? How would it do to meet at Waggoner's house a week from tonight. The ninth?"

"I'm free," said Tyler. "I'll be there unless I hear otherwise. Now, is that all you had on your list?"

"That's the menagerie," Paul said. "From Drake to Ochs."

"Good," said Tyler. "Let me buy you a drink at the Faculty Club."

III

When they had all stopped talking and turned towards Bill Waggoner who sat with a sheaf of papers in his lap in the leather chair, Tyler could hear the small voices of all the clocks, ticking off the seconds, moving their small hands towards the hour of eight-thirty.

Waggoner scanned the human faces with his eyes. "Five out of the six," he said. "Cos Cobb, as you know, is out in California. In his absence, I've asked Ed Tyler to take over as secretary pro tem." He looked over the top of his glasses—just the way, Tyler thought, that old Irving Babbitt used to do at Harvard. "Do you have that list of inside people, Ed? I mean those who survived the last screening?"

148

"I have the list," said Jim Sloane. "In case you don't find it there."

"It's here," Tyler said. "Not counting Cos Cobb, we had got it down to nine candidates. Ten, if you include Cos. You recall we did that job at the December meeting. This paper is in Cos's handwriting, and at the top it says 'Fourth Meeting —December.' Our fifth meeting was the one in Bishop Hall with Mr. Martin. So this meeting is the sixth since we began. Meantime, of course, Bill Waggoner has heard that the trustees are interested in several outside people."

"Let's have their names," said Jim Sloane.

Waggoner shuffled the papers in his lap and drew one out. "Ochs of Louisiana," he said. "Naylor of Tecumseh—he's an Enfielder—"

"Let's call him an outfielder," said Eaton, laughing.

"—And this man Fuller," said Waggoner. "The foundation executive."

"That's the lot?" said Sloane, scribbling quickly.

"That's the outside group," Tyler said. "The outfielders. Now the infielders, utility and otherwise, total up to nine. A ball team. We haven't put them in any order yet, but I'll read them out."

"Slowly, if you please," said Abel Vincent.

"Not counting Cobb," said Tyler, "we have Noel Hatch in the Department of Classics—Sinclair Appleton in Physics— Dave Ridder, David O. Ridder, in Chemistry—Jim Howarth in History—Cass Daniels in Chemical Engineering—John Webb in English—Everard Sturgis in Philosophy—Gus Atterbury, I mean Augustus P. Atterbury, in Biology—and Oliver Buell in Astronomy. Nine men."

"Any discussion?" said Waggoner.

"Could we have those again, Ed, with the departments? They came a little fast for my old rheumatic fingers," said Abel Vincent.

Tyler repeated the names and their departments. Five scientists, he thought, and four humanists. Nary a social scientist, unless you counted Jim Howarth in History. The slate ought to please Jim Sloane. As he looked up from the sheet of paper, he could see Jim leaning forward, fixing him with the eyes under their shaggy eyebrows.

"We're supposed to cut this list down, right?" asked Sloane. "Mr. Chairman, I'd like to ask our secretary pro tem just how good he thinks Webb is. Didn't I read somewhere he had been writing some poetry?"

Here we go, Tyler thought. Sloane is out to clear the list of humanists. "That's right, Jim," he said. "The *Eagle* had a story last week about Webb's long poem on the French and Indian Wars."

"That's what I mean," said Sloane. "Do we want to recommend a poet for president. I've got nothing against poets, but I can't see a poet as President of Enfield. I'd like to hear some discussion."

"Why not?" asked Paul Eaton. "Uncle Homer did some translations in his youth. From the Greek Anthology. Pretty juicy stuff, some of it. It hasn't seemed to cramp his presidential style."

"My point is," said Jim Sloane, "that it might have been all right thirty, forty, years ago, when this place was a college of liberal arts. But times have changed. This is a great university now. And the president of a great university doesn't have time to fool around with roses and lilies. He's got to be out gathering in the old mazuma, if you know what I mean. Not bouquets."

"Fooling around with roses and lilies," said Paul evenly, "sounds to me like the definition of a botanist, not a poet. Would you want to exclude a botanist on the same grounds?"

"Don't be silly, Paul," Sloane said. "You know what I mean about the poetic type."

"Sure I do, Jim," said Paul. "And I don't agree with it. You have some kind of stereotype of the poet. Long hair and knee breeches. Ever look at Webb's hair?"

"I don't know him," Sloane said.

"If you did," said Paul, "you'd know he has other gifts besides poetry. He reorganized the whole humanities curriculum almost singlehanded. He's written three excellent books. He's much in demand as a public lecturer. In fact right now, this winter, he's been asked to give a series of three lectures at the Library of Congress."

"What's his subject?" said Waggoner.

"I think they're on modern poetry," said Tyler. "Fairly tough material."

"It sure is," said Paul Eaton. "He's a very able guy, Jim. As cleancut as they come. He could easily be the next Dean of the Graduate School—if some other university doesn't buy him away."

Sloane leaned back in his chair, apparently satisfied. If this went on all evening, Tyler thought, it would be midnight before they left. He thought of the lectures he had agreed to do in Georgia late in February, and for a moment panic seized him. One of them was in his typewriter now, up in the office in Trask, no more than a third finished.

"I have a very tentative suggestion," Abel Vincent was saying through a cloud of pipesmoke. "Since I understand our job is to pare this list down to size, and since Cos Cobb is going to be on it, do we want to recommend two biologists?"

"Who are they?" said Sloane, leaning forward again.

"I was about to suggest," said Abel, "that the whole slate might be a little better balanced if Gus Atterbury's name is taken off. I believe he isn't very well. Physically, I mean. And though I respect him highly, I'm not sure that his constitution would be able to take the wear and tear of the president's job. Well, there are two reasons."

"Any discussion?" said Waggoner. "Shall we go round the circle?" He looked at Eaton.

"I agree," said Paul. "For the reasons given."

Waggoner looked at Sloane, who shrugged and spread his hands. "I'll go along with that," he said. "You can't fight illness."

Tyler, next in order, merely nodded.

"Atterbury goes off the list, then," Waggoner said. "And of course Cobb goes on, if you don't already have his name. Now, any other de-nominations?"

Sloane looked elaborately puzzled. "Denominations? What is this, religion?"

Waggoner smiled, uncrossing his legs. "Excuse me, Jim," he said, mildly. "I just meant nominees that we might want to un-nominate."

Tyler and Eaton laughed and Abel Vincent smiled, his long face lighted from within before it turned somber again.

"I have another suggestion," said Paul. "With Buell of Astronomy you run into a different sort of problem. He's such a damned good scientist, so necessary in this 'peaceful atom' business, that it would be a shame to demote him into a university presidency. If *demote* is the word, Jim."

Sloane smiled faintly. "Demote is right, I guess. Much as I hate to say it, I agree that Ollie is better off working on his crash program than he would be in straight administration."

When Vincent and Tyler nodded approval, Waggoner said: "That makes it unanimous, Ed. We're down to seven. Eight, counting Cobb. Now, who else gets the guillotine?"

"I seem to be the headsman around here tonight," said Paul. "So I'll put this question: would we really want to see Cass Daniels in the Parthenon? His only claim to it, really, is his given name—Cassius Quintus Daniels. I don't for a minute deny that he's a very good chemical engineer. But he's not a real scholar, is he? And his administrative experience is practically nil. Though I like Cass—"

"You're sound on that, Paul," Sloane rumbled. "His field touches mine. He's much respected by the industrial chemists. Does a lot of consulting. But he's not a real pioneer. Never has been. Fact, he came out of industry in the first place."

"Daniels out then?" said Waggoner. The others nodded. "All right, Ed, a blue pencil through that one. That brings us down to seven, including Cobb."

"Lucky seven," Paul said. He rose and moved towards the walnut side-table where the silver ice-bucket and the whiskey-bottles stood waiting. "How about a seventh-inning stretch, Bill? This is wearing work."

"We'll have to do some more cutting," said Waggoner. "But it's true. This kind of responsibility breaks you up into small, bite-sized pieces. Help yourselves, gentlemen. You'll find some soda and ginger ale in the cupboard. I forgot to get it out."

"There's no reason why you should be stuck for this, Bill," said Paul. "We'll take up a collection at the end of the evening."

"Oh, this is on the trustees," Bill said. "The last time I saw my old student Jumping Jack Martin he offered us a modest expense account. He wasn't sure whether we'd be insulted or not. But he said something to the effect that good liquor, in moderation, had oiled many industrial wheels."

"I've seen some of the big industrial wheels in my travels," said Paul. "Haven't you, Abel? Big manufacturers from Omaha, for example. Very well oiled indeed. Getting primed to pinch bottoms in night clubs. It was not pretty. Tyler, what will you have?"

"I should probably stick to water," said Tyler. "But you can put a little Bourbon down under the water."

"Coming up," said Paul. He handed the glass to Tyler and began to fill the other orders.

Was this break, Tyler wondered as he sipped his drink, a part of Paul's political strategy? He remembered Eaton in the austere office, slapping the neat desk, insisting that severe cuts were necessary if the infielders were to compete with the out-fielders. The cutting tonight had gone better than you might have expected. From ten to seven in about an hour, including the argument on John Webb, the English Department poet. But if a thing like this were pushed too fast, the committee might begin to move the other way. Particularly when they reflected that they were eliminating a man from so important an opportunity without more deliberation. You might get that tightening-up which means a group of men taking back its voting-rights, saying (in effect): "This far, no further."

Tyler had seen it work often enough, and in various ways. Suppose a great tension had developed, become actually visible in the drawn faces around a committee-room table. Or suppose someone had got out of hand and anger had begun to flicker along the edges of the spoken sentences. A good chairman could often handle it, deflect the lightning before it struck. But sometimes, too, any welcome interruption, a well-placed joke, the hostess (if there was one) coming in with a tray, could lower temperatures from the boiling point as rapidly as a plunge into cool water in the summer. After the break, Tyler had noticed, the tension or the anger might begin to build up again. But it seldom reached the boiling point. The clouds bearing the lightning rolled away and the skies cleared.

Had Paul sensed the possibility of some incipient tightening-up process—one that would slow the work of cutting down the list to size—one that might even make the Committee refuse, under any circumstances, to reduce the list of recommended candidates below seven? Or had Paul decided that seven was about the right number? Tyler sipped his drink and waited to see.

Eaton finished handing round the drinks and took up a station, legs apart, before the fireplace, facing the room. Sloane and Vincent, glasses in hand, were conversing near the door to the front hall.

"How are your young lovers, Bill?" said Paul. "What is it you call them—Paolo and Francesca?"

"Lately," said Bill, smiling, "they've been quiet as mice.

She's quite a charming girl. Her name really is Frances, too. His is Edgar. Edgar Rosenthal. Speaking of mice, did I tell you the mouse story? Did I tell you, Ed? It's rather nice. Frances, the bride, wraps the garbage and puts it into an open can under the sink in the little kitchenette. A mouse— maybe it was mice—naturally began to take an interest, and Frances, like all brides, is afraid of mice. So it occurred to her that if she left out some food, cheese and such-like tidbits, the mice would avoid the garbage. For quite a while, evidently, she left a saucer in the middle of the kitchen floor, and it was always empty in the morning. Edgar likes a late-evening snack and often kicked the saucer in the dark. I could hear him cussing, and once he stepped directly on it and cut his foot." Bill began to laugh his odd, snorting laugh.

"And they came to you for first aid," said Paul, grinning.

"No, Edgar just limped for a few days. They quarreled about it—audibly. But Frances stuck to her plan. The pied piper couldn't have done it better." Bill Waggoner got out his handkerchief and wiped his eyes. "Finally the little creatures got in here, too. The upshot was that Papa Waggoner had to import an exterminator from Rahway."

Vincent and Sloane had stopped talking to hear the story. Paul Eaton still stood before the fireplace. "We could use an exterminator tonight," he said. "Or an eliminator."

Bill Waggoner returned his handkerchief to his pocket. "Probably we ought to start eliminating some others," he said. "Seven is a very pretty number, but it's probably too many still. The trustees have those three outsiders under careful consideration."

Sloane cleared his throat. "Four," he said. "Remember I put in the name of Clem Shaw."

156

"I must have missed that," said Abel. "Who is Clem Shaw?"

"Haven't you heard of Shaw?" said Sloane. "He's the great organic chemistry man at Harvard. Nobel Prizewinner, and all sorts of other medals. I wrote Martin about him some time ago, and he acknowledged the letter with a promise to add Shaw to their list."

"Jack hasn't mentioned him to me," said Waggoner. "I didn't know you had written to Jack." He looked around the circle. "I had thought our recommendations would all come from the committee. Has anyone else written a separate letter?"

Tyler and Vincent shook their heads. "Of course there was the letter I wrote about Cos Cobb," said Paul. "At your request, with our typed signatures. He's the only member of this committee we have nominated."

"That was a committee action," said Waggoner. "Well, then, the trustees have at least four outsiders to look at. Maybe more. Or possibly they have already eliminated some of them. What do we do about further inside eliminations?"

"There's one prior question," said Abel Vincent suddenly. "We're all friends here, and there's no cause for embarrassment in raising a delicate question. The fact is that Cobb is so far the only nominee from our own committee. Several of the members fall within the presidential age group. For example, I'm fifty. Jim Sloane is fifty-one."

"Fifty-two in April," said Jim.

"I don't know how old you are, Paul, or you, Bill. But Ed is in his forties."

"I'm almost fifty-three," said Paul. "But I choose the role of king-maker. Or maybe critic-at-large. I am not, as the fellow says, the man who would be king."

"I share that view," said Abel. "But we still have Sloane and we still have Tyler. Is it fair to keep them out of the running merely because they're on this committee?"

"As the grandfather in this group," said Waggoner, "I'm happily out of it. I'm due to retire in eight years. I'm glad you raised the point, Abel. It's one we've never faced—except in the case of Cos Cobb."

Tyler twisted in his chair uncomfortably. "We're on the spot, Jim," he said. "Cobb is my candidate. We'll look a long time before we find another as good. My own ambition is to be a good professor. If they were ever foolish enough to offer it to me, the whole thing would be over inside of five minutes. Cos is our boy."

All the eyes went to Sloane. "I'm on the spot, now," he rumbled bearishly. "A man's pride—well, this is pretty silly. I'm bound to say that if they ever offered it to me, I would be sorely tempted. There are a lot of things that need to be changed around this university. I—in fact, any of us—could do this job. I'll be frank. I'd take it on a straight reform basis, but—" he swept the room with his deep-set eyes and thrust out his lower jaw,—"we're just wasting our time. None of us will get the nod. Let's get on with the meeting."

Waggoner looked at Paul Eaton, who still held the position in front of the fireplace.

"Mr. Chairman," said Paul, immediately, "I have a suggestion. Nobody here aspires to the Parthenon. Cos doesn't know we're pushing him in that direction. The trustees have four outside candidates. We have seven insiders, counting Cos. My suggestion is that we try a straw vote on the seven men, and that if everyone agrees, we consider the idea of eliminating the three men who get the fewest votes."

"What do you say?" asked Waggoner. "Any objection? All right, hearing none, I call for a vote. Ed, how about some ballots?"

Tyler got up and handed round the sheets. "What do we do, Bill, just list them in order of preference?"

"I should think so," Waggoner said. "We'll score seven points for the top man, six for the next one, and so on down. Agreed?"

The room fell silent except for the small clock-voices. Under the lamps, faces intent, all five bent forward. Vincent whistled softly under his breath. One by one they finished and looked up, folding the sheets of paper. Tyler collected them, and with Waggoner began the master-list.

"I'm no good at figures," Bill said. "You read them out, I'll write them down, and then you can add them." They conversed for five minutes in low voices. Then Tyler handed the master-list to Waggoner.

"I hadn't noticed until now," said Bill, laughing, "that we have a Cobb and a Webb on this ballot. That ought to entangle the trustees. Anyhow, the results are fairly clear. Cobb gets sevens right across the board, with a final score of 35. Howarth is second with twenty-eight units. Webb and Hatch are tied for third with seventeen each. Then Appleton sixteen, Sturgis fifteen, and Ridder twelve."

Paul Eaton refilled his glass and sat down. "The people have spoken," he said. "Cobb and Howarth, with Webb and Hatch in a tie for third. Then Appleton, Sturgis, and Ridder. The next question, Mr. Chairman, is whether we want to draw the line after Webb and Hatch. That would eliminate the last three men, and give us a slate of four."

Jim Sloane came over to Tyler's chair and set down his glass. "Mind if I have a look?" he said. Tyler handed him the scribbled ballots, and Sloane leaned under the lamplight to study them. In a moment, without a word, he handed them back.

"All in order?" said Tyler.

"Looks all right to me," said Sloane, almost curtly. He went back to his chair.

"The two remaining scientists," said Abel Vincent, "would be eliminated if we followed Paul's suggestion. How about leaving the list as it is, and notifying the trustees that this is our preferential rating? Or we could draw the line after Appleton. That would make five insiders, including one scientist."

"Let's leave it at the first four," Sloane said. "Cobb is a scientist. Four is an even number of insiders to match the four outsiders, man for man. If I'm in order, I so move."

Tyler looked across at Sloane with curiosity. Jim's face was impassive.

"I'll second Jim's motion," said Paul Eaton. The vote was taken, and the motion lost, three to two.

Tyler, recording the motion and the vote, looked at Sloane again. Why the reversal? All through the earlier sessions, Sloane had seemed to champion the scientists and to raise doubts about the humanists. Even tonight he had brought up that silly argument about Webb's poetry. Yet in the discussion that followed, he had readily agreed to remove Daniels, Atterbury, and Buell, who were all scientists. Now he had made—

and lost—a motion which would have wiped the slate clear of Appleton and Ridder, the only two scientists remaining. He was against the humanists. That was clear enough. But he did not seem to be strongly in favor of any of the scientists.

"Now where are we?" asked Bill Waggoner. "A second motion seems to be in order."

"Then I'll move," said Paul Eaton, "that we draw the line after Sink Appleton." Vincent quickly seconded and the motion was carried. Sloane, Tyler noticed, did not vote.

The banjo clock on the wall behind Waggoner's head slowly struck eleven. As if by some pre-arranged signal, the meeting dissolved. All the men rose, stretching arms and legs. Vincent went to the fireplace, cleaning the dottle from his pipe. Tyler saw that the air in the room was blue with drifting tobacco-smoke.

One of the smaller clocks chimed eleven. "I take it," said Waggoner in a tired voice, "that we stand adjourned. Thank you all." They drifted towards the hall where the coats hung.

"We seem to have a thick fog," said Abel Vincent, opening the front door and moving off. "Good night all."

Jim Sloane jammed his gray fedora onto his head and buttoned the topmost leather button on his overcoat. "Good night," he said in his bearish rumble. His tall figure disappeared down the walk.

"Are you all set, Bill?" said Tyler. "Want any help?"

"All set," Waggoner said. "Except for what I'm afraid is a slight cold coming on. I'll write all this to Martin tomorrow. Paul, you handled things well. We got the job done."

"*You* did, you mean," said Paul. "I was just the democratic

whip, or whatever you call it. Ed, have you got your car tonight? Come on, I'll ride you home."

"I have the car," said Tyler, wrapping the muffler round
his throat. "But I'll walk you to it. Good night, Bill."

"Good night," Waggoner said. He looked old, standing in
the doorway, his vest awry, his pants bagging at the knees.

Under the streetlight the two remaining cars stood twenty
feet apart. "That was quite a session," Tyler said. "I watched
your operation with interest."

"What operation do you mean?" said Paul. "The guillotine?"

"The way you kept things rolling," said Tyler. "What
puzzled me was Sloane. He was anti-humanist, but when the
chips were really down he didn't seem to be strongly pro-
scientist. He's changed his tactics since our other sessions."

"That's easy," Paul said. "Bill's anti-everyone except the
man he named tonight. Shaw of Harvard. And why is he
pro-Shaw? Very simple. Sloane's daughter is working in Cambridge, and the story I hear is that Shaw is courting her.
Sloane was pushing his potential son-in-law. It's as simple as
that."

IV

In the cushioned and comfortable seat, with its view of the
plane's right wing and the acres of concrete beyond, Tyler
slumped with fatigue while the motors roared their pre-flight
warm-up and the two hostesses began to move up the aisle,
checking on the seat-belts. "Good," he said, half aloud. "It
won't be long now." Or maybe it would. He watched the two

shuddering motor-nacelles and the silvery circles of the whir-ring propellers. Like the right wing, stretching widely away in rivet-studded strength, they looked efficient, shipshape, and trustworthy. Too bad the airline wasn't equally efficient. They were already forty-five or fifty minutes past the scheduled time for the take-off.

One of the hostesses leaned towards him briefly, flashing the smile they all cultivated. The reassuring smile. "Fasten your seat-belt, please," she said. "As soon as we are aloft we'll be serving lunch." Tyler nodded as she went along to the next seat.

Lunch. Probably fried chicken. If it was, that would make the fifth or sixth time in the four-day lecture tour. The faculty wives who were entertaining the visiting Yankee had naturally supposed that real southern fried chicken would be a special treat. But they all lived in different towns—Atlanta and Deca-tur, Athens and Rome—and they hadn't compared pros-pective menus. "Boy, you had tha-at?" his last host had said. "And ah'll bet you had aigs for breakfast, too. Boy, you be sprouting pin-feathers time you get back home." Tyler chuckled. It would be good to get back to Alice's cooking after all the banquets.

The plane roared again and began to move, gathering speed, lifting strongly. Tyler looked down at the busy airport, then at the streets of North Atlanta with the cars and buses steadily diminishing in size as the plane climbed higher. Then the country-side, patched green and brown under the pale February sun, then the first cloud, light as smoke, curling under the wing, and finally the enormous billowing floor of cloud, well below them now, and stretching in all directions as far as you could see. The plane levelled off and began to drone steadily northward.

He ate the lunch from the compartmented tray: some kind of steak, a scoop of rice, flaccid green beans, chopped lettuce with an oil dressing, the hard roll baked, no doubt, in some Atlanta oven just about the time he was getting to bed after the last discussion, the last thin swallow of Bourbon-and-branchwater. He drank the coffee and opened the ice-cream cup. It contained machine-made chocolate pudding and a swirl of frozen whipped cream. He closed it up again and signalled the hostess.

"Would you like a magazine?" she said, lifting the lunch-tray. He shook his head, pointing at the newsmagazine on the seat beside him. "We have word," said the hostess, "that the International Airport has bad weather. We're now heading for Pittsburgh. Idlewild may clear later. I'll keep you informed."

Yes, thought Tyler, keep me informed. It will only take me all night to get from Pittsburgh to Enfield. He pictured himself calling Alice from the Pittsburgh Airport. Well, tomorrow was Saturday. Maybe he might take the day off and remove that platform from the pine tree in the back yard. He unbuckled the seat-belt and stood up to remove his jacket. The plane, he saw, was only about half full. Outside the huge plain of billowing clouds still spread out like lumped cotton. Once, through an opening, he caught a glimpse of brown fields and a house with a fence around it. Then the fleece stretched solidly once more. He glanced towards the newsmagazine. "No," he said, half-aloud. He felt his lids closing. The plane droned on.

* * * *

Much later he felt the hand on his shoulder and heard the voice mention the safety-belt. Half-awake he buckled it and leaned forward in the seat. Pittsburgh, no doubt. No snow here. They came in over the low hills, the gray and brown houses, the metallic roads, and sat down easily on the concrete. He felt the air-draft as the door was opened, and half-staggered down the ladder-steps with the other passengers, pulling on his jacket, sniffing the cool west wind. The pilot, clipboard in his hand, blue cap aslant on his head, was walking towards the terminal.

"How are things in New York?" said Tyler.

The pilot glanced at him momentarily—one flick of the cold eyes. "We're checking now," he said, striding on.

When Tyler came out of the washroom, one of the other passengers hurried up to him—a short, plump man in a wrinkled brown suit. "Any word?" he said. "Do we go on or do we hop a train from here?"

"I haven't heard," Tyler said. "The pilot is checking. I hope we can fly over."

"Pea soup, they tell me," the little man said. "If it's pea soup over there, I'm hopping the choochoos." He hurried into the washroom. Tyler went outside where he could see the plane, the ladder against its side, the dark oblong of the open door. They were refueling, he saw. Probably they would go on. He sat down to smoke a cigarette. The wind had freshened slightly. In five minutes the mechanical voice from the loudspeaker named his flight. He climbed the steps into the plane, looking around for the man in the brown suit. He was nowhere in sight.

For half an hour after the take-off, Tyler read his magazine. The news items were dull and the style, as always, irksome. His head began to ache slightly and he closed his eyes again. When do we get in, he wondered, and where? Would they land at Newark if Idlewild was blanked out? Or La-Guardia? Sleep moved across his brain like the clouds down below. He opened his eyes once and looked over the side. The blanket still held solid. He closed his eyes and slept.

For a long time, in his dream, he thought they were circling, circling. There was not a sound except the steady drone of the engines. Across the aisle he could see Jim Sloane, fast asleep, his jipper-jaw protruding. Beside him sat Bill Waggoner, peering out of the window. He looked up as Paul Eaton came down the aisle, jaunty in the blue pilot's cap. "Fasten your safety-belts," Paul said. His voice sounded unnatural, not like his. Tyler opened his eyes as the hostess leaned towards him.

"We're over New York now," she said. "Fasten your belt, please."

Groggily, Tyler bent to look from the window, clipping the belt. The plane, he saw, now flew in a layer of clear air between two thick blankets of cloud. Far below, seemingly close to the gray sea of vapor, he saw a tiny plane with four engines. Up ahead, but still far below them, was another plane. "They're all circling," he thought. "They're all waiting for the signal to come in through the cloudbank. Instrument landing." The other planes were no longer visible now. The palms of his hands felt sticky and wet, but he noticed that his head-ache was gone. The plane began a long slow glide. Soon they were in the midst of thickening fog. Drops of water shuddered on the gray glint of the wing. A whole line of lights showed under them. The heavy air was the color of chocolate. The wheels touched on the runway and the plane, roaring and whining like a banshee, taxied quickly towards the terminal where lights dimly gleamed.

* * * *

Alice's husky voice sounded faintly and far off. "How are you, Ed? And where are you? I was just beginning to worry."

"I'm calling from Penn Station," said Tyler. "We were late getting into Idlewild. The weather was closed in all the way from Atlanta, and we took a dog-leg detour to Pittsburgh."

"Pittsburgh!" said Alice. "How was Georgia? Did you have a good time? It's raining here now."

Through the earpiece Tyler heard a babbling in the background.

"I have a message for you," said Alice. "The boys are right here beside me and they want you to hurry home."

Tyler heard their clamoring voices in chorus: "Hurry. Hurry home."

"Tell them I'll hurry," said Tyler. "Give them a hug for me. Alice, I'll eat somewhere around here and catch the seven-forty train. How are you? Any news?"

"Nothing special," Alice said slowly. "Oh, one thing. We've got a dinner invitation. To the Parthenon. I haven't answered yet. I didn't know if you were free. It's the night of March seventh."

"I'll check when I get home," Tyler said. "Take care of yourself, now. See you soon."

He hung up the receiver, slid his bag into a pay-locker, rode the escalator, and walked out into the damp air. A block away was the small hotel where he had once stayed overnight during a New York meeting of the Modern Language Association. He waited for the lights to change, hurried across the wet macadam, and entered the street door of the hotel coffee-shop. "One?" said the head-waitress, coming up. Her pancake powder was all in place, her eyebrows forbiddingly pencilled, the henna hair coiled round her head. "Right this way, sir."

The print of the menu swam before his eyes. The slight head-ache had returned, and he felt the heaviness in his legs that meant too many late hours, perhaps a shade too much of the Bourbon-and-branchwater. He was not hungry at all, but he ordered ham and eggs, and sat smoking nervously. The old wound in his right thigh was beginning to throb insistently. "Hurry home," he said, half-aloud.

His chair faced the street-door and, after a time, while his waitress served people at the nearby tables but failed to return with the ham and eggs, he began to amuse himself by watching the people as they came in. A pair of Jewish girls in transparent raincoats and bright scarves, dressed to the hilt, talking with animation. A little man, fat and dumpy, who might have been his worried friend at the Pittsburgh airport, except that this man walked with a cane, wore a gray suit, and was obviously not aboard the eastbound choo-choo cars somewhere around Harrisburg. A woman who looked like a gypsy, accompanied by a pale dark man who coughed erratically, holding a handkerchief to his mouth. Tyler looked for his waitress with the order. She was nowhere in sight. He tamped out the cigarette in the glass ashtray, and looked back towards the street entrance. In spite of himself, Tyler froze. A man who looked exactly like Cos Cobb was standing in the doorway. Beside him, her face turned up to his, talking steadily, her hand on his sleeve, was a strange girl.

Tyler shook his head and looked again. It was Cos, all right. He was wearing the familiar gray tweed suit and in his hand he carried the gray snap-brim felt hat. Close to his skull clung the crisp hair—"lichen on a granite boulder," Polly had called it. But the girl was not Polly. She had the look of— what? A lioness, thought Tyler. Besides the thick, tawny hair and the belted coat of yellowish wool, there were the eyes. From where he sat, Tyler thought they also looked tawny. And cold. Somehow predatory.

Still searching the room for the head-waitress, Cos swung his head in Tyler's direction. For one split second his eyes looked at Tyler's face, held, then moved on. Tyler almost waved, thought better of it, and glanced back over his shoulder towards the head-waitress, who was returning now to her station near the cashier's desk. When he looked back to the street door, Cos and the girl were gone.

The waitress brought his platter. He cut into one of the eggs with the edge of his fork. The liquid yolk spread slowly. For some reason the phrase "Love lies a-bleeding" sprang into Tyler's mind. He could not eat the eggs, but he made a sandwich with part of the ham and drank the coffee. Then he lit another cigarette, signalled for his check, and sat deliberately for five minutes, smoking.

Outside in the street a light rain had begun to fall and the taxi-tires sizzled on the macadam like frying meat. He retrieved his bag, bought a newspaper at the stand, and walked towards the usual gate. The lighted red sign was already in place and he went down the stairs. The train was crowded and he went through two of the smoking cars before he found a single seat, lifted the suitcase into the rack, and slumped down on the dirty plush.

What the hell, he thought. It's nothing. You're just tired and you're making a mountain out of a molehill. Maybe it was Cos's sister. But he had never heard Cos mention a sister and besides, if it had been a sister or even a girl cousin, they would have come over to his table. If Cos recognized him. And surely he had. His expression had not changed but his eyes had held steady on Tyler's face for long enough. Plenty long enough.

Cos's girl, then. Or some female biology professor from one of the women's colleges in New York. She's a professor of biology, all right, thought Tyler, bitterly. Like hell she is. With that possessive hand on his coat-sleeve she was not talking to Cos about the laws of genetics. Or was she? He saw Cos's sardonic face under the gray hat-brim in the driver's seat of the car that afternoon earlier in the month. Before he went to California, Cos had said, he was going to stop off in Chicago for a couple of days. On a matter of genetics. In a manner of speaking you could call it genetics.

Tyler sat up so suddenly that his newspaper fell from his lap to the floor. Cos's first wife, then. The one he never spoke of: Polly's nameless, faceless predecessor. The other half of that war-time marriage that went on the rocks. Tyler bent to pick up the newspaper. Now the girl had a face: the face of a lioness. Appointment in Chicago, appointment in New York. The lioness was creeping closer. Cat and mouse. Cat and squirrel. But Cos was neither mouse nor squirrel. He was an eminent professor of biology and a candidate for the presidency of Enfield.

If that was it, it might be nasty. Demands for more alimony, maybe even some form of blackmail. A tawny blight on the

Cobb household. "Don't dramatize it," Tyler thought. "It's probably nothing. Nothing at all. You're tired from the Georgia lecture-tour and from the plane-ride. You're seeing things in the road that aren't there."

He glanced at the newspaper headlines, and turned to the crossword puzzle. The car was dryly overheated, and his head and thigh were both beating steadily now. The small print of the crossword definitions swam before his eyes, and he found he could not concentrate. "Hurry, hurry home," the turning train-wheels said. "Love lies a-bleeding, a-bleeding," they said. Tyler shrugged and folded the newspaper. The hell with it. The very hell with it. Am I my brother's keeper? The train-wheels clacked, and he could hear the rain brushing the windows. Far up ahead the diesel engine whonked for a crossing. You bet you are, thought Tyler. You bet you are.

I

TYLER thrust the sheet of departmental stationery into his typewriter, loosened the clamp, straightened the paper, tightened the clamp, and sat staring at the printed mast-head. "Enfield University," it said, and an inch below and to the left, "Department of Modern Languages and Literatures." He slid the carriage left and slowly typed in the upper right-hand corner: "Friday, 3 March." He turned the roller three spaces down and pulled the carriage to the right. "Dear Dean Baer:" he typed. And stopped.

Now, what do you say? he asked himself. What explanation do you offer? Do you try pinning the dean's ears to the wall? You could, you know. The dean made the mistake of writing a letter when he was angry. The language he used was rough. There was no more excuse for that kind of language than there had been for Don Drake's handing the Campbellite farm-boy a strong martini, or whatever it was. But Drake had done it, and Baer now rose in righteous wrath. All right, Tyler, what do you write in reply?

172

What a day, he thought ruefully. For that matter, what a month! Not three days old and it brings you the lovely cases of Donald Drake and Giorgio Renzulli. And the Ides of March still to come. He picked up the dean's letter to read again. "Take it easy," he said, half-aloud. Read it now in calm of mind. Your ears were flapping this morning in the hot Baer blast, but now it has blown away. It started out politely enough, the good dean leaning carelessly on his detonator handle, chipping away at the rock as he planted his charges. The big boom came in the end. The concussion blew in your ear-drums. You lay barefoot and bleeding on the field of battle. It was doubtful if you would ever rise and walk again. Yet here you were, without visible evidence of your ordeal by dynamite. Only your soul was bruised. Or what the young critics were now calling your sensibility.

"Dear Professor Tyler:" it began,

"You are aware, I am sure, of the unfortunate events sur-rounding the dismissal in January of Dr. Donald Drake whom you and several other senior members of your department had strongly recommended to us as a prospective instructor. In the event that you are not, I shall rehearse them briefly. This young man induced one of our students to partake of alcohol in his living-quarters. The results of this thoughtless act were unhappy in the extreme. When summoned to this office, I am glad to say, Dr. Drake immediately made a clean breast of the whole affair. I had, however, no option but to request his immediate withdrawal from this campus and this town. He complied with my request, not without some surliness, and has now, I believe, returned to his home in Nebraska.

"He has lately written to Professor Leveque, head of our French Department, and asked for a letter of recommendation.

This suggests that he is now seeking another position, and he no doubt plans to use the same set of credentials which you at Enfield sent to me at the time of his appointment here. Professor Leveque has come to me in some distress, being naturally at a loss to know how to recommend Dr. Drake to some other institution. He has also returned to me the Enfield credentials, and I have just reread them. It is about these that I now write.

"I write, I am obliged to confess, in some dismay. For it has recently come to my attention, through a mutual friend, that you and other members of your department *were fully cognizant of Dr. Drake's unfortunate taste for alcoholic beverages long before you recommended him to me.* Indeed, I have some reason to believe that you at Enfield relieved him of his teaching duties there *for habitual and chronic drunkenness.* Since hearing of this, as I pointed out above, I have reexamined his papers with some care. *Not one word about drinking appears in any of the letters of recommendation.*

"What puzzles and angers me is that you should have been party to so obvious a misrepresentation of the facts. Your name is known and respected in the profession. You must have guessed that Dr. Drake's drunkenness would recur, and you might have expected that it would involve innocent students. It is, I submit, a singularly unhealthy situation when members of the teaching profession are unable to trust one another. And I cannot forbear to say that the case before us reflects upon the honor, not only of the profession, but also upon the good name of Enfield University, and upon you, sir, as a man of truth.

Very truly yours,

Harold M. Baer, Dean."

Tyler had cooled off enough to chuckle. The good dean's final blast had carried him away from the rules of syntax, and the whole letter was roughly twice as long as it needed to be. Still, it was quite a letter. If you listened carefully, you could hear it crackle. Somebody had given the great Baer a bum steer and he was happily, or sadly, crunching its bones.

He held his fingers poised over the typewriter keys and after a moment began to write. "I have your loud and ear-flapping letter," he wrote, and sat staring at the words. Then he set the capital key and X'd the sentence through. That would never do. Better play it straight. "I have your letter of March 1," he wrote, "with its clear indication that you have been most unfortunately misinformed." He X'd out the dependent clause and typed a period heavily over the comma after *March 1*. "It contains a very serious accusation, involving professional, institutional, and personal honor. I have to inform you that the mutual friend is wrong. Donald Drake is not a drunkard. I have never seen him intoxicated. He drank quietly among his colleagues here; as far as I know he never offered a drink to one of our students. In this university, as elsewhere in the country, a certain amount of social drinking does occur. Unless the recommender is specifically asked whether or not a candidate drinks, he is not likely to make any allusion to it. In Drake's case, no allusion was made to his mild social drinking because it did not occur to anyone that this was worth mentioning."

Tyler read the sentences he had written. They would not do, either. They suggested that the Enfield faculty was a bunch of topers, and that unless a man went reeling across the campus brandishing a bottle, his drinking habits would pass unnoticed. There was obviously nothing to do but begin again. He ripped the sheet out of the typewriter, crumpled it,

175

dropped it into the wastebasket, and inserted a fresh one. Voltaire, Voltaire, he thought—a kingdom for your powers of expression. Grant me the precision of your *Philosophical Dictionary* and I will skin this Baer and tack his hide up on the door.

He typed the date and the salutation on the fresh sheet of stationery and began again. "I have your letter of March 1. I am heartily sorry for the incidents that caused you to write it." Ah, that was sound. Part of it was even prayer-book language. "But I am happy to say that you have been misinformed. Dr. Drake performed very creditably as a teacher during his stay at Enfield, and at no time was there any indication of the 'chronic' slavery to alcohol to which your letter mistakenly alludes. We failed to renew his contract simply because he had done no scholarly writing whatsoever. It seemed to us that his talents as a teacher could be best employed at some institution where scholarly publications were not a necessary prerequisite to academic advancement."

Tyler reread the paragraph. A little stiff, but it would do. He began to write another paragraph, diagnosing Drake's trouble as a bad case of Enfielditis. It was probably, he guessed, Drake's failure to readjust to new conditions, his disappointment at being cut off from his many friends at Enfield, which had led to this social blunder. Such a situation as the Dean had described was not likely to recur. "Once Baer-bitten, twice shy," thought Tyler, but he did not write it down. This letter had to be rational, had to be polite—a cool and decent rejoinder to the hot blast, a balm to Baer's hurt feelings.

Quickly he wrote a concluding paragraph in which he agreed with the Dean on the necessity of honest dealing among the academic brotherhood. The Dean was mistaken, he suggested, in supposing that the recommenders had been other than frank and straightforward in the preparation of Drake's credentials. Tyler paused and reread the whole letter. Do we close with a request for an apology? No, let that one ride. If Baer chose to apologize, that was his business. If not, not.

He pulled the sheet from the machine and took it down the corridor to Mrs. Rhodes's office. Her typewriter was going as he entered, but she stopped and looked up.

"Here's a letter," he said, "on the sad case of Donald Drake. Could you make a fresh copy—better make two carbons—and then destroy this messy original?"

Mrs. Rhodes could and would. "I hope you were firm with the Dean," she said. "I was shocked at what he wrote. It was just terrible."

"You can see what you think of my answer," Tyler said. "We'll try it, anyway. Any news of Giorgio?"

"The nurse," said Mrs. Rhodes. "I called the infirmary around three, and the nurse said they had given him a blood transfusion and something to make him sleep. You know they always say people are resting comfortably. He was asleep. Poor man."

"On my way home, I'll swing over there," Tyler said. "What about Mrs. Renzulli?"

"Oh, they gave her some pills and Dr. Maynard drove her home," said Mrs. Rhodes. "She's probably asleep, too. It must have been an awful shock to her. Poor woman."

"You handled the whole thing like a commanding general," said Tyler. "It must have been quite a shock to you, too. But you kept your head."

Mrs. Rhodes flushed pleasurably. "I must say I was startled

when that student came busting—burst in here," she said. "It must have been eleven-fifteen. Everything was quiet. 'The professor has fainted, the professor has fainted,' the boy kept saying." She laughed her high-pitched laugh. "Lucky for me, I remembered my spirits of ammonia. We rushed down the hall and there he was on the floor behind the desk. Some of the students were there. They had loosened his tie, and one was taking off his shoes." She laughed again. "His shoes, can you imagine? So I just step up with my little bottle—"

If her narratives went on for more than a few sentences, Mrs. Rhodes was likely to adopt the historical present. She enjoyed talking, since she spent most of every work-day alone in her office. Now she warmed to it, her wrinkled face grew animated under the crown of white hair, and she gestured for emphasis.

"I lift his head—oh, he does look terrible, all the color of putty and breathing loud—and hold the bottle under his nose—"

Just about there, Tyler thought, was where I came in. That murmur in the Trask hallway during a class-hour had been so unusual that he had opened his office door to see what was happening. The little group of students down the corridor were talking excitedly and leaning to peer through the doorway of Room 201. One of them beckoned and Tyler went down the hall. Giorgio lay on his back with a student's rolled-up jacket under his head. His color was better, Mrs. Rhodes had whispered, but to Tyler the skin of his face looked green, his lips were ashen, his ears like wax. His shoes were off, placed neatly side by side on one of the chairs, and there were holes in both his socks.

Giorgio coughed, and Mrs. Rhodes removed the ammonia bottle from under his nose. Tyler knelt down beside him just as one of Giorgio's arms lifted convulsively. As gently as he could, Tyler seized the upraised wrist to lower it to the floor. Under the soiled French cuffs of Giorgio's shirt a handkerchief was loosely bound. He saw that it was the same with the other wrist, and that both handkerchiefs were stained with dried or drying blood. Warily, masking his act from Mrs. Rhodes and the students, he lifted the edge of one of the handkerchiefs. The flesh of the wrist was crisscrossed with slashes that could only have been made with the blade of a razor.

II

"Oh, I think he's much better," Miss Mackenzie said. "Very much better." Her white shoes with the thick gum soles squeaked rapidly on the polished floor of the corridor—*wek wek wek*—and Tyler lengthened his stride slightly to keep up. You had to hurry when you walked with Miss Mackenzie. Her broad Scotch face shone up at him. "He's had his Sunday dinner and a little nap and I think he's very perky."

She said "perrrky" with the merest survival of a Scottish burr, and smiled happily at the news she was purveying. She had small, uneven teeth, and her face was plain, but you thought of her as rather pretty. Something shone inside her mind like a light. It's probably dedication, thought Tyler. It's probably what you have to have to be a nurse all your life, like Florence Nightingale and the others. All the undergraduates worshipped Miss Mackenzie, though a few were satirical at first about her winsome manner. Anyhow, Tyler thought, this is just what Giorgio needs. That and the nap and the Sunday dinner. Yes, the Sunday dinner. Even the infirmary Sunday dinner.

"Right in here," Miss Mackenzie said. The door was ajar and she pushed it gently open. "A visitor for you, sir." Giorgio lay on his side facing the window. Outside the bare boughs tossed in the March wind. At the sound of her voice, he rolled over, his hair showing coal-black against the white pillow. She straightened the sheet, yanking it firmly to Giorgio's chin, tucking the edge under the mattress.

"Didn't I tell you he was looking better?" she said. "Very much better." She filled the water-glass at the sink, inserted the bent glass tube, and held it to Giorgio's lips. He sipped gratefully and his eyes followed her as she left the room.

He needs nursing, thought Tyler. "She's right, Giorgio," he said. His voice boomed in the small room. It sounded too jovial for the circumstances, something he always had to watch when he visited a hospital. "You do look better. Are they taking good care of you?"

Giorgio nodded. "Good. They are kind. I ask to get out tomorrow."

"No, Giorgio. Not tomorrow. Tomorrow is much too soon. Give it a week. It won't cost you anything. You want to get back in shape."

Giorgio's hands moved on the sheet. They still looked like yellow beeswax. Both wrists, Tyler saw, were wrapped in clean gauze. "I must teach," Giorgio said.

"No, we've got your classes covered," said Tyler. "Weinberg and Teale are splitting your upperclass hours. Lever has the beginner's section. They all came in Friday afternoon and volunteered. They insisted. Everyone sends you greetings."

Giorgio swallowed and looked out of the window, then back at Tyler. His slim mustache showed black against his pale face. "Ed," he said, "I am sorry. You have great trouble. This is a mess."

"It's nothing," said Tyler. "Never mind, Giorgio." Again his voice was beginning to sound hearty. "We're all pulling for you," he said, keeping his voice low. "You just have to rest and eat and get back in shape." You sound banal, now, he told himself. You sound like Old Mother Hubbard. You sound like the old lady's home.

"Last Thursday night," said Giorgio, suddenly, "I decide to do it. For a long time, I have this plan. I work on it in my mind. It is a good plan. So that night, Thursday, late at night, I go to the Inn. They do not know me there. I never go there usually. I sign with a false name. I get a room and bath."

"Don't talk about it now, Giorgio. Never mind. Wait a while. It will keep. Nobody knows except Maynard and Miss Mackenzie—and me. And your wife."

The muscles in Giorgio's forehead contracted and he shut his eyes. There will be tears, thought Tyler. But when the eyes opened again they were dry. "The plan is good," he said. "I lock the door, lie on the bed, look at my wrists. I take my fountain pen and mark the right places to cut. In my briefcase is the shaving kit. I smoke cigarettes and wait. For a while I read. Then I fall to sleep."

All right, Tyler thought, let him go. He has to tell it. His voice even sounds stronger.

"My dreams are bad," said Giorgio. "I sweat. Outside is

dark when I wake up. It is cold in the room. A dog is barking. I smoke some more. The cigarettes are use up. Now I will do it. I fill the tub with warm water and I get the razor."

Giorgio lay quietly for a minute or more. On his forehead a thin film of moisture showed in the pale light from the window. Shut him up now, Tyler thought. Say you have to leave. He'll tire himself. Say you will listen to the rest of it in a few days.

"I open the razor," Giorgio said. "In the bathroom the floor is made of tile. Easy to clean up. I get undressed, put the shoes under the bed, put the clothes in my briefcase." His voice stopped again.

He's tiring now, thought Tyler. Tell him you can imagine the rest. Change the subject.

"Now the rest is quick," said Giorgio. "The rest is a big laugh. I get in the tub. I cut the left first. The right hand is strong. I slash and cut as deep as I can. The blood comes fast. It spreads out in the water. Now the left hand will not hold the blade to cut the right wrist. I hold the razor in my teeth, and I run my right wrist on it. I press hard, but it does not cut deep enough. I taste the blood. I am sick in the water. I pass out."

His head fell back against the pillow, and he lay without moving, his eyes on the ceiling. He's said all he can say, now, Tyler thought. Poor Giorgio.

"It's a big laugh," said Giorgio, as from far off. "The plan is good, very good. Warm water to make the blood flow. Hot water cooks, cold water stop the bleeding. Warm is best." He lay silently again, with his eyes closed.

He's asleep, now, thought Tyler. He's said it, and now he's asleep.

"I do not know the time," said Giorgio in a tired voice. "The time I cut, the time I pass out. Much later I wake. I hear the dog still barking. The water is cold, I shiver. I feel dizzy in the head, sick in the stomach. There is much blood all over."

Silence. Outside, the wind still tossed the black branches. It must be getting towards sunset.

"The plan is no good. It is foolish and silly. I move my legs in the water. I start to get up and the bleeding starts. I place a towel on the edge of the tub and hold the arms tight against the towel. I rest. Then I bend the knees and work them under me. I swing around. I slide like a *biscia,* a serpent, over the edge, and fall on the floor. In a while I get another towel and bind the wrists. I crawl to the bed. I fall asleep."

It's almost done, now, thought Tyler. He still could not think of what to say. Maybe there was no need to say anything. Whatever you said would not apply.

"Past nine," Giorgio said, "I wake up. I am very hungry. The wrists do not bleed. I take two handkerchiefs and tie them up. In the tub I run water, wipe it with towels. I get my clothes on, and think 'Giorgio, what do you do with the bloody towels?' There is nothing to do. I put them into the brief-case. I ring for the elevator. I ride downstairs and pay for the room. I walk down the street to Joe's place and eat some breakfast. I am not hungry as I thought. Nobody notices me. I think I can handle the one class. I rest in my office. Then I go to the class."

All right, Giorgio, Tyler thought. Now you've got it off your chest. What was Baer's phrase? You've made a clean breast of the affair. You tried it on Miss Mackenzie but she would not listen. Now you have found someone who would listen.

Giorgio had closed his eyes. The room was almost dark now. He did not say anything more but lay quietly, his two hands relaxed on the bedsheet on either side of his body.

"Better catch a little sleep now, Giorgio," Tyler said. "Take it easy now. I'll see you again tomorrow."

Giorgio's left hand lifted a little as if in answer. But he still said nothing. Tyler patted the hand once and tiptoed from the room. There was no one in the corridor, and he let himself out of the heavy front door. After the warmth of the infirmary, the outside air felt bracing. The sun had set, and the wind had died down.

Tyler buttoned his coat and walked out of the pebbled driveway into College Street. A student passed him walking north, shoulders hunched in the fur-trimmed jacket, heels clicking rapidly on the cement. In the dormitories a few lights burned, and from one of the open windows he caught a snatch of music. A few of the offices in Turner Hall were lighted, but Trask, when he came to it, was entirely dark. He glanced up at his office window, then swept his eye down to the big double-doors on the College Street side. Under the streetlamp the brass fittings gleamed. The doors, he knew, were locked up tight. That's where they carried him out Friday morning, he thought. That's where they put him into the ambulance.

III

"Do you really like this dress?" said Alice. "I mean really?"

"You look positively classical," said Tyler, swinging the car into the curved driveway of the Parthenon. The frozen gravel crunched under the tires. Two porch-lights twinkled coldly behind the tall columns. He let Alice out by the granite steps and parked the car quickly farther down the drive. When he returned, she was shivering beside one of the columns.

"Who else is coming tonight?"

"The Eatons," said Alice, her teeth chattering. "Marianne called this afternoon to see what I was planning to wear. I don't know who else. Let's get inside before I turn into an icicle."

The gray-haired maid answered the bell immediately, and waved Alice to a second-floor tiring-room. Tyler surrendered his coat, tugged once at his black tie, shrugged the dinner jacket into place, crossed the entrance hall, and stood waiting on the top step of the conservatory. In the dim light of the huge room he could see the rubber plants and the jaded palm-trees, coiling up from their molded cement tubs against the stucco walls. Under the high domed skylight, a few refectory chairs were arranged stiffly, and on one of the marble-topped tables he could just make out the parrot's cage, partly hooded in a heavy brown cloth.

He's probably asleep, Tyler thought. But he performed the well-known ritual, tapping his foot on the tile step and whistling softly. The parrot immediately whistled back, adding a phrase that sounded like *awhaw*. Still at it, is he? thought Tyler. The undergraduates called him Old Neverfail, distant cousin of Poe's Nevermore. He was an Enfield institution, and the heel-tapping, followed by the whistle, was by way of becoming an Enfield tradition.

When Alice's footsteps sounded behind him, he turned to

watch her approach. She walked confidently, like the dancer she had once wanted to be, and the black velvet sheath set off her brown beauty. He tapped his heel on the step again and whistled softly. The parrot whistled back.

"He saw you coming," Tyler said. "Did you hear that wolf-whistle?"

Alice only smiled and squeezed his arm as they followed the maid down the hall and into the study. Homer Vaughn and the Eatons sat talking by the fireplace, and Dod, the wizened little butler, was passing canapes.

"How are you?" said the president in his loud and jovial voice. "Come over and get warm, Alice. I've just been hearing about the Committee of Six, Ed. Alice, that's a very becoming dress."

"Thank you, sir," Alice said. "I'm doubly flattered now. Your parrot just whistled at me."

"Alice, you just listen to me, instead," Uncle Homer said. "Pay no attention to him. That other old bird whistles at all the girls."

"He certainly didn't whistle at me," said Marianne Eaton from her chair by the fire. She wore a navy-blue dress with a triangular rhinestone brooch at one shoulder. As she spoke she tossed her head in mock derision, shaking all the soft gray curls which covered it.

"All the parrot said to Marianne was 'Beat Princeton'," Paul said. "The signals got mixed somewhere."

"Think nothing of it, Marianne," the president said in his best avuncular manner. "That's just a vulgarism he picked up from me. I often go out to the conservatory to practice my cheering and singing. Superb and flattering acoustics. On a

186

good day I can sound like the whole Enfield cheering section, can't I, Dod?"

The little butler cleared his throat and grinned his bleak old grin. "It's sometimes so loud that we worry about the skylight falling. The parrot can't stand it. He puts his head under his wing." He pronounced it *poots,* and almost, not quite, dropped his h's.

Vaughn roared with hearty laughter. "What are the ladies having, Dod? You don't even need to ask these men. These are whiskey men, Dod, and all you have to know is how they want it."

"The ladies," said Dod, "are having sherry. I think Mr. Eaton likes a little soda. And Mr. Tyler?"

"Yes," Tyler said. "It's a good whiskey night, at that."

"Same for me, Dod," said Vaughn. "Ed, Paul tells me you're making real progress." He lowered his hearty voice. "And you notice I'm keeping out of it, except to bring you here to pump you. If the trustees should ever ask me point-blank, though, I could tell them about one of their outsiders. Of course I shan't interfere, but in my private Louisiana bestiary, the ox is an ass."

Paul chuckled. "The great Dean Ochs, eh? Good. We'll carry the message back to the committee, Ed. Only, like all committees, they'll want a little more elaboration."

"To elaborate," the president said, "would be to interlope. And I'm already off base. I'll only add that to know Ochs is not to love him. Jack Martin won't pause long down there among the Louisiana bayous."

From somewhere down the hall a bell sounded. "That," said Vaughn, "will be the Cobbs."

187

Tyler stiffened slightly. He had not seen Cos since that night in New York. The night of the lioness. If Cos had really seen him, sitting there waiting for his ham and eggs at the coffee-shop table, he might try to explain. But not tonight, thought Tyler. Some other time. Tonight we pretend that the lioness wasn't there.

He watched Vaughn cross the room as Cobb entered. Cos was alone. For a minute or two he leaned towards Vaughn, speaking quietly and earnestly. Then he waved at the women on the long divan and came over.

"Good evening, men," Cos said. His hand was cold. "We ought to have a rump session. Half the committee is here."

"Oh, the rump session is already in session," said Paul. "One rump is over the barrel right this minute. Where's Polly?"

"She's not feeling well," Cos said, shortly. "One of these March viruses. She's a little better tonight, but not enough to venture out." He took the highball from Dod and at once drank half of it. He was facing the fireplace and stood gazing at the leaping flames.

Eaton winked at Tyler. "Mr. President," he said, "maybe you could save the committee, and the trustees' committee, a lot of time. Do you know any other outside candidates?"

Uncle Homer sipped his whiskey, looking more than ever like a well-shaved and portly Grover Cleveland. "I'm all ears," he gaily boomed. "My curiosity is a bottomless well. Trot out the names, Paul. Of course you realize," he said, "that this is exactly why I planned this evening. The Vaughn pumping station is all primed."

"What do you think of Henry Fuller?" asked Paul.

188

The president looked serious. "I heard they were thinking about Henry. Of course I know Henry well, served on his board of governors ever since the war. A very good man, Paul. He's come up fast and in my judgment, he'll stay up. Works hard, has brains, knows how to handle people——"

"Would you call him a scholar?" asked Cos. It was the first time he had spoken since he had mentioned Polly's illness.

"Not in the strictest sense, no," said Vaughn. "He taught for a few years before the war. Still, you can't be with him five minutes before you see that he has the scholar's point of view. Vision, I think you'd call it. The mind of the frontiersman—the only kind of frontiersman we have left these days. Among the foundation men I know, and I think I know most of them, Henry's one of the best."

Cos looked at Eaton. "We'd better report that to the trustees," he said.

"I'm sure they know my views on Henry already," said Vaughn. "Harrison Caldwell brought his name up some time ago. You realize, gentlemen, that I haven't kept entirely clear of the Great Search." He beamed around the circle. "I used my tomahawk on some of Jack Martin's earliest candidates. To very good effect. Of course that's strictly off the record, and I'd deny it if you quoted me."

"We won't quote you," Paul said. "Except to Mr. Martin. What about Joe Naylor, the President of Tecumseh? He's an Enfield man, about the right age, a former scholar. Obviously an administrator."

Again the president's face looked serious. "Joe Naylor? He must be a recent addition to Jack's list. Joe's doing fine where he is——"

"Sir, you sound a little doubtful," said Tyler.

"I was just thinking," Vaughn said slowly. "Sometimes you run into the problem of personal ambition. You don't sit where I've sat for thirty years without being slapped in the face with it. There's a good ambition, and another kind—"

"Where do you put Naylor?" asked Paul. "Type one or type two?"

"Anyone who wants my job ought to have his head examined," said the president jocosely. He glanced quickly at each of his listeners. The old eagle's eye, thought Tyler. He's typing us.

"I'll make one sage observation before we go in for dinner," Vaughn continued. "I'll even claim the presidential privilege of speaking in parables: find me the man who wants this job—and I mean flat-out anxious, avid to take over, setting his cap for it—and I'll tell you the man you shouldn't take under any circumstances. Come on, men, bring your drinks to the table. Dod's giving me the Indian sign."

He turned his broad back and walked quickly towards Alice and Marianne. "Age longs for beauty," he said, like a Roman. "I can see those professors any day. It's you I long to talk to."

"Let's keep the old boy on this line after dinner," Paul whispered. "What we get may be prejudiced, but it will be a firm opinion, anyhow."

Tyler nodded and turned to speak to Cos Cobb. But Cos was already out in the hall. Vaughn had seized Alice and Marianne and was piloting them along, his voice booming. Cos followed alone.

All through the dinner, which began with oysters and ended with a complicated dessert which fascinated Alice and

Marianne, the president kept up a continuous flow of talk. Cos sat at the end of the long table facing the president. The women flanked Vaughn. Tyler, across from Eaton halfway down, tried speaking to Cobb several times. Cos said little. He ate sparingly and was breaking his dinner-roll into small pieces. Worrying about Polly, Tyler wondered, or about the lioness? Probably both. There might even be some connection between Polly's sudden illness and Cos's New York woman. Polly wasn't looking well these days. The last time Tyler had seen her—on Main Street a week or two ago, carrying the basket of groceries, with Cornie pulling at her skirt—Polly's eyes had shown strain. Tiny v-shaped wrinkles under them. You couldn't tell, of course. They weren't always up to par.

"How's Giorgio Renzulli?" Paul was asking from across the table. "I heard he was sick, too."

"Yes he was," Tyler said shortly. "Something of a siege. He's due back at work Monday."

Don't elaborate, he told himself. If you don't elaborate, you won't have to lie. Nobody knows yet except you and the medical people and the Renzullis. If you commit any sins, commit the sin of omission. How many secrets are you keeping now, anyway? Giorgio and the razor, Cos and the lioness. Alice's possible pregnancy. All the names of these presidential candidates, inside and outside. Even that presidential proposition from the Schuyler College people. He had not thought of the Schuyler business since they wrote him in reply to his own long letter. They had been very decent about it. They understood perfectly, they said. They respected his motives. They were glad of the chance to meet and talk with him, anyway. They wished him luck.

Luck is what I need, he thought, with all these damned secrets. Some damned and some not so damned. Call it the information necessarily withheld from general circulation. "You were less than honest," the good Dean Baer had implied, "in not advising me of Drake's chronic alcoholism." Alcoholism, hell. One swallow didn't make a summer, and a couple of martinis didn't make a Bacchanalian orgy. Tyler had withheld no known information about young Donald Drake. Not from Baer, anyhow. But it might be necessary if some other prospective employer wrote in. No, Tyler thought. Tell the new employer, if there is one, the whole story. Don't keep *that* secret. You don't want any more Baer-type letters.

He glanced down the table at the president, who was leaning forward between Alice's brown head and Marianne's gray curls, telling them some long story. The women were listening attentively. How many secrets does that old boy know? he wondered. After thirty years in office? But if the secrets he knew weighed him down at all, he wasn't showing it tonight. The president finished his yarn and Marianne choked with high giggles, throwing back her gray head and reaching for her water-glass. Under that silver sound Tyler could hear Alice's contralto laughter, like a violin obligato under the trills of a flute. The old boy's in good form tonight, Tyler thought. He's obviously enjoying himself.

Cos, he saw, was smoking morosely. When they left the dining-room for coffee in the study, he lingered by the sideboard for a moment and walked out beside Eaton and Tyler, listening to Paul's crazy story about the horse who liked to sit on grapefruit. But he only smiled at the end of it. In the study he refused coffee, and after a suitable interval he shook hands with the president, bowed goodnight to the others, and left.

When Alice and Marianne went upstairs to repair their make-up, the president came over to Eaton and Tyler. "What about a brandy?" he said. "Ed, Paul? Take a little spirits for thy stomachs' sake." When they agreed, he went off happily in search of the bottle.

"How's your pump, Tyler?" asked Paul. "No, I mean your informational pump. Can't we tap the president's bottomless well of wisdom?"

Tyler suppressed a yawn. "If I can keep awake, sure. I ate too much. But my second wind may be just around the corner."

When the president returned with the brandy, Paul said, "Sir, I wonder if you know Shaw, the Harvard professor."

"Shaw," said the president. "Shaw? No. What's his racket?"

"Winning Nobel Prizes, I guess," Paul said. "And courting Jim Sloane's daughter."

"Good for him," said Vaughn. "Very pretty girl. I guess I've heard of him. Chemistry, isn't it? I'll say one thing: some of these scientists are good presidential timber. They make their marks early as scientists. Much earlier than the humanist or the social scientist usually does. And then you have them supervising big project research operations. They don't work on the line quite so much. But they set the problems, point out the way to subordinates, run the show from a higher echelon. And some of them turn out to be first-rate adminis-trators. Like Cos Cobb out at San Diego during the war. Or like you, Tyler, with that language institute."

"I'm no scientist," Tyler said. "Not even a linguistic

scientist. But Cos's experience as a wartime administrator hasn't spoiled him for straight, on-the-line research. He's still a very active contributor."

"Point of information," said Paul. "We had an argument about that matter in the Committee of Six. The opinion seemed to be, saving your presence, sir, that any active research man who took a college presidency was *ipso facto* accepting a demotion. We said something to the effect that his scientific knowledge was a living sacrifice on the altar of power."

"Very pretty phrase," said Vaughn. "Shows a touch of the Aztec influence. And of course I've heard that argument before. It's not immediately a question of power, though power enters in. I'd call it a question of a man's obligation to society. You'll always have your new scientists coming along. Otherwise we're certainly pouring a lot of millions down the rathole. And the new ones are going to get the jobs done, whatever they are, all in good time. Now let's just suppose that the Enfield trustees, after a long and hard search, decide to offer this job to a scientist—a Shaw. Could you honestly advise him to turn it down and get back to his test-tubes?"

"Or his project research," said Tyler. "I think I would. It takes years to train a specialist. There are never too many of the really good ones. You nurture a man along, spend a small fortune getting him educated to the point of epoch-making productiveness—and then you yank him out to run a university. It seems wasteful to me. The hardest job in the world is to be a good professor."

"Or a good doctor, or priest, or judge," Vaughn said. "Or, forgive me for saying so, a university president. All the hard jobs are hard, and they all have their rewards. Maybe not in cash, but certainly in satisfaction. They all require, too, the possession and exercise of power."

"There are different kinds of power," Paul said.

"Don't gang up on me, you men," said the president, laughing. "Can you both stand there and honestly tell me that the power a college president is called on to use is any less important than the power a judge uses? Or a doctor? Or even a professor?" Vaughn's eyes flickered with amusement. He was obviously enjoying the argument.

"I think I would have said so," Eaton answered. "Again, saving your presence. If we rob Peter to pay Paul, and I'm not alluding to Paul Eaton, the whole teaching profession suffers. I don't say this for flattery, but when you took over at Enfield thirty years ago, the profession lost a damned good classical archaeologist. The president stopped digging."

"But I'm still digging," cried Vaughn with delight. "I've only transferred the scene of my operations from classical antiquity to present-day America. Instead of old coins, I dig up new talent. I carefully exhume the living tissue of talent and genius, not the charred bones of pre-Homeric Greeks. And I don't have to leave my find in a box in some museum. I have the infinite satisfaction of watching it walk away under its own power. Maybe it even thumbs its nose at me over its powerful shoulder. And very often, in a place like this, it walks right out to those frontiers of knowledge we hear so much about. As if they weren't located in our labs and libraries, or inside the original ivory towers."

"Original ivory towers?"

"The craniums, boy," cried the president. "The living skulls of the local geniuses."

"You know, don't you," said Tyler, "that we strongly recommended Cos Cobb to the trustees. There's a case in point. Cos was quoting Henry Adams to me a while ago. 'A friend in power is a friend lost.' Now of course he doesn't know his name is in the presidential pool. What I think he was meaning to mean is that the faculty friend who takes the job of president is lost to his profession. At the door marked *Administration*, the man's lifework stops. When he sits down at the president's desk, a light goes out somewhere on the frontiers of knowledge."

"All very eloquent," Vaughn said. "All easily disprovable. I admire young Cos Cobb, and within limits I admire old Henry Adams. I'm sure that, whatever Cos meant, Henry didn't mean it that way. He was a little sour about the political scene in London and Washington. And he tried to elevate his own bitter experience into a universal law. The law is false. Do you think Abe Lincoln should have turned down the presidency so he could get to be a first-rate county judge in the great state of Illinois? So he could work out on the frontiers of the legal profession? Not on your life. When Abe took over the presidency, or at least after he'd learned the ins and outs of it, he transcended the legal profession. We owe him both the preservation of the union and the emancipation of the slaves. There's a frontier for you! Sure the legal profession lost, or seemed to lose, a good man. Sure Lincoln lost friends and friends thought they had lost him. But in the long run we all benefitted."

"You're talking about the Presidency of the United States," said Paul. "Not the presidency of a university."

"No," said Vaughn, smiling. "I'm talking about power. I used to think—and don't think I didn't—that my archaeological digs were the umbilicus of the universe. I had a self-portrait of myself, a cinematic reel in glowing technicolor, in which I had become the greatest living classical archaeologist. In my colored newsreel, I kept getting decorated by the King of Italy, the Prince of This, the Grand Factotum of That. Over in one corner of the film was a great pile of honorary degrees, like a cord of wood, all neatly stacked. And I'd earned them, I thought, all by myself. They weren't simply the complimentary stock-in-trade that one university president deals out to another on a *quid pro quo* basis. Don't laugh—"

Eaton's head was thrown back and he shook with laughter. Tyler was smiling. The old boy was going along well. He had a good satirical vein.

"Don't laugh because I'm dead serious," said Vaughn, laughing. "I kept telling myself that the only kind of power I wanted was brain-power. As a matter of fact, it still is. But it's what you do with the brain-power that counts. Put your friend Cos in power, or persuade the trustees that he's the man for the job, and you won't lose him as a friend. Maybe you won't see him as often. He won't be around the Student Union gassing with the boys in the late afternoon. He'll be fending off a drunken alumnus in Peoria, Illinois, who wants to know what the hell happened to the football team in the last Dartmouth game. But he'll still be your friend, even in power. He's working with human beings rather than guinea pigs. He's diverting his powers to a noble purpose."

The president glanced over his shoulder as Alice and Marianne came back into the room. "Here come your beautiful wives and here goes our beautiful argument," he said. "But you tell Cos what I said if he ever throws Henry Adams at you again. Tell him his power-argument is a two-edged sword, like that one in the Faculty Room across the way. Tell him he must take the job if they offer it to him." He grinned at them and went over to Marianne and Alice.

IV

"Emergency situation," said Bill Waggoner. "First you tell me if you can do it, then I'll explain. Can you go to New York with me on the three-thirty train?"

"Today?" said Tyler in surprise. He had been catching up with his day-book. Now he put it on the telephone table and leaned forward to look at his desk calendar. "I don't see how I can today, Bill. There's a professors' meeting at three which I called myself. Sort of an emergency, too. I don't see how I can cancel it on such short notice. What's your emergency?"

"Can't you tell those damned linguists of yours to go away and come back another day?" Bill was puffing with disappointment. "I'll tell you what it is. Cos and I were supposed to go in there this afternoon to have a dinner session with the trustees' committee."

"Yes," said Tyler. "I knew that. It looked like the perfect chance for them to have a close look at Cos without his suspecting."

"Maybe so," said Waggoner. "All I know is that Martin asked us in. Just the officers, he said, not the whole committee. Now we've hit this snag."

"What's the snag?"

"The snag," Waggoner said plaintively, "is that Cos can't go. He just called. He has an emergency, too. Something about Polly and a doctor's appointment. Has Polly been sick?"

"She had a virus a week or more ago," said Tyler. "I haven't seen Cos to talk to for quite a while. What time were you supposed to see the trustees?"

"Five or a little earlier," said Bill. "As soon as we could get uptown from Penn Station. At the Century Club. Century Association. Can't you muzzle those foreign desperadoes of yours and come along?"

"If five wouldn't be too late, we could drive in," said Tyler. "I can run the meeting off in about an hour. I'll call Alice and if there's no problem there, I'll pick you up wherever you say a little after four."

"Remind me to present you with that water-carrier print from my bathroom," Bill said. "As a reward for moral support. This could be an important meeting. I'll wait in your departmental office, and we can leave right from Trask."

"All right, Bill."

Tyler depressed the cut-off and then dialed his home number.

"Alice, my dear."

"I just kissed you goodbye," said Alice. "Not an hour ago. What do you mean, calling at this hour?"

"Emergency situation," said Tyler. "No, nothing very important. I just have to drive Bill Waggoner to New York this afternoon. The trustees are having a dinner session."

"What's all this New York mystery?" said Alice. "Polly Cobb just telephoned to ask if I could take care of Cornie today. Maybe overnight, too. She and Cos are going in on the noon train. She has to see a doctor, and they may have to stay overnight."

"It all fits," said Tyler.

"What fits?" said Alice. Her voice sounded edgy.

"I mean this," said Tyler. "Waggoner just called in some desperation. He and Cos were supposed to go to see the trustees. But Cos just called Bill a while ago and begged off. Mentioned Polly's appointment with the doctor. Asked me to take Cos's place with the trustees. So it all fits."

"It'll drive me into fits," Alice said. "So mixed up. Why do you have to go?"

"I wish I didn't," Tyler said. "I'm getting rapidly sick of the whole damned thing."

"Don't swear," said Alice.

"Anyway," said Tyler, "I'm committed to going in with Waggoner. And of course I'll need the car."

"Well, all right," Alice said. "But it all sounds damned odd to me."

"Don't swear," said Tyler. "It is odd. But that's the way it is."

"I won't need the car," said Alice. "The Cobbs are bringing Cornie down here before they go. What time will you be down to get it?"

"The car?" Tyler said. "Around two."

When he came into the house, Alice and Cornie were sitting on the couch in the living-room, stringing red wooden beads onto a long white shoestring.

"We're just playing a little," said Alice, "and then Cornie is going to take a nice nap. She's a very good girl. She knows all about beads."

Cornie smiled without self-consciousness, and Tyler caught a glimpse of her wide-spaced baby teeth before she ducked behind Alice's shoulder.

"Come out, come out, Rapunzel," said Tyler, "and let me see your long golden hair."

"I'm not Rapperzell," said Cornie in a muffled voice. "I'm a princess. I'm making beads."

"Don't you wish we had a little girl?" said Alice.

"Maybe we will," said Tyler. "The odds favor it."

"Not this trip," Alice said. "Not the way I feel right this minute. I'm as nervous as a witch."

"You don't look like one," said Tyler.

Cornie's tow-colored head reappeared, close to Alice's brown one. "You're not a witch," she said. "You're the princess's mother. You don't look like a witch."

"Thank you, Cornelia," Alice said.

"I agree with you, Cornie," said Tyler. "Be good, you girls. I have to go put on my dark suit." He moved towards the stairs, shucking off his jacket.

"Wear that new tie," Alice called after him. "You want to look nice for the trustees."

Upstairs, Tyler stepped into the shower, dried and dressed quickly, and was knotting his tie when Alice led Cornie down the hall to the guest-room.

"You look sleepy, Cornie," said Tyler. "Are you going to take a good nap, now?"

"Maybe I am," said Cornie. "If I like the bed I will. When will Tommy be here?"

"He'll be home from school soon," said Alice. "Just about the time you wake up." She unlaced Cornie's shoes, put them on a chair, and covered the child with a light blanket. "Take a good nap now," she said.

"Good night, Cornie," said Tyler from the doorway. "See

you later." He took Alice's hand as she came out and closed the guestroom door. "I'll see you later, too, my dear."

"How late will you be?" she asked.

"Hard to tell. Nine, maybe ten. It all depends."

"Are they going to make you the president?" said Alice suddenly.

"God forbid," said Tyler, laughing. "They know I'm not a candidate. Whatever gave you such a silly idea?"

"So I'm silly, am I?" Alice said, stiffening in his arms. "That's pleasant news. Thank you for the kind words." She pushed his arms away and smoothed down her dress. "Tell them you won't take it because you have a silly wife."

"No quarrels," said Tyler, grinning at her. "Good luck with Cornie."

"Good luck, indeed," said Alice. "I was hoping you'd be here to help out."

"Let her play outdoors with the boys," said Tyler. "It's a nice day. Hadn't you better try a nap yourself?"

Alice straightened the knot in his tie and quickly brushed his cheek with her lips. "I am a witch," she said. "But I know I'm not a pregnant witch. Drive carefully, now."

v

Tyler accelerated gradually until the speedometer showed sixty and then glanced over at Bill Waggoner, slumped in the front seat beside him.

"Another meeting down the hatch, Bill. How many does that make?"

"Seven or eight, I guess." He had scarcely spoken since they

202

had emerged from the tunnel. His voice sounded distant and tired. "I can't say this one proved much. The Century is a pleasant place. They've got some very good pictures on the walls there. And the dinner, of course, was just right. But it seemed to be much ado about very little. I wouldn't call it an emergency meeting. Do you really think they've made any progress in the last couple of months?"

"Mostly in a negative way," said Tyler. "If you can call that progress. It was very clear that Brother Ochs was out of the picture."

"Yes, and just possibly Brother Naylor of Tecumseh, too," said Bill. He drew a long breath and expelled it. "They're still hot on the trail of Henry Fuller. He looks to me like the potential winner. At least right now. I was surprised at how little they had to say about Cos Cobb."

"Did you get that impression?" said Tyler in surprise. "I had just the opposite idea. Dr. Macy buttonholed me right after dinner and we had a long talk over on that leather couch. It might have been a psychiatrist and a patient except that we were both sitting up. Fifteen or twenty minutes, and all about Cos. How would the faculty feel about a scientist in the front office? Did I think Cos's work in San Diego was a real administrative operation? Why hadn't Cos ever been chairman of the Biology Department? What kind of national reputation did I think Cos had? And so on. The works."

Tyler shot the car into the right-hand lane as the huge trailer-truck barreled past, big as a house, roaring like a dragon. Two passenger cars rushed by in the truck's wake, doing seventy or seventy-five. Just ahead and to the right he could see the control tower of the Newark airport.

"No, Bill," he said. "Cos Cobb must be strongly in the running."

"Well, fine," Waggoner said. "That's good news. They asked me a little about Shaw. I was very ignorant, I'm afraid. But they hinted that Shaw was still in their minds. Another scientist alongside Cos Cobb. They may have decided that, since this is a scientific age, a scientist belongs in the driver's seat. If they ever committed themselves to that point of view —I mean in so many words—I could give them an argument. But they didn't come right out with anything. They didn't even say positively to me that Naylor was eliminated."

"Oh, yes," said Tyler. "I got that straight from Jarvis Eames. I sat beside him at dinner and he said it flatly. Naylor's a dead duck."

"They were more candid with you than they were with me, then," Bill said. "Who else got you into a corner?"

"The Philadelphia banker," Tyler said. "What's his name —Sibley. He missed our first meeting in the fall, and I hadn't met him before. Very bright man. Seemed to be very well informed."

For a time Bill sat silent, watching the patterns of the colored lights far off across the flatlands. The moon, Tyler saw, hung coldly in the winter sky. It silvered the factory rooftops. His headlight beam picked up the roadsign that marked the Enfield exit. One mile. He shifted his cramped right leg and lit a cigarette with the lighter in the dashboard.

"I see we've got a moon," said Bill. "Seems to be on the wane—like me. A March moon. I can never understand why the early Romans thought of March as the first month of the year. To me it seems like the bloody bottom of the barrel."

MARCH

"Bloody is right," said Tyler. "At Harvard we used to call it the month of suicides. The blood is for the god of war."

"Martius," said Bill. "Kalends, Nones, Ides. Cheer up, Ed, we're past the Ides of March and nothing's happened yet."

"Not much, anyway," Tyler said. He had a fleeting glimpse of Giorgio's face against the infirmary pillow. "Not much tonight, at least. Maybe later. Around the Ides of May the trustees may tag somebody or other." He swung the car up the exit ramp, leaving the turnpike road behind them. In the moonlight, the land lay quiet. He paid the toll to the lonely attendant, and rolled up the window again.

"They can't let it go much longer," Bill said. "June, as the poet says, comes hard upon the heels of May."

They fell silent again, watching the Madison Street houses as the car sped past. Tyler took the short cut past the infirmary and pulled up before Waggoner's small brick house in Lackdale Road. No lights showed.

"Home again," said Bill. "I guess my young lovers have hit the hay. Thanks, Tyler. That was a lot faster than the train. And pleasanter. I don't know about you, but I'm for bed."

"Good idea. I'll be seeing you next week. Good night, Bill."

He sat for a moment as Bill stumped tiredly up the walk. Then he made a U-turn, swung left into College Street, and made for home. When he passed the Parthenon, bulking huge and dark on the hill in the waning moonlight, he glanced up momentarily. "We're trying, Uncle Homer," he murmured, half aloud. "You can't say we're not trying."

Tyler ran the car into the garage and locked the door. Limping stiffly, he went up the narrow cement walk towards

205

the back door, turning for a final look at the peaceful yard. By the Ides of May it would all be in bloom. The leaves would be out on the plum tree, and there would be apple-blossoms like snow on the greening grass. Now, just past the Ides of March, the pine tree stood tall and black against the high sky. The moon looked as if it were caught in the branches.

In the kitchen he poured and drank a glass of milk, standing by the small table. Lying there, tossed carelessly, was a string of red wooden beads. Cornie's work. He rinsed the glass at the sink and had just turned off the kitchen light when Alice came in from the front hall.

"Alice. You startled me." She was wearing the plum-colored housecoat over her pajamas, and she felt soft when he put his arms around her. "How'd you get along with your baby-sitting?"

"Baby-sitting indeed," said Alice. "I heard you come in." He noticed that her voice had lost its afternoon edge. The warm huskiness was there again. "It was quite a day." She took his hand firmly and led him to the couch in the living-room. "Sit down, dad," she said, "and I'll tell you about what a day it was."

Tyler grinned and pulled her down beside him. "What kind?" he said. "Long, busy, harrowing, never-ending—— I know it wasn't lazy or easy."

"You didn't name it exactly," said Alice. "It was awful. At least it was awful all the morning because of the way I felt, and it got worse after Cornie was hit. But it's all right now."

"Hit?" said Tyler. "A car? Hurt? Who hit her?"

"Nobody," said Alice. "It was an accident and it was very

bloody and it might have been serious. But she's fine now. She's upstairs asleep. The doctor—"

"Poor Alice," said Tyler. "What happened?"

"It was that pine tree," said Alice. "I'm going out there tomorrow and cut it down. After Tommy got home from school, I woke Cornie up and put on her snowsuit. She and Tommy went out to play in the yard. Susie Coxe came over from across the street and I guess they decided to play house." Alice chuckled softly. "Two wives for our Tommy, Susie and Cornie. Susie evidently went home and got her doll-stove, and they must have decided to set up housekeeping in the tree. On that damned platform," Alice said fiercely. She looked Tyler in the eye. "You remember the platform?"

Tyler swallowed. "Yes," he said. "That damned platform."

"So Tommy apparently began to carry the dollstove up the tree and of course the two girls had to stand right under him. The first thing I knew, Susie was screaming at the back door. 'Cornie's bleeding. Cornie's bleeding.' Tommy had let the dollstove slip and it smacked Cornie on the head. If only she'd kept on her snow-suit hood—"

"Tommy didn't mean—"

"No, it was an accident," said Alice. "He said it slipped. But you know how scalp wounds are. There was blood all over her collar and the snowsuit and the ground, and the poor little thing was just standing there dazed."

"Poor Alice," said Tyler. "Poor Cornie. Poor Tommy."

"The doctor had to take eight stitches," said Alice. "And Polly and Cos in New York, and you in New York, and me without a car, and Susie screaming, and Tommy crying. I always wondered what I'd do, how I'd act, if something like this happened. I surprised myself. I was quite calm. I could see the Coxe's car in their garage and I knew Betsy Coxe was home from high school because I'd seen her going in with her armful of books a few minutes before. So I wrapped Cornie's head in a bath-towel—she was wonderful about it— and telephoned Betsy. She drove us to the doctor's on one wheel and they let us right in, right past a whole waiting-room full of people." Alice took a deep breath. "Eight stitches."

"Good girl," said Tyler.

"I was really very self-possessed," said Alice. "Cold calm, in an awful sort of way. But Cornie was the best. The doctor spoke to her very softly and said he wouldn't hurt her. And while he put the stitches in he said, 'Now that doesn't hurt, does it, Cornie?' And Cornie sat up there with one tear on her eye-winkers and said 'Yes, it does. It certainly does.' But she didn't even whimper. Ed, I want a little girl. Starting next week let's have a little girl. I love little girls."

"I love one big one," said Tyler, hugging her. "If we ever have a little one, I've got a name for her."

"Already?" said Alice, smiling broadly. "What? What do you want to call her?"

"Little Ida."

"Little Ida!" said Alice. "Oh, no. Whatever made you think of that name?"

"We'll call her little Ida," Tyler said, firmly. "In memory of the Ides of March. Come on, brave one. Let's get to bed."

SEVEN *APRIL*

I

THURSDAY morning already, thought Tyler, and classes due to reconvene next Monday. Where was that thing called a holiday? Or, as Cos Cobb was fond of exclaiming, how tempus does fugit! Here it was another year, here it was the end of another spring vacation. And the awful Monday approached with the inexorability of a juggernaut. The year varied, but the basic pattern stayed the same, like familiar moth-holes in the pants of history.

And we know exactly how it will be, he thought. The Monday atmosphere will be suffused with gloom. It will almost certainly rain, and the air outside will be so dark that we will wonder if it's really morning or just some elongation of the night. Lights will be needed in the classrooms. When the students enter, their clothes will steam. There will be a pervasive smell of wet wool and wet leather. People will tend to snap at one another. The janitors will angrily survey the corridors they mopped up the last Saturday of vacation. The floors, like our souls, will be streaked with gelid mud.

Students will suppress yawns, yawn broadly, or fall frankly asleep. Especially the wealthy or merely adventurous worthies with the deep and dirty tans who spent the week on Bermuda or Florida beaches and drove all night to get back for the first class. There was an official rule which called for a fifteen-dollar fine if you missed your Monday class, but it said nothing about being prepared. Very few will have read their assignments. Some of the gifted double-talkers will try to cover their ignorance; others will gaze at you vacantly if you are so foolish as to ask a point-blank question. The whole scholarly community will be tacitly agreed on one major principle: the Monday morning after spring vacation is an annual horror that must be got through however one can.

The faculty always staggered in to that Monday morning with an air ranging from simple resignation to quiet desperation, having just passed through the process which Bob Schaeffer called, in that army parlance that had now passed into academia, Operation Mop-up. This meant simply that you planned to use the spring vacation for catching-up. All winter, scurrying along on the quotidian tread-mill, the faculty had been laying things aside for the spring holiday: the pile of papers from the graduate seminar, the junior essays, letters that could wait, committee reports not due until May or June. "I don't have an answer for you on that one yet," Dean Schaeffer would say. "I'm saving that job for the Easter recess." By Easter, of course, the detritus on every desk was mountain-high. The faculty approached the Monday-morning-after as a drunk approaches an expected hang-over. "I've worked like a beaver," said Paul Eaton, "and my gums are sore from gnawing my way through the spring back-log."

Faculty wives resented this faculty habit. "When is your spring vacation?" they said. "Let's go to New York some night and see a show." Or they said, "I've always wanted to see Williamsburg. Couldn't you drive me down to Williamsburg?" Or they said, "I'm sick of keeping house, I'm sick of cooking, I'm sick of winter—couldn't we have a little change for a change?" And the husbands answered, "Fine, but what do we use for money?" Or they said, "My dear, I wish I could but I don't see how I can." Or they said, "I promised the Dean the report will be done." Sometimes, shrugging off the winter's incubus, they would say, "All right, let's go. I feel like a change, too. What are we waiting for?" By the Monday morning re-opening of classes the incubus was back, astride the victim's shoulders, whanging away with the mallet, the hammer, or whatever it is that incubi slug you with. And nothing mopped up, either.

Things in general, thought Tyler, are running absolutely true to form. The form, we will say, of the vernal equinox, the Easter rat-race. Including the usual insomnia. He had awakened that morning at half past five, tense and restive, thinking of the day ahead. Thursday already, and most of the bark still on the backlog. His tossing and turning woke Alice, who stirred, rolled over, and sat up, leaning on one brown elbow.

"What's the matter, Ed?"

"Nothing."

"It must be something."

"It's nothing."

"Nothing but waking me up in the middle of the night," said Alice. "Are you worrying about something. Have they secretly offered you the presidency and you're not telling your wife?"

"Don't be silly, Alice. I tell you everything you need to know."

"I need to know about that."

"There's nothing to know. Except that I wouldn't touch it with a ten-foot pole."

"That's what you said about being chairman. Now who's chairman?"

"That was different. That was nothing special. Just a job that someone had to take."

"So is the presidency."

"Oh, Alice."

"All right, Ed. But I know something's bothering you."

"I'm not bothered about anything but getting it cleaned up."

"Getting what cleaned up."

"That pile of stuff in the office."

"You work too hard. You need a day off."

"There aren't many days."

"There's today. It's going to be fair. Couldn't you take the day off and work outside? The back yard needs raking. We could—"

"It will be too muddy from the rain. A raking now would tear up all the grassroots."

"What about that tree-house? Aren't you going to get that down?"

"Yes, but not today. I don't see how I can do it today."

"What time is it, anyway?" said Alice.

"Almost six. Maybe a little after. I think I'll get up now and get an early start."

Alice sighed. "All right, Ed. Please don't wake the boys."

"I'll be quiet. You stay in bed. I'll get the breakfast."

"No, I'll get it. Let me have the bathroom first. I'll have breakfast ready by the time you're shaved."

"Alice, you're a paragon."

"I'm gone, all right," Alice said, getting out of bed. "The wives—well, never mind. We all give our all for dear old Enfield."

He worked up a lather and shaved with quick strokes, cutting his chin. "Take it easy," he said to the face in the mirror. You never cut yourself unless you're tense. He looked with distaste at his long face, the grooves in the cheeks, the suggestion of pouches under the gray eyes, the thinning hair with deep recessions above each temple, the crimson blood running down the narrow chin. He rinsed off the lather, dried his face, combed his hair wet, and poured out a palmful of witch hazel. The alcohol stung the fresh cut but the bleeding stopped. He decided not to take time for a shower.

Half an hour later he was out in the cool morning. Enfield Avenue was deserted. No one was raking the lawns of the empty fraternity houses. The hedges looked ragged, last fall's leaves crammed soddenly around the roots. The grass was mushy after the days of rain: the winter's debris of dirt-speckled candy-wrappers, raddled newspapers, fallen branches, and the inevitable empty beer-cans lay strewn where they had fallen. The tiny hammers of the pelting rain had beaten everything into the spongy soil. Except the oak-leaves, he noticed. The little tree on the Alpha Delt lawn still bore its tattered ensigns. They rustled in the fresh morning breeze.

He spent the first half-hour catching up with the day-book entries, neglected for two weeks, and then attacked the pile of seminar reports. By half-past nine he had read and graded the last of these, and he closed the manila folder while the ink of his commentary was still undried. He went down the hall for a drink of water and returned to write two recommendations—one for Alph Kramer to the Columbia Graduate School, one to the Curtis Publishing Company for Jim Crawley, who thought he wanted to work for the *Saturday Evening Post*. Nine-fifty.

There were three letters of application from people who wanted to teach in the department next fall. A Mr. Svensen, who described his virtues in a four-page letter that read like a Papal Encyclical. A Mr. Altgeld, who was fifty years old, had no doctorate, and was being fired from some Teacher's College in upstate Michigan, cause unstated. Fighting with the president, probably. A man from South Carolina who signed himself Speedy Ford, assuring all chairmen in a bright and slangy letter that he was a real good buy, and would prove himself in the first two weeks of classes. Do you suppose his name is really Speedy? Tyler wondered. He sounds like an automobile advertisement. He took a red pencil and wrote "Form Rejection" on the bottom of each letter. Mrs. Rhodes had the text of the polite reply that went out to most applicants. Ten-fifteen.

He charged and lighted his pipe and reached for Fenelosa's senior paper on Voltaire and Jefferson. The boy had done it well, after all the backing and filling. He had even taken some cuts in February and driven down to Charlottesville, where a friend of his went to school. A girl named, astonishingly, Virginia Hamm. They had driven up Jefferson's little mountain and gone over the house from garret to cellar.

Fenelosa had come back with a thick sheaf of notes. "Too bad," he said, "that I can't fly over to France: I'd really do you an original paper." Still, it was a good job, seventy-two pages, all neatly typed. He had read as far as page sixty-eight, and he began the final drive to finish it.

The phone buzzed and he lifted the receiver. "Hello."

"Professor Tyler."

"Speaking."

"Oh, hello, Ed. Didn't recognize your voice. Milton Fletcher."

"I had a pipe in my mouth, Milton. How are you?"

"As well as can be expected. I'm running to catch up."

"It's the seasonal disease. Are you all set for the faculty meeting?"

"The minutes of the March meeting, I'm glad to say, are all typed and proofread," said Milton, with satisfaction. He lowered his voice. "Are you alone?"

"Alone with my pile of debris."

"I wanted to raise one piece of new business with you, Ed. Can you hear if I speak this softly? I'm calling from Enfield Hall."

"I can hear."

"It's about the president's retirement," said Milton. Tyler could hear him breathing into the phone. "Some of us thought that the faculty, of course subject to faculty approval, ought to offer a complimentary resolution to the president at the last faculty meeting in June. We'd print it up nicely, and if we can arrange it, everyone would sign it. Then we'd read it out and hand it to him during the last faculty meeting. Kind of a surprise gesture," said Milton, breathing heavily into the mouthpiece.

"Fine idea," said Tyler. "Where would that come, Milton? Under new business or under old business?"

Milton considered the problem, breathing hard. "I guess you could put it under new business," he said seriously. "Or under reports of special committees. We'll have to work out the details. I think we can."

"Don't you have a classification called 'New Business about Old Business'?" said Tyler. "Thirty years of old business?"

Milton chuckled. "That's about it. Now, Ed, I'm coming to the hard part. We wanted to ask you if you'd be the chairman of a small committee to draw up the resolution."

"I'd be honored," said Tyler. "Who are the others?"

"I thought I'd check with you. We had in mind Webb and Howarth."

"Fine," said Tyler. He leaned forward to look at his desk calendar. "Are you going to call them? How about asking them if we can meet here around two next Tuesday. We may as well get it cleaned up."

"I'll do that," said Milton. "And on Monday, we'll get faculty approval. The president is out of town and Bob Schaeffer will be chairing the faculty meeting. So it's a good time. Thanks very much. I'll see you after the faculty meeting if any hitch develops."

Tyler sighed and hung up the receiver. He picked up Fenelosa's paper again. "Both Voltaire and Jefferson," he read, "believed in the existence of God as Creator. However, the Sage of Ferney was far more outspoken—"

The buzzer sounded.

"Greetings, Ed. Paul Eaton. Won't keep you a second. Point of information. Isn't it true that the trustees meet tomorrow?"

"I think so, Paul. Friday and Saturday. To approve promotions and raises for next year, and to transact such other business as may come—"

"What about the Committee of Six? Do you think Jumping Jack Martin will want to see us?"

"I've had no notice of any meeting, Paul. Probably not. They're cleaning up debris, too. I doubt if they'll have any time."

"Well, good," said Paul. "Marianne and I want to run down to Annapolis for a couple of days to see young George. We haven't seen our budding admiral since Christmas."

"How's your desk looking these days?" said Tyler.

"My desk? You know my desk. Clean as the mind of the Dean of the Chapel," Paul said. "But you ought to see the top drawer. It looks like the Enfield town dump."

"Give my best to young Admiral Eaton," said Tyler. "When does he graduate?"

"This year," said Paul. "God and Eisenhower willing. He's done pretty well. Marianne's brains and my charm. We expect him to take command of a light cruiser sometime in July. He's promised us a boatride. So long, Ed."

Tyler looked at his watch. It was already almost eleven. The five hours since he had crawled out of bed seemed like a thousand years. Outside in the corridor he heard Ernie's quick footsteps. A new batch of letters appeared in the mail-slot and plopped to the floor. He let them lie where they had fallen and picked up the Voltaire essay again. By eleven-thirty it was done. He had smoked too much, as usual, and his stomach felt empty. He picked up the mail without looking at it, laid it on the desk-corner, and went down the hall for another drink of water. When he returned, he still did not look at the mail. He swiveled his desk chair around to face the typewriter and began to write the comment on Fenelosa's essay. "You are to be congratulated," he wrote, "on having brought a fresh and original subject to so firm a fruition." Nuts, he told himself. Who sounds like a Papal Encyclical now? He canceled the sentence with X's and M's and began once more. By the time the noon whistle blew from its high tower on the Enfield Pottery, he was well down into the fourth paragraph. He wrote rapidly for a few more minutes and then paused as a tiny wave of nausea struck and broke over him. Time for lunch, he thought. Fill that gaping maw. You can finish the commentary after you eat.

The buzzer snarled. Bill Waggoner's voice sounded faint and distant.

"Dr. Tyler, I presume."

"In the jungles of darkest Enfield. How are you, Bill? You sound as if you were calling from Mars."

"I'm home," said Bill. "Reading art term-papers. It is very depressing. I'm a throat-reader, I think. My vocal cords feel stretched. Does spring vacation depress you?"

"No, but it makes me hungry. I was just about to get some lunch. Don't you want to take a break and join me at the Faculty Club?"

"I am resolved," said Bill, "to sit right here on my you-know-what until these papers are finished. Tonight, if I continue in my present state of mind, I am resolved to get plastered. I called to tell you that our friends in the upper echelons wish to see us once more."

"The trustees? My God, when?"

"My God, tomorrow afternoon," said Bill. "At five in Bishop Hall."

"Poor Paul," said Tyler. "He and Marianne were going to go to Annapolis to see their son George. Now I suppose they'll have to call it off. Why can't they give us more advance notification?"

"Paul can go to Annapolis, all right," Bill said. "It's just us."

"Just us?"

"They just want to see you and me," said Waggoner. "I gathered they are pretty far along and they just want to do a final rundown on our faculty candidates, including Cos."

"Five o'clock tomorrow, then," said Tyler. "See you there, Bill."

"If I'm alive," Waggoner said.

"Never say die, Bill. We're not dead yet."

He slapped the telephone into its cradle and swiveled back to his typewriter. "All right, let's clean it up," he muttered, half aloud. For a full minute he sat staring at what he had written; then the whole final paragraph took form in his head and he raced through it in a series of clattering bursts. He had come to the bottom of the page and when he reached to re-move it, it slipped from his hand and fell under the desk. Retrieving it, he bumped his head, swore briefly, reached into his drawer for a paper clip, and attached the sheet to the front of Fenelosa's essay. His eye fell once more on the title-page epigraph, the last stanza of Auden's poem on Voltaire.

"So, like a sentinel, he could not sleep. The night was full
    of wrong,
Earthquakes and executions. Soon he would be dead,
And still all over Europe stood the horrible nurses
Itching to boil their children. Only his verses
Perhaps could stop them: He must go on working. Overhead
The uncomplaining stars composed their lucid song."

Tyler stared dully at the excellent words. He could not
take them in. A hunger-pang gnawed at his stomach. He
glanced at the pile of unopened morning mail, shrugged into
his jacket, and went to lunch.

II

All through Monday morning, while rain splattered the
east windows and the cold sky lowered darkly, Tyler sat in his
office answering mail and trying to contrive rhetoric suitable
for the faculty resolution on Homer Vaughn's retirement.
"It's too bad it's such a day," Mrs. Rhodes said, bringing
him the sheaf of correspondence to sign, "but it will be a
bright day for some of the men, anyway. The letters are in
from the President's office."

"Good," said Tyler. "That'll be a good Monday morning
pick-me-up."

They all thought they should thank him. Periodically
would come the knock on his door. "Ed, may I come in? Just
to say thanks for the raise?" Simeon Strong was first. Tyler
knew what his notice had said. *"Dear Professor Strong: I have
the honor to inform you that the Trustees of Enfield University, at their annual spring meeting, have approved your*

promotion to the rank of Associate Professor of Modern Languages and Literature, effective July first next, at a salary of $7000. May I add a personal word of congratulation to you, with my most hearty thanks for your years of thoughtful service. Faithfully yours, Homer Vaughn." Now Simeon sat there in his wet raincoat, beaming happily.

"Don't thank me," said Tyler. "This was unanimously recommended by all the full and associate professors, to say nothing of Dean Schaeffer, Dean McClure, President Vaughn, *and* the trustees. You've earned it twice over. Maybe you and Liz can afford to move, now."

"Maybe we will," said Simeon. "Maybe we'll have to, just for reasons of space. Liz is expecting a baby."

Lever came in shyly. "Thanks for the raise, boss," he said.

"I'm not the boss," said Tyler. "Just the liaison man. I wish the raise could have been bigger."

"So do I," Lever said. "So do I. Still, it's very welcome."

Teale, blustering in, his old army trench-coat flapping as he waved his long arms, was as breezy as ever. "Now I can buy that yacht, Ed," he said. "Nine hundred footer. Sixty knots. Overnight to the gambling tables of La Habaña."

Tyler laughed. "And lose all your raise in three throws! We ought to pool our resources and buy a departmental island in the Lesser Antilles. We could all go down week-ends in your new yacht."

"With all this dough," said Teale, flapping his arms, "we won't have to use the yacht. We'll all fly down in my Stratocruiser."

And Giorgio. He entered with dignity, slender frame held

stiffly, dark pale face composed. During the vacation, Tyler saw, Giorgio had shaved off his thin black mustache.

"Well, Giorgio," Tyler said, heartily. "I see you made a New Year's resolution."

"What is that?" said Giorgio quietly.

"The mustache."

"Oh, that. I am sick of it. I get rid of it. What you call a new facial deal." Still he did not smile.

"I hope you got the notice about your new financial deal," said Tyler.

"What is that?" said Giorgio again.

"The raise," said Tyler. "Didn't you get the letter? Didn't they tell you?"

"Oh, yes," said Giorgio. "The letter from the president. That came this morning. Very, very nice." He looked at his hands in his lap. "Ed, I cannot accept it."

"Not accept it? Of course you can, Giorgio. It's all yours. It's all set. The trustees approved it Friday."

"Yes," said Giorgio quietly. "It is nice of them—nice of you. But, Ed, I must leave. The radio offer is still open. I take that."

"Radio Free Europe?" asked Tyler. "Better think twice. You'll miss the teaching here, Giorgio. And what happens to the Dante book?"

"Since October," said Giorgio, "nothing has happened to the Dante book. Since October I have not written one line of it. The teaching I will miss. But Dante needs some change of geography. Now he is only going around the circles." He smiled faintly for the first time. "You know about the circles, Ed."

222

"Yes," said Tyler. "I guess I know about the circles." He waited a suitable interval before he said, "What about Giulietta?"

"Milano," said Giorgio briefly. "It is her native home. She will go there. She has arranged passage already. For June. They have promised her translating work."

"I'm sorry, Giorgio. I won't argue the point. Maybe this is best after all."

"Yes," Giorgio said. "It is best."

Getting no answer to his knock, Tyler dropped the minutes of the Friday meeting through the mailslot in Bill Waggoner's office door and turned away. The minutes, such as they were, said very little. The trustees were politely interested in the faculty candidates, and Dr. Macy and Jarvis Eames had spoken very enthusiastically about Cos Cobb. But the meeting had been what the politicians called unilateral. He and Bill Waggoner had simply answered the trustees' questions. In less than an hour the meeting had broken up. And nothing concluded. If the trustees had made up their minds, they gave no hint. Well, let them set their own pace. It was their affair.

With fifteen minutes to go before the faculty meeting, Tyler stood for a moment on the granite steps of Roberts, gazing across the sodden campus. There were no visible signs of approaching spring: to all outward appearances, it might be the middle of winter. The phoenix sun-dial pointed skyward, the marble flame burning whitely through the curtain of gray rain that still finely fell, dripping down the roofs and walls of the lighted buildings, glistening on the parked cars, making the pavements gleam in golden pools wherever a lamp-post stood. Coming past the nearest of these, Tyler saw the tall figure of Cos Cobb, gray hat aslant, black Navy raincoat shining with wet, moving towards the steps of Enfield Hall.

"Cos," he shouted. "Hello, Cos. Great day."

"It certainly is a beauty," Cos said. "How are you, Ed? I've been wondering about you."

"Those are the words I was going to say to you," said Tyler. "Where have you been keeping yourself?"

"Today," said Cos happily, "I have been keeping myself in the lab. All day long. And with what looks like very happy results. How about you? Any news on the Guggenheim?"

Tyler held up crossed fingers. "It isn't official, yet. But it looks as if it might come through."

"Hooray, brother," said Cos. "I'll hoard congratulations until it becomes official. Not to jinx it, I mean."

"Why go to a faculty meeting when you're on leave, Cos?"

"I'm beginning to get curious about what's going on," Cos said. "I've been in and out of town all winter."

Joe Grandi took their coats and hats at the Faculty Room door. "Puffess Tyler," he said. "Puffess Cobb. You coming early today. Look, I putting your coats where you could get them easy." He hung them at the end of the long portable rack, his rainy day responsibility.

"Thanks, Joe," they both said, and went into the white and gold room. A few men were there already, scattered along the mahogany benches. On the rostrum Milton Fletcher was checking through a pile of official documents.

"How about this side, Cos? Do the scientists ever sit over here?"

"Why not?" said Cos, grinning. "I can admire my fellow-scientists across the way. Distance lends enchantment. When are we going fishing, Ed?"

"It's getting on into the season, come to think of it," said Tyler. "How's the ice in the lake?"

"Gone. Melted and gone. We were up there Saturday and Sunday. As long as the sun shone, things looked fairly spring-like. When the rain closed in, we were back in the middle of March. How's your schedule, Ed? Want to take a week-end off later in the month?"

"It's an idea," said Tyler. "When do you think?"

"Let's wait for some good weather. How about the twenty-third?"

"I'll put it down. And we'll hope the trustees won't decide on a meeting for then."

"How are they doing, anyway? They haven't peeped in over a month. And I haven't thanked you, Ed, for taking my place that day in March."

"It was nothing," said Tyler. "The meeting was inconclusive. We went over the outfielders once more. Henry Fuller still looked like the man to bet on. How is Polly? We've missed you both. We haven't seen her at all. Alice called—"

"She's been away," said Cos. "Didn't I tell you? At her ma's house in Massachusetts. With Cornie. I thought I mentioned it to Alice when I picked Cornie up at your house. I may not have, though. Things were confused then. I drove them up."

"And Cornie? How's her head-wound?"

"All healed long ago. She's in fine shape. Her grandmother has been spoiling her. I stayed up there a while and worked in Cambridge. Since then I've been working here, doing the long commute over week-ends. I know the turnpike system like the back of my hand. Polly and Cornie just came back Saturday. We had a homecoming up at the lake. Now we're back in business."

He seems exuberant, thought Tyler, more like his old self. Perhaps the trustees had approached him already. But probably not. A good day in the laboratory could lift a man's spirits. So could the satisfaction of a reunited family. He would not tell you if you asked him. Cos was a firm believer in the policy of the closed mouth. He'd talk, of course. After a couple of whiskeys, he had been known to talk very volubly indeed. But not, as a rule, about his personal affairs. Only his manner revealed his state of mind. And even that only if you knew him well.

Whatever the trouble had been, back there in the winter, it was now apparently gone. Neither of us, thought Tyler, has ever raised the question of the lioness in the coffee-shop. If that was a question. Nor the question of why Polly had the emergency appointment with the New York doctor. If she really did, thought Tyler. Anyway, you can't figure it out. There are too many unknowns. Leave it alone for now and see what happens.

He glanced past Cos's profile towards the empty president's chair. He found that he could not picture Cos sitting there, running a faculty meeting. Probably no one else could, either. From simple habit you expected to see the face of Homer Vaughn. It would take a while to get accustomed to any new face. Cos would look good there, though. Cos would do the job well.

The Faculty Room was no more than a quarter full by the time Bob Schaeffer came in to run the meeting. He banged the gavel and called in his harsh voice for the reading of the

March minutes. Milton Fletcher was brief. So were McClure and Woodruff with their dean's reports. Sam Buck read a memorial minute on the death of old Jildo Cameron, who had been retired so long that everybody was surprised, not so much at his death as at the fact that he was still alive at all. The faculty quickly approved the names of Tyler, Howarth, and Webb as the committee to prepare the resolution on Vaughn's retirement for the June meeting. The gavel banged again and they stood adjourned.

"That was fast," said Cos. "And I learned very little. Except that Jildo Cameron is dead and that you're going to write the resolution for Uncle Homer. That's hardly worth the price of admission."

"I got caught up on the Cobb family, anyway," said Tyler. "Give our love to Polly and the princess."

"The spoiled princess," said Cos. "Cornie's got the world's worst case of grandmotheritis."

"Alice wants a daughter just like Cornie," said Tyler.

"For a small fee," said Cos, "we'll rent her to you any time until grandma wears off."

"Not till I demolish that tree-house," said Tyler.

Cos buttoned his black raincoat and moved off down the steps. "Remember," he said. "We've got a date to demolish some trout. Keep it open."

"I'll put it down," Tyler said.

III

Slowly, because his right hand held the large hammer and his left the small crowbar, Tyler made his way up the pine tree. Tommy was nowhere in sight, but Toby stood against the garage, partly resentful at not being allowed to assist in the act of destruction, partly angry that it had to be done at all, and partly pleased (Tyler guessed from the boy's mixed expression) at the spectacle of the old man unfamiliarly ascending the familiar pine tree.

Now he came forward and stood underneath Tyler, looking up. "Put your right foot, there, Dad," he said. "No, not there, silly. On the big limb."

"Don't boss your old man, son," Tyler said. "And don't call me silly. That might make me angry. You'd better stand back, Toby."

"There, see," cried Toby. "You boss me, you boss me all the time."

"All right," said Tyler, sharply. "Here's one more time, Toby. You stand back now. I've got a hammer and a crowbar here. If either of them fell, you'd have a dented skull, boss or no boss."

Toby backed off four or five steps. "Can't I come up there with you, Dad? I want to help pull out the nails."

"Fraid not, Toby," said Tyler. "There wouldn't be enough room up here for the two of us working side by side. We'll save the boards and the two-by-fours. Then you can make something else. Something on the ground."

"It's no fun on the ground," said Toby. "That's where you're born, on the ground. On the ground is for ants and stuff. Boys like trees." He went back to lean against the garage.

On the ground is for ants and professors, thought Tyler. He reached the platform and sat gingerly on one edge of it. It creaked under his weight and he saw that it probably would not hold him.

"Look for my jack-knife up there, Dad," called Toby. "I think I left it up there."

"Not here now," said Tyler. He looked down at Toby's upraised face and then around at the yard. He had never seen it from that angle before. He thought of telling Toby that he agreed with him about the fun of being in trees. Then he thought better of it and began to pry up the boards of the slender platform. The nails gave, screeching. He hit the board to start the nailheads, yanked them out with the hammer-claw, and dropped the bent nails into his pants pocket. Toby, he saw, was backing his red bicycle out of the garage, preparing to ride.

"So long, Dad."

"So long, Toby."

A warm finger of sunlight slanted through the branches onto the back of Tyler's neck. He paused to look around and his eyes roved the quiet yard. Under the drying sun, it looked ragged and disorderly. An old newspaper had blown up against the privet hedge and hung there in yellow tatters. Old leaves were scattered in the flowerbed; dry twigs and branches, pruned from the trees in the gales of March, lay where they had fallen. The yard, he saw, was dry enough to rake, and he turned back to the work of demolishing the platform, hurrying the job in order to leave time for the raking.

Cleaning up and tearing down. How much of a man's time —even the time of mankind—was spent doing one or the other. Both literally and metaphorically. Take the case of Voltaire. Who enjoyed cleaning up and tearing down more than Voltaire? Or did it better? There was pleasure in both. The professional housewrecker, sitting there in his cab last week down behind the chemistry building where the old heating-plant was being razed. Manipulating his battery of levers, raising and swinging the heavy iron ball to crack and smash the thick wall of brick. Obviously enjoying it. Or those three men last fall, tackling the dead elm at the corner of Madison and Main. They had lopped the higher boughs and were taking the tree down in sections. A huge twenty-foot chunk, controlled with ropes and pulleys, was about ready to topple, and the men bounded back and forth with complete and earnest absorption. Only part of it was for the onlookers' benefit. They were enjoying the complexities of the art of destruction. *Ecrasez l'infame! A bas Le Bastille!* Every day, for someone somewhere, was a new July 14th. Down with the old, up with the new.

Tyler dropped the loosened boards to the ground and opened his knife to cut the rope-lashings which held the two-by-fours in place. The boys had built it well, considering their age. The lashings, even after a winter in the open, were firm. But it would have to go. They were young. There was plenty for them to build. He slid the loosened two-by-fours across the boughs until they fell, and climbed down after them.

When he had stowed the wood in the small lumber-room behind the garage and returned the tools to the rack behind his work-bench, he took the rake and began to pull the dead leaves from the flowerbed. Under their faded brown matting the soil lay moist and dark, and he saw that the first shoots of the daffodils were well up from the ground, pale green nipples under the pale April sun. Off with the old, up with the new.

He took one of the bushel baskets from the garage and stuffed it with debris—the faded newsprint, a raddled cardboard carton, the paper-like leaves, the twigs of plum and apple. The larger branches broke easily across his knee, brittle and dry as they were. He criss-crossed them on the basket-top and in the middle of the driveway built a fire, leaning the branches wigwam style against the mounded leaves. Smoke struggled in gray wisps, leaves faintly smouldered. The newspaper caught and blackened with invisible flame; hot tongues licked and licked the twigs until they squirmed; leaves dried, leaped flaming in a gust of breeze; broken branches crackled; the loose wigwam collapsed; and over the whole pyre, sweet and sharp, hung the autumn smell of the burning leaves.

At the rasp of Alice's shoes on the dirt of the driveway, he turned to see her looking up into the pine tree. She had an envelope in her hand. "Oh, good," she said. "You took the tree house down. And I saw you raking. Aren't you the industrious fellow?"

"Today I'm a destroyer," said Tyler, smiling. "Today the Bastille fell."

"*Le jour de gloire est arrivée,*" said Alice, smiling back. "The mailman just came. You got a letter."

Tyler leaned his rake-handle against the garage door and took the envelope she held out. The John Simon Guggenheim Memorial Foundation. He ripped it open. "Dear Professor Tyler," it began, "I am happy to inform you that—" His eyes skimmed on down the formal page.

"We got it," he said, handing the letter to Alice.

She read it quickly. "What did I tell you?" she said on a note of triumph. "*Le jour de gloire.* Now we can go to France."

Tyler took the letter back from her and read it again. "Yes," he said. "Now we can go to France."

IV

In the glen among the boulders just below the wooden bridge, Cos Cobb leaned his rod against a still-leafless sapling, yanked his waders up around his thighs, and fastened them to his wide leather belt. The battered felt hats of both men were gay with troutflies. Tyler finished threading the line through the eye-guides and knotted the leader. Fine rain fell in a down-moving mist. It formed small pearl-shaped drops on the sleeves and shoulders of Cos's khaki fishing-coat and clung wetly to the rough wool of Tyler's faded old peajacket. Whenever he bent forward, he felt it sifting coldly on the back of his neck.

"If you don't mind, Ed, I'd like to try it first under the bridge," Cos said. "Then I'll work upstream as far as the dam. Do you want to walk down from here along that far bank and work back up?"

"Sure," said Tyler. "I'll start close to the river, and come on back. If you fall in, just set up a yell."

"You, too," Cos said. "Better keep back from the river. It's too high and fast and the boulders will be slippery. If I fall in, I'll shuck these waders fast. I saw a man drown once in swift water. Tomorrow morning we'll try the lake." He moved off upstream.

Trailing his rod, stepping high over the fallen trees on the trail, Tyler moved down along the brook. The brown water roared over the stones with a high music. When he stepped knee-deep into the stream half a mile below the bridge, he could feel the scurrying water through the waders and the woolen socks, cold against his ankles and his calves. There was an open space where tall trees stood, shorn of their lower branches, with plenty of room for a back-cast. He bent his wrist and snapped the rod, dropping the light fly well downstream, reeling in slowly. Try a few here, then move along. He had passed some good spots on the way down. Somewhere there, noses upstream, strong tails flicking, fins braking and ruddering, invisible as secrets in the heedless dark water under the always-transient-always-present bubbles of foam, feeding like kings on the delicate debris the water bore down to them, were the fish he was after.

By five-fifteen, with the light gone to gloaming under the wet trees, he had four fish in his creel. It was too early for the sweet fern he used to wrap them in later in the season. They lay now cold and silvery, couched on the handfuls of withered grass Tyler had pulled along the bank. He hooked the fly into a guide-ring and tightened the line with a quarter-turn of the reel. Among the hemlocks the fine mist still feathered in as he walked tiredly and lumberingly in the waders back along the trail towards the bridge. Cos stood on the bridge, casting from the roadway into the wide brown pool beyond. His creel and the rod-case lay on the bank.

"About ready to quit?" he said. "How'd you make out? I thought I'd try in here again. I got one here just as we started —on the very first cast—but it wasn't a keeper."

Tyler bent to unhook the wader-straps from his belt. The back of his right thigh beat slowly with the low-grade pain he was used to. "Got four," he said. "Threw back two or three. Didn't connect on a couple. How about you?"

"One good one," Cos said. He reeled in his line and stood

looking down towards Tyler. "The rest are edible. Had enough now?"

"With this rain it's getting dark now," said Tyler. "Under the trees it's hard to see what you're doing."

"Guess you're right," Cos said. "Would you bring up my creel and the rod-case? It's close to time for a drink. Let's wait to stow the rods."

They tossed the creels into the back of the jeep, and wedged the butts of the rods under the front seat. They did not wait to change the waders. Cos flicked on the headlights and started the jeep. The wheels spun on the gravel as it bounced up the hill from the glen.

"We got us a good breakfast," Cos said.

When they reached the cabin, Cos eased the jeep into the narrow door of the woodshed. Stacked neatly almost as high as the rafters, the split and corded firewood hemmed in the jeep-space on either side.

"You didn't burn much of this last winter," said Tyler.

"What with one thing and another," said Cos. "we hardly got up here at all. I figure this for a two-year supply, the way we use it. And as much again lying ready in the woods. You earned some of this, Ed, with the sweat of your brow. We'll load up the back of the jeep on the way home. Keep you in fireplace fuel the rest of the spring."

"I've still got some left from the last time," said Tyler.

They got out stiffly and went around through the thin rain to the heavy stormdoor on the lake side. Cos's keys jingled against the padlock. A heavy mist grayed the lake over and you could not see the low hills across the water. Inside the cabin the air smelt dank. Cos lighted the overhead lamp and knelt before the fireplace. He rolled a newspaper into a loose cone, lighted it, and warmed the flue, then thrust it under the kindling on the andirons. Flames licked up crackling and the seasoned logs caught quickly. In a few minutes the room was warm.

Tyler stood his waders in the far corner, and got the bottle from his canvas kit-bag. He poured two amber drinks into the heavy tumblers and added cold springwater, using the ladle in the white pail on the draining-board beside the sink. He handed one of the glasses to Cos and raised the other in a quick salute.

"Down the hatch, Cos. Here's to breakfast."

"Here's to dinner, first," Cos said, grinning. "Here's to that steak." Unwrapping the butcher's paper, he laid it out flat on the drainboard. "Polly sliced us some onions to go with it," he said, and held up the large waxed-paper bundle from one corner of the food-carton. He lifted the cylindrical chimney from around one of the burners and lighted the circular wick of the kerosene stove. "We could broil it over the fireplace," he said, "but with the onions we may as well use the pan."

From its hook above the stove he lifted down the large black frying pan and set it over the flame. When it was hot, he slapped the steak in and dropped in an egg-sized dollop of margarine. In three minutes he turned the steak over, and shook in handfuls of the sliced onions. "How about another snifter?" he said. The room was filled with a delicious smell and the sound of frying.

Tyler poured out two more drinks and ladled in springwater. The whiskey felt warm in his stomach. He unwrapped the long French loaf and cut half of it into good-sized chunks, buttered them on both sides with margarine, and slid them into the oven to warm on a pie-plate.

Cos drank half the second drink, and deftly turned the steak with a long-handled fork. He began to hum a tuneless tune. The onions in the frying pan were turning from white to brown. He mounded them with a spatula and patted the mounds flat again, fringing the steak like surf around an island. "How about this?" he said happily. "Did you ever see a steak like that?" He hummed softly to himself.

At either end of the kitchen table near the fireplace Tyler laid a steak-knife, a kitchen fork with a black handle, and one of the stainless steel spoons. Beside the forks he put two large paper napkins. He sluiced springwater over two large white plates from the cupboard, wiped them dry with one of Alice's dishtowels from the food carton, and set them ready on top of the oven. He poured out two more whiskeys and stood Cos's tumbler within reach on the window sill near the stove.

"How about some peaches?" he said. He could hear the beginning of a hint of thickness at the back of his tongue. "Should we break out the peaches?"

"The peaches," said Cos, gaily. He patted down a mound of simmering onions with the tip of the spatula. "By all means the peaches. Let us have large orders of Mrs. Tyler's special peaches." He took another long swallow from his tumbler.

Tyler unscrewed the top of a mason-jar of the home-canned peaches, and poked the edge of the lozenge of paraffin. It sank and the opposite edge lifted. He laid it carefully unbroken on the drain-board, licked the sweet juice from his thumb and forefinger, rinsed his hand with a ladleful of spring-water, and began to spoon the peach-halves into the white cereal bowls. He could smell the crusty smell of the bread in the oven.

v

Cos finished cleaning the last of the trout and laid it with the others on the waxed paper.

"There they lie," he said. "The Committee of Nine. The headless wonders." He rolled up the bloody newspaper and sluiced the sink and his hands with lake-water from the tap. "With any luck tomorrow morning, we'll yank the presidential candidate out of that lake."

"The big one," said Tyler, grinning. He stretched his legs toward the fire. "Wherever he lurks. Your friend in power."

"The bigger they are the wilier they are," Cos said. "The big ones aren't easy to catch. The best ones don't want to be caught."

"I can't say I blame them," said Tyler. "Out of the deep blue lake and into the frying pan."

"That's right," said Cos, grinning. "The hot seat. You don't ask what's cooking in that job. You know it's you."

Tyler leaned forward to stir and replenish the fire. If the trustees had already approached Cos about being president, he had either turned them down or he was putting up a front.

"What happened last Friday, Cos?" he said quietly. "Bill told me they had you in for another parley."

Cos did not answer. He was running cold water into the dishpan. When it was half full he put the trout into a crockery bowl, set the bowl in the dishpan, and covered the top with a plate. "There," he said. "Primitive refrigeration. As good as on ice."

Try him again, Tyler thought. "Didn't you and Bill have a session with the trustees last week?"

"Oh, that. It only lasted a half hour, and they gave Bill and me only about a half hour's notice. I got the impression, Ed, that they're marking time. We went over the list of insiders. Jack Martin seemed to be especially interested in Howarth. Wanted to know how Jim had made out as a departmental chairman. We both said fine."

"He did, too," said Tyler. "He ran the department for ten years."

"Poor Bill Waggoner was put on the frying pan," Cos said. "Jack Martin asked him if he thought a departmental chairmanship was a major administrative responsibility. Bill said he didn't think so. Then you could see the wheels turning in Bill's head. He was obviously thinking that it might queer Howarth's chances for the presidency. So he mumbled that he guessed a chairmanship was a good preparation after all. That's the way it went. Yes but, either or, maybe and probably. I finally told them what I thought."

"What did you say?"

"I said the foundation man—what's his name? Fuller— would be the best choice. He could start fresh. I couldn't exactly tell them that I hate to see a good man kicked upstairs from a professorship to a presidency. You don't run that risk with a man like Fuller."

"Uncle Homer likes Fuller," said Tyler. "He told us so that night at the Parthenon. But he'd want to give you an argument on this idea of professorial demotion. He gave Paul

238

Eaton and me a long and eloquent dissertation on the doc-
trine of transcendence."

"You mean how to go to presidential heaven?" said Cos.

"No," said Tyler. "On this question of power. Power can
be used or it can be abused. If you use it rightly, if you tran-
scend the base uses of power, you can do a lot of good. Uncle
Homer cited Abe Lincoln. Union and emancipation. If Abe
had remained a country lawyer, he couldn't have made
either of those doctrines stick. No matter how much brain-
power he had, he wouldn't have been in a position to use it
for a purpose as high as that."

"How did you answer him?" Cos asked. "I would have
given him the answer that no purpose is higher than the
search for truth."

"He'd agree with you," said Tyler. "But he'd want to add
that the search for truth is the university president's whole
business. He just goes about it differently. He takes his Geiger
counter and goes prospecting for professorial uranium. He
lines up his personnel. He sees that they get the books and
the laboratories and the money. He runs the whole shebang
in such a way that he helps others in their search for truth.
Not just in your subject—biology—nor in my subject—
literature and literary biography, or whatever the boys are
doing. But in all the areas. All the departments and divisions.
The works."

"You sound convinced," said Cos, shortly.

"Well, no," Tyler said. "I'm not. At least not entirely. I'm
just giving you Uncle Homer's argument."

"You'd throw Voltaire out the window and start riding the
alumni circuit?"

"We're not talking about me," said Tyler. "We were talking about the uses of power."

"Listen," said Cos. "Don't tell me about power. I—well,
look, Ed. When Polly aborted in March, I didn't hire the
director of the New York hospital. I hired the best surgeon
I could find with the only kind of power we needed: what you
could find in a surgeon's hands and his brain. I never looked
at the front office of the hospital, except through the window
where I paid the bill."

Tyler leaned forward to knock out his pipe on one of the
andirons. "Of course that was right," he said lamely. "A matter of life and death. I hope your man did a good job."

"The best," said Cos. "That's my point. Sorry, Ed. I didn't
mean to embarrass you with a personal example."

"It's a good example," said Tyler, quietly. "How's Polly
now?"

"As good as new. But it was a rough winter. What with one
thing and another." He sat gazing into the flames.

Tyler glanced at Cos's profile, ruddy in the firelight. "I
guessed it was, Cos," he said. "What with one thing and
another."

Even in the firelight he could see the flush spread up over
Cos's face. "If I catch the intonation," Cos said, "you mean
the lady in the coffee shop. I was quite sure you saw me. I
spotted you. I would have come over but it was no night for
introductions."

"She was very handsome," said Tyler.

"She's handsome, all right," Cos said. He still gazed into
the fire. His mouth, Tyler saw, was clamped firmly, the jaw-
muscles working. That's the end of that story, Tyler thought.

Look at that mouth. This is the man who believes in the closed secret.

Cos got a drink of springwater from the bucket by the sink. He found his pouch on the mantel-piece above the fireplace and began to fill his pipe. He took a flaming spill from one of the split logs in the fireplace and lighted the tobacco. Then he turned to face Tyler.

"She's handsome, all right," he said, quietly. "She's one of the most original-looking women I ever saw. You only got a glimpse. But did you notice those eyes?"

"It was only a glimpse," said Tyler, "and you were across the room. But I got the impression of a lioness."

"Or a tiger," Cos said. "The lady and the tiger. The lady tiger. Ed, her eyes are actually tawny. Damndest color I ever saw. Almost the same shade as her hair."

"I couldn't see the color of her eyes," Tyler said. "They were fixed on you at the time."

"One way and another," Cos said, "they were fixed on me all winter. What they call renewal of hostilities."

"Hostilities?" said Tyler.

Cos leaned down to slap Tyler's shoulder. "Don't look so worried, Ed. Yes, hostilities. That was my ex-wife. Name of Carlotta. She's what our friends in the Psychology Department call a very mixed-up girl."

"What's her problem?" asked Tyler. "Trying to get you back?"

"I'm not sure she knows what she's trying to do," Cos said. "But she sure ruined this last winter. She did it in two long hops."

"Hops?"

241

"Hops," said Cos. "From California to Chicago, and from Chicago to New York. She must have spent a fortune in telegrams."

"Where is she now?" asked Tyler. "Back in California?"

"I think she's in Miami," Cos said. "But with that lady you never know."

"She was working close to home when she hit New York," said Tyler. "Is that why Polly lost the baby?"

"She lost one before Cornie came," said Cos, "so you can't be absolutely sure. But the doctor talked to her, and then we had a long talk after the operation. He thinks Carlotta was a major factor."

"That's too bad," said Tyler.

"It's worse than that," Cos said. "Because it's my fault for teaming up with a girl like Carlotta in the first place. Anyhow the team didn't last long. She left me in San Diego for the golden marts of Culver City. They took her on as a starlet. Her tawny qualities charmed some scout or other, and she screen-tested well. Pretty soon she had one of those lawyers working on a divorce. I didn't contest it. I was too disgusted, and too busy with the Navy in San Diego. So we were put asunder after ten months of not exactly bliss."

"When was that, Cos?"

"Another winter. Forty-three. Only then there was nobody else to worry about. I hadn't met Polly."

Tyler was staring into the fire, his elbows on his knees. "I'm sorry I didn't know about this before, Cos. You never let me in on it."

"There wasn't a thing you could have done," said Cos. "Except what you did do after you saw me with the lady in New York."

"What do you mean?"

"I mean sit tight and wait for me to let you in on it. Which you did. For which, thanks. I don't like to talk about it: it's against my operating rules."

"But I blundered into it, Cos."

"It was strictly my blunder," Cos said. "From start to now. The worst of it is she could come back into the picture any time. You know what set this one off? They voted me a medal for being a good biologist, and there was an advance notice in a California paper about it. Somebody we used to know in San Diego sent her a clipping. It said I was teaching at a place called Enfield. That started things. Telegram Number One arrived."

"What did she want?" asked Tyler.

"Said she must see me. Said she had just read I was to be on the coast at such and such a date." Cos grimaced. "Said she could cry her eyes out—that's one of her favorite expressions, by the way—because her studio was sending her east to Chicago just when I was coming. Said she had to make a personal appearance at a movie premiere in Chicago. So she would miss me in California. But there was something very important she had to talk over. Couldn't I meet her in Chicago?" Cos spread his hands. "That's where I made my mistake."

"What mistake? Did you see her?"

"I didn't know what to do," Cos said. "It was a real problem. Polly was pregnant. If she knew about this, she'd worry. If she worried, she'd get sick. If she got sick, she might lose the baby. There were some fellow-biologists I could see at Evanston on the way to the coast. I wired Carlotta that I'd meet her in Chicago. One more time."

"I remember the time," said Tyler. "It was that time you

243

gave me a ride up the street one afternoon. Before you took off for Newark."

"That was the time," Cos said. "I saw the people at North-western and then came in town. I remember it was snowing. She was staying at one of those old hotels in the Loop. I forget the name. I invited her to dinner and she met me in the hotel lobby dressed like—well, she was all dressed up. She turned on the charm. And, Ed, she has charm. Of a certain kind. But it is also a charm that you can be impervious to. It's transparent."

"What did she want?"

"That wasn't very clear. Mainly she wanted to prove something, I thought. To show me how a successful starlet looked. To prove it had all been worth it."

"Is she?"

"Is she what?"

"Is she a successful starlet?"

"No," said Cos, flatly. "That was one of the transparencies. She had been sick for awhile. She already showed the wear and tear under the make-up."

"Was that all?"

"Well, no. Not quite all. Somewhere in the back of her slightly dazed mind she had alimony ideas. Her second marriage had broken up. I was Old Faithful, or so she thought. I told her no. She didn't turn a hair, didn't even seem to mind. Just went on gabbing brightly there at the table. She made no proposals. I saw her back to the German hotel. Is there one called the Bismarck?"

"I think so."

"And the next day I flew to the coast," said Cos.

"And collected your medal."

"Yes, the good old medal. Then I came back home, feeling like a heel. Carlotta had not let well enough alone. When I got home I found she had called Polly from Chicago. Person to person. Polly was in ruins."

"Didn't Polly know she existed?"

"Oh, yes. Polly knew about her. I told her the first part of the story before we were married. But Polly, you can imagine, was in no condition to be reminded of it. So what was there to do? I sat and waited until Hop Number Two."

"To New York," guessed Tyler. "Poor Cos."

"In a D-C Seven," Cos said. "Heralded by a 200-word night letter."

"And that was—?"

"And that," Cos said, "was when you saw me with her in the coffee shop of that hotel. I was giving her—I mean I was about to give her Dinner Number Two and the bum's rush."

"Did Polly know about this one?"

"Yes, she knew. Polly wanted me to come in. To see if Carlotta wouldn't go away and mind her business."

"Would she?"

"She had an engagement in Miami the following week," said Cos. "Around the first of March. As far as I know she kept it. I've had no word since. But the hell of it is, to coin a phrase, that there may be word any time. And meantime, of course, Polly lost the baby."

"Can't you muzzle her some way, Cos?"

"What do I use for a muzzle?" said Cos, quietly. "Money? After the years in southern California, Carlotta's ideas might be fairly high-flown. The law? That costs money, too. As a generalization, I would say professors are well advised to stay out of lawsuits."

"The law is the way to handle it, though," said Tyler. "She hasn't, obviously, a leg to stand on. You ought to get some legal advice."

"You tell me where," said Cos, with a touch of bitterness.

"I've known some faculty men to get help from some of the doctors on the Board," said Tyler. "Why not one of the lawyers?"

"On the Board of Trustees?" said Cos, laughing. "Can you imagine a trustee like our man from Philadelphia messing in a tawdry melodrama?"

"No," said Tyler. "No, I guess I can't. Still, Cos, there are plenty of other lawyers."

"If it keeps up," Cos said, "I may be driven to it. I just have a holy terror of the publicity. Not for me so much as for Polly. It's a mess, all right. I'm just hoping she stays in Miami, or points west. The farther west the better." He laid his pipe on the mantel, stretched his arms, and yawned. "That's enough on Carlotta," he said. "The hell with it. I brought you up here to fish and now I feed you tripe."

"No," said Tyler. "I'm glad you told me. But it's an unendurable situation, Cos. For you, for Polly, for Cornie. You can't go on inventing this way forever."

"It won't be forever," said Cos. "We'll fix it some way." He had the air of a man ringing down a curtain. "Wonder how the weather is. If the rain is still falling, it can be damned uncomfortable in the boat."

"Let's check, then," said Tyler. He went to the door and threw it open. Cold night air rushed in. With Cos behind him he stepped out onto the pine needles before the house. A mist hung low on the lake, but now the hills on the far side had come into view. The rain had stopped. Overhead a few stars showed faintly. "We've got stars, Cos," he said.

"It looks good," said Cos. "It will be fair tomorrow. We'll clean up on that lake tomorrow, Ed. Let's get rolling early."

I

SUDDENLY, as by pre-arrangement, the leaves came out. Three days ago, two days, yesterday, they had been ready and waiting but they did not appear. Last week, looking down any street in town, one saw the ruddy mist of maple buds beginning to blur the sharp outline of bare limbs. Along the River Road wherever vistas opened, a green haze plumped the tops of distant trees. The twisted stems of apple and pear upheld their rime of blossoms. Dogwood and magnolia swelled and bloomed. Closer to the ground the lesser shrubs rioted. Forsythia blazed in the dooryards; lilac coned tall in white and purple. On College Hill the mountain laurel massed and rhododendron waxed as if it would never wane. Peonies fattened in the chocolate gardens; tulips and blue-flags called for admiration. Violets clumped in shaded corners. Wistaria festooned gray buildings and climbed the porches. Every lawn-plot was studded with dandelions, spiked with wild onion. White clover grew and flowered in the fresh grass. But the leaves waited for their time. The weather warmed, held warm, persisted in warmth. Mild airs moved among the

248

maple branches. Noons turned hot; nights were not cold. And in the end, without a sound, the bonds loosened and burst. The leaves came out.

Alice sat down beside him on the front steps.

"What's the news?" she said.

Tyler slid the morning paper into her lap. "Nothing much today. It says the weather will be fair and the temperature around seventy-five. The Russians are quiet. The book review is dull. Oh, and my old professor is dead."

"What professor?"

"Alcide Turcotte."

"Oh, did he run off again?"

"No, nothing spectacular at all. It says he died in his sleep following a long illness. He hasn't been sick, really. The illness, of course, was old age."

Alice looked up at the new leaves. "What a time to die," she said.

"It's as good a time as any," said Tyler. "For him, for his sister, it couldn't be anything else but a blessing. There was nothing ahead for him except slow decay. A gradually deepening senility."

"We'll have to send flowers."

"Yes, and I ought to attend the funeral. It's at eleven on the eighth. That's the day after tomorrow. We'll send some flowers, and if I can go up, I'll go."

"Where will he be buried?"

"The paper doesn't say. Probably here. They might take his ashes to France. As a young man he spent some time in the west of France, but all he ever said about it to me was 'Après être allé en Normandie, je suis allé en Bretagne.' He did the Voltaire over here."

249

"La Jeunesse de Voltaire?"

"That's the monumental one. There was an earlier, much shorter study on the Bastille business. And some other books. The one on Stendhal is only fair. There's a good little survey on the Encyclopaedists. The big Voltaire is his real monument."

"Professors are lucky," said Alice. "They can write their own monuments and people will always read them."

"Not all the people."

"The best people, then," said Alice. "The teachers. The students. The fusty, dusty, lovely old scholars with their courtly ways. The dusty old Turcottes and Tylers."

"We're dusty, all right. Both now and finally."

"What a thought for a May morning," said Alice.

"All right," said Tyler. "Let's think about some breakfast."

II

When he got back to the office after the May meeting of the Committee on Discipline, Tyler glanced over his desk for the usual pile of mail. There was only one letter on the blotter. Attached to it was a note from Mrs. Rhodes which said: "This was *all* your mail today. I'm sure you will agree that this is a red-letter day."

He glanced at his watch. Ten after four. If it was a routine letter, he could answer it and get it out of the way before the first of the freshman theme conferences began. The postmark was blurred at the top but the underside was legible. *3:30 pm May 10 South Carolina.* He opened it and read:

"Dear Professor Tyler:

Please thank your secretary, Mrs. Rhodes, for sending me, at my request, the credentials of Dr. Donald Drake, which include your own testimonial letter. I have examined them carefully and it is my considered opinion that we would be most fortunate to secure the services of Dr. Drake, beginning next fall. He seems to be quite learned in French language and literature, and in my single interview with him, he struck me as the possessor of an engaging, if rather tense, personality. As we move into a period of expansion here, we shall be very much in need of competent teachers, particularly if (as I assume from his own remarks to me) he is not without some skill in minor administrative operations.

"The one problem which gives me pause is what happened in his previous post. I lack full details, but it has come to my attention that he was dismissed for consuming alcohol. Personally I must say that I do not consider this an offense of the first magnitude. Professionally, however, I would have to say that we could not condone such an act here. As a church-affiliated college, we naturally must set forth certain ground-rules, and one of them specifically indicates that faculty members must not indulge in alcoholic beverages in the presence of students, nor be in the presence of students after having recently indulged. I should go on to say that I recognize the absurdity of many of our social attitudes. But we must hold the line on this regulation.

"Mrs. Rhodes's note which accompanied the credentials suggested that I should address you personally if we were at all interested in Dr. Drake. Accordingly, though I know this is a very busy time of year for you, I must turn to you for a more detailed estimate of his character, particularly as it bears upon his ability to adapt himself to conditions as they obtain here. With renewed thanks, I am,

> Sincerely yours,
> Axwell Enders Troube III
> Chairman"

Some more of the same, thought Tyler. This is your disciplinary afternoon. Two to four: Committee on Discipline, Enfield Division. Four-ten to four-thirty: Committee on Discipline, Southern Branch, Mint Julep Division. All right, son. You have fifteen minutes to solve the tactical problem. The brother-keeping problem. You are the judge and the jury. You are the responsible officer. How do you help Brother Drake to get a job? And how do you keep Brother Axwell Enders Troube III from incurring the wrath of his dean when Brother Drake shows up at a faculty tea next fall with a couple of martinis under his belt? You're the friend in power. Go ahead.

Tyler swung around and faced his typewriter. After a minute he inserted a sheet of stationery and began to write:

"Dear Professor Troube:
Under the circumstances, I think it would be unwise for you to offer Dr. Donald Drake a position on your staff. He is an able teacher and he is certainly not a drunkard. Yet I cannot promise you that he will not drink. If drinking is against your faculty regulations, he will probably break the rules sooner or later. I am sorry that you will lose his services, and sorry too that he will lose the job. But you can probably locate a good man who doesn't drink, and he can probably find a place where drinking is permitted. With all good wishes,

> Yours sincerely,
> Edward B. Tyler"

He signed it with his fountain pen just as the first freshman knocked on his door. The boy's name was Edward Congdon. Tyler found his essay in the folder. He had marked it with a large red A and the legend: "Very sound organization, good writing, substantial thinking. This rounds out a fine record for the term." Tyler handed him the essay with a smile.

"Thank you, sir," Congdon said. He smiled back. He had regular negroid features and his dark bronze skin shone cleanly. "I'd just like to say how much I liked the course."

"You did a good job, Ed," said Tyler. "How have you liked your freshman year?"

"At first, not," Congdon said. "I felt out of it. Now I'm beginning to feel sort of in it. Not all the way, but enough."

"That's the way I felt at Harvard," Tyler said. "It was a long time ago, but I remember it clearly. I think it's the best position by far, and you put it well. 'Sort of in it. Not all the way, but enough.' When you feel as if you're all the way in it, it's time to start looking around you and wondering if that's the place to be. On the outside looking in is a lonely position, at least for some men. But on the inside looking out can make you very stuffy indeed. Not you, I mean. I mean men in general. Not all the way in, but enough: that gives you a little psychic distance."

"Yes, sir," Congdon said. His brown hands held the theme in his lap. "I know what you mean. In high school I used to worry about being popular. It wasn't until I stopped worrying about being popular that I got to be. I mean, sort of. Then I can remember thinking maybe I didn't want to be so popular. It used up all your time."

"I see your name is Edward, too," said Tyler. "Maybe it's the name that makes us think along the same channels. There isn't anything wrong with that essay of yours. I marked a couple of spelling errors in the margins."

Congdon looked serious. "I have to look up the doubtful words," he said. "I learned to read wrong. I mix up the vowels because I learned to recognize words by the consonants. But if there are only two errors, that's pretty good, for me."

The knock at the door meant that the next freshman had arrived. Tyler said "Come in," and held out his hand to Congdon. "Ed, keep up the good work. I wish you a happy sophomore year. I've been lucky enough to get a leave, so I won't see you around until you're a junior. I've enjoyed having you in the course."

Congdon shook hands warmly, with only a shade of embarrassment. "As I say, I enjoyed the course," he said. "I wish you luck next year." He nodded to the tall, thin boy who stood in the doorway, and went out.

"So long, Ed. Come on in, Oscar. You're right on time."

The tall boy had metal braces on his teeth. His brown hair stuck out in all directions. He spoke with a slight lisp, perhaps because of the braces. And he was probably, thought Tyler, the best poet Enfield University had had in twenty years. At least since the war.

"When a poet is on time," said Tyler, "that's news. Oscar, how's the boy? Have a seat and I'll get out your latest opus."

Oscar Black blushed wordlessly. He dropped from his great height suddenly into the chair. They're getting taller, thought Tyler. Every freshman class looks taller. It must be the cod-liver oil and the orange juice we give them. For a brief moment he pictured Toby and Tommy ten or eleven years from now, sitting in some college professor's office, tall and strong. He looked over at Oscar Black sitting there in the chair. With his long legs folded, he looked a good deal smaller. And younger, thought Tyler. He found the essay in the manila folder and handed it across to Black. The buzzer sounded at his elbow, and he picked up the telephone.

"Yes."

"Professor Tyler? Oh, Ed. Jack Martin speaking. I just called your home and Mrs. Tyler said you were still at the office. Hope I'm not interrupting anything. Could you possibly spare us a few minutes, Ed, on a pretty crucial issue?"

"You mean right now?"

"Within the next few minutes, yes." Martin didn't offer any further explanation. He's used to getting his way, thought Tyler. The Chairman of the Board of the paper company has the habit of the senior executive. Want to talk to an employee? Call him up. Let him drop whatever he's doing and hotfoot it to the boss's office.

"I'll try to get there," Tyler said. "I'm right in the middle of some freshman theme conferences. Right now I'm starting to work on our best campus poet." He winked at Black, who blushed and averted his eyes. "It shouldn't take too long to polish him off. Then I'm supposed to have one more man, who's due at five."

"I'm truly sorry to interrupt, Ed," Jack Martin said. "We've bitten a big chunk out of your time this year, I know. The only thing is, Ed, we're near the end of the line on our special business, and this is sort of urgent. Is there any chance of your asking the five o'clock scholar to come back later on?"

"I could do that, yes," said Tyler. "It's getting close to final examinations now, Mr. Martin, and I wanted to get these conferences finished up first. I guess I can fix it up to see the man next week."

"If you could," said Martin. His voice sounded the slight note of command, but he kept it warm.

"I didn't know you were meeting today," said Tyler, "or I would have arranged—"

"Sure, Ed," said Jack Martin. "I know you have to do the job. But you can appreciate that we're anxious to get on with ours—with our job, too."

"All right," said Tyler. "Where are you now, Mr. Martin?"

"Conference Room in Bishop," said Martin pleasantly. "The old hang-out, you remember."

"Please go ahead with the meeting," said Tyler, "and I'll get there in about ten minutes. Or maybe sooner. Would that be all right?"

"Fine," Martin said. "See you in ten minutes. My best to the poet."

"All right, sir," Tyler laughed. "I'll give him your regards."

He heard the click at the other end of the line and turned back to Oscar Black. "Did you look over the paper, Oscar? Did you see the remarks in the margins?"

Oscar blushed for the third time. "Yes, sir," he said.

"I didn't mean them to sound rough, Oscar. You see, with a man like you, a man, I mean, who really has a sense for language, you have to watch yourself especially. You get so pleased with the way words sound, you get so involved in the process of manipulating words for themselves, those small black tuneful groups of letters—that you can sometimes forget what the words mean. You lose sight of your object, I mean, which is communication. Then you get empty rhetoric. I don't say it doesn't sound wonderful. It falls musically on the ear. But sometimes it doesn't mean very much."

"Yes, sir," Oscar said again. He did not blush this time. He shifted his long legs disconsolately.

"I don't mean to belabor the point," said Tyler. "Meaning, and communication, are a matter of degree. But anyone who doesn't keep his eye on the thing or the idea that he's trying to communicate can get easily charmed by sound-patterns. Your friend Baudelaire had a musical ear. Sometimes he followed it too far off the track."

"Yes, sir," Oscar said. He glanced at Tyler and then looked away.

I wish he'd argue back, thought Tyler. Let's try him again.

"It's a matter of power, Oscar," he said. "Rhetoric which is only rhetoric is like a steam turbine hooked to a generator when all you do with the power you generate is to send it back into the ground. It's a bunch of crackling sparks with no gap to leap. It's a waste of power."

Oscar said: "I've thought about power. Word-power, but other kinds, too. I think power is made to be wasted. In our physiology class, we had a big discussion about it. The professor said—" he swallowed and looked at his large shoes "—I mean he told us that when we go to lift our arms, we always use much more power than the lifting really needs. And then in nature, outside nature. A tree throws seeds all over, and each seed has power, but only one or two out of thousands of seeds are going to take root. In a way, it's wasteful. Shakespeare used words the way a tree uses seeds. He scattered them wide and let them fall all over the ground."

The boy gestured awkwardly with his long arm, like a man sowing seeds.

"Yes, and there's a lot of empty rhetoric in Shakespeare, too," said Tyler. "When his plays were translated into French, that was evident. Still, when the old boy was really in the groove, nobody could be more wonderfully direct than he was. He harnessed his power. He brought it right onto a specific dramatic purpose. He chose words the way a college chooses its faculty—or tries to. He tried to make every word count. You're working on the waterfall theory, Oscar."

After his outburst, Oscar sat silent again. He wrinkled his forehead and glanced at Tyler.

"A waterfall," said Tyler, "is very beautiful. All that white water diving for the lowest level. It flows, but unless you direct it, it flows away towards the big ocean and gets lost."

Tyler discovered that he was very tired. His mouth was dry, and the damned trustees' meeting was over there gabbing away. Anyway, this was the time to stop. Black was a sturdy enough character, but you didn't want to discourage him.

"I'm afraid I've got to go, Oscar," he said. "That phone call was about a meeting, and I'm a little late for it now. I hope you won't be discouraged by what I said. I think you're such a good writer that I wanted to tell you about those marginal comments on the essay. What the scrawl was meant to mean. It's still a good job, though. Your writing has real character, and you know I've thought so from the beginning of the term." He paused. Shut up, he told himself. You talk too much.

Oscar untangled his long legs and stood up. "Yes, sir," he said. "Thank you, Mr. Tyler. I've got to try a lot of theories.

This spring I got interested in that one. Maybe this summer I'll try the dynamo theory. I hope to write a lot this summer."

"I hope you do, Oscar. Good luck. I look for great things from you." He held out his hand.

Black shook it awkwardly. "I'll try to use the dynamo on the final exam," he said, blushing.

"You do that, Oscar," said Tyler. As soon as the door closed he reached for a sheet of paper and wrote a note to Selbourne, the five o'clock appointment. He straightened the knot in his tie, got into his jacket, hung the note on the door, got a drink from the water cooler, and went down the stairs of Trask.

The campus lay green under the late afternoon sunlight. Long beams slanted through the trees. The sculptured figure on the top of the phoenix sun-dial glowed in the westering light. The days were getting longer now. The clock on the chapel showed five-ten. Tyler hurried down the front steps of Trask and turned left towards Bishop Hall. He disliked being late, but what the hell could you do on ten minutes' notice? He pictured the men around the table, Committee of Six and the trustees, approaching the end of the line now, about set to give the nod to Cos Cobb or Henry—what was his name?—Henry Fuller, the foundation man. Or Howarth, the good gray historian. He felt tired and his leg ached, but he began to feel the slow beat of excitement as he climbed the steps of Bishop. What dynamo are you going to harness, boys? Who's the new inhabitant of the Parthenon? Or have you made up your minds? Are you still sweating it out, weighing this man's merit, that man's scope, dealing in those intangibles of power that make all the difference?

The brown door stood closed. Tyler could hear behind it the murmur of voices. When he knocked the murmur ceased. Almost at once, Jack Martin's close-cropped gray head appeared. He held the door partly closed, peering out at Tyler in the darkness of the hall.

"Hello, Ed. Glad you're here. Come in." He swung the door wide and stepped back out of Tyler's way.

Around the table the men were seated, all looking in his direction. In a flash he saw that the other members of the Committee of Six were not there. Martin took his elbow and steered him towards an empty chair at one end of the long table. "Sit down, Ed," he said kindly. "Did you send the poet on his way?"

Tyler swallowed and sat down. "Yes, sir," he said. He looked around at the other faces. Eames, the man from Standard Oil, nodded and smiled from Tyler's right. "Good man, is he, Ed? A good poet?"

"I think he's the best we've had in years," said Tyler. "And he's only a freshman. He doesn't always seem mature, but as a poet he certainly is."

The others were smiling and nodding: Caldwell, up the table next to Eames, sat alertly behind a pile of papers, straightening them with his long white fingers; Dr. Macy the surgeon waved at him; Sibley leaned forward, smiling.

Martin sat in the chair at the other end of the table and looked down at Tyler. "Some of us have to catch the six-ten train," he said, "so we'd better get down to business. Ed, we wanted to consult you on this crucial matter. As you know, we've spent a good many hours on it. In committee and in private conference. Some of us have traveled to the coast and as far south as Louisiana. And under the guidance of your faculty committee, I think it's fair to say we've screened the country, up and down and across." He looked around at the group. They were all watching him.

"I want to make it plain," Martin went on, "that we have made no offer to anyone, as yet. We wanted to be sure that when we finally made up our minds, we'd have a single candidate who would be our absolute first choice. One we felt could take over the presidency. Though, of course, we had to make a list of runners-up, in case something happened." He looked at the pile of papers in front of Caldwell, and his face hardened momentarily. "We have that list, and we are sure we have found our Number One candidate."

Tyler nodded, but said nothing. The pain in his leg beat steadily. He shifted his position in the chair and lighted a cigarette. Come on, Jack, he thought to himself. Let's have it. You've got to make that train, and I'll agree to whoever it is. It's your business, and you look like the man who could transact it. He did, too, thought Tyler. The big Cromwell head. The confidence of the commander.

"The choice," said Martin, "was not easy. Some of the strongest candidates, as we thought from the beginning, were right here on your own faculty. *Our* faculty. Jim Howarth, for one."

So it isn't going to be Howarth, thought Tyler. Well, good. Jim can get on with his history of Enfield instead of beating his brains to make history for Enfield. But Howarth would have been a good man for the job.

"We think very highly of John Webb, also," Martin was saying. "And the other literary man—" he glanced at the papers in front of him—"Noel Hatch. It isn't relevant, but we found that Hatch comes of an Episcopalian family which has been associated with Enfield in every generation since its founding."

Dr. Macy moved his surgeon's hands on the table and sat forward, clearing his throat. "Hatched a lot of Enfield eggs," he said.

The men laughed gently and Tyler could feel the tension relaxing in the room.

Martin, who had not laughed, smiled at Macy. "We also considered—and eliminated—a good many outside candidates," he said. "I think you on your committee have been calling them the Outfielders."

Eames nodded and smiled at Tyler.

"That's right," said Tyler. "We leaned towards the Enfielders because we knew them best, but we liked a few of the Outfielders, too."

Inside the well-tailored jacket of his suit, Martin hunched his broad shoulders and bent forward. His chin was nearly on the table-top. "Picking up your analogy," he said, "we were after the man who could play, not only first base or shortstop or center field, but all the positions on the team, including especially manager. We considered Dr. Shaw—" he looked around and smiled grimly— "and we thought he was a very good strong second baseman. For a long time, Mr. Fuller held our attention, too. We decided against him finally, though his name is still on the list of runners-up, because we found a better man. Your own committee has been strong for Cos Cobb from the first."

"Yes indeed," said Tyler. He took a final puff and tamped

out his cigarette in the glass ashtray. "Cos Cobb has been my
personal first choice right along. I didn't think it was wise or
fair to rule out the others because there were a lot of good
men there, but I think Cobb is an extremely good man."

"We certainly agree with you," said Martin. He paused
and looked at the other trustees. "I can say it was no surprise
to me that the strongest local candidates should also be members of the Committee of Six."

Tyler's heart leaped in his chest. "Cos is certainly the ideal
man for the job. This makes me very happy. Have you approached him yet?"

Martin hesitated again. "Not yet," he said finally, speaking
slowly. "He and all the other members of the Committee of
Six agree with us that you are the man for the job."

III

Tyler's heart sank. He could feel the warm flush rising up
his neck. His mouth went dry. His voice, when he listened to
it, sounded like a gasp. "Me?" he said. "I—" A lump rose in
his throat and he could not force out any more words. He
bowed his head and picked up the ashtray in both hands. His
hands, he saw, were trembling. After what seemed a long time
he managed to mumble, in a voice that did not sound like his
own: "I'm not the man for the job." He stopped.

Harrison Caldwell bent forward in his chair and caught
Martin's eye. Martin nodded.

"Ed Tyler," said Harrison. "We don't believe that. We
think you are. We all recognize that this comes as a surprise.
We had to keep it very secret, as you'll appreciate, until we

were sure. We're also sorry to bring it up just at this time—
out of a clear sky—with no advance hinting or preparation.
And especially, I may say, since I didn't favor this method of
notification, just at the end of a working day, the end of a
week, and close to the end of the term. If you're like my
people at the seminary, and I know you must be, your tail-
feathers are dragging on the deck. You can't think clearly
when you're fatigued and when you have to fight your own
emotions. You look like the man the roof fell in on, and I
can't blame you."

They all laughed at that, quite loudly. Martin grinned, and
reached over to pat Caldwell's sleeve. "You can see, Ed, that
Brother Caldwell was not in favor of broaching it to you this
way. We had a little argument over that one—" he laughed
deep in his throat—"to say the least, Harrison." The trustees
laughed again.

Tyler felt the lump receding, summoned all his powers, and
found his voice. He even squeezed out a smile. "I guess the
time doesn't matter," he said. "I appreciate your kindness.
I'm sorry to be so—so taken aback."

Eames smiled and nodded again. "Take your time, son," he
said kindly. "Get those rafters combed out of your scalp." The
men laughed again. Tyler found that he could take a deep
breath. He took one, let it out, and began again.

"It is really a surprise. I can't believe my ears. The other
committee members never even breathed me a hint. All
through last winter I felt very sound and secure. I never
wanted to be president, never dreamed of being president.
Like everyone else on the committee, even Cos Cobb, I wasn't
in any contest, and I had no ambitions—I mean, no ambition

to be president of Enfield." The title sounded so hollowly in his ears that he stopped. "President of Enfield," he made himself repeat. "We—I said from the first that all I wanted to be was a good professor. When a man gets to my age, he ought to know what he's cut out to do. Excuse me, but I'm cut out to teach and write a few books. It's the life I wanted. All my eggs are in that basket."

He glanced up at the faces around him. They were all listening seriously. The room was very still. He felt some of his strength flowing back. "It isn't," he said, "as if there were no other qualified people. I think Cobb is the best choice—"

"May I interrupt?" asked Sibley, politely. "I want to interrupt, Ed, to point out that you are practically echoing Cobb's own words about yourself."

Harrison Caldwell spoke quickly. "Sibley means, Tyler, that Cos *wrote* us those words in one of the committee letters. The men on the Committee of Six were unanimous for you, and Cos, as secretary, simply added his personal opinion as a postscript." He gestured towards Sibley. "I just wanted to point that out, Sib, so that Ed wouldn't think we had brought Cos in here to make him an offer."

Sibley blushed. "Right, Harrison," he said. "Of course I didn't mean that Cos—I didn't mean it any other way." He sat back, still blushing.

Martin cleared his throat. "Coming back to your point about the eggs in your basket, Ed," he said quietly but with force. "The eggs are one of the reasons we chose you. Several of the reasons. Your books, your brains, your hard work, your administrative experience here and elsewhere. Your army record. Two of the eggs say 'North Africa' and 'Sicily'. You have the respect and admiration of your colleagues on the faculty. You're a father. You've got a fine wife and family. You're a scholar and a teacher."

Tyler opened his mouth but could not speak. Martin noticed it and lowered his voice.

"I don't want to embarrass you, Ed," he went on. "But I will say this one thing more. Wherever we gathered information, and don't think we didn't run plenty of crosschecks, the answer was the same. Around the country, I mean. Don't let any doubts hold you back. Or loyalty to others you think are better qualified. You're the man the lightning hit. You're the man called to serve."

Tyler swallowed and reached for a cigarette. Eames held a lighter out and spun the wheel. Tyler could not hold the cigarette steady in the small flame. At last one edge caught and he drew back, puffing hard. He looked at the glass ashtray on the table in front of him. It held the ashes and the butt of his old cigarette. The new one trembled in his hand.

"Do I have to decide—" he began. "I mean when do you have—" He stopped again.

"Of course you'll have to think it over, Ed," said Martin quietly. "We know it's a surprise. What the hell. We planned it that way because we had to. And of course it's a very big step. No bigger than some others you have taken, but still a big step. We all realize you'll have to sleep on it, talk it over with Mrs. Tyler. We certainly can't insist on an answer today or tomorrow. We had in mind to ask you to bring in a verdict by about Monday or Tuesday. But we'll wait until you're ready. And when you are ready, I'll come down here, if you like. Or I'll see you in New York. Or you can telephone or wire or write me there. And if you have questions about it—matters like salary, repairs at the Parthenon, nature of the duties, and so on—you can ask any of us and we'll try to answer. How's that? Would that give you enough time?"

"Yes," said Tyler very quietly. He stood up. "I don't know just what else to say now," he said. "Except to thank you. And to let you know one way or the other."

"That's all we want," said Martin. "That, and your acceptance. We want you to be the next president of the best university in the country."

They had all risen now. Martin came around the table and shook hands, looking straight into Tyler's eyes. The others followed. Tyler smiled—he hoped not too bleakly—at each of them.

"All right," he said, turning to the door. "And thanks. I'll let you know."

He went out and closed the door behind him.

IV

Before the small white frame house at the southern end of River Road, Tyler stopped and sounded the horn three times —the pre-arranged signal. He leaned over on one elbow and fixed his eye on the curtained glass of the front door. Almost immediately the door opened and a hand appeared. The hand waved up and down. It wore a white glove. Then it withdrew and the door closed noiselessly. Now she's pinning on the hat, thought Tyler. Now she's looking around for the wicker bag.

He could feel the sun warm on his hand and arm. On either side of the front steps the hydrangea bushes had begun to put out broad leaves. The small dog that smiled was asleep on the rubber doormat beside the two empty milkbottles on the top step. The tiny grass-plot, he saw, had recently been cut. In the cinder driveway, gleaming in the May morning light, clean as a whistle, stood the new Pontiac sedan.

Tyler glanced with momentary disgust at his own dirty hood. Beyond it, down the hill from the side yard of the house, the river made its wide westward sweep. A clump of willows, freshly green, billowed on the far bank. Appearing and disappearing behind them, a red tractor moved back and forth across a field of brown loam. He could not hear the sound of its motor.

When the door opened again, he looked up. The dog scratched to its feet and began to caper enthusiastically. The woman's bulk nearly filled the small porch of the house. She wore a blue print dress as big as a puptent, a small round hat sat well forward over her looming features, her slender ankles were encased in short white socks, and on her hands were the white gloves. She carried an enormous wicker bag and was beginning to move forward with a rocking motion.

He got out to help her down the steps. "The top of the morning to you, Mr. Tyler," she yelled. Her florid face bloomed like a rose.

"And to you the same, Mrs. DeNew," said Tyler, loudly. The dog stood grinning on the top step, its muzzle pulled back in tight wrinkles, all its tiny front teeth bared in the terrible smile. "And to you, too, Petal," Tyler added.

Mrs. DeNew paused part way down and gazed with pleasure at her dog. "Now, Petal," she said, in the special falsetto she reserved for pets and small children. "You be a good girl, now,

Petal." Petal grinned, her stump tail wagging, the pink hinder parts wriggling, the front paws spread for another caper. Petal was easily, thought Tyler, the ugliest dog he had ever seen.

Tyler assisted like a votary as Mrs. DeNew wedged her vast bulk into the car-seat. When he slid into the driver's seat to start the car, the first wave of perfume hit him powerfully. Never mind, he thought. It's what they used to use in France in place of baths. All Voltaire's girl-friends were that way, or worse. Let us get moving and stir up a Maytime breeze. He leaned forward and opened the ventilator—not, he hoped, ostentatiously.

"And did you notice my son across the river?" said Mrs. DeNew. She pointed to the brown field with one of the white-gloved hands. "That's Joey's tractor. You see there?"

"I saw it," Tyler said. "How is your son and how is Mr. DeNew?"

"Joey's all fine," said Mrs. DeNew. "My daughter's with us now and we all have high old times." She began to grub around in the wicker bag and soon drew out a small handkerchief. It was covered with purple flowers. Mrs. DeNew, bearing down hard, ran the handkerchief quickly over her forehead, under her ears, and around the back of her neck. Then she took a corner of the handkerchief and began to fan her pink face daintily. Fresh waves of perfume inundated Tyler. "And Mr. DeNew," she said. "Like always he's full of yarns." She pronounced it *yarrens*. "Where he picks them up I don't know. I tell him it's in bars and beer-joints." She chuckled in a high key.

Mr. DeNew was a character: a small, wiry man like a jockey,

who wore red suspenders and was never without the large, well-bloused cloth cap, indoors and out, winter and summer. Mr. DeNew was a foreman in the State Highway Department; from years of experience as a raconteur he had mastered the dead-pan delivery. Beside his wife he resembled a cock-sparrow beside a barn. He walked with a lordly strut. In the kitchen of the small house he could entertain her for hours, while they drank strong tea by the potful.

Tyler swung the car east on Main Street. "Any good ones lately?" he asked.

"I'll tell you a true one he told me this morning," said Mrs. DeNew, waving the handkerchief under her nose. "Course you know Ike Bower the butcher. I don't know as you know Mrs. Falconi, she's a friend of mine."

Tyler shook his head.

"Mrs. Falconi was sick this spring. She was under a doctor's care. She was operated on. So she calls up Ike Bower. 'Ike,' she says, 'send me a good pot-roast,' she says. 'Send it up in your delivery wagon,' she says. 'I can't come for it meself,' she says. 'I'm under the doctor.' 'Well,' Ike says, 'that's a hell of a note for a decent married woman,' he says. 'You better get the hell out from under,' he says."

Mrs. DeNew erupted with her high strangled laugh. She fanned herself vigorously with the purple handkerchief. "Oh, Mr. DeNew, he keeps my daughter and I in stitchuzz. 'You better get the hell out of there,' Ike says. 'It's no good place for a married woman to be.'"

Tyler laughed with her and waited. She clutched the wicker bag to her bosom and made the sounds of strangling. "She meant to say she was under the doctor's care," said Mrs. De-

New. " 'Deliver my pot roast, Ike,' she says. 'I can't come for it meself. I'm under the doctor.' Meaning, of course, that she's under the doctor's care."

"Ha ha," laughed Tyler. "You tell that to Mrs. Tyler. I'm sure she'll get a kick out of that one."

"There's nothing like a good story," said Mrs. DeNew, "for starting or ending the day." She was simmering down now, recovering her breath. The purple handkerchief flapped idly. "Oh, ho," she laughed gently. " 'I'm under the doctor,' she says. 'I can't come for my pot-roast.' "

Tyler pulled the car close to the curbstone. "Just a minute now, Mrs. DeNew. I'll come around." He opened the door on her side and held his palm under her elbow as she hitched around and billowed out, clutching the wicker bag. She gained her small feet, bent slightly forward from the perpendicular, and began the slow rocking motion that would presently bring her to the front steps.

"And how are Toby and Tommy?" she said, rocking along. Her voice took on its special falsetto. "Bless their little hearts," she said.

"They're fine," said Tyler. "I think they're playing somewhere in the neighborhood. We'll round them up before we leave. Alice —Mrs. Tyler will tell you about them. We'll be home again tomorrow night. We're all glad you could stay with the boys."

He cupped her elbow in his palm again and lifted strongly as Mrs. DeNew rocked vastly up the steps. At the top he held the door open while she sailed through like a full-rigged ship. Alice had seen them coming and was in the hallway.

"Good morning, Mrs. DeNew," Alice said, brightly. "It's

nice of you to come and take over. Would you like to get settled in your room now? Or I have a pot of tea in the kitchen."

Mrs. DeNew looked up the stairway, set down her wicker bag, and began to remove her white gloves. "Tea, is it?" she said. She raised her large arms and lifted the small hat from her head. "Mrs. Tyler, I'm always ready for a pot of tea. And we'll settle the state of the world." She followed Alice grandly into the kitchen.

Tyler sat down on the couch in the living-room. The two suitcases stood ready in the middle of the rug. As soon as Alice was finished with Mrs. DeNew, they could get into the car and go. To get perspective on it, he thought. To get up there and think about it from a distance. To cover the ground. To go over the arguments, pro and con.

He found that he could not sit still. Stop thinking about it, he said, half aloud. Push it down out of sight. Let it wait. You have all day today and tonight and tomorrow and Monday if you need it. Forget about it now. Get out from under it.

But in the back of his mind it still turned and twisted. He could not keep it still. He went out to find the boys and to tell them goodbye.

v

By the time he turned the car's nose into the black macadam of the final stretch, keeping the left front tire on the sinuous winding track of the white center-line and slowing down for the dangerous curves, the sun was low in the sky, it was after five, and neither of them had spoken for what seemed an hour or more. On either side of the road the familiar landmarks appeared, held, and faded away behind: the mustard-colored house with the red barn and the ancient blue Buick still mouldering (as it had been doing for years) just over the worm fence in the rocky pasture; the jerry-built, beer-signed hovel which served as the regional liquor store and was run by a gross and red-faced giant who looked like a criminal but was only a slob; the three well-landed farms, owned by cousins who never spoke to one another, each with a huge, square-cut house under its elm-tree, its yard well-tended, all the front windows blankly curtained like blind eyes; and the worn store at the cross-roads, dominated by the black-and-white sign which proclaimed: "MEATS AND GROCERIES   ASA P. HARRIS, PROP." And finally the gradual hill from whose level and treeless top you could see, far away, blue, rock-punctuated, and vast, the ocean.

He glanced toward Alice, who was quietly asleep, her head resting on the back of the seat, her lips slightly parted. All morning, even after lunch at the roadside stand when she had taken the wheel for a couple of hours and he had fought with drowsiness, Alice had been alert and talkative, obviously pleased to be making the trip, obviously determined not to interfere in the decision. She had recovered quickly from the shock of his phone-call from the office, agreed to the long drive up here, and by the time he reached home, his head still whirling, had arranged with Mrs. DeNew to stay with the boys over Saturday and Sunday.

So here they were, the professor and the professor's wife, topping the rise, rolling down the long hill towards the white village, and nothing was settled except that on Monday he would make an appointment with Jack Martin in New York and there, on the twenty-ninth floor of the Wall Street office building, refuse the presidency as gracefully as possible.

Alice had taken the good wife's stand. If he was going to be president, she would gladly be the president's wife; if not, they would go on happily as before. "There's only one thing," she had said, with an air of determination. "Sometime in the next two years, I want to have a girl-baby. I don't care whether her father is a professor or a president, though if she were to be born in the Parthenon we'd have to give her a classical name. Like Antigone," she had said, giggling. "Antigone Tyler, isn't that nice? Tiggy for short."

Now Tyler touched her cheek. Her lips closed and her eyes flew open. "We're almost there," he said. She sat up, smoothing back her hair with both brown hands.

"I was asleep," she said. She looked out. "There's Quimby's store," she said. "He's still open. Don't we want to get some food for breakfast?"

"Mr. Bowen got some stuff today," said Tyler. "When I called him I suggested it. Oranges, eggs and bacon, coffee, a loaf of bread. He can have what we don't eat."

Alice had opened her handbag and was applying lipstick. "Good," she said. "We'll have what Mrs. DeNew calls a high old time."

Tyler turned down the narrow graveled lane between the clumps of rose-bushes and they both looked towards the house, whose low roof showed above the tall grove of sumac.

"It's still there," said Tyler. "Like the ocean." As he turned the car into the grassy driveway and stopped, they saw the ocean, blue and gold in the westering light, the humped masses of the rocks along the shore, the sea-grass waving where the lawn stopped, and on the horizon the faint blue blur of the Gay Head end of the Vineyard. A tanker was moving up the coast, heading for Boston or Portland.

A light showed faintly at the far side of the house where the small apartment was. "I guess he's there, too," said Tyler. "He's probably too deaf now to hear us." He opened the door of the car and got out, stretching. The breeze flowed all around him, laden with the brine-smell, cold and sweet. "Smell that air," he said.

Alice stood still on her side of the car, face lifted, brown hair blowing back. "It's the best air there is," she said. "Let's retire up here in about twenty-five years and breathe it all the time. Here's Mr. Bowen."

The old man had come silently around the corner of the house. In the light of the late afternoon, his seamed face looked like leather. He wore the familiar long-billed sword-fisherman's cap and a fawn-colored sweater with all the buttons buttoned. They both shook his knobbly old hand, cold and dry as a tree-root.

"Glad to see ye, Alice. Ed. I judged ye'd git here about now. Got your groceries inside. Fire's a-going in the stove. Beds is made up clean."

Alice ran her arm through his and held his hand. "Aren't you smart?" she said. "Aren't you industrious?" She turned momentarily to wink at Tyler. "Mr. Bowen, how old are you now?"

"What's that?"

"I say, how old are you now?"

Mr. Bowen stood still. He lifted the fisherman's cap off

275

with a thumb and forefinger, scratched his head with the other fingers, and yanked the cap on again. "I'm seventy-eight years, three months, and five days," he said. "Going on seventy-nine."

Tyler took the suitcases from the trunk and they moved towards the house. "Mr. Bowen," said Alice, "is Ma Carey's place open?"

"What's that?"

"Ma Carey," Alice shouted. "Is she open now?"

"Why I guesso," Mr. Bowen said. "I guesso."

"Ed and I are going to go down there to eat tonight," said Alice, loudly. "Can't you come with us?"

Mr. Bowen jingled his huge key-ring and unlocked the door. "I thankee," he said. "I wouldn't care to, I guess. I've et a-ready."

While Alice unpacked and changed in the still-musty-smelling bedroom, Tyler made the circuit of the comfortable living-room on the ocean side, lifting and putting down the familiar objects. The sea-clam shells that Toby had gathered for use as ash-trays, the sweet-grass mat on the broad table where last summer's magazines were neatly arranged. He glanced into the coat-closet where the oil-skins still hung. An old pair of Tommy's sneakers, worn out at the toes, covered with dry salt-crystals and specks of sea-sand, stood side by side in the corner. He thought of the boys, eating in their pajamas at the kitchen-table at home, while Mrs. DeNew gabbed away at them from her post by the stove. Enfield seemed far off. The problem was nothing but a shady blot in the back of his mind. He went to the stair-well.

"Alice," he said. "Alice. Come on, girl. Let's go on down there. I'm hungry."

276

"Coming," Alice said, and he heard her heels clicking on the bare floor of the upper hall.

He lay tense in the dark room listening to the sound of the sea. The roar of slow breakers on the shore, the shuffle and whisper of the water's withdrawal, the onset renewed, the endless rhythm; dependable as the beating of a heart. Three thousand years, he thought, four thousand, more years than you could imagine, that breaking thunder, that outflowing, the crash and the sigh—older than Enfield, older than any of its presidents, older than the civilization along this coast or inland, older than France, older even than Gaul or the Caesars or the Phoenicians. Crash and flow, crash and flow.

Dr. Johnson came into his head. Voltaire's enemy: the moralist, the Great Cham. Some argument with little Boswell, fidgety over a problem. "Consider, sir," said Johnson, "how unimportant this all will seem a hundred years from now." Or something like that. And so it would, if you measured by the time of the sea. Or by human generations, stretching back and back, their costumes gradually changing: pepper-and-salt suits, knee breeches and wigs, doublet and hose, tanned leather jerkins, skins of wild animals, or the thick home-grown pelts, rank as a bear's den, in which those squat prognathous men, ugly as baboons, had met the onslaughts of the age of ice.

He turned on his side and wrenched his mind back to the present problem. Catch the eight-forty for New York and the subway to Wall Street and the elevator to the twenty-ninth floor. Mr. Martin, I wanted to see you personally to tell you what there is to tell. Ever since Friday I have thought about it continuously. Except for a little eating and sleeping. And

277

driving. My wife and I went up to our summer place in Massachusetts. I needed time to think, and the perspective of distance. We went over it again and again, backwards and for-
wards. It is a great compliment. My wife and I are grateful
for it, for your confidence, for your kindness. But a man
knows what he's cut out to do, what he wants out of life, by
the time he's past forty. Even before the war I knew I wanted
to teach and write in some good and lively university. The
war confirmed it. I could hardly wait to get back; it took me
one minute flat to accept the assistant professorship; the years
since then have been lucky. I'm glad of the chance to work
here: the work is completely absorbing, it's a beautiful place.
The students are good. We complain about the amount of
work, we bitch and moan like the G.I.'s or the factory workers
or the house-wives. But unlike most of those, we wouldn't
have it any other way. It's hard but absorbing. It takes all our
time, but we give the time with a sense of constant profit. We
look for truth and we look to hand it on to the boys. It's the
kind of life I have learned the value of, know I want, would
not exchange for any other. But thank you, thank the trustees
for the honor and the confidence.

You sound smug, said Tyler inside his head. You sound con-
descending and holier-than-heaven. You sound like the dedi-
cated soul. That's not the approach. It's negative. Be positive.
Go up there and tell him that Cos is the right candidate. Cos
is the friend to honor with the power. His name is on your
list, Mr. Martin. He belongs in the front office. He's a real
man, a proved administrator, a distinguished scholar. You are
making a mistake to pass him up. He would take the job and

do it well. He would head a strong team. People like and respect him. He's a man's man for a man's university.

Somewhere outside, above the rise and fall of the ocean, a gull whawked. Like a crow, thought Tyler, without the hoarseness. He turned on his other side and drew up his knees. After the day of driving, the back of the thigh was beating slowly. Not pain, really, but you knew it was there. He reached a hand down and gripped the muscles where the criss-crossed scars lay corded under the cloth of his pajamas. Cos went to San Diego, I went to Africa and Sicily. Only as far as that field in Sicily. We came back, like the others. Like some of the others. We put on the civilian clothes, picked up our jobs, began to build our families, worked our way in. Like Eddie Congdon. Not all the way in, but far enough. Involved with the work, poring over the work, bending over the cage in the laboratory, bending over the book or the typewriter. But keeping perspective, too. Able to stand off from it, evaluate it, see it for what it was—not only a job but a way of life. Not only a way of life but the one way you really wanted.

And now they said, come off it. Now they said, change horses in the middle of the stream. Now they said, drop what you're doing and scurry over here: there's a vacancy at the top, a vacuum in the front office. And you said, I'm where I want to be right now, thanks. You said, the hardest job in the world is to be a good professor. You can get someone else to come over there. I'm not all the way in, but far enough. Uncle Homer said, yes, the hardest job is to be a good anything: a doctor, a lawyer, an Indian Chief, even a college president. You don't have a right to refuse. If they offer you the job it means that you're the man. You ought to rise to the occasion. Ecce Homo.

How do you know the cup is bitter? It may be bitter and it may be sweet, or more likely both, but you won't know until you try. Try.

Tyler turned on his back, stretching his feet down to the cool place at the bottom of the bed. Beside him he could hear Alice's measured breathing. If you want to be a college president I will be a college president's wife. If you want to be a professor, I will be the professor's wife. I love the fusty scholars with their courtly ways. The fusty-dusty professors who write their own monuments. The Tylers and Turcottes. Uncle Homer said, I thought my archaeological digs were the center of the universe. I had my honorary degrees in their green tubes piled like the cord-wood in Cos's shed, and I had earned them with the sweat of my brow. They weren't handed to me as a token honor that one college president gives to another. But Lincoln, said Uncle Homer, took the cup. Lincoln transcended country lawyerhood. Lincoln left the country better than he found it. Yes, he left it, all right. On a stretcher out the back door of Ford's Theatre. That's right, yes. But now he sits in the temple, huge and brooding, and all the world makes a path to the door of his shrine. But I don't want to be a shrine. Let me write my own monuments, such as they are. My dusty monuments. *Voltaire en Angleterre* and the others there beside it on the dusty shelf—my five-inch shelf of books. And still others conceived but not yet born. You think it was easy? It was not easy. No, never. To avoid the rhetoric, to channel the idea, to harness the energy and direct it, to persevere until it was done and then to go through it again, and again, until it was perfect. No not perfect. Just not too imperfect, the monument not too lopsided. My own Parthenon, with all the columns in their places, and my own

gods inside. Literary and otherwise. Godlike and otherwise.
But mine.

He turned again on his side, facing the windows where the
sea lay heaving under the moonlight.

"Can't you sleep, Ed?" said Alice softly.

"Not yet."

"Oh, that air," said Alice. "That wonderful air. I've had
the most delicious sleep and you feel so nice and warm and
you can hear the ocean."

Tyler turned on his back and slid an arm under her shoulders. She moved towards him and her cool hand rested inside
his pajama coat on his chest. He did not say anything.

"Haven't you been to sleep yet?" said Alice.

"Just thinking," said Tyler. "Just chewing the cud, like
old John Henry with his quid. Just thinking up arguments
for Jumping Jack Martin."

"You ought to stop," said Alice. "You hardly slept at all
last night, either."

Tyler kissed her forehead. "You tell me how. Maybe you
can tell me how. I have counted sheep, I have made Uncle
Homer jump over the fence nine hundred times. I have dis-
sected the Parthenon stone by stone—"

"You poor dear," said Alice. "You just come here. You just
come here a minute."

When he awoke a long time later he did not know where he
was. Then his mind snapped awake and he raised his head
from the warm depths of the pillow. The white curtains
moved. He saw that outside the moon was still shining and
under it all, like breathing, he heard the ocean.

Tell them to give it to Cos Cobb. Tell them—but of course

you couldn't tell them. If the top name was stricken from the list the next one might be Fuller, not Cobb. Or they might get together again and revise the order. It was their business. But you could advise them to take Cobb. And then what about the lioness? In Miami, in Chicago, in New York or out there in Culver City she would read the paper, see the news, and the two-hundred-word night-letters would begin again. "Congratulations, Professor Cobb. Are you coming to Chicago on university business? It just so happens that I have to be there next week. Please give me a call."

"Oh, God," said Tyler, half-aloud. Professor Cobb, biologist and woodsman, fisherman and presidential candidate, you are licked. Even if they make you the offer, you are licked. Suppose they agree to my proposition, call you over to Bishop Hall in secret session next week, sit you down in that chair at the end of the table, and give you the works. Suppose you go out of there and call Polly from the lab; suppose you all pile into the jeep and head for the lake. And have supper and go to bed and turn and toss through the moonlit or the rainy night. And the loon calls like that gull, and Polly wakes up and is sweet and kind, and afterwards you go to sleep and before dawn you wake again. And then what do you think, Cobb? Of all this and the lioness, too. Of the beast in the jungle waiting with the night-letters. And you say no. I could do it but I won't. I could open the university to the breath of scandal, but I won't. I can tell the trustees about the lioness, but I won't. I'll simply refuse the job, and let the ex-wives fall where they may. "I don't believe," said Cos, "in airing dirty linen."

All right, Cos, so you don't become the friend in power.

Then Henry Fuller, the foundation man. The one you've never seen, except in that newspaper picture of an owlish man, forty-five-ish, well-dressed, the Yale who won his Y in Life, sitting by the clean desk, half-smiling through his polished glasses at the crouching camera-man. Are you our man? Ecce Eli. Or suppose he says no. Then where are we? Knocking on the office door of Professor Howarth of the History Department. The good gray Howarth. Or Webb. Or Hatch. While Edward Bennett Tyler gets his Guggenheim, packs his trunks, gets his immunity shots, renews his passports, collects his wife and children, and sails away for a year and a day to the land where Voltaire grew. And completes the big book at the age of forty-five or forty-six. The tome. The monument.

He opened his eyes again and looked towards the window. The quality of the light had changed and the sea was hushed. Quietly, swinging out of bed and tip-toeing to the window, he saw that the tide was out and that the dawn was nearly ready to break. There was no breeze: the sea-grass down the hill near the rocks was scarcely moving. A few gulls flapped silently across his line of vision, heading up the coast. As he stood watching, the red edge of the rising sun lifted over the rim of the sea. So it was here. Sunday, May fourteen. D-day. The day of decision. *Le jour de gloire. Der Tag.* He shivered and went back to bed, cold stone awake, permanently awake, sandy-eyed awake, never-to-sleep-again awake. And in five minutes was asleep.

When he stirred again and sat upright, Alice was gone. A smell of coffee and bacon drifted up from downstairs. He heard voices—Alice's laughter, Mr. Bowen's old man's voice chattering away. He shaved, dressed quickly in old slacks and a sweater, and went down to breakfast.

VI

Back from the tan ribbon of the curving beach stood the low dunes, covered with sea-grass. Where the grass stopped and the dry sand began, the irregular line of last winter's driftwood showed, as far as the eye could follow. He kicked at a green bottle which lay there on its side; around its neck a frayed rope-end was tightly knotted; the bottle was corked and empty. Through the valleys between the humped dunes he could see the low ridge beyond, dotted with bayberry and jackpine.

To seaward the sky was hazy; the sun glared; you could not see the Vineyard. Under the quartering wind the waves ran in crazily, at odd angles to the shore. On the north-east horizon clouds were banked like ragged mountains. The tide was rising. Fifty yards out, a few terns were fishing. The cocked heads, the quick-fluttering hover of wings, the plummet dive, the splash in cold water. Sometimes they rose with a prize in their beaks. More often, they did not. They moved down the shore, searching.

"Let's walk on the hard sand while we can," said Tyler.

The wind blew Alice's brown hair forward around her face. She pulled the suede jacket around her chest and shivered momentarily.

"That wind is cold," she said. "It's not like summer."

"A few weeks will warm it up," said Tyler.

"And crowd it up," said Alice. "With summer people,

284

muscling in on winter people." She ran a few steps forward and then walked backwards, facing him. "Let me see how you look now," she said. "How do you feel?"

"Much better since breakfast. I like this buffeting breeze—and the empty beach, with you in the foreground."

"It's empty all right," Alice said. "But it's lonely. Like you last night, with your problem."

"I'm not lonely now. I have a crowd in my head."

"A crowd of presidents?"

"A crowd of presidential arguments," said Tyler. "Mostly negatives. Ever since Friday I've been thinking in negatives. The big no."

Another gust of wind blew Alice's hair, back from her ears this time. Her cheeks glowed. Still walking backwards she said, "Why don't you develop the negatives? I want to see how the pictures come out."

"They'd all be sunstruck," said Tyler. "The positive prints would be dim and hazy. You couldn't recognize the protagonist."

"Try it anyway," said Alice. She turned and let him catch up with her, then walked beside him. "Let's see how the picture looks."

"I've got a color photograph of you in the Parthenon," said Tyler. "You look very gracious. You're serving tea in the presidential study."

"Never mind me," said Alice. "Do I look very gracious, like a grande dame?"

"Yes."

"All right, then, never mind me. We're talking about you."

"Oh, I could do it, I guess," said Tyler. "It's probably hard but it could be done. A man could learn the ropes. Most of the machinery runs by itself. You sit there and make decisions. You go away and make speeches. You worry. You confer with deans."

"That sounds like what you've been doing," said Alice.

"But presidents don't teach. They don't learn. Neither do they write—unless you count speeches and baccalaureate sermons in that rhetorical language, that circumlocutory presidentese that they all acquire, sooner or later."

"Don't presidents keep on learning?"

"Oh, yes. I meant learning about Voltaire or Shakespeare or natural laws or why crowds behave as they do on beaches."

"Maybe not that, but they learn."

"Yes, they learn," said Tyler. "How to handle people, how to wield the power vested in the office, how to keep the big machine running smoothly, how to keep it inching forward, how to choose and keep a faculty, how to take a firm position and stick with it. And how to compromise with necessity."

"That still sounds like what you've been doing."

"On a smaller scale, yes. But I don't want that much power over others. The power I want is inside."

"What good is it if it's inside?"

Tyler stopped and leaned to pick up a clam shell. He scaled it into the breakers, which were running higher now. "Alice, are you trying to push me into the Parthenon?"

She laughed. "Whatever gave you that idea, professor? I'm just trying to get a positive print of your well-developed mind. Honestly now, haven't you ever thought of living in the Parthenon? Or sitting in the president's chair at faculty meetings? Or getting an honorary degree from Harvard?"

286

"Not the honorary degree. But the others—oh, sure. Since Friday. Maybe a few times before that, in my weaker moments. It would be nice for you to have a maid and for us to have some more money."

"And a butler," said Alice. "Wouldn't it, though? Of course, no matter how much you earn, you never have enough money."

"Your wants expand with your ambitions," said Tyler. "I'd rather keep the wants ultra-simple. And the ambitions, too." He turned to gaze seaward. The tide was coming in fast, pushed by the wind. Over the horizon the bank of clouds was rising and spreading. Somewhere off there was the lightship, invisible in the haze. That's where the dory tipped over, thought Tyler. That's where you hung on in the green water, surprised and dripping, with the icy bolus of seawater in your stomach.

"I guess what I don't like about it is the way it sneaked up on me," he said, after a moment. "Out of nowhere, like John Henry's squall. Unsuspected and unanticipated. Unwelcome and unbelievable."

"Now we're getting the positive," she said. "Four negatives make a positive. Surely you must have known it might possibly happen to you. It wasn't, it couldn't have been completely unsuspected. You and the others were fixing things so it would happen to Cos Cobb. Why not to you?"

"I guess I thought it could. Never that it would. I was for Cobb. I was for some of the others, too, but chiefly for Cobb. I was thinking positively about him, negatively about me."

Alice skipped two steps and stood squarely in front of him. She put her hands on his arms. She spoke slowly, choosing her words. "Are you sure it wasn't this way, Professor Tyler? I mean as follows. Are you sure you didn't think to yourself, 'I don't want this to happen to me?' And then, in the next thought, you assumed that it wouldn't? And then refused to consider, even to recognize, all the signs that it might happen?"

Tyler grinned down at her. "You've got the old man all figured out, have you? The Prince of Naiveté. The Lord High Self-deceiver."

Alice looked serious. "I don't mean that you're naive, Ed. I guess it's modesty or something. You don't see these things as happening to you. That's what happened about the chairmanship."

"The chairmanship wasn't a life sentence," said Tyler. "The presidency is."

"Don't get me off the point," said Alice. "It's hard enough to stick on it as it is. Let me be a professor and cite you an example. You are walking along a trail and something big is following you, off there in the bushes. It is after you, but you won't look towards it. You say, 'Why should it want me?'— and then you go on about your business as if it weren't there at all."

It's true, thought Tyler. It was true in that squall out there by the lightship when the dory turned over, and it was true in that filthy field just outside Messina in Sicily when the kid tripped the anti-personnel mine where they said it had all been cleaned up. And the junk hit you in the tail and the back and the thigh, especially the thigh.

"Maybe you're right," he said. "It's probably not modesty, though. Call it my sanguine nature."

288

"No," said Alice. "It's some form of modesty. You don't like surprises, even nice surprises. You run away from surprises."

"You're a surprise," said Tyler. "You're even a perpetual surprise. I didn't run away from you."

"Oh-ho-ho," laughed Alice. "You ran away from me for a year and a half. I thought I'd never catch you. I followed you along that trail for a long time and you didn't know I was there. Or if you did you wouldn't admit it to yourself."

"Then you sprang out?"

"Like a lioness," said Alice.

"Not like a lioness, no."

"All right, like a cheetah. But I mustn't reveal my womanly secrets. Should we turn back now? We can have the picnic lunch on the rocks and leave about two or three."

"Let's go as far as the lighthouse," said Tyler. "It's only about twelve." He took her arm and they walked faster along the narrowing rim of hard sand where the tide was rising. For a long time neither of them spoke.

She's right about one thing, he thought. You don't take kindly to surprises. You never have. You don't care for unknowns: you like to see ahead. You like to plan out your life and pursue your own business. So when the surprises come along, your impulse is to reject. What you have planned to do, you will do gladly. You do not like the unplanned.

Take that interview in New York when you moved into Cos Cobb's place at the last minute. Your first impulse was rejection; you agreed to go only to help out Bill Waggoner. All the time the trustees talked with you about Cos, they were looking you over, sizing you up, and you ought to have known it. But would you consider that as a possibility? No, you wouldn't. It didn't occur to you. Cos was the one who was supposed to be there. And Cos, though you didn't know it then, was pacing up and down in the corridor at the hospital where his wife was losing her baby. You took his place innocently. And now you are asked to take his place permanently. If that New York interview was the turning-point in the presidential contest, fate played Cos—or you—or both —a dirty trick.

Don't think about fate, he told himself. You don't believe in fate. You believe in chance. Or rather you know that chance operates in human affairs. And you believe in change. Or rather you know that changes are bound to occur. Changes of mind, of status, of occupation, of clothes, of architecture, of heart. Chance and change are two of the laws of human life. Here is the chance that beckons you to change. Are you willing to change? No. Are you willing to give up the trip to France and the Voltaire book and the Guggenheim fellowship and the leave of absence and the teaching and the good life of the professor? No. Do you really mean it, or are you just sore at the way it sneaked up on you, unawares, like the offer from Schuyler College, which you rejected? I'm not sore at that especially. Things happen. The unlucky, the unwelcome, the bad sneak up, like the sudden squall at sea or the sudden explosion in a Sicilian field. And you do what you can to meet them. But the lucky and the good surprise you, too. Suddenly they are there, and after you have really earned them they are yours for ever, or for as long as you live. Like Alice, like the boys, like the girl if we have one. The good chances and the bad chances, and how do you know that the bad chances always turn out badly? I don't, he thought. And the future is always different from the past, and the past is called the past because it is past.

"Here's the lighthouse," said Alice.

They looked up at it, standing gray and weatherbeaten, abandoned now, its old red door carved with generations of initials. The door was spiked and bolted and padlocked shut. To keep out children and lovers and suicides, thought Tyler. He bent down and ran his fingers over the scaling paint.

"My initials used to be here somewhere," said Tyler. "I carved them when I was a boy."

They looked all over the door but could not find the initials.

"It's too bad they aren't there," said Alice. "They might be famous some day."

He glanced at her, but she was looking out to the ocean. The cloudbank was rapidly advancing now, moving towards the zenith. The tide had nearly covered the narrow ribbon of hard sand. The walking would be harder than it had been coming up the beach. While he watched the sun went under and the air turned gray.

"Let's go along now," he said. "It's not going to be good weather for a picnic."

"No," said Alice. She took his hand and held it and put it into her pocket. "I guess we won't have any picnic," she said. "But we'll have fun anyway, won't we?"

"Yes," said Tyler. "We'll have fun."

NINE *JUNE*

I

As HE passed the granite steps before the Faculty Club, Tyler saw the tall, thin figure of Abel Vincent emerging from the front door. He stopped to wait as Abel came down the walk.

"Abel," he said. "Are you going where I think you're going?"

Vincent came slowly down the steps, his skull face gleaming like parchment in the afternoon light, the dark circles showing almost purple around his deep-set eyes. Those eyes, thought Tyler. They're like two fires smoldering in caves.

"If you're going where I think you're going, I'm with you," said Abel in his deliberate voice. "It's all very mysterious. I gather, Ed, that we are scheduled to get a tall snort of Waggoner's Bourbon and possibly some information. The one is certain, the other problematical. Did Bill tip you off at all?"

"All he said was that something was in the wind," said Tyler. "Either he is enjoying the role of Sphinx or he's still in the dark himself."

"One thing came to light," said Abel. "This is the last meeting of the Committee of Six. Almost seven months to the day

292

since we first convened. This sounds like the seventh-inning stretch."

"Here's Lackdale," said Tyler. "A pleasant street." They turned the corner. "Do you know, it's actually hot this afternoon?" He ran his handkerchief over his forehead and returned it to his pocket. Abel, pacing along deliberately, looked down at him.

"You are warm, aren't you?" he said. "I'm comfortable. You've been walking while I've been sitting. I just spent the last two hours in a cool, quiet corner of the Faculty Club with my Sunday afternoon vice."

"What's that?" said Tyler. "Marijuana or old Doctor Mercer?"

"Neither of those," said Abel, laughing, "though I guess they have about the same effect. No. My sin is venial, I hope. It consists in reading every scrap of information in the financial section of the Sunday *Times*. Did you ever read the pages on *Business Opportunities?*"

"Never did," said Tyler. "My departments are Education and the weekly Book Review. With a glance at early season baseball."

"You'll never win there," said Abel. "You ought to look at the financial section. It makes you into a prophet. Somewhere in that twenty-page mass are the clues to what may happen tomorrow, or next week, or in the second part of the fiscal year. It's fascinating. Charts and statistics. News-stories on credit and discount rates and sales across the country. Success-stories from rags to riches. Bankruptcies. Plant expansion plans and vital shortages. Wholesale wants and offerings. And of course the trading summaries for the week on the Stock

Exchange. And *Business Opportunities*—that'll set you dreaming."

"How are they this week?" asked Tyler.

"Everybody will sell you something at a sacrifice," said Abel. "Either yours or his, but he says it's his. Do you want to buy a diner, a campsite in Vermont, a nightclub? Just look there. Maybe you'd like to own a motel. You can get one on a busy highway for only seventy-seven thousand and some odd dollars."

"I have the odd dollars," said Tyler.

"Or a dog-kennel with thirty dog-runs," said Abel. "And a five-room house attached so you can keep the little darlings in view. Complete with meat-grinder. And then there's a nursing home."

"The nursing home sounds good," said Tyler. "We could use it for professors just after the final exam period."

"And a day nursery," said Abel enthusiastically. His deep-set eyes were twinkling. "We could use a day-nursery for some of the students."

As they turned into Waggoner's front walk they heard a sound of hammering. In the grass-plot near one back corner of the house stood a heavy-set young man in a T-shirt and khaki pants, hammering an iron fence-post into the ground.

"Looks as if Bill has bought a dog-run," said Tyler, "and someone to install it." He pressed the front-door bell and heard the chime-notes sound their gentle tune: *"How dry I am."*

"Da da da da," said Abel, off-key. "Very appropriate for a warm afternoon. Here comes Eaton, looking dry, too."

"The top of the evening to you," said Paul, easily. He

strode up the walk. "Were you taking my name in vain? What goes on in the back yard?"

"We think it's a dog-run," said Tyler. "Do you know the young man?"

"That's Waggoner's tenant," said Paul. "Hello, Bill. What's happening back there?"

"A fence is going up," said Waggoner, holding the screen door open while they filed in. "It's a secret weapon. Come on in. I'll tip you off."

The living-room was cool and the clocks ticked away industriously in the brown gloom. Ice and whiskey stood ready on the side table and there was a pitcher of martinis.

"Step right up, men," said Waggoner. "I've just iced those martinis. Anybody who's for whiskey, there's the Bourbon—courtesy of Jack Martin."

"I'll tend bar," said Paul, quickly. "What'll it be, gents?"

Tyler and Waggoner took highballs. Vincent stood before the cold fireplace sipping a martini. Paul poured a martini.

"Who do we lack?" he said. "Cos and Jim. Are they coming?"

"They're supposed to," said Waggoner. "Cos may be a little late. He's had his family up at that lake where they go for week-ends. He promised to leave his woodchopping early and drive back."

The screen-door slammed and Sloane came in. "Greetings," he said. "I heard you and just walked in."

"It's all right," said Eaton. "You're still a member of the inner circle. The Mafia. The Rover Boys at Waggoner's Farm."

"What's that feller doing in your back yard?" said Sloane. "Are you going to raise milch-cows?"

"We've been trying to pump Bill," said Eaton, "but the pump is dry. The fence is probably to hang paintings on. Waggoner's one-man art show. Right, Bill?"

"Ah, boys," Waggoner said, mysteriously. "That's my secret. Did you recognize the young man?"

"Your tenant," said Paul quickly. "Mister—er—Blumenthal, is it?"

"Rosenthal," Waggoner said. "Now what would you guess he is doing?"

"Building an elephant-trap," said Paul.

"No."

"A cow-pasture," said Sloane. "That's clearly what it is."

"No," said Waggoner. He was obviously enjoying the game.

"A dog-run," said Tyler. "Abel and I thought it was a dog-run."

"That's close," said Waggoner delightedly. "Jim, did you get a drink?"

"I never drink before five," said Sloane. "What time is it?"

"Ten after," said Paul. "So you're safe. Martini or Bourbon?"

"Bourbon if you please," said Sloane. "On the rocks. Bill, you say a dog-run is close. Would it be a puppy-run? Or a cage for Uncle Homer's parrot?"

Waggoner looked mysterious. "What is it," he said, "that squawks like a parrot, moans like a puppy, drinks like a calf, and is more trouble than an elephant?"

"A baby," said Paul, laughing. "Are you a father, Bill?"

"I'm about to be a grandfather," said Waggoner, grinning. "By adoption. You ought to see the nursery they've fixed up. They even have something called a bathinette. Did you ever hear of a bathinette? Fascinating thing."

296

"Aren't they?" said Tyler. "Will they let you change the baby, too? There's an art you'll have to master, Bill."

"I haven't volunteered on that one, Ed," said Bill, looking gloomy. "Safety pins scare me. I understand they do need to be changed."

"You'll have a lot of explaining to do when that mauve and pink diaper-service truck stops at your door," said Paul. "Which do you want, a boy or a girl?"

"If it's a boy, they're going to name him for me," said Waggoner. "Isn't that wonderful? William Waggoner Rosenthal. A very euphonic name."

"The little stranger," said Paul. "The new president of the Waggoner household. The presiding officer who ignores Roberts' Rules of Order. The little king. Tyler, what's the name of those savages in Swift?"

"The Yahoos?"

"That's it. The little Yahoo. Which will arrive first, Bill, the new baby or the new president?"

Waggoner's pale face took on its mysterious look once more. "It will be close," he said. "The new baby could come any time now. But unless it arrives sometime tonight, I rather think the new president will win."

"Tell us," cried Eaton. "Isn't that what we're here for? Who's the lucky man? Cos Cobb?"

Waggoner refilled his highball glass and sat down. He looked around deliberately. "That is the question," he said, after a moment. "I had hoped that Cos might be here by now. There's a sort of time-schedule the trustees want to follow. Would one of you want to look out and see if Cos's jeep is anywhere in sight?"

"I'm nearest," said Sloane. "I'll look." He went to the

front door and returned. "No sign of Cos on the horizon," he said.

"Maybe we'd best go ahead, then," said Waggoner. "Jack Martin has written us all a letter. Probably the best thing to do would be to read it out loud. Then we can pass it around."

Tyler saw Paul looking at him fixedly. He averted his eyes and watched Waggoner fumbling in his pocket for the letter.

"Here it is," said Bill. "It's addressed to me as chairman of the Committee of Six, and it begins very formally: 'Dr. Waggoner and Gentlemen.' It is signed by Jack as Chairman of the Executive Committee of the Board of Trustees. Jack writes as follows. Paragraph one. 'I know that you and the other members of your hard-working and infinitely patient committee will share the great pleasure of your alter egos on the Board of Trustees at the news I have to divulge.' "

Bill paused, and Tyler glanced around the room. They were all watching Waggoner and listening intently. In the brown atmosphere they might have been statues.

"Paragraph two," said Waggoner. "Jack says, 'Our long labors are now at an end. We have decided on the successor for Homer Vaughn. We have approached him in secret session and he has agreed to serve. The members of the Board of Trustees of Enfield have voted unanimously to confirm his appointment. They share my belief that we have located an extremely able man—the best man for our purposes anywhere in the country. I feel certain that when you know his name you will agree with us that he very fully conforms to all the requirements which we laid down in our initial meeting. I am very happy in the choice we have made.' "

"Nobody can say Jack isn't happy," said Paul. "He makes that plain enough. So what's the man's name?"

Waggoner grinned and looked around the circle of intent faces. "Paragraph three," he said. "And I may say, gentlemen, that this letter is really precision-built, like our new fence in the back yard. Paragraph three. Jack goes on, 'You will understand that a certain degree of circumspection is indicated as we move towards the time of public announcement. The national press will naturally carry the story, and it is essential that no news-leak, such as the one in the *Eagle* which embarrassed us earlier, should now occur. It is likewise essential that the members of the faculty shall be notified in advance of the release of the news to the press.' Close quote."

"End of paragraph three, is it?" said Jim Sloane in his rumbling voice. "Precision-built isn't even the word for it. This is honed to a fine point."

"Paragraph four," said Waggoner. "Quote: 'After a good deal of discussion among the members of the Board,' says Jack, 'we have determined on the release date of Monday, June 5.' "

"That's tomorrow," said Paul.

"Yes, tomorrow," said Waggoner. "Continuing with paragraph four: 'The news will be released in three stages. First, assuming the concurrence of the members of the Committee of Six, I shall meet with them at noon on the fifth in the Conference Room in Bishop Hall—a spot already hallowed by our many meetings there. At that time I shall reveal the name of the new president to them. It seems only fair that they should be the first to hear the news, since they have worked so hard to make this day possible. The second stage will coincide with the June meeting of the University Faculty. At that time, President Vaughn will notify the members of the faculty, who will be advised through each departmental chairman that an announcement of importance will be made at the meeting. The third stage is to release the news to the press. This will be done in such a way that the faculty will be in possession of the story prior to its release to the town and the nation.' End of the fourth paragraph."

"Is there any more?" said Paul.

"One more," said Waggoner. "It's apologetic. Martin says he's sorry that he cannot tell us now, in this letter. He goes on to say: 'With the kind of three-stage program we have worked out, however, I hope the members of the committee will understand that we must hold the line against the possibility of a prior leak. It implies no lack of trust in your excellent committee; we are simply determined that no feelings shall be hurt anywhere among the faculty, and we have asked the press representatives to respect our release time absolutely. It would be unfair to the papers if we arranged it so that any of them could scoop any other.' "

"That's sensible," said Abel. "It seems to me Jack and the others have worked it out very well."

"But no news for us yet," said Paul. "Today is Bourbon day. Tomorrow the world."

The door chimes sounded. "That'll be Cos," said Waggoner. He went into the hall, returning immediately with Cos behind him. The bridge of Cos's nose showed sunburn, and he was wearing a brown sport shirt and slacks. He stood out from the paler group around him, Tyler thought. He made Abel Vincent look more like a ghost than ever.

"Sorry to be late, Bill," Cos said. "We lost Cornie up at the lake and it held us up starting home."

"She's all right?" said Tyler.

"Oh, yes. She was down in the woods picking flowers and didn't hear us. Or so she said."

"I had just finished reading Martin's letter," said Waggoner. "Here, you can read it faster yourself."

Cos took the letter and read it through rapidly. He handed it back to Bill. "Quite a system," was all he said.

"So we all assemble at high noon in Bishop," said Waggoner. "And that's the news for today. Such as it is. Cos, you'd better have a drink after the drive home. Who else is ready?"

The meeting dissolved in companionable talk. Now that the decision was made, they stopped speculating about it. The die was cast. They would be on hand at noon tomorrow. Now they spoke of other matters. Abel got going about the financial section of the *Times;* Cos had a story about a fish that got away; they asked Tyler about the complimentary resolution for Homer Vaughn, to be read out in faculty meeting by John Webb; Waggoner told about the household scare at three on Saturday morning, when Mrs. Rosenthal thought she was in labor.

"Bill, I've got to go," said Abel at last. "Very pleasant party. I take it this is the final meeting of the Committee of Six— this noble group. We ought to pass a resolution of self-commendation. Assignment completed." He shook Bill's hand and moved towards the door.

"Good luck with your grandchild," said Paul. "I'm off, too. See you tomorrow." He went out with Sloane.

"Ed, how about a ride home?" said Cos. "If you don't mind the open jeep. I didn't change cars at home."

"Thanks, Cos. Fine. Take care of yourself, Dr. Waggoner."

"I will, Ed. Goodbye, Cos."

301

The jeep was parked across the dappled street. The leatherette seats were warm from the sun.

"How did you find things at the lake?"

"Practically perfect," Cos said. "Only one minor tragedy yesterday. Cornie found that her summer doll had been pretty well chewed up by some small animal. Squirrels or mice. Otherwise things were fine. Polly caught a good-sized fish for the first time this year, and it was very good for her morale. We cooked a steak outdoors. It was what you might call a wedding celebration."

"Anniversary?"

"Not exactly," said Cos, smiling. "There may be a first anniversary about a year from now, or again there may not. I would almost bet not. This was a celebration for my first wife's wedding. You remember Carlotta. She has taken unto her bosom a third husband. Name of Hugo."

Tyler clapped Cos on the shoulder. "Hurray, Cos," he said. "That called for a celebration. The lioness is caged, is that it?"

"I don't know for how long," Cos said. "But while it lasts, I like it. I even hope that Hugo likes it. For as long as it lasts."

"I hope forever."

"Nothing is forever," said Cos. He braked the jeep to a stop in front of Tyler's house. "Anyway, I can't complain about the last couple of weeks since we heard the news."

"Congratulations, Cos," said Tyler. He swung out of the jeep and stood on the curbstone. "And thanks for the lift."

"Any time you want a lift," Cos said. He grinned, raised one hand in salute, put the jeep in gear, and went off down the street.

302

II

"Thanks," said Tyler. "Thank you very much." And returned the receiver to its cradle. How many times have you said that and done that? he thought. And how many times more? And that is how it's going to be—the signature of the future, as far as a man can see. You are on the receiving end, and that's where you're going to stay. And giving, too, he thought. The giving end, though not the kind of giving you had planned on, not what you had been led to expect.

Led? Led to expect? Who led? He looked down at his desk, covered with a litter of books and papers. In some of the books, small pieces of torn paper marked the degree of his progress. On the papers, in scrappy longhand or the greater formality and order of typescript, were the notes he had put down and put away at various times in the past. In the typewriter, staring back at him like the eyes of a statue, was the half-finished page. Led? Led to expect? Who expected?

He read the title, in spaced capitals at the top of the page: NOTES ON A REVOLUTION. A good title, he thought. I'll will that to somebody. Someone can use it. It's as good a title as that one you were going to use for the mystery story you never wrote: *A Matter of Life and Death*. Only some writer scooped you on that one, he thought. You saw the title in a bookseller's bin outside that little shop just off Washington Square. All right, who cares? There are a million titles. What's a title, anyway? What you build under the title is what makes all the difference.

The typed epigraph under the title was a sentence from John Morley. "What ought to have gone on, and would have gone on, as a process of soft autumnal dissolution, was converted by the infection of Voltaire into a stained scene of passion and battle." He gazed at the words. Morley was deceived by his metaphor, he thought. The seasonal metaphor. You know the leaves of autumn fall, and you know the spring is going to come. You watch Louis's civilization disintegrate and you say to yourself, 'Ah, yes. But spring is just around the corner.' But is it? Is it necessarily? There may be winters as long as a thousand years. Morley, you slipped there. How do you know the dissolution would have continued, the new order have arisen, without man's stir? And what about those buried metaphors of Morley's—*infection* and *stain*? Can we never change without some kind of infection? Is there always a stain?

He thought, illogically, of the mown field in Vermont, that afternoon in summer, walking with Alice. She noticed in the grass a thumb-shaped, half-dried bundle of gray and white fur, and flipped it over with the toe of her sneaker.

"What's that, Ed? A dead mouse?"

He bent to look. It was not a mouse: it had neither eyes nor tail or even a life-like shape. The thing lay at the edge of a small irregular circle on the stubble, and though the area had been gleaned and licked over, every scrap consumed, the tips of the grasses showed the tell-tale stain.

"It's the coughed-up caudle of a well-fed owl or a fox," said Tyler. "This is a crumb from his dining-table. Something died here to keep the owl or the fox alive. Something ended here, and you can see the stain."

Passion, he thought. Battle. Must there always be the stain, the conflagration, the ache and agony, before we come out on the other side, resurrected, new-fledged for new flight, or simply well-fed? Probably, thought Tyler. That's why they used that phoenix on the sun-dial in the middle of the campus. Not only for the old college buildings that went up in acrid smoke that December night in the Eighteen-eighties, but also for the other destructions and constructions. All the fires that have destroyed the old and prepared the way for the new on this very campus. That fire in the brain, for instance, which makes men swink and sweat away in labs and libraries: the flame no fire-hose can quench, the inward agonizing roar and fall of towers and cave-in of walls that you have to have before people are ready for a change of architecture. Before man's knowledge of himself and his world can inch forward another notch.

Maybe you're right there, Morley, thought Tyler. The causes of change, minor or epochal, lie deep among the paradoxes of human action. Sometimes it is easy. Everything clicks into place. It makes you suspicious; you wonder if it can be true—or, if true, right. Then again, you push the sunken wheel and it will not move. You labor at the oars, and the opposing wind prevails. You plan for peace, and find yourself at war.

Tyler mopped his forehead and got up to turn on the fan. The June humidity was thick as syrup. He stood looking at his desk with distaste. What a mess of words and of unborn— or stillborn—ideas. How many trials before the final heat. For Cos Cobb and Homer Vaughn, for men like Giorgio Renzulli and Don Drake, for old Turcotte whose trials were done, or for kids like Toby and Tommy and Cornie, whose trials were just beginning. For George Woodruff, cajoling his students into line and for Bob Schaeffer, riding herd on his faculty inside the budgetary corral. All the brethren, thought Tyler, for better or for worse. He glanced up at the bust of Voltaire, which stared back at him with blind plaster-of-Paris eyes.

The buzzer made him jump, and he cleared his throat before he spoke.

"Is that you, Ed? It doesn't sound like you?"

"Just a fog of humidity, Alice. How are you feeling?"

"Not exactly calm," said Alice in her husky voice. "What about you?"

"The same. What's up?"

"Nothing much, except that it's almost five o'clock. Couldn't you come home now and take a shower and get cool?"

"I'll be home soon. Just clearing up my desk a little. How are the boys?"

"They've been playing in the sprinkler. Now they're drinking Kool-Aid on the back steps. Mrs. DeNew is going to give them their supper if they have any appetite left. Have you had any other phone calls?"

"Plenty," said Tyler. "Everybody and his brother. I mean the three deans and the Committee of Six. The ones who have heard. Except for Cos Cobb."

"Several of them called here first. I said you were in Trask. What about Cos?"

"I don't know. I suppose we'll see him at the president's house later on."

"I should think he would have called you first of all."

"He's probably busy."

"Can't you stop being busy, Ed, and come home?"

"In a little while."

"Your dinner jacket is ready. It looks too hot. Please leave time to rest and cool off a little. You want to look nice for the trustees."

"Where did I hear that before?" said Tyler, laughing.

Alice chuckled. "You'll hear it again, Mr. President. Hurry home."

"In a few minutes," said Tyler. He put down the telephone and sat looking at it, silent in its cradle. He might have called while I was getting a drink from the cooler, he thought. The others got right on the wire after the noon meeting. All inside of an hour. Eaton bubbling, Abel serious and deliberate, Waggoner mild as May, Sloane rumbling out congratulations like a bear in a bee's nest. But no Cos Cobb.

He swung his chair back to face the desk and the litter of books and papers. Under his eye was a scrawled note in long-hand, a quotation from Morley. One of the epigrams. He leaned forward to read it. "Where it is a duty to worship the sun, it is pretty sure to be a crime to examine the laws of heat." He swung back to the typewriter and typed it onto the half-finished page. It fitted the half-made paragraph neatly. A way of summarizing the conflict of religion and reason in Voltaire's France. He sat staring at the words, push-ing them around in his mind. What else could they apply to? Where else would they fit?

He took a pencil and a piece of yellow paper and wrote: "Where it's a duty to worship power, it's a crime to speculate on the laws of friendship." Does that fit? he wondered. He read it over in the humid air. Never mind, he said, half-aloud. If he calls you, well and good. If not, there's a reason.

Adams was wrong—or at least you hope he was wrong. We don't worship power around here, we harness it. We use power to spread what light we have. The Enfield Power and Light Company. We're all on the board of directors.

The buzzer burred, stopped, burred again. Tyler picked up the phone hopefully.

"Professor Tyler," the woman's voice said. "Just a moment, please. President Vaughn would like to speak with you." There was an interval and a click.

"Oh, Ed," said Homer Vaughn's voice loudly. "I just wanted to make dead-sure we had our signals straight. You're keeping away from the faculty meeting. Right."

"Yes, sir."

"And you understand that we expect you and Alice at the Parthenon around six-thirty?"

"Yes, sir. We got Mr. Martin's note and also his phone call."

"Double check," cried the president. "This Board of Trustees doesn't fool. Now how are you feeling this muggy day?"

"All right. Except that I'm shaking in my boots."

"Oh, you'll have some blisters," said the president. "It'll get harder before it gets easier. But they picked the right man. Ed, in about ten minutes, I'm due to go into the faculty meeting and tell your colleagues all about you. Milton Fletcher, who arranged the thing, says he expects quite a crowd. If you should feel your ears burning around five-twenty, that will be the old president praising the new one."

"It's too early for praise," said Tyler. "Can I come talk to you—can I get to see you next week after things calm down?"

"You not only can, you must," said Vaughn. "I'm making a list of tips for Tyler. No, Ed, I'm at your service. That's what the presidency is about. See you in a couple of hours or less."

"Yes, sir," said Tyler again. He rang off and sat quietly, Vaughn's loud voice still ringing in his ears, Vaughn's words still echoing hollowly. You'll have some blisters. It will get harder before it gets any easier. At your service: that's what the presidency is about. After a minute he reached out for the worn book in the red binding. All right, Morley, he said, half aloud. What do you say? Anything about blisters? He opened the book to the first chapter: "The Ideal Man for the Time." Maybe so, he thought, and maybe not. He flipped through the pages idly, reading the passages he had under-scored in ink or in red pencil long ago. Nearly every page carried annotations. These might do for a commencement address, thought Tyler, or a baccalaureate sermon. That's the way you have to teach, now. Lecture at them. Sermonize at them. And speeches are what you write from now on.

He read on quickly, turning the pages, pausing to read the lines he had marked. Halfway through the chapter, a phrase caught his eye. "The book-writer," he read, "assures men that the sacred bard is a mightier man than his hero. Voltaire knew better. . . . He rated literature, as it ought to be rated, below action." Probably true of Voltaire. Was it also true, as Morley said, in general? Tyler turned the page, his eye hurrying through the words he had underscored in red: "Let us make our account with the actual, rather than seek excuses for self-indulgence in pensive preference of some-thing that might have been."

All right, Morley, thought Tyler. There's our blister, you old moralist. There's our Victorian sentiment of up-and-at-'em. Say not the struggle naught availeth. Smite the furrows, boys. Westward, look, the land is bright.

He closed the book and put it back on the shelf. Time to go home. Time to shove off and smite the furrows of that shower-bath. The brethren would be gathering in the Faculty Room in Enfield Hall. Ionian white and gold. The dignified figures slumped in various attitudes on the mahogany benches. The fathers staring down from the gleaming walls. Milton Fletcher reading out the May minutes. Schaeffer and McClure and Woodruff presenting the deans' reports. John Webb rising up at the appropriate time to read the resolution in praise of Uncle Homer. And then Vaughn himself, going to the lectern beside the silver sword of office, fiddling with the papers in his hand, saying, "Gentlemen, you have heard that an announcement of some importance is to be made this afternoon——"

He jumped again at the sound of the buzzer.

"Hello."

"Edward, this is Cos. Alice told me you were still up there. Let me be the latest to congratulate you."

"You're early, Cos. Thanks. It's a relief to hear you. Only I wish it had been the other way."

"What other way?"

"Me congratulating you. The way it ought to have gone."

"No," said Cos. "Not at all in any way. You're the man. We never had any doubt that the trustees would see it that way."

"I had plenty of doubts," said Tyler. "Still do. Especially in the light of old Henry's idea."

"Henry? Who's old Henry?"

Tyler laughed. "Sorry. I meant Henry Adams. Friend-in-power Adams."

"Oh, that," said Cos, chuckling. "A friend lost, you mean. Never mind, Ed. Henry could have been wrong, or just too exclusive in his choice of nouns. Friends have been lost for other reasons. Plenty of other reasons. Women, for instance."

"Yes, and fame. And religious belief. And money. But also through accession to power."

"And gradual growth apart," Cos said, "like two limbs from the trunk of a tree. Don't let Henry worry you, Ed. It's nothing but a slogan, and slogans are made to be disproved."

"Maybe it's more than a slogan, Cos. Maybe it's a basic law of human behavior. It can't help changing relationships, Cos. I'm only determined that it won't."

"*Can't help* and *won't* are ancient enemies," Cos said, slowly. "I don't know that we can ever promise much beyond tomorrow. And expect the promises to work out as promised. It could be the best plan to bow to the inevitable and go on from there. Which, of course, you have done and will do."

"Wearing doubt like a raincoat," said Tyler.

"A very useful garment, Ed. Keeps your humor dry. I can assure you that no one else shares your doubts. You ought to have seen Martin beaming when he told us the news at the noon meeting. He looked like the sun at the zenith, and so did all the others. Sorry, by the way, that I couldn't call you earlier. Except for that meeting in Bishop Hall, I've been with the Navy all day."

"The Navy?"

"One Rear Admiral. One very bright Commander. Classified project. I just put them on the train a few minutes ago, and I'm heading for the showers. What are you doing, working so late on a day like this?"

"I'm just putting Voltaire on the skids," said Tyler. "Not, as the man says, without some reluctance."

"Won't they give you any time to finish your book?"

"I didn't ask for any time, Cos. There's too little time to learn what I have to learn this coming summer."

"Never mind, son," said Cos. "It's in a good cause." His voice was tired.

"I hope so, Cos. It had better be."

"Well, I just wanted to call you before I get into that shower. You'd better move on home, boy. And congratulations."

"Thanks," said Tyler. "Thank you very much."

For what he hoped would be the last time that day, Tyler returned the telephone to its cradle. He looked at his watch and saw that it was already well past five o'clock. Time to go and change. Change? Yes, change. He gathered up the scattered books on the desk-top and one by one returned them to the shelves. He stood for a moment in the cool breeze from the fan, then clicked it off. It slowed down and stopped. The notes still lay helter-skelter. He swept them into a pile and looked for a paper-clip. In the typewriter was the half-finished page. He ripped it out so quickly that it tore in his hand. Smoothing it out, he laid it on top of the pile of notes, clipped them all together, and dropped them into the left-hand drawer of his desk. For a minute he stood looking around the office. Then he picked up his light jacket from the back of the chair and went out.